To those who guide the future,

the Master Rays

of the Cosmic Logos,

from whence all imagination,

inspiration

and wisdom

comes.

Traci Harding, best selling author of 'the Ancient Future Series', has published in excess of twenty books through through HarperCollins/Voyager Australia, Brio Books and Bolinda Audio. Her work blends fantasy, fact, esoteric theory, time travel and quantum physics, into adventurous romps through history, alternative dimensions, universes and states of consciousness. Her books have been published in several languages throughout the world.

**To find out more about Traci and her books
visit her website at:** traciharding.com

For autographed copies of Traci's books visit her store at:
allthingstraci.com.au

Get Exclusive Content at Patreon:
patreon.com/user?u=20034469&fan_landing=true

Find Traci on Facebook at:
"Mastering Your Reality with Traci Harding" Group -
All Things Traci Store - Traci Harding Fans - Trazling

Traci is also on:
Twitter: @tracharding
Instagram: traciharding_author
YouTube: youtube.com/c/TraciHardingChannel
& Redbubble: redbubble.com/people/traciharding/shop?asc=u

OTHER BOOKS BY TRACI HARDING

The Ancient Future Trilogy

The Ancient Future: the Dark Age (Book One)

An Echo in Time: Atlantis (Book Two)

Masters of Reality: the Gathering (Book Three)

The Alchemist's Key

The Celestial Triad

Chronicle of Ages (Book One)

Tablet of Destinies (Book Two)

The Cosmic Logos (Book Three)

THE COSMIC LOGOS

LOGOS

BOOK 3 OF THE CELESTIAL TRIAD

TRACI HARDING

Voyager

An imprint of HarperCollins*Publishers*

Voyager
An imprint of HarperCollins*Publishers*, Australia

First published in 2002
by HarperCollins*Publishers* Pty Limited
ABN 36 009 913 517
A member of the HarperCollins*Publishers* (Australia) Pty Limited Group
www.harpercollins.com.au

HarperCollins*Publishers*
25 Ryde Road, Pymble, Sydney, NSW 2073, Australia
31 View Road, Glenfield, Auckland 10, New Zealand
77–85 Fulham Palace Road, London, W6 8JB, United Kingdom
Hazelton Lanes, 55 Avenue Road, Suite 2900, Toronto, Ontario M5R 3L2
and 1995 Markham Road, Scarborough, Ontario M1B 5M8, Canada
10 East 53rd Street, New York NY 10022, USA

National Library of Australia Cataloguing-in-Publication data:

Harding, Traci.
The cosmic logos : book 3 of the celestial triad.
Bibliography.
ISBN 0 7322 6667 X.
I.Title. (Series : Harding, Traci. Celestial triad ; bk 3).
A823.3

Cover and internal design by Darian Causby, HarperCollins Design Studio
Typeset by HarperCollins in Goudy 11/13.5

In the Ancient Future
there was an Echo in Time,
when the Masters of Reality
were called forth
to record a Chronicle of Ages
with the aid of the Tablet of Destinies,
and serve the divine purpose
of the great Cosmic Logos.

CONTENTS

PART 3: MASTERS

Acknowledgements

At last the final instalment of this Triad/series has arrived. As per usual there are many to whom I owe my gratitude for making this book happen, so here goes ...

Firstly, I must thank my poor, overworked husband, David, who has gone well out of his way to ensure I had the time to write this tale and put up with my grumpy moods as I struggled to process all the heavy research material. Many blessings to my nanny, Mo, and my mother, Toni, for taking care of my daughter, Sarah, while I grabbed some time in front of the computer.

On the research front I must thank my new friend, Dianna, for introducing me to the Reverend Michael King of the Melchizedek Synthesis Light Academy (www.aussiemsla.com). Michael aided me with some of the heavy research and was kind enough to proofread this manuscript. The Reverend's assistance is most appreciated. I must also thank Dr Joshua Stone (www.drjoshuadavidstone.com) for his kind invitation to the Wesak Celebration in California this year, I greatly look forward to the experience.

I must also take time here to credit my clairvoyant, (another Michael — must be something in the name?), whose insight and words of guidance have contributed greatly to these tales over the years and to my life.

Next, my gratitude goes to the great gang of people who have been frequenting the message board at my new web site, which the HarperCollins multimedia team set up for me this year: Dianna, Sautia, Rob, Cally,

Corrina, Clair, Michelle, Olivia, Melissa, Sharon, Karita, Rebecca, Christine, Beki, Amanda, Guin, Chi, Haze, Fiona, Annie, Starmie, Leah, Leigh, and all the other regular message posters, many thanks for your wonderful support, ideas, views, stories, poems and encouragement. Also, to our fairy webmother, Deb, a big chug on the shoulder for a job well done, and thanks to Andrew, Laura and Fiona for their assistance as well. Thanks, too, to all those readers who have emailed me during the years that this series has been in publication; your feedback has been invaluable.

To that wonderful gang of authors at the Sassy net, I thank you also for your words of wisdom and for sharing your experience: Kim Wilkins, Ian Irvine, Graeme Hague, Louise Cusack, Richard Harland, Tess Williams and all our new members too — you are wonderful authors and I highly recommend you to all readers. I cannot credit this esteemed list of colleagues without crediting our fearless leader and agent, Selwa Anthony. Words cannot express how much I owe and adore this woman; she is my idol, my friend and my guiding light.

Speaking of guiding lights, thanks to my editors, Sue and Steph, for negotiating a tighter editing schedule than usual, as this tale was a real monster to write and took longer than usual. I'm sure readers appreciate your efforts to get this tale to the bookstores as soon as possible.

As for the rest of the team at HarperCollins, especially Linda and Midge, what can I say but it's been a real pleasure and I look forward to working with you all for many, many years to come.

PART 1

PLANETS

CHARACTER LIST

PART 1

Leader of Alliance	Brian Alexander (Lahmu)
Governess of Kila	Candace
Vice-Governor of Kila	Rhun
Ex-Governor of Kila	Maelgwn
Ex-Governess of Kila	Tory Alexander
Leader of Falcons	Sparrowhawk
Leader of Leonines	Bast
Leader of Centaurs	Thais
Leader of Delphinus	Zabeel
Lord of the Otherworld	Gwyn ap Nudd
Gwyn's apprentice	Avery
Avery's twin sister	Lirathea
Tutor of the Chosen	Noah
Daughter of Lahmu	Fallon
Night Hunter's secretary	Templeton
Head of the Third Ray	Master Rakoczi, 'the Count' (Mahachohan)
Chohan of the Seventh Ray	The Master R's Apprentice
Synthesis Chohan	Djwhal Khul 'the Tibetan'
Chohan of the Second Ray	Kuthumi
Chohan of the First Ray	El Morya

Prologue

She had an idea for a new film script, which had been evolving for some time now. The heroine was a martial artist misplaced in time. The main character had been a hero originally, but she'd rethought this idea, considering that it would prove far more challenging and interesting if the warrior-hero was a female. Such a woman would be able to physically defend herself, no matter which of history's dark ages the writer decided to cast her into.

Speaking of the Dark Ages, the writer was very interested in this period of British history. Still, the last thing the world needed was another Arthurian tale, even if this one would have a rather strange twist. According to the few historians writing during the purported era of Arthur's rule, like Bedi, Gildas and Nennius, King Arthur and his Knights of the Round Table had never existed, as the legend had failed to score so much as a mention in the histories of the time.

Merlin, or rather Myrddin, was documented as having aided King Ambrosius to victory over the Roman tyrant, Vortigern — could the former have been the true Arthur? Even if he had been, this tale had also been done to death by novelists over the past few centuries. What this writer wanted was a new hero with a new legend to tell. There must have been mighty Kings who performed the great deeds and fought the bloody battles that had long since been attributed to Arthur. The writer made a mental note to seek out more research material on the early Kings of Britain during her forthcoming trip to the UK.

She wasn't too sure how her, as yet nameless, heroine had become misplaced in time. The date and place of her transcendental episode of bio-location was still a mystery. The writer supposed that the answer to this conundrum would be answered during a good research session at some distant point in time. Work had begun on her second serious attempt at a film script and the tale was proving to be rather intriguing, immersed as she was in the realms of the denizens of the nature kingdoms.

Still, all her writing was going to be put on hold for the next month or so, as she was off to the UK to raise interest in her first attempt at a feature film. She was also going to view locations, and get costings on the section of the film that would have to be shot in the UK. This film explored past lives and karma, and although much of the footage could be shot in Australia, it was hard to fake a castle. And why would you want to, when the UK had so many breathtaking castles on offer? Appointments with the relevant custodians had been made in advance to view the locations, as it was the middle of the cold season and thus estates were closed to the public. It would have been nice to have been able to hold out and visit the UK during a more accommodating season, but the Gulf War had driven the price of a ticket overseas to an all-time low, so for the young and rather broke film writer, opportunity beckoned.

I

THE APPOINTED

'Knowledge dwells in heads replete
with the thoughts of other men …
wisdom in the minds attentive to their own.'

'An insightful thought from one of Gaia's fifteenth century philosophers —' Noah stopped short of naming the source, noting that one of his students was eager to supply the information. 'Yes, Avery.'

'The Honourable Frances Bacon, En Noah,' the blond-haired lad with the twinkling violet eyes responded.

'Exactly right,' Noah stated, proud of his student's firm grasp of the human history of the planet that Avery's forefathers had called home. 'I felt this was an appropriate quote with which to conclude your tuition. For, with all the lessons I have given you, you alone can transmute that knowledge into wisdom. And I am confident that each of you will do exactly that.'

The Sage broke from his formal address to approach each of his five graduates in turn.

The first of these was a fiery young Leonine female named Bast, who was as unique in character as she was in appearance. Her dark, straight hair and piercing blue eyes made her one of a kind among her people, but her abundance of pure-hearted amorous charm was fast marking her as the most desirable single female alive. The fact that she was heiress to the Leonine kingdom and was to be the voice of her people in Lahmu's senate only added to her eligibility.

'Dear Bast,' Noah began, smiling broadly as he took up her left hand and held it in his. His right hand enfolded the three-sided pyramid, engraved with ancient hieroglyphs, which hung on a chain around his neck. This ancient divining tool was known as the Tablet of Destinies and had been a gift to the Sage's first human incarnation from the divine Logos, Anu. It had been handed down through the ages to each of the guardians of mankind and had found its way back into his possession twenty years ago, when Noah's super-conscious link to the Cosmic Logos had been restored. 'Before you leave our fair planet to assume the Governorship of Nugia, my parting advice for you is ...' He allowed himself a graceful pause, which amused his students greatly.

This was a game that they had played throughout their schooling, which was nothing more than good old fortune telling — Noah had learned to make his guidance fun, lest it go unheeded. The prophet would give his students one insight into their future each year, and at some time within that year a situation would arise where the advice could be put to good use.

'Don't tease me, En Noah,' Bast implored him, dying to know the prediction.

'Although men will be falling all over themselves to court you, Bast, true happiness lies with a man whom you will have to pursue,' he concluded, inspiring a round of applause and laughter from the other four students, who knew the Leonine lady well.

Bast screwed up her nose, disappointed. 'I won't be interested in a serious relationship for years, but even so I was kind of hoping he'd be tall, handsome and courageous, not forbidding!'

'Courage would be a must,' agreed Avery.

'All right,' Noah cautioned him, ahead of turning back to Bast. 'Don't be blinded by glamour, Nin. Physical beauty can be a great deceiver and can only bring a fleeting happiness, for all physical beauty will perish in time.'

Bast sat tall in her seat and, crossing her legs, she placed both hands on her hips. 'Not my beauty,' she debated in fun, her black lion's tail twitching playfully as she spoke. 'We Chosen are immortal and thus eternally young and beautiful, are we not?'

Noah's mouth curved into a half-smile, as he realised that she was still too new to the physical world to appreciate the argument he was trying to put forward. 'Nothing in the whole of creation remains the same forever, Bast. If it did all would be stagnant. One day even you shall tire of your physical form, as becoming as it is.'

Although Bast couldn't imagine ever feeling as Noah described, there were some among the Chosen who were losing their affinity with physical plane existence, such as Avery's and Lirathea's parents. 'Perhaps I should have said I am looking for a man who is wise, loving and true, En Noah,' the Leonine female resolved, knowing what her tutor would want to hear.

'That would serve you better, Bast,' he agreed. 'But only if that is what you truly will for yourself. What I want for you will have very little effect in your reality.'

'Point taken,' Bast conceded, a little ashamed for attempting to fool En Noah. He always knew when he was being mocked.

The Sage moved on to the verbal extrovert of the class.

'I know what life holds in store, for I am the force behind my own manifestation,' Avery stated, proudly. 'But any advice you or the Tablet of Destinies may have for this soon-to-be Otherworldly lord, En Noah, shall surely prove insightful.'

Avery was apprentice to Gwyn ap Nudd, the current guardian of the Otherworld. Too much of the lord's confidence and mischievous nature had rubbed off on the youth during his tuition. For, although Avery had proven himself very adept at commanding wisely the various inhabitants of the etheric realm, he had a tendency to be far cockier than an older, wiser man might be.

Noah gripped Avery's hand and advised. 'You have many selves, on many different levels of existence, all pouring energy into your manifestation. If you are putting out the right messages then they shall surely heed your will. But beware what you *will* to manifest.'

'Is that the prediction?' Avery queried.

Noah shook his head. 'My advice is this ... when your words conflict with what is in your heart, know that a great rivalry will be avoided by putting your ego aside and telling the truth.'

'Ooooh ...!' Avery's fellow students murmured, thinking that the prophecy was a rather ominous one.

'Shall I be rewarded for telling the truth?' Avery wasn't satisfied. He wanted something to look forward to.

Noah smiled a knowing smile. 'The truth always brings its —'

'Own rewards,' Avery concluded in unison with his tutor. Having studied under the Sage for twenty years now, he knew Noah's predictable response to his stupid question. 'I walked right into that one.'

Noah raised both eyebrows in agreement before moving on to Lirathea, Avery's twin sister and his opposite in most regards. Avery liked action, whilst Lirathea personified tranquillity. He was forthright, self-promoting and mischievous, whereas she was meditative, selfless and as close to a saint as anyone Noah had ever known. They did look remarkably alike, however; white blonde hair and violet eyes were traits the twins inherited from their infamous mother, Tory Alexander. Avery had his parents' warrior form and

Lirathea had a body that was waif-like, which she commanded with all the grace of a prima ballerina. Her vocation in life was also Otherworldly. Where her brother would soon command the denizens living in the etheric realms, Lirathea had an affinity with the spirits in the higher mental realm and beyond. In days of old, the young woman would have been regarded as a Priestess or a Druidess, but Lirathea preferred the term oracle. Both brother and sister were to assume seats on Lahmu's council — Avery was to represent the Otherworld and Lirathea would be the voice of the spirit world.

'You are probably more adept at soothsaying than I am these days, Lirathea,' Noah granted as he came to a stop in front of the angelic maiden.

'Please state my fate according to the Tablet, En Noah, for although I have many guides, you are one of those whose advice I most cherish.' Lirathea had an expectant smile as she offered her hand to the Sage to participate in the game.

'Ah!' He teased her in fun and she cowered behind the long fine hair that fell dead straight to her waist, suddenly sorry she'd insisted. 'Being born perfect is a curse,' Noah continued, cracking a gracious smile. 'For a state obtained must be maintained and herein lies your challenge. Do what you must without regret, and thus conserve your energy for grander pursuits. Never feel sorry for knowing your own mind and the will of the Logos.'

Lirathea was rather enchanted by his counsel. 'I shall do my best, En Noah.'

'And that has always proven more than sufficient,' he said gently.

Sparrowhawk, as always, was alongside Lirathea, and although the younger Falcon male was only her half-brother, he had far more in common with Lirathea than her twin brother did. From different human tribes, one never would have guessed them to be of the same family, but their mother's violet eyes made their kinship more obvious. This set Sparrowhawk apart from his breed, for he was the only Falcon who had pupils of such colour. The lad inherited the deep brown wings that sprouted from his back, and the shoulder length quills of the same colour that grew on his head, from his father, Hawk — an infamous space pirate turned diplomat.

'So what do you foresee for me, En Noah?' Sparrowhawk gripped the Sage's hand firmly.

This young man was making a fine show of repressing his sorrow. Tomorrow he would depart for Tarazean to take over the leadership of his people from his father, and the Falcon seat on Lahmu's council. But it was not the pending responsibilities that hung so heavily on his heart, nor was it leaving his training ground on Kila. It was the thought of leaving Lirathea that was distressing him so deeply.

'I know you are going to miss Kila, Sparrowhawk, and we here will miss you,' Noah admitted and the girls in the class all agreed.

'Ha, speak for yourselves,' Avery scoffed, and was hushed by all present.

'But destiny is not taking you from us so that you can spend all your free time thinking of us,' Noah insisted. 'Your brain space will be better employed looking to the future rather than dwelling in the past ... and your heart shall be more contented too.'

Sparrowhawk was a little disconcerted by the soothsaying, but cracked a resolute smile to quickly cover his distress. 'I am sure Tarazean's governmental affairs will leave me very little time to ponder missing anybody.' He glanced at all his classmates, but his gaze fell on his sister beside him, who leaned her head upon his shoulder and threw an arm across his back to give him comfort.

'We'll be lucky if he even transmits us a message,' Lirathea joked, and nearly choked on her words; she was losing her best friend.

'I doubt that you have need to fear on that count, dear sister,' Avery quipped, a little concerned about the close association between his sister and their half-brother.

'No,' Sparrowhawk agreed, pretending not to notice the implication in their brother's tone. 'None of you need fear, as I fully intend to drive you nuts with correspondence.' He threw an arm about his sister and returned her hug.

The tension between the lads was nothing new. They had always been competitive when it came to their sister's attention. The rivalry was of little concern to Noah, for he knew Avery and Sparrowhawk would have far more important affairs into which to channel their energy, once they assumed their forthcoming appointments.

The last of Noah's five graduating students was

Fallon, the daughter of Brian and Candace Alexander. Unlike her half-sister, Bast, and every other student in her class, Fallon was not destined to take up a great appointment upon graduation and her coming of age. Her name and chart had given very little insight into her future vocation, for her name simply meant 'daughter of the ruler'. Her father, Brian Alexander, was Lahmu, the supreme head of the senate of the interplanetary human alliance. Fallon's star chart and her studies had revealed an aptitude for humanitarianism, the psychic arts, leadership and protocol, but she had yet to decide what avenue she would pursue as a career. Thus, schooling had proven more of a struggle for Fallon than for her peers, as she had no fixed idea of her future endeavours and could not channel her energies into the subjects that would prove most beneficial to her cause. Still, she had studied hard and managed to graduate despite her want of a calling.

'Let me guess, En Noah.' Fallon pulled her mass of dark curls into a ponytail as her tutor approached her. 'You cannot foresee my future, for that is for me to decide.'

Yes, her lack of destiny had definitely made her a cynic. 'On the contrary,' Noah assured as he held her hand and focused his mind to perceive the Tablet's counsel. 'I can see you averting a great calamity, Fallon.'

'Really?' She was intrigued by his claim, then thought better of it. 'There is no such thing as a great calamity, so far as we Chosen are concerned ... for what situation could possibly arise that my father and his great council could not handle?'

'Fate picks its own warriors,' Noah told her surely. 'But you must keep your heart and mind open to the higher purpose. Malice will confuse your perception for a time, making the right decision and course of action unclear.'

Fallon didn't know what to say, for it seemed her future was more complex than she had imagined. 'I hold no real malice towards anyone, En Noah.' She gazed up at him with her piercing blue eyes, the only trait that both Bast and Fallon had inherited from their father.

'That is true,' Noah seconded, 'but when situations get twisted and the whole truth is not known, sometimes we jump to conclusions that would not normally be our own.'

The young woman frowned and forced a smile to concede she would commit the advice to memory. 'In that case, I shall always try to get my facts straight. If, at any time, I feel I have not, then I shall come see you, En Noah,' she resolved, with a lighthearted laugh — the Sage's prophecies always sounded more ominous in the telling than they actually were in reality.

'I shall always be here for your counsel,' he assured, as he let go of Fallon's hand and addressed all five of his graduates. 'It has been my honour and privilege to be your tutor these twenty years past. Go now, and rise to the challenge of your individual pursuits in the knowledge that I have prepared you well for what lies ahead. Be proud of your perseverance, for your efforts hail the dawn of a new era of prosperity and peace for humanity. The allied council of Lahmu will finally realise its full potential in accordance with the will of the great Cosmic Logos.'

'So be it!' all five students responded as one, and they rose to leave the Institute they had frequented all their lives — the day had finally come to pursue their aspirations.

2

KINDRED SPIRITS

No sooner had Avery been dismissed from the Institute, than he'd willed himself back to the Otherworld. He imagined that Gwyn ap Nudd would be waiting to give him some last-minute tuition, for Avery would soon undertake the formal initiation that would prove him worthy to succeed the lord as ruler of the dominions of nature and their realm of higher activity. It was a great honour that was to be bestowed on Avery, for the etheric world appointment had never before been awarded to a human being.

Gwyn ap Nudd was the last of the race known as the Nefilim. He was still operating below the mental plane of awareness and, understandably, he longed to ascend and join his kindred who were dwelling on the threshold of the causal plane of existence. This was the intermediary realm between the lower triad spheres pertaining to mankind, and the higher triad planes that played host to the hierarchy of the divine creator of the universe. Upon Gwyn ap Nudd's retirement, his soul group would spend thousands of years immersed in a deep cleansing sleep, whereby all their beneficial dreams, talents and aspirations would be realised and perfected in preparation for the next evolution conducive to their level of awareness.

Avery felt confident of fulfilling all expectations in regard to his forthcoming appointment. Gwyn ap Nudd may have ruled the realm of emotion, but the Nefilim had never been very emotionally inclined as a species; they functioned primarily through their mental awareness. For the first time, rule of the Otherworld would rest with an emotional creature who was sympathetic to nature's cause and humanity's cause.

Upon willing himself to his mentor, Avery arrived in a lovely valley located upon the planet Gaia's etheric body, which was where Gwyn ap Nudd chose to base himself.

In the physical realm Avery would have been in some abandoned town in lower Wales — the land in which his famous time hopping father, Maelgwn Gwynedd, had ruled as High King during the Dark Ages. In the etheric world, however, it was a lush valley filled with colourful blooms and huge enchanted trees, the like of which only existed in the fairy tales of Gaia's physical consciousness; every atom of every manifestation in the valley was luminous because they absorbed the ultraviolet light beaming forth from the heart of the Logos via the rays of the sun, which was less

21

harmful on the eye here than in the physical realm. The landscape was alive with colour day and night. The build-up of the absorbed divine light resulted in an energy-mist that arose from the body of Gaia and floated out into the cosmos in all directions, advancing the energy exchange between all beings in the cosmos. Negativity could not exist here, but there were dangers in this realm, the most delusional being 'glamour'.

Avery floated over to the babbling brook by which the Lord of the Night was seated. Avery had mastered the art of flying on both the etheric and physical planes of existence, which accounted in part for Avery being nicknamed Pan by his mother. When he was a child, Tory had told him the adventures of Peter Pan and, feeling a kinship with the legend from Never Never Land, Avery still bore the nickname with pride.

'There is something I have been meaning to ask you, Night Hunter.' Avery used the title bestowed upon Gwyn ap Nudd by the Celtic peoples of ancient Briton. 'Why, out of all the planets in the known universe, do you choose to base yourself on Gaia's etheric manifestation? There are other locations in our realm that are far more wondrous.'

This is the planetary body that needs the most attention. The mortal Homo sapiens have made it necessary for me to keep a constant eye on them. Praise the Logos that they are all still confined to this star system. The lord conveyed his viewpoint using telepathic projection, as was his way. *Your forefathers have a lot to answer for and humans are only just beginning to atone for the rape and devastation of the lovely Gaia.*

'Her physical body is a mess,' Avery had to admit. 'I must say I am hard pressed to fathom my forefathers' reasons for poisoning the planetary body that nurtures their existence. Especially with no means to move elsewhere!'

His mentor explained that the devastation on Gaia was all part of the evolutionary learning process designed to develop the courageous human souls who had inherited the nightmare. *Without great evil and adversity to overcome, no great good can be achieved, no huge lessons learned. One force without the other renders the whole of physical existence redundant … for nothing can evolve without the cause and effect set in motion by these opposing forces.* Avery's frown prompted Gwyn to expand his theory. *A large part of Gaia's population is now devoted to healing the planet and their children will inherit conservation sense and so on. The evolution of the mortals of this planet is finally beginning its upward spiral. A new Ray is coming into force with your appointment. The time of 'the devotee' is coming to a close and the Violet Ray, the Ray of 'the ritualist' will soon hold more sway on Gaia; this is the same Ray that governs the Chosen Ones.*

'Ray, lord?' Avery had never heard him use this term before. 'Are you talking about the celestial light of the Logos?'

Gwyn nodded, but sucked in his cheeks as if dissatisfied with the vague definition. *The Rays express themselves through the light of the Allied Logoi, but more specifically they are the seven aspects of the Almighty, through which creation was brought into being. The seven spirits before the throne of God channel the universal will into the myriad of forms operating on all levels of awareness. Without the interplay of the seven Rays of Life on every plane of existence, evolution would not be possible.*

Avery was frowning again.

Is the explanation too vague? the Lord of the Night inquired, but then he heard the faint call that echoed through the ethers.

'Avery! I know you can hear me.'

'It's my sister, lord,' Avery advised, a mite embarrassed to interrupt the important tutorial with mundane considerations. 'She probably expects me to go out and celebrate graduation, before our little brother leaves for Tarazean. I'd be glad to put her off.' Avery fished for permission to get out of the engagement, as Fallon was sure to be going and he hated the way she hung on his every word all the time.

No, no, insisted the lord. *You should take time to celebrate life with your friends, before your adult responsibilities make it impossible to organise.*

'But I'd much prefer to hear your tuition, Night Hunter,' Avery appealed. 'I don't want to —'

Ah! Gwyn held up a finger to caution him. *In the future you shall be glad to have such carefree memories. Best look after your physical body for a change. Your mental and spiritual bodies are overloaded.*

'But I can take more,' the lad said eagerly.

Gwyn shook his head. *Take a break and enjoy it. That's an order.*

With a cringe and a moan Avery willed himself home.

* * *

For a student studying at any of the Institutes, 'Patrick's' was the in place to go to eat and socialise. Patrick Haze and his husband, Season, had been running the place since the Chosen had landed on Kila. It had been the first restaurant to open in the city. It was the perfect arrangement for the gay couple, as Season loved to cook and Patrick loved to play host. But the best thing about eating here was that Patrick had a sixth sense where food was concerned and could order for you if you chose.

With full bellies and faces aching from laughter, the five young graduates stood on the pavement outside the restaurant contemplating their next move. Fallon, Bast and Sparrowhawk were a little wobbly from the Bahula (deadly joy water) they'd been drinking. Avery was only pleasantly tipsy and even Lirathea, the saint, had been talked into having one glass, which had given her the giggles.

'I'm not too smashed to know I have to pack.' Sparrowhawk leaned on Lirathea, but she was as unstable on her feet as he was and they both fell about laughing until they steadied themselves.

'I'll give you a hand,' Lirathea offered. 'I think I need to get home before I embarrass myself *badly*.'

'Aw,' whined Fallon, figuring Avery probably wouldn't stay unless Lirathea did. 'Must we retire so early?'

'Well, just because these two want to pike out, doesn't mean we all have to.' Bast nudged Avery, who had been rather charming and chatty all evening. 'What do you say we continue on, old chum?'

As Fallon had not been as adoring as usual and had even been pleasant company, Avery nodded. In any case, Bast was always good for a laugh. 'I get to pick the destination,' he proposed.

'You're on!' both girls agreed, as Avery's choice was sure to be exotic.

Thus, with a girl on each arm, Avery bid his brother and sister goodnight. 'Be good,' he cautioned them, going out of his way to make the comment sound like a jest.

Lirathea did not take it that way. 'You're telling us to be good? You're so deluded, Avery.' She rolled her eyes and taking Sparrowhawk by the hand, turned to make her way home.

The Falcon lad smiled back at his half-brother as he was led away. 'See you ... if I do?' Sparrowhawk waved, knowing Avery probably wouldn't come to the spaceport to see him off in the morning — they just weren't that close.

'The blind leading the blind,' Avery muttered under his breath as he watched his brother and sister stagger up the road together. *We'll see who is deluded ... and I know it isn't me.*

'So where are you taking us?' Bast prompted. 'Somewhere Otherworldly?'

All the Chosen had mastered the art of physical teleportation but to differing degrees. Some could only achieve the feat within the star system. The fourteen appointed ones of the Allied Logoi, which included Maelgwn, Lahmu, Tory and En Noah, could teleport themselves to any known destination or person within the galaxy. But only Avery and the Night Hunter himself could access any destination in the etheric world.

'Want to go to a concert, ladies?' Avery invited them

winningly. He drew their attention to their feet, and both girls gasped and burst into delighted laughter upon realising they were floating.

'You're not going to fly us there, are you?' Fallon clutched Avery tighter as they continued to rise.

'Hardly,' Avery scoffed, as the blue-white light of the ethers engulfed them and they were spirited off to the mysterious destination.

When Bast and Fallon found themselves standing on the top of a remote mountain peak in the physical realm of their home planet, the girls were clearly disappointed.

'I don't think the musicians are going to be able to haul their gear up here.' Bast scoffed at Avery's promise of a concert.

'Trust me.' Avery parked his butt on the ground and leaned back on his elbows to gaze at the sky.

Bast looked at Fallon, who shrugged in blind faith and sat down beside Avery.

'Come on.' Avery patted the ground to the other side of him, urging the suspicious Leonine to be seated also. 'Quickly ... before the mist comes and you get lost.'

Stay standing, Fallon wished to herself, wanting nothing more than to lose her flamboyant sister so as to have Avery all to herself.

'All right, Pan man, but this had better be good.'

Before Bast had even got herself comfortable a bright celestial light erupted in the sky, flashing white, and then red, and then green.

'Oh, how beautiful!' Fallon uttered, delighted by the spectacle.

'It's a solar flare shower, so what?' Bast flopped flat onto her back, unimpressed.

'Allow me to turn up the volume a little,' Avery offered, as the mist of a thousand flowers came sweeping over them.

'Great ... now I can't see anything,' Bast chided, inwardly excited by what was occurring.

'That aroma is heavenly.' Fallon fell onto her back and breathed deep the scent. Her eyes had closed to fully appreciate the bouquet that was very arousing to the senses and was all the more so for feeling Avery's gaze upon her.

The dress of shimmering black, which Avery knew Fallon had worn for his benefit, fitted her shapely torso rather snugly and seemed to be accentuating her cleavage, as she stretched out on the ground beside him. Maybe it was just the alcohol or the celestial light, but she really did look rather scrumptious this evening. Bast looked fabulous too, but then she always did. This was a new look for Fallon and her personality had taken a swing for the better this evening as well. She was actually pretty cool when she wasn't adoring him like a love-sick teenager — it was kind of nice that he could do a little silent admiring for a change.

A stirring synergy of sound could be heard arising, and as the mist cleared it became apparent that each different note sounded from a different colour as it burst forth in the sky. Now the phenomena in the sky radiated with fluorescent colour that danced in an overawing collage across the sky.

'The sky is singing?' Bast found her tongue first.

'Not just the sky,' Avery explained. 'What you are hearing is the music of the spheres. Each atom in creation resonates to a particular note in accordance with its vibration and movement, which results in the great symphony of the cosmos. This is the most acoustically correct spot, as it were, from which to listen, as this is the most distant location on Kila from our city of Chailida. Civilisation tends to drown out the performance, even in the otherworld and hence I come here for the best seats in the house. I also find a solar storm is a very dramatic addition to the planetary repertoire.'

'Wow, it's just incredible.' Fallon held her hands to her heart, moved to tears by the experience.

'It's certainly not boring,' Bast admitted.

'Let it never be said that I don't know how to show a girl a good time.' Avery lay down between the sisters, feeling rather gratified by their delight.

'Oh, I feel sure that will never be said,' Bast retorted in a very fresh tone of voice.

It infuriated Fallon when her sister flirted with Avery, which Bast only did to mock Fallon's feelings. Bast hogged every man's attention just because she could, and Fallon deeply envied her sister's abundance of charisma and her confidence in wielding it. Fallon knew that if she'd ventured to make the comment first, it would have come out sounding corny instead of seductive.

A shadow fell over the three of them and a deep grunt startled the girls into a standing position, which spurred Avery to laughter. The sisters, upon spying the upper body of a large stone creature protruding from the ground, began to scream.

'Avery, do something.' Bast gave their amused host a kick.

'Sorry, ladies.' He composed himself and arose. 'I know Grom looks ominous, but I assure you he's harmless.' Avery addressed the creature directly. 'What's up, my stony friend?'

You know how you wanted me to tell you if I ever saw your brother and sister getting cosy?

'Yes,' Avery queried warily.

They're looking pretty cosy now.

'Really?'

'Really what?' Bast interjected, as all she heard from the beast was grunts and moans. 'What's it saying?'

'I need to nick off for a bit.' Avery backed away. 'I'll be back before long, but you can will yourselves home at any time.'

'I'll wait,' Fallon responded ... a little too quickly she decided in retrospect.

'Is there any more like him lurking about?' Bast inquired, pointing to the huge rock creature as it curled back into the boulder from which it had appeared.

'Everywhere!' Avery grinned as he began to fade away. 'But not to worry, I would never leave you two unsupervised in my realm ... that would be an accident waiting to happen.' He chuckled at the thought.

As Avery vanished, so did the breathtaking Otherworldly surroundings and Bast threw her hands up, most put out to find herself back on the earth plane.

* * *

As they strolled through Central Park on the final leg home, Sparrowhawk and Lirathea's pace had practically come to a stop, as they laughed and joked about their unseemly state.

'I don't want to leave,' Sparrowhawk protested, and suddenly losing his good cheer, he came to a complete standstill. 'Why don't you come with me to Tarazean?' he asked, knowing it was an impossible suggestion.

Lirathea gave him that 'good sense' expression of hers. 'I am currently working through the energies of a site on Kila. You know I can't leave here now, as I truly feel I'm on the verge of a breakthrough in communications with Devachan!' She announced her results with great excitement, although Sparrowhawk only managed to force a smile at her news. 'Spiritually speaking, this is a very big deal,' she added, hoping to stir up some sort of enthusiasm in him.

'I know ... your research is the most important thing,' he agreed, although his tone was that of a man rejected.

Lirathea folded her arms, annoyed by his self-indulgent attitude. 'I support you in your endeavours, Sparrow, I thought you might have been happy for me.'

'I *am*,' he admitted, albeit grudgingly. 'I just wish —'

'I know what you wish,' she injected, her tone soft and heartfelt. 'And we both know it can never be.'

'Only me, Thea?' he asked, unable to keep the desperation from his voice.

Lirathea took a deep breath. Every time they spoke in this way, she felt herself on shaky ground, and having had a glass of Bahula, she was not thinking as clearly as usual. 'I cannot bring myself to pour energy into something that can never be.' She backed away from him a couple of steps.

'What kind of an answer is that?' Sparrowhawk was offended by her cool indifference. 'Are you afraid to just tell me plainly how you feel? Or do you think you are protecting me from myself by refraining?'

Tears were welling in her eyes. Lirathea had wondered if this subject, which they'd been evading all their lives, would come to a head this evening. Perhaps she'd even willed it; in fact, she must have desired it for it to be happening at all. 'If I could fall in love with you, I would.' Her voice quivered as her emotions surged forth and she struggled to repress them. 'But earthly love is not on my agenda.' Her resolve hardened once more, and Lirathea held out a hand to keep her brother at bay. 'My life's ambition is a solitary one and must be so to be achievable. I am entirely devoted to the service of the Allied Logoi.'

'I understand that,' he confirmed, frustrated with his lot. 'But surely one kiss would not ruin your standing with the powers that be?'

'No ... no it wouldn't,' she admitted, exhausted by the situation. 'But it would be the beginning of the end of sanity, for the both of us,' she concluded soberly, before turning and walking on.

'My sanity left me years ago,' Sparrowhawk muttered under his breath.

The sincerity of the statement took some of the wind out of Lirathea's sails and she stopped dead in her tracks. After a long pause she finally spoke. 'Mine too.'

She turned slowly around to face him, ashamed to be admitting her secret when she'd sworn to herself that she would remain strong and pretend not to feel the electricity that danced between herself and her half-brother.

Up until this moment, Sparrowhawk had never in his wildest dreams suspected his sister of lusting after anyone, and his heart soared with pride and joy to think that he held the affection of such a blessed creature. 'We are in so much trouble,' he uttered, straining to keep the smile from his face as they closed the distance between them.

Lirathea held his face in both her hands. 'I am going to miss you terribly.' Her announcement was accompanied by a flood of tears, but she kissed him anyway, swept away by emotion.

They endeavoured to express a whole lifetime of forbidden affection in that one kiss, both knowing the memory would have to last a lifetime.

'Is this one of my delusions then, dear sister?'

The sound of Avery's voice brought the heart-stopping encounter to a grinding halt.

'You're a sick bird, Sparrow.' Avery approached to pry them apart. 'She's your sister!'

'Half-sister,' Sparrow corrected, evading Avery's attempt to strike him by backing away. 'In ancient times on Gaia it was the done thing.'

'But we have supposedly progressed since then.' Avery chased his brother further away from his twin.

'We were just saying goodbye, Avery,' Lirathea stated quietly, in the hope of getting him to lower his voice.

Avery got her message and walked back to her to quietly advise: 'I saw you kissing him, and the general vibe was not goodbye.'

'But that's what it was … okay?' she appealed with a sniffle. 'So, if you've quite finished proving your superiority and making us feel guilty, we'll just leave it at that, shall we?'

The hurt in her voice persuaded him to back off. 'I won't tell anyone,' he vowed.

'Much appreciated.' She forced a smile and moved to catch up to Sparrowhawk.

'This time,' Avery added in caution.

Lirathea paused in her advance a second, but did not look back at Avery. She wanted to suggest that he get a life and stop interfering in everybody else's, but she knew that would simply be taking out her frustration on her brother for *her* mistake. As infuriating as it was to admit, Avery was right — that kiss should never have happened and it must never happen again.

Much to Fallon's delight, Bast got fed up with having no male to impress and so was threatening to head home.

'If I know Avery, and I do, he's not coming back,' she advised her love-struck sibling. 'Don't embarrass yourself by waiting too long.'

'I'm still enjoying the show.' Fallon looked at the sky, attempting to hide her contempt for her sister's thoughts. 'But you run along home. I know you have an early flight to catch.'

'Yes,' sneered Bast, folding her arms, 'and you wouldn't want me to miss it.'

'Well, destiny waits for no woman.' Fallon looked back to her half-sister and forced a smile.

'Oh, fear not, mine will wait for me.'

Fallon was glad when Bast disappeared; she lay down, stretched out and enjoyed the peace and quiet.

'I thought she'd never leave.'

Startled, Fallon turned her head to find Avery lying on his side next to her. 'I was under the impression you and Bast were chums?' she commented, proud of how calmly the words slipped from her mouth in the presence of her sweetest dream come true.

'Three's a crowd, don't you find?'

As he leaned closer, Fallon's heart began thumping in her chest, inducing a mild panic; this was too good to be true. She leaned aside to avoid the kiss and quickly raised herself to kneeling. 'You've never thought so before.'

'Of course I have.' He sat up to confront her. 'I just never said so.'

'Why not?' Fallon persisted, loving every minute of the attention.

'I wanted to get graduation out of the way before distracting you with more compelling issues.' His voice dropped to a whisper, his lips poised close to hers.

His explanation was not really convincing, but in Avery's case Fallon wasn't going to query her luck twice. She closed the gap between her lips and his and, once engaged, their kiss was far more passionate than she'd imagined. Before she'd even realised they'd moved the ground was at her back. She felt Avery's hand pass over her right breast trapped beneath the shimmering black material that hindered their delight. But in a daring move, he slipped the strap from her shoulder to expose her breast and her nipple hardened in the cool night air, and again when encompassed by the warmth of his hand. Only as a moan slipped from her lips did Fallon realise they were no longer being kissed. Avery's attentions were moving downward. As his tongue toyed with her nipple, he was already reaching a hand up under her skirts. Although her head was swimming in a sensual delirium and she wanted nothing more than to oblige him further, this encounter was moving way too fast.

'Avery!' She gently pushed him off of her and replaced the strap on her shoulder. 'Perhaps we should both take some time to sober up and then reconsider our position?'

'You think I'm drunk?' Avery began to chuckle, but suppressed his amusement to explain: 'One does not need booze to seduce a *beautiful* woman.'

Fallon was stunned. 'You think I'm beautiful?'

'No,' he replied. 'I know that you are more comely and radiant than even the glamour of the enchantress sirens of the Otherworld.'

Fallon suppressed the urge to gasp at his flattery, as she had always feared comparisons to the waifs of the kingdom Avery was to rule.

'I don't want an illusion, I don't want a planetary ruler, I want a woman of flesh and blood, who loves me for who I am and not what I represent.'

He has to be drunk. Fallon couldn't think of any other explanation for the sudden swing in his attitude towards her. 'If what you say is true...' Fallon rose to standing, '...then surely you would be willing to formally court the woman you want so badly.'

'If I must.' He rose and was overpowered by a hug.

'Oh Avery ... do you really mean it?' She held him at bay to look into his eyes as she received the answer, but the coloured light in the sky ebbed at that moment.

'It's destiny,' he replied.

Avery thought he'd best make an appearance at the spaceport this morning. His mother would be furious if he was not there to bid his little brother all the best for his Governorship before he left for Tarazean. He also wanted to catch up with Bast before she left for Nugia and apologise for not making it back to them last night. He expected both Bast and Fallon were probably furious with him for just abandoning them like that, but after his run-in with Lirathea and Sparrowhawk he'd needed to seek some Otherworldly repose.

When he spotted his mother hugging Sparrowhawk, Avery made his way over to the family gathering. He was surprised not to find Lirathea present and equally surprised to get a smile instead of a frown from Fallon. Bast looked pretty annoyed at him though.

'I know,' he stressed, as he approached the Leonine female. 'I'm so sorry I never made it back to you last night, but I had to take care of some rather pressing affairs.' His attention shifted to Sparrowhawk, who glared back at him, then to Fallon who winked at him, and, not knowing what to make of her resolve, Avery looked back to Bast.

'Goddess, how I pity the woman who marries you.' Bast gave him a squeeze, suddenly realising how much she was going to miss him. 'I expect you to visit after your appointment, you hear?' She pulled away and slapped his chest hard. 'Don't disappoint me, Pan man.'

'I wouldn't dream of it,' he replied, winded. Bast was quite the warrior woman — she was very much her father's daughter.

It was her father, Brian Alexander, who came forward and took his daughter under his arm. 'Come, Bast. If we don't get on that flight we'll never get off Kila.'

'Bye everybody.' The young ruler-to-be waved as she was lead away. 'See you all in the senate.'

Avery turned about, figuring he'd better say something to his brother before his parents got suspicious. 'Haven't you gone yet?' he jested, moving over to ruffle the quills on Sparrowhawk's head as he knew nothing would annoy Sparrowhawk more. 'Geez … what have I got to do to get rid of you?'

Sparrowhawk brushed off his brother's annoying intent and forced himself to smile — when all he really wanted to do was smack Avery in the head. 'I won't miss you either.' He held his hand out and shook Avery's — they even came at a hug for the sake of appearances. 'I'll see you in the senate.' Sparrow echoed Bast's sentiment, unable to think of any other kind words.

'Not if I see you first,' Avery joked as their mother tapped his little brother's shoulder to let Sparrowhawk know it was time he got moving. She served Avery a look of scorn, but said nothing as she accompanied Sparrowhawk to his transport.

'Hey, remember me?' Fallon waved a hand in front of Avery's face to get his attention.

'Oh ... hey, Fallon, what's up?' he queried, looking back towards his parents as they saw his brother onto his flight.

'Nothing much.' She played along and in the spirit of the game she dropped her voice to a whisper. 'I was just wondering when you were planning to tell everyone?'

'Tell everyone what?'

'About us, of course.'

'About us!' Now Fallon had his attention. 'What about us?'

'*What about us?*' The joy fell from her voice and Fallon realised that what had happened last night had been as she feared. 'Then it was just the drink and you didn't really mean it?'

Avery pressed all ten of his fingertips into his skull. 'Fallon, did I miss something?'

Fallon took a breath to refrain from slapping his face. 'Deny that you desired me last night?'

Avery's jaw swung open at the question, dumbfounded by her presumption. Sure, he'd thought she looked a bit of all right, but a thought didn't constitute an affair and certainly not a commitment! And unless her psychic aptitude had improved somewhat of late, how could Fallon have known what he was thinking anyway? 'I do most certainly deny it,' he retorted and realised he wasn't telling the whole truth. '*Beware when your words conflict with what is in your heart.*' En Noah's warning ran through his mind and he cringed. *This was not what he meant*, he assured himself on the quiet, when a stinging sharp slap to his left cheek brought him back to reality. 'Hey, wait a minute,' he called after Fallon as she stormed off. 'What the hell was that for?'

'I wish you could remember,' Fallon called back to him. 'It was really beautiful.' On the verge of tears, she buried her face in her hands and hurried away.

'What the ...?' Avery, who was never lost for words, held his cheek, amazed. Fallon seemed genuinely upset, so he thought he'd best wait before attempting to extract an explanation from her.

'What was that all about?'

Avery turned to find his mother, arms folded and glaring at him. 'I have no idea.' He pleaded ignorance. 'The girl has gone insane!' He appealed to his father, Maelgwn, knowing he'd have a better chance of getting him on side.

'Has she now?' His mother wasn't convinced. 'Have Sparrowhawk and Lirathea gone insane, too?' Tory queried him further, and he looked a little stumped by the question.

'I don't know what you mean?'

'I mean ... you don't seem to have many friends this morning.'

'Is that why Lirathea isn't here, because she doesn't want to see me?' Avery assumed that saying goodbye to Sparrowhawk in public would prove too difficult for their sister and that she was using him as an excuse not to be here.

'Now why would you wonder that, if you've done naught to offend anyone?' Tory proffered.

'Perhaps they offended me?' Avery was rather disturbed at always being the first one accused whenever there was trouble.

Maelgwn kissed his wife's cheek to distract her from the interrogation and save his boy. 'Why don't you go home and see if you can't cheer Lirathea up?' he suggested, moving to take a firm hold of his son around the back of the neck. 'I'll take Avery to lunch and we'll have a little *chat*.'

'Ah! Good plan, father,' Avery squeaked, pained by his father's grip, which made it obvious how annoyed he was with Avery. 'I'm sorry I snapped at you, mother,' he stated, hoping to appease his father, who released him. Avery braved planting a kiss on Tory's cheek.

Her look implied that she hoped he was telling the truth, but she was far from believing him.

Praise the Logos for dear old dad, Avery decided as he sidestepped his mother's wrath to go to lunch.

It had taken some time to convince his father that he hadn't done anything to warrant Fallon's outburst at the airport this morning.

Fortunately for Avery, his parents were souls of high spiritual morals, for they could read the thoughts of whomever they chose, but refrained to engender trust and encourage those in question to offer up the truth for themselves. None of the fourteen blessed guardians of the Logoi ever abused their additional psychic talents; these gifts were reserved for times of crisis and were used only to serve the higher purpose of the Cosmic Logos.

Avery had nothing to fear for himself, of course. He was more concerned about giving away Lirathea's secret. He had kept the conversation over lunch way off the subject of his falling out with his sister. His father didn't mention it either.

However, Avery had vowed to Maelgwn that he would head straight over to see Fallon and get to the bottom of her strange behaviour.

Fallon seemed to have mixed feelings about Avery's visit. 'Have you come to apologise or get hit again?' she asked as she settled on a chair in the lounge room, having shown him in.

Avery remained standing. 'I'm still not too sure what I was hit for,' he ventured to explain politely, but the look Fallon gave him told him this was not the response she'd been hoping for.

'Oh, come on, Avery, you can drop the act, *we're alone*,' she stressed the point, 'just like we were last night. I haven't planted any secret surveillance to entrap you or —'

Avery pulled her up. 'We were never alone last night. I left you with Bast and that's the last I saw of you.'

'Oh no,' Fallon shook her head slowly and calmly, unable to support his claim. 'You saw more of me than that.'

Her voice and manner had a seductive edge that Avery found both becoming and alarming.

'You really don't remember, do you?' Fallon sounded almost sympathetic suddenly and Avery thought he had best take the path of least resistance.

His shook his head, not needing to fake his bemusement as he took the seat opposite her. 'Would you be so kind as to refresh my memory?'

Fallon blushed slightly, which set a seed of fear burning in Avery's chest, and as she told of how he'd returned last night to seduce her, he didn't know what to think. Avery knew it hadn't been him, as he'd been otherwise detained with a beautiful forest nymph at the time.

'And you're sure you didn't imagine this?' Avery probed, his concern mounting.

Fallon had to refrain from hitting him again and in desperation she removed the thought-wave neutraliser from her wrist and held out her hands to him. 'Take hold if you don't believe me.'

Desperate to know the truth Avery removed his thought-wave neutraliser, so as to perceive her memory. What Avery didn't consider was that, in opening her mind to his, he also left his mind open to her.

As he viewed Fallon's memory of their encounter, it stirred Avery deeply and he began to wish that he had returned to her last night — but he hadn't, so who was this impostor?

'You're right, it was beautiful,' he said as he let her hand go, afraid to look at her face and see the hurt there. A slap across the cheek made him braver and he looked at Fallon as she stood to yell down at him.

'You slept with a wood nymph last night after you left me?' Fallon burst into tears. 'How come you remember that encounter so clearly? Am I so forgettable?'

'No.' Avery found himself on the defensive, as his feelings were all in a muddle.

Fallon's misconception would cause her less worry than the truth — that some impostor had molested her in his stead. This realisation made Avery jealous, knowing the passionate encounter he hadn't had. He'd never before suspected that he could feel this way about Fallon. It was all too confronting; time to retreat.

'I'm sorry about everything, Fallon.' Avery wondered why, when she'd hit him twice for something he hadn't done, that he was the one apologising?

'Sorry doesn't really cut it, Avery.' She placed both hands on her hips, whilst she visibly got her anger under control. 'I can't tell you how happy I am that I stopped you last night ... that is the last time I ever share anything intimate with you.'

Avery remembered dreaming of escaping Fallon's adoration once they graduated and now that his wish was unfolding, it didn't look very attractive any more. En Noah had warned him to beware what he willed to manifest. Avery realised his heart was aching at the thought of losing her love. 'Fallon, please —'

'Please leave.' She cut him off and, bursting into tears once more, she headed for another room. 'Just go.'

Avery raised both hands to his head, shell-shocked from the encounter. 'My perfect existence has turned to complete shit in a matter of hours ... what the hell is going on?'

3

GLAMOUR

'Frankly, I'm worried,' Avery stated, having reviewed what he'd discovered with his father, who was reclining on a lounge, wearing a smug smile on his face.

'Yes, I can see that.'

'Well, who do you think it could have been with Fallon last night?' Avery stopped floating about and lowered himself onto a seat to be still.

Maelgwn raised both brows and took his best guess. 'It could have been you.'

'Me!' Avery was excited by the supposition only a second. 'How could I have been in two places at once?'

'If the nymph you were with was playing you for sport with her glamour, you would only remember what she wanted you to,' Maelgwn reasoned. 'Ask En Noah, he knows all about being glamoured by a siren.'

'En Noah has been seduced by a nature elemental?' Avery found the premise hard to accept.

Maelgwn nodded surely. 'Oh yes. His past life incarnation, Selwyn, near stole the heart of Gwyn ap Nudd's queen ... before Amabel was the Night Hunter's wife, that is.'

'I don't remember much of Amabel,' Avery commented. The fairy queen of the Otherworld had achieved a four-fold elemental state of being when Avery was still a boy and so had passed on to the next stage of elemental evolution before he'd really had much of a chance to get to know her. 'I remember she was very beautiful,' Avery stated and then smiled. 'Who would have thought En Noah could have charmed the greatest charmer of them all?'

Maelgwn was amused by his son's astonishment, but felt obliged to point out, 'But Amabel was not Noah's soul-mate and thus their affair brought him nothing but grief and distraction for twenty years.'

'But I have been trained all my life to detect glamour, both Otherworldly and material,' Avery defended, knowing that his father was headed toward a lecture on the error of seducing Otherworldly maidens. 'I am the master of glamour, for heaven's sake ... I would've known if Didi was playing me for sport last night and she never has before.'

'*Before*, Avery?' His father prompted an explanation.

Avery shrank from the question. 'It's not like I force myself on them, father,' he defended. 'They pursue me!'

'That's not the point, and well you know it.' Maelgwn became very adamant suddenly. 'The only time you should ever get intimate with a female is if you love her. Not like her a lot ... think she is sweet, hot, charming, persuasive! For only love will ever steer you right, all other motives lead to disaster.'

'You sound like you're speaking from experience, father,' Avery noted and braved a query of his own. 'How many women did you know intimately before mother?'

'That was over a hundred and fifty years ago for me, Avery. You can hardly compare the morals of modern-day Kila to the Dark Ages of Gaia.' Maelgwn brushed off the question.

'I'll assume you knew many,' Avery smiled, having got his answer.

'Look, your cavorting last night has landed you in strife,' Maelgwn sat up to emphasise his point, 'when you could have been in love.'

'No, I don't think so.' Avery resisted the idea strongly.

'Okay, then.' Maelgwn changed tack. 'Let us consider the possibility that it was an impostor with Fallon last night, because any of the Chosen who know you are capable of assuming your form.'

'Then I would have the culprit drawn and quartered.' Avery stood, unable to think of anyone who would do such a thing. 'If Fallon hadn't been so chaste the bastard would have —' Avery got so angry he couldn't speak.

'It could have been a woman,' Maelgwn suggested.

Avery couldn't come at the idea. 'Bast might be cruel and game enough to spite her sister like this, but ...' He thought back over Fallon's sensual little memory and shook his head. 'I'm betting the impostor was a male.'

'Sorry to interrupt, fellows.' Tory came to a standstill in the middle of the large archway that led into the lounge. 'The Governess has summoned all of us to an emergency meeting.'

Maelgwn stood, concerned by the curious request. 'But we have been retired from political life for twenty years?'

Tory shrugged, none the wiser herself. 'Best go and find out what the problem is, I guess.'

Candace had also summoned En Noah, her historian, Rhun, the Vice-Governor of Kila, and Floyd, their head technologist to the boardroom at Government House.

'Thank you all for coming so quickly,' Candace began, as everyone was seated around the boardroom table. 'I wish I could say *good* afternoon, but I've had a communication from the Delphinus chieftain, Zabeel, that suggests otherwise.' She remained standing to say: 'The Aten has been stolen from Lura.'

Everyone in the room gasped at the announcement. The space and time hopping Aten had been the brainchild of the Nefilim Lord Marduk, and he'd utilised the space station's unique capabilities to bring about the realisation of his dream, the immortal race of Homo sapien legends, now known as the Chosen Ones.

'And that's not the worst news,' Candace forewarned

everyone before dropping the bombshell. 'Zabeel's wife, Cordella, was on board the Aten at the time and has been kidnapped along with the vessel.'

As the father of Zabeel, the immortal half-caste Delphinus-Homo sapien ruler, Maelgwn was concerned for his daughter-in-law's welfare. 'Has anyone claimed responsibility? Has there been a ransom note?'

'No,' Candace informed him matter-of-factly. 'No one has claimed responsibility. There has been no ransom note, nor were there any witnesses to the theft.'

'How can there have been no witnesses?' Maelgwn contained his frustration beautifully. 'The Aten is the size of a small moon. Surely someone saw the pirates who commandeered it, or something of their craft at least! I doubt that the culprits are of the Chosen breed, so they must have used a vessel to execute the hijacking.'

Candace shook her head. 'According to Zabeel, the Aten simply vanished, with no warning and no witnesses.'

'Do you have a plan of action?' Tory asked, heading off another interrogation from her husband. Realising he was being overzealous, Maelgwn contained himself.

'As we all know, the Aten has an excellent cloaking system. However, as a safety precaution, Zabeel recently had a tracking system designed to track the elestial crystal emissions that radiate from the Aten's unique drive system. Naturally, this system can only track the Aten across space. If the thieves have taken flight into time, the system cannot track them. We are hoping the hijackers are not aware of the full potential of the vessel they have stolen, and that their timing for the theft was just an unhappy coincidence.'

Rhun felt sympathy for his Delphinus half-brother. 'Well, surely we can assume that if the tracking system can't pin down the Aten, then the hijackers have fled into time?'

Everyone around the table nodded to agree with the Vice-Governor's summation, except Floyd; Candace looked to him to explain the hitch.

'That's the theory. The problem is that the tracking system has yet to be completed.' Floyd outlined the problem.

'That's what I meant when I said we're hoping this theft was just a fluke, as the timing was uncanny,' Candace added.

'So how long until the tracking system is up and running?' Maelgwn voiced the pertinent question.

'Naturally Zabeel has given it top priority, and I shall leave for Lura to see if I can't speed things along as soon as this meeting is adjourned ... we hope to have the system operational asap,' Floyd assured his old friend.

'In the interim, we were counting on,' Candace's eyes turned to Noah, 'the Tablet of Destinies ... might it be of some aid in locating the Aten's whereabouts?'

Noah looked a little doubtful. 'I shall certainly consult the Tablet on this matter,' he offered. 'I can put forward the Aten as my current concern, and see what we come up with, but as Tory will tell you, understanding the Tablet's predictions is not always immediate.'

'This is probably a stupid question ...' but Avery had

to ask it anyway. 'Have any of the fourteen guardians of the Logos tried willing themselves after Cordella?'

It was too risky for any bar the fourteen of the Logoi, and the Night Hunter's apprentice, to attempt pursuit, for only they had been granted the ability to teleport themselves safely between star systems.

'I tried to locate her psychokinetically but was unable to,' Candace informed them regretfully. 'We suspect a NERGUZ module is being used to conceal her.'

'I thought we'd disposed of all those wretched things,' Tory scowled.

'So many modules had been black-marketed by the end of the Pantheon's rule that it has proved impossible to get them all out of circulation.' Candace defended her government's efforts. 'I was surprised by just how many of the devices we did manage to recoup … it seems that just about everybody had visions of bringing the Pantheon down.'

'And now someone wishes to bring us down,' Maelgwn stated warily.

'We don't know that,' Candace argued. 'They may not have known Cordella was on board, or the capabilities of the vessel they were stealing.'

'And they just happened to have a NERGUZ handy?' Maelgwn posed. 'I don't buy that.'

'Our terrorists may have skipped through time already.' Rhun voiced another possibility. 'Not even the fourteen of the Logoi have the ability to fold time without Otherworldly aid or technology.'

'I do,' Avery boasted, although he hadn't done much time travel yet — there was so much of the Otherworld to explore and Avery found the physical realm mundane no matter what point in time. 'From the Otherworld I can gain access to history past and future. And I shall endeavour to seek out our dear sister-in-law at the first opportunity.' Avery looked first to the Governess and then to his father to reassure them.

'But who would do this?' Tory appealed for possibilities. 'Lahmu has brought freedom, peace and prosperity to the interplanetary alliance, and we haven't had so much as a whiff of discontent from any quarter of humanity, mortal or not.'

Everyone dwelt long and hard on the question, and no one could suggest there was even a fraction of discontent, and certainly none so large or organised as to be able to hijack an entire space station undetected.

'But even if you do get the tracking system operational, they won't be able to track the Aten through etheric space?' Avery sought clarification from Floyd.

'That is correct,' Floyd confirmed.

'I shall spread the word throughout the Otherworld ... if they pass through my dominion, I shall know about it,' Avery vowed and Rhun gave him a sideways glance.

'I don't believe you are the ruler of the Otherworld just yet, or have I missed news of your initiation with the Night Hunter, little brother?'

'Any day now,' Avery warranted, and Rhun nodded to himself as if not entirely sure about that.

'I shall accompany Floyd to Lura.' Maelgwn stood up, wanting to aid Zabeel through his crisis. 'I'll report back to you if there is any news,' he advised Candace, as Tory approached to bid her husband goodbye.

'I should go also.' Avery requested the Governess's leave, even though he was not yet officially part of Lahmu's council.

Candace granted his request with a nod. 'I had best inform my husband of the event.'

Avery couldn't help but suspect a connection between Fallon's mysterious admirer and the disappearance of the Aten, as in both instances superhuman ability had been required to execute the deception and none of the Chosen were corrupt enough to have committed the crimes.

He sought his mentor at his favourite Otherworldly haunt on Gaia, and was surprised to find the Lord of the Night absent — this place may as well have been Gwyn ap Nudd's office and it was always business hours.

Night Hunter? Avery telepathically requested the lord's presence or alternatively, for Avery to be willed to his mentor, whichever was more convenient for the Otherworldly ruler in this instance. In all of his fifteen-year apprenticeship with Gwyn ap Nudd this technique had never failed him; therefore, Avery was deeply shocked when nothing happened.

He's not here, young master, informed Templeton the old willow tree by the river.

The upper body of the nature spirit protruded from the tree that once represented its body in the physical world, although in Gaia's current age nothing remained of the tree at all. A mass of matted twigs sprang from Templeton's head and his facial features were long and drawn. Green glowing were his eyes, as his spirit was saturated with earth energy. His arms resembled branches and stick-like hands and fingers extended from these two appendages. If this place was Gwyn's office, then Templeton was the Night Hunter's secretary.

Avery found the claim amusing and thought he knew better. 'Of course he's here. Why doesn't he want me to locate him? Is this a test? My initiation, perhaps?'

The master said you had nothing left to prove. He has gone, Sire. The Night Hunter said that you were in charge now.

'What!' Now Avery really was alarmed. 'But I need his assistance ... there are still so many things about this realm that I don't know. Templeton, please tell me you're joking.'

I am just the messenger, Sire. Templeton pleaded ignorance. *If you have any problems, Gwyn suggested you speak with the presiding Ray, Master R.*

'The Ray,' Avery mumbled, remembering Gwyn had said something about a new Ray coming into power at the time Avery would assume rulership of the Otherworld. 'And how do I communicate with this master? Does he manifest, or —'

We have been known to.

The voice seemed to fill the Otherworld and emanate from everything within it, including Avery. Out of the running river rose a brilliant, celestial body of flaming ultraviolet fire that had a heart of yellow light. It was not composed of etheric substance, but of some matter from beyond the lower planes of existence. The body of the winged being was only vaguely apparent within its celestial aura, which radiated beyond the field of Avery's vision. Once his eyes adjusted to the lustre of the presence, he came to focus on the features of the face.

'Father?' There was questioning in Avery's voice, only because there was a softness about his father's appearance that wasn't evident in his physical manifestation, and his form appeared not so warrior-like.

Sometime, responded the master, *and mother, too.* The features of his face transformed into those of Avery's mother, Tory, but the celestial body, clothed in fiery ultraviolet vapour remained completely sexless.

'Mother,' Avery mumbled as he collapsed onto his knees, realising he was in the presence of a truly divine being of whom his parents were only one tiny aspect.

The apparition floated over to settle alongside the overawed lad. *Perhaps you would be more comfortable if I chose another incarnation to assume, and perhaps a body of lower order. One moment whilst I transfer myself to your plane of demonstration.*

The bright aura of the master retracted into a male physical form with only the glow of an enlightened being about it. He appeared to be about thirty-five years old, of slender form and average height. There was a striking intellectual and regal countenance about the man, although he was only dressed in a robe of violet that was trimmed with gold. His hair was long, straight and dark, falling to below his shoulders, and he had a tiny moustache and a triangular beard on his chin. When he smiled he displayed a perfect set of teeth, and his eyes of soft blue sparkled brightly.

'The Comte de St Germain,' he announced verbally, much to Avery's astonishment. 'But you can just call me "the Count". Everybody else does.'

'Everybody else?' Avery ventured to ask.

'The Members of the Great White Brotherhood, the other Chohans, my co-workers and adepts,' the Count explained.

Avery understood that by Chohans, the master referred to the master souls who had ascended beyond the sixth initiation of the Logos, the same initiation Avery was approaching himself. 'So you are the Chohan of the Violet Ray of whom Gwyn ap Nudd spoke?'

'Not for very much longer,' the Count explained. 'I too have an Apprentice, who will assume the role of the Chohan of the Seventh Ray of the Violet flame very soon. I am still aiding the new Seventh Ray Chohan to hold and process the patterns for the principles of freedom and liberty in the physical world. It usually takes many years for a new Ray Master to become conditioned enough to hold and process so much energy alone, but I am very pleased with my apprentice's progress so far.'

Avery floated to a standing position. 'And what will you do then, lord, move on to the higher work?'

'Well, in truth, Avery, I have already assumed the appointment of the Mahachohan — The Lord of Civilisation for the physical world. I'm at the Head of the Third Ray Department of Active Intelligence. This means that I am responsible for the evolution of human civilisation. The four sub-rays of attribute ... art, science, religion and transformation are channeled through my department to collectively influence civilisation.'

Avery boggled at the lord's responsibilities. 'Can you instruct me as to how to find my sister-in-law if she has been abducted and hidden in time?'

The Master R is the authority on time travel, Sire, Templeton boasted on the lord's behalf. *He created the concept. For among his many titles and responsibilities he is the Lord of Time.*

'It is true,' the Count confessed in a modest fashion. 'But you have much to learn about a great many things before you will become a Lord of Time. I am here to help you prepare for your forthcoming initiation.'

'My initiation?' Avery was confused. 'But Templeton here said that Gwyn ap Nudd has handed the Otherworld over to my guidance, because I had nothing left to prove?'

'Nothing left to prove to the Night Hunter,' the Count clarified. 'But still you must prove your worth to the Cosmic Logos.'

'But, if Gwyn ap Nudd has gone, what shall happen if I fail my test? Who shall manage the Otherworld then?'

The Count chuckled away the lad's concerns. 'Gwyn has not gone altogether, think of him more as ... taking a vacation, so that you can have the opportunity to try Otherworldly leadership on for size. And you need have no fear of failure. I am a very good teacher,' he assured Avery. 'But you must put aside the affairs of the physical world for a time and concentrate on the bigger picture.'

'But I have made promises to my Governor to help find —'

'You are not ready to face your earthly foe,' the Count informed abruptly, albeit kindly. 'You have already admitted that there are things you still don't know about the realm you are to rule. For you to rush off and attempt combat with physical world affairs at present would be like sending a carpenter to build a dwelling without his tools.'

'But Gwyn has taught me so much.' Avery didn't like to argue with an obviously superior being, but he felt like he was being asked to abandon his kin.

'Gwyn has taught you how to utilise the beings within your realm,' the Count concurred. 'I am here to enlighten you about the existence and purpose of your allies dwelling beyond the planes of demonstration with which you are familiar, and to make you aware of how to best utilise the light within yourself. Only once you have learned to detach yourself from earthly affairs will you be able to aid your kindred.'

'Well, there is still one thing I can do. Templeton ...' Avery approached the willow to give his instruction. 'Send out word throughout our realm that if anyone spots the Aten space station, I want to know about it.'

Yes, master. Anything else?

Avery looked to the Count to see if he had any suggestions, but the master only smiled and shook his head, as if Avery was wasting time. 'Make it clear to everyone that I am not to be disturbed from my tuition with the Count,' he added. 'I'll report to you to be updated about the Aten, as soon as I have the Count's leave.'

The Count closed his eyes and gave a nod, pleased by Avery's resolution.

* * *

Noah had never used the Tablet of Destinies for detective work before and, concerned about understanding its insights, he had asked Tory to be present when he consulted the tool on the issue of the vanished Aten.

'Tea?' Rebecca, Noah's wife, offered as Tory took a seat on the lounge in Noah's private chambers at the Purcell Institute of Immortal History, which bore his name and was dedicated to him.

'Afterwards perhaps,' she smiled, knowing Noah wanted to get on with the task at hand.

'Right, then.' Noah lowered himself into a seat, as did his wife, as he detached the three-sided pyramid from its setting that hung on the chain around his neck.

Anyone could see the pendant engraved with ancient hieroglyphs and fashioned from Orichalchum — the strongest metal known in ancient Gaia — but only Noah could touch the tool or see what it divined and so it would be until the Sage passed it on to the next keeper.

Noah held the base of the pyramid against his third eye area, between his brows. Eyes closed, he focused on the cause of his concern, and within moments the pendant drifted away from him and began to unfold, expanding in size ten times over. The sides of the pyramid fell flat to form a large triangle, with four smaller triangles contained therein; this was positioned so that the lone triangle crowned the lower three. The Sage opened his eyes to take in what the divine tool disclosed as it hovered in midair before him.

Tory and Rebecca waited patiently for Noah to speak. His eyes drifted from the central triangle where he saw the Aten, the cause of his concern, to the quarter depicting the best that could eventuate, at which he'd smiled warmly. The joy fell from his face as he viewed the worst outcome, and as he viewed the crowning pyramid depicting what would come to pass should no action be taken, the Sage went into a trance. This might have alarmed some people, but, having previously been a keeper of the tool, Tory had experienced similar episodes.

'Oh, Goddess!' Noah gasped as he was released from the mental grip of the Tablet's prophecy.

'Are you all right?' Rebecca urged him to speak of his experience.

Tory added in encouragement, 'What did you see?'

'I saw, I saw ... I'm not entirely sure what I saw,' Noah said, momentarily dumbfounded.

'How about you just start at the best outcome and work your way from there?' Tory suggested.

'In the quarter depicting the best outcome, there was ...' Noah suddenly came back to the present and looked at Tory to inform her, '... a vision of Sparrowhawk getting married.'

Tory was bemused to hear this. 'What could the Aten being stolen have to do with my son getting hitched?'

'I have *no* idea,' Noah emphasised, having already explained that not a lot of what he'd seen made sense to him. 'Perhaps the connection lay with his bride, but I didn't glimpse her face.' He shrugged apologetically. 'In the quadrant that divined the worst outcome I saw the Chosen fighting a holy war, against —'

As the Sage gasped to a pause, Rebecca pressed for an answer. 'Yes?'

Noah had seen more in this segment than he was prepared to tell Tory, for it had been Avery he'd seen leading the army of darkness against them. 'It was hard to see,' he said finally. 'A veil of darkness shrouded our adversaries. But I got the distinct feeling that they were immortal, like us. It was as if they'd ingested Charichalum Orme, as the Goddess Aya did in an attempt to postpone her destiny.'

'Heaven forbid! I don't see how that incident could have become common knowledge.' Tory shuddered at the thought, thankful that only a handful of the most adept of the Chosen had borne witness to the event.

Aya had been one of the Nefilim who, during the fall of the great Pantheon twenty years ago, had ingested the substance produced by reducing the metal Charichalum to its purest form.

ORME was the abbreviation for the process of the purification of base metals — Orbitally Rearranged Monatomic Elements. Gold subjected to the Orme process produced what was variously known to the ancients on Gaia as 'the Water of Eternal Youth', 'the Philosopher's Stone' or 'the Alchemist's Key'. If this substance was introduced to a human body containing a dormant immortality gene, passed on to a select few humans by their Nefilim forefathers, then the gold Orme activated the dormant gene to bring about a quickening of the subject's psychic talents and an accelerated spiritual enlightenment. The atoms of the body, now in a high spin state, became magnets for the cosmic light of the Logos. The atoms, after drawing in the vital life force, project it back into totality with love, via the heart centre of the subtle body. This explained why the Chosen Ones were felt to exude such a positive, calming and inspiring energy, for their chakra centres spiralled outward, projecting their goodwill to all around them. This kind of spiritual enlightenment was not exclusive to the Chosen, of course; any human being could become adept by devoting themselves wholly to the divine will. However, the discipline required was such that a spiritual adept was a rare occurrence among mortal men. A heart that loved more than it feared was the key to maintaining the immortal state induced by gold Orme. On a more mundane level, gold Orme defied gravity and had major super-conductive properties and applications.

As opposed to gold, Charichalum was the densest, darkest, strongest substance in the inhabited galaxy and yet it was incredibly lightweight. The pure Orme derived from this metal was found to have the opposite properties to gold Orme in many regards, save three. These were that Charichalum Orme still defied gravity, granted life eternal, and was super-conductive.

But Charichalum Orme absorbed light and energy continuously and this was the way of the inward spiral, the way of the destructor. Any human taking this substance to achieve an immortal state of being pledged themselves to the dark arts and powers derived from the Planes of Density that existed below the physical.

Charichalum Orme production would have ceased under Lahmu's government — to curb the risk that the substance posed to the future of humanity — but Charichalum Orme was needed to power the shield that was currently protecting one quadrant of the galaxy from the radiation of a dying star. The shield completely encompassed the sun, Anu, that would otherwise be a black hole in space if not for the thousands of brightly lit shield generating stations that surrounded the black orb.

'But none of the Chosen would choose the dark path, and nobody else has the immortality gene in their DNA.' No sooner had Rebecca finished her claim than she realised it was false. 'Except —'

'The children of Dumuzi,' they concluded at once.

'Yes.' Noah was shocked to a standstill by the implications. 'In order to orchestrate a challenge against the Chosen, our opposing force would have to have significant numbers and there could be hundreds of the Nefilim lord's offspring by now.'

This ascended Nefilim lord had been the God of Fertility in ancient times and living up to his name, Dumuzi had seduced many human women and produced half-caste bastards of nearly every breed. Sexual relations between immortals and mortals were forbidden under Pantheon law, but Dumuzi repented the error of his ways and had been forgiven his indiscretions. His soul-mind had ascended from the physical realm with the last of the Nefilim, twenty years ago. In the wake of the Nefilim departure, the existence of a spaceship of potential demi-gods of questionable moral upbringing posed somewhat of an ethical dilemma to Lahmu's government. Looking at the big picture, all of Dumuzi's bastards should have been killed, to ensure none took the divine plan into their own hands by activating the dormant immortal gene in their DNA. But at the time there were over a hundred children and grandchildren that had been spawned by the lord, and Lahmu could not bring himself to murder so many — nor even one innocent soul, if the truth be known. Instead, Lahmu decided not to inform any of the souls in question about their hidden potential and had given them free passage throughout the inhabited galaxy. They were forbidden to go to Numan or Anu, as was anyone not working on the sun-shield project, Numan being the planet where Charichalum was mined and the dark Orme produced.

Only one of Dumuzi's children so far had been recognised as one of the Chosen. She was the wife of Zabeel, Cordella, who had gone missing along with the Aten. Thankfully, Cordella was not one of the handful of souls who knew about the human applications of Charichalum Orme, but the Delphinus Governess was living proof of gold Orme's superhuman properties.

'If the descendants of Dumuzi were the ones who stole the Aten, that would seem to explain why they kidnapped Cordella.' Tory feared the track her thoughts were taking. 'Some of her kindred are probably wondering why, in twenty years, Cordella has not aged a day.'

'If a person carrying the dormant God gene in their DNA was of low morals and hateful intentions, gold Orme's superhuman effects would be short-lived, Rebecca outlined. 'However, if such a person had a large stock of the substance they could take it indefinitely, just as some of the Nefilim did, but then they would also run the risk of overdosing and accidentally enlightening themself.'

Noah was turning pale and shaking his head. 'And would you say Gaia has the largest population of undeveloped souls in the galaxy?'

Tory was startled by his query. 'What has Gaia to do with any of this?'

'That's what I was wondering,' Noah commented, not eager to disclose his concern. 'In the quadrant of the Tablet that foretells of what shall happen if no action is taken, I witnessed a great division in the human consciousness on Gaia.' He looked Tory in the eyes, looking forlorn as he understood what it meant. 'Our foe won't try and take Kila or any of the other planets within Lahmu's alliance straightaway, as there is too much goodwill among the human inhabitants. On Gaia, the Dark Lodge knows it has a chance of winning the fight for control of human consciousness, as it has partially succeeded before.'

Tory thought back through her history. 'The fall of Atlantis,' she gasped.

'The witch hunts, the great world wars!' Noah listed a few more instances.

'But Doc has reported great progress on Gaia,' Tory argued. 'With the co-operation of Gwyn ap Nudd and his dominions, most of Gaia's body will soon be repaired and many of those humans who have assisted with the renewal of the earth have achieved great leaps in spiritual awareness.'

Noah nodded, allowing that her claims and Doc's were quite true. 'Still, inside Gaia's great biodome cities, moon colonies, space and sea stations, all the lower desires still thrive,' Noah was sad to concede. 'I feel we, the Chosen, are to blame for their lack of comprehension. If every other human race in the galaxy can benefit and learn from our example, then we should have made an effort before now to bring Gaia's children into our alliance.'

'We've been working towards that,' Tory defended.

'Obviously not fast enough.' Noah was annoyed that over the years he'd foreseen these problems arising, but had hesitated to voice his concerns, trusting that the government knew what it was doing. 'The Dark Lodge has a perfected form of mind control at use on Gaia now. Back in Atlantis you had to study to become a devotee of the dark arts. Now you can be seduced to the dark path and not even know it.'

'What are you talking about?' Tory had lost his train of thought.

'Glamour,' he announced. 'The same glamour that you and I and everyone on Gaia were seduced by before we were called to the service of the Logos.'

'I understand Otherworldly glamour, but by physical world glamour, do you mean magic?' Tory frowned in question.

'Perhaps I should have said glamours. Magic is a form of physical world glamour whereby you fall victim to the illusion of another; this is also the case with the glamour of the Otherworldly inhabitants. But more often in the realm of matter, it is material world desires that cause us to inflict self-induced glamours upon ourselves. The media on Gaia is what makes glamour there so pervasive, and there are so many forms of glamour to choose from ... such as the glamour of physical strength, ambition, personal wisdom, aloneness, the love of being loved, selfish unselfishness, self-importance, personal comfort, devotion, sentimentality, narrow vision, popularity, sex-magic, excess, and a million other distractions that make glamour such a problem on Gaia, and indeed everywhere. My attachment to this Institute, and my library, is a glamour of sorts,' Noah admitted. 'In the knowledge that everything in manifestation is but an illusion and a transient tool for creation to learn and evolve by, I would like to think that if this Institute was destroyed tomorrow I wouldn't give my creation a second thought. Still, I fear I would mourn the loss of my glamour as all victims do.'

'So, only when we are completely detached from everything in the material world, including our own bodies and kindred, can we truly be sure we are walking the path of light.' Tory had known all this for a long time, but even the advanced spiritual soul found it difficult not to become entranced by matters of the physical world. Noah was nodding and seemed to be rediscovering the meaning of life too. 'So,' Tory continued, 'in reality, we should not be worried about the theft of the Aten or how its misuse might alter the quality of life that we have worked so hard to achieve. Rather, we should allow events to unfold as they may ... for no matter what happens, good or bad, we shall learn from the experience and that is the purpose of creation.'

Noah stopped nodding and raised both brows. 'That's how the Cosmic Logos will be viewing this instance. Fortunately, we are the tools of the master artist and not the brain.'

'I don't think I'll ever make a very good Ascendant Master,' Tory sighed. She did long to move on to more meaningful work in the universal scheme of things. 'I fear I shall always fail on the emotional attachment front. I do care about what happens to my kindred and the peoples under my brother's rule.'

'Ditto,' Noah stated. 'But somewhere in creation we don't judge matters of the physical world as good or bad — we only know the challenge of change in the great tides of consciousness.' Noah stood perfectly still to focus himself, for he knew he was digressing from the matter at hand. 'I believe I should speak with Lahmu.'

'I agree.' Tory was a little spooked by what the future held in store. 'I'll wait for permission from my brother before taking our suspicions to Maelgwn and Zabeel. And when we get a moment, it might also serve us well to pay Gaia a visit.'

With a firm nod, the Sage and his wife seconded her proposed course of action.

4

EXPOSING A LEGEND

As bold as brass he strode up to the counter of the library at the Institute of Immortal History on Kila, safe in the knowledge that his disguise would grant him safe passage.

'Good afternoon, Avery.' The woman behind the counter greeted him warmly. 'What can we help you with today?'

'I was looking to do some research on my grandfather,' he informed, hoping his smile wasn't too smug.

'Myrddin,' she assumed, rather than queried.

'No, Caswallon,' he corrected. 'What text has En Noah scanned onto orb pertaining to Caswallon's rule of Gwynedd? I was particularly interested in the uprising of his brother, Cadfer.'

'That *is* obscure.' The librarian's eyes boggled. 'I'll see what I can find.' She sounded a little doubtful of finding anything, but moved off to check her database.

How dumb can you be, he thought, *leaving such a prime information source open to the enemy? The good of heart are far too trusting.*

'Well, what do you know,' the librarian informed him, as her soft-light screen filled with data. 'There are a few references listed.'

'I'm looking for dates.' He got more specific.

'These are the orbs concerned.' She gave her database a mental command and three PKA (PsychoKinetically Activated) orbs appeared on a small teleporter plate on the counter in front of him. 'You can check the index for specific references,' she told him, and then realising who she was talking to, added: 'But you know that, Avery.'

'I do. Thank you kindly.' He scooped up the orbs. He knew that none of the orbs were allowed to leave the building, and so found himself a quiet corner in which to do his research.

When Fallon spied Avery in the library, she wasn't sure if she was pleased by his presence or not. She had to admit that she didn't expect to find him in the Institute now that they had graduated. She thought he'd be dedicating every spare second to his Otherworldly studies.

'This is an unpleasant surprise,' she bowed down to whisper in his ear. He was seated on a lounge chair, absorbing information from a PKA orb.

He was startled by the interruption and, looking up, was rather taken by the sight of the girl who was frowning down at him. 'Unpleasant?' he queried, not sure what his assumed form had done to offend the girl.

'Has your memory had another lapse?' Her eyebrows raised in question.

'I ... I?' He hesitated to respond, but resolved to be charming, as that was the best course of action where females were concerned. 'I could hardly forget anything that passed between us.'

Fallon's frown deepened, as she figured he was being smart. 'I haven't forgiven you,' she informed him, just in case he was mistaking the conversation as a sign that he was back in her good books.

Forgiven me? He had a feeling that he might be in trouble here. 'I didn't expect that you had,' he smiled meekly.

'What are you doing here, anyway?' Fallon caught a glimpse of a scrap of paper with some numbers on it before Avery tucked it into his pocket. It read 519–14 = 505. The digits had to stand for dates, she reasoned, and only Gaia had so many years of history.

'Just some research.' He gathered up the orbs to return them to the counter.

'Into your father's rule of Gwynedd?' Fallon guessed, and was surprised to note the alarm in Avery's face, as he rarely showed such an emotion.

'Yes, of course.' He brushed off her query and stood to take his leave.

'But why?' She suppressed an urge to laugh. 'You know it all backwards, forwards and sideways.'

'No time to explain.' He began to back up towards the counter. 'I'll see you around, okay?'

As Fallon watched him return his research tools and exit the library, she concluded that his behaviour was somewhat odd. She was not as outstanding at history as Avery was, and was unable to recall what was happening in Gwynedd in 505AD — or, at least, she was assuming AD if Avery had been researching his father's life.

The librarian smiled as Fallon approached the counter.

'Could I please take a look at the orbs that Avery was just referencing?' Fallon requested, whereupon the librarian handed them over. 'Thanks.'

In 505AD, Avery's father, Maelgwn, had been but fifteen years old. His mother, Queen Sorcha, had been murdered in the uprising of his Uncle Cadfer that year. With the aid of an evil crone, Cadfer had led an uprising against his brother Caswallon. He had succeeded in taking Gwynedd, jailing his brother the King, and murdering Sorcha when she would not submit to Cadfer's intent to claim her as his own. Maelgwn, with the aid of his father's champion, Sir Tiernan, and the High Merlin of Briton at the time, Taliesin, defeated Cadfer and freed his father.

'Why, in heaven's name, would Avery be researching this period?' Fallon wondered, but then most things about the man were a mystery to her — that's what she found alluring about him.

Brian was disappointed to be forced to leave his daughter's inaugural celebration before the festivities had even begun. He considered that he should have known that some major disaster would rear its ugly head and prevent him from enjoying the momentous occasion when the government of Nugia was finally handed from the Leonine leader, Tyrus-Leon, to Bast, their daughter.

In order to introduce the immortality gene into the gene pool of the Leonine race, Brian Alexander had artificially fathered the child of Tyrus-Leon's wife, Samara. For Tyrus-Leon was a living mortal incarnation of Brian's soul-mind, just as Samara was a living mortal incarnation of Brian's own wife, Candace. Thus, Bast had always known two sets of parents — as, indeed, did Sparrowhawk — one set belonging to the Leonine race and the other set belonging to the Chosen breed.

As Brian prepared to leave Nugia, he felt consoled by the fact that since Tyrus was remaining for the ceremony, all Brian need do was a little past-life regression and he too could bear witness to the ceremony he was about to miss.

'I'm so proud of you, princess.' Brian hugged his daughter in parting. 'I know you are going to be an outstanding Governor to your people and I'm so very sorry that I'm going to miss your big moment.'

'No, you won't.' Bast held him at arm's length as her eyes turned to Tyrus-Leon who was standing close by. 'You're always with me, in one body or another.' She smiled, doing her best to suppress her disappointment.

'And yet, you'd do just as well without me.'

'Perhaps.' Bast was flattered. 'But I like having the ruler of the known universe behind me for support. It's very confidence building.'

'Like your confidence needs any boosting.' He kissed her cheek and turning his thoughts homeward, he served Bast with a wink of encouragement and vanished.

In the conference room of Government House on Kila, Brian found his wife and Vice-Governor very pale in appearance as they spoke with his sister, Tory, and the historian, Noah Purcell. After hearing the news of the missing Aten and the suspicions they were entertaining about the identity of the thieves, Brian himself paled.

He stood, gripping the edge of the table and staring hard at it as he assessed his own feelings on the matter. 'All those who knew my ruling on the children of Dumuzi was going to come back to haunt me, please raise your hands.'

Tory was the only person present who did not raise her hand, thus Brian looked to her. 'Ethnic cleansing is never an answer, as it stems from intolerance, ignorance and fear. If the children of Dumuzi are set to oppose us, then it was meant to be. I feel we made a mistake leaving them to their own devices, though. They should have been educated in the secret mysteries and encouraged towards taking up the cause of the Logos.'

'They didn't want to be integrated into our society, Tory,' Brian defended. 'They just wanted to continue as they were.'

'But they had no idea of their hidden potential,' she argued. 'With the proper guidance —'

'It looks as though they do know of their hidden

potential and intend to activate their immortality without any guidance or permission from us.'

'But we don't know it was they who stole the Aten,' Tory pointed out. 'This is all just an educated guess.'

The Governor looked to Noah for his feelings to be made known, but the scholar's mind seemed to be elsewhere. 'Kila to En Noah, are you with us?'

Noah broke from his contemplation and smiled broadly. 'I don't know why I didn't consider it before, but do you think Myrddin's old time hopping chariot might be able to speed me to the current location of the Aten?'

'Yes! Brilliant!' Tory jumped up, suppressing a cheer. 'After all, both vessels have the same drive system.'

'Hmmm.' Rhun sounded wary. 'Imagine all the damage the children of Dumuzi could do if they got their hands on the chariot as well.' Everyone's spirits deflated at the very possibility. 'I quietly considered this avenue at our last meeting, but I never suggested it due to the danger.'

'He's right.' Brian hated to pass up such a promising solution. 'It's too risky.'

'But we always have the backup chariot that Inanna constructed illegally. We could use it to track down the first chariot, should it go missing.' Noah suggested and all his associates looked stunned.

'We have possession of the other chariot?' Tory got out the question first.

'Yes,' Noah confirmed. 'Inanna gave it to Maelgwn to speed him between Tarazean and here when the revolution against the Nefilim first broke out. I've had it in storage with the original ever since.'

Brian looked to Rhun to see what he thought in light of the new information.

'Sounds like we might have a plan,' he granted.

Beneath the Institute of Immortal History was a vault only Noah and Maelgwn, the ex-Governor, knew about. The Governor and Governess, the Vice-Governor and the ex-Governess all felt like mischievous school children as they followed the Sage through the depths of the building.

'This is much more fun than playing politician,' Brian commented. He would've felt guilty abandoning his duties to go on an adventure, had this not been the most pressing matter on his agenda.

'I agree.' Rhun kept pace with the Governor. 'I feel almost compelled to volunteer to go.'

'No way.' Brian flattened the idea — if he wasn't allowed to go because of his position, he wasn't going to let Rhun get away with it either.

'I shall go.' Noah concluded the argument, or so he thought.

'Noah?' Tory sounded surprised that he'd volunteer. 'But, you've never done any physical time travel in your life.'

'High time I did, don't you think?' He grinned back at her. Twenty years ago he would not have felt confident to execute such a mission, but his experience in the Sensor-sphere had changed him; he knew no such fear any more.

The Sensor-sphere, like the Tablet of Destinies, had been a gift from the Nefilim Logos, Anu. A high-level spiritual learning tool, the Sensor-sphere was located in the Otherworld — out of the reach of mortal man. This Otherworldly technology offered a crash course in cosmology and granted insight into the pertinent eras of the development of human consciousness into matter — it was a universal bible, experienced first-hand via all one's senses. But more than this, the tool was an initiator of the soul that awakened a deeper universal purpose in all who braved the course. Noah held the only key to the Sensor-sphere, and only those persons who he knew were spiritually and intellectually advanced enough to cope with the Otherworldly school's doctrine had been admitted. Everyone present had qualified and graduated.

In response to Noah's mental command, the wall at the end of the corridor vanished to disclose a chamber beyond. 'Here we are,' the Sage announced as the lights came on.

The two chariots sat side by side and looked not unlike a couple of large, hovering, hi-tech motor scooters. Both vehicles sat inside a floor-to-ceiling box of light that constituted both the alarm system and an electric shield, which could inflict enough pain to deflect even an immortal attempting to breach the system.

Noah shut the defence system down with a thought.

'Now, I want you back here immediately,' Brian instructed Noah, as he seemed to be determined to go. 'You will yourself to Cordella, grab her, get back here, and then we discover what she knows before we attempt anything else. Is that clear?'

Noah nodded as he climbed on board.

'You're sure you don't want me to go?' Tory was hopeful that the Sage might be swayed, as she hadn't done any time travel for ages, and she missed it.

'I know you are the expert, Tory,' Noah granted, 'and probably a far better warrior than I if a considerable force is guarding Cordella. Still, who shall we send after you, should you go missing? Better that I test the waters and then we have an experienced swimmer to send in after me, if I fail to surface.'

'You shall not fail.' Tory allowed him the adventure despite her lust for the quest. Noah was right — it was high time he took the journey of journeys.

'All right, here goes.' Noah placed his hands on the chariot and closed his eyes to focus on his target. After a few moments he opened them once more to find the Governor and company still staring at him. 'Would a NERGUZ module prevent me finding her this way?'

'Maybe,' Tory warranted, and then clicked her fingers with another solution. 'But you can still locate the Aten.'

'I am not familiar with the space station.' Noah was clearly disappointed that he might have to forfeit his quest.

'I am,' Candace spoke up, 'and I should be able to direct you telepathically.' She racked her brain a moment for a safe place to hide the chariot whilst Noah searched for Cordella. 'I know, Gibal's old laboratory. I very much doubt that any of Dumuzi's children are interested in science, and even if they found the chariot there, without knowing what it was it would just look like another incomplete project the lord had left lying around.'

Brian kissed his wife's cheek. 'Beautiful and *brilliant*.'

Noah stepped out of the chariot. 'But once I get to the Aten, how am I to search it? The security system has probably been altered to suit the thieves, so if I attempt to open any doors, they're going to be alerted to my presence. We need to send someone who is intimately familiar with the control centre of the station.' Noah's eyes came to rest on Candace. 'Someone who can will themselves from place to place to avoid detection.'

Candace couldn't contain her smile when she realised the scholar was right.

'No way!' Brian put his foot down. 'No way.'

'We have no choice.' Candace ignored her husband and began willing forth a few essential weapons to take with her, just in case she ran into trouble.

'Then I'm coming with you,' Brian insisted.

'No way!' insisted everybody else.

'Shit!' he protested loudly, having predicted the objection. 'Why did I turn out to be Lahmu?' he whined, feeling that he was never permitted to do anything exciting any more.

'Oh, do stop complaining!' Candace calmed Brian with a kiss and then informed him, 'Noah shall go with me.' She nudged the grinning historian back towards their transport. 'Let's go.'

Arriving in the large abandoned laboratory on board the missing space station, Noah removed the crystal that was the heart of the chariot's drive system, and Candace found a large dust cover that was draped over one of the many incomplete inventions lying about and threw it over their transport.

'I'd say that's pretty secure.' Noah felt confident about leaving his precious treasure here.

Candace nodded. 'Now, it's my guess that our foes are all going to be hanging out in the Star Chamber and its affiliated chambers.' It was far too risky to teleport them straight into the high-security areas without knowing the number of thieves they were dealing with. 'The dock ... too far away,' she mumbled, as she assessed the possibilities and then startled Noah when she clapped her hands. 'I've got it ... the security station.' She pulled the two PKA sonic pulse blasters from her belt and, setting them to stun, handed one to Noah, who looked a mite overwhelmed by the notion of a shoot-out. 'There will be two guards at most,' she informed him in a routine fashion. She extended her left hand to Noah, as he needed to capture her memory of their destination in order to be teleported along with her.

He took hold with his left hand, gripping his weapon in his right and preparing to fire upon arrival.

In a dance-like motion they turned outwards, to defend each other's backs.

'Ready, friend?' Candace gave notice of their departure.

'I was reborn ready.' Noah picked up on Candace's mental image of the security station, and the laboratory in which they stood became saturated with the blue-white etheric light of their passage.

* * *

As Candace had predicted, there were only two guards in the security station, both of which the Governess managed to blast into unconsciousness before they even knew they had company.

'These are Dumuzi's offspring all right.' Candace noticed the vague Nefilim genetic traits in their physical appearance as she hoisted them out of the control seats.

Their eyes were larger and more almond-shaped than those of humankind, their features were a little pixie-like and they were tall and slim of stature. The Chosen Ones had not inherited Marduk's Nefilim features as he'd always assumed a human form, right down to a cellular level, when spreading his seed among humanity. The only genetic difference Marduk maintained during his intercourse with humanity was that of his God gene, to ensure that his immortality was passed on to the Chosen Ones, but his genetic features were not. This ensured Marduk's offspring remained outwardly undetectable from any human being. Dumuzi had not bothered taking any such precautions.

Candace concealed their victims in a storage cupboard before taking a seat in front of the wall of soft-light screens that were monitoring the interior of the Aten. To her surprise the Star Chamber that contained the quartz throne, the command seat of the vessel, was currently empty. 'Damn it!' She'd felt so confident of learning the identity of their major adversary. 'Where's the ringleader?'

As Noah was viewing the screens monitoring the exterior of the vessel, he had other concerns. 'Holy cow, that's Gaia.' He vaguely motioned to the monitor displaying the image. 'We're parked in orbit around her.'

Candace willed her hover seat closer to the external monitors to take a look for herself.

'Oh, Goddess!' Noah startled himself as he noted that there were no city lights illumating the darkness on the night side of the planet and the same was true of the dark side of the moon. 'No cities, no moon colonies ... when on earth are we?'

'Maybe ...' Candace searched for another explanation, 'the power grid is down.'

'Where is the orbiting power station, and all of earth's satellites?'

All they observed on the monitors was virgin atmosphere, uncluttered by human space debris.

'My husband told us not to get sidetracked.' Candace brushed off her curiosity and returned to her search of the interior. 'We have to locate Cordella.'

She was right, of course, and Noah joined her in front of the screens to help with the search, until he came up with another idea.

Dragging one of the unconscious thieves — they were both a Falcon-Nefilim mix — from the storage cupboard, Noah placed the unconscious man's hand on the PKA control plate of the security database and then placed his own hand over the top, being sure not to touch the control plate himself.

'Will that work?' His lateral thinking amused Candace.

'There is a chance it won't, I guess.' Noah hesitated, even though he felt they were pressed for time. 'I've never tried projecting my will through somebody else's body before. Do you want me to refrain?'

Candace shook her head. 'Continue.' She rose from her seat and drew her weapon. 'If we set the alarm off, head straight back to the chariot.'

Noah instructed the database that he wished to be advised of the location of Cordella, Governess of Lura.

'Excellent.' Candace understood the garble of information the database spat forth onto the soft-light screen. 'They've got her in a cell on the prison levels. Request a visual on security camera PL5–92.'

Noah did as Candace bade him and they both smiled broadly upon seeing Cordella pacing her prison cell alone.

Candace pulled an Enzu-Guz from her toolbelt. This handy little device had been developed for the removal of NERGUZ modules back on Gaia, when the psychic restraining device had first been introduced as a weapon. The NERGUZ had a tiny needle on the inside of the wrist module which penetrated the skin of the prisoner; the Enzu-Guz severed this pin and freed one from the NERGUZ's restraint. Candace had not had to use an Enzu-Guz since the time of the great Gathering on Gaia, which was over seventy years past.

'I'm going to get her,' Candace instructed. 'You keep watch until I return and then we'll all head to the chariot together.'

Noah served her a reassuring nod, quietly formulating another plan.

Candace left his presence and reappeared on the soft-light screen. He observed the two women as they briefly embraced. Candace cut the Delphinus Governess loose of the device that was restraining her and immediately teleported them forth from the cell to appear before him.

'En Noah,' Cordella gasped, when she saw the great Sage. 'I am so indebted to you both.'

'Thank him later.' Candace gave Noah the nod to proceed to the chariot.

'May I have the NERGUZ you cut off, Cordella?' Noah asked upon their arrival in the laboratory.

'Why?' Candace frowned, as she ushered Cordella into the chariot ahead of her.

Noah's physical form transformed into that of the Delphinus Governess. 'I'm going to stay with the Aten and keep track of the time hopping adventures of our foe. If I replace Cordella, then there's a good chance our foe won't even know we've been here.'

Candace's jaw dropped. She wanted to forbid it, but she could not when it was actually the sensible thing to do. She handed over the deactivated NERGUZ, which looked untampered with once it was snapped back onto Noah's wrist.

Cordella was speechless as she watched the Sage conceal his weapon under the long skirt of the dress he now wore; her dress, in fact, on her body! 'Thank you for getting me out, En Noah,' she finally found her voice. 'But I fear you should come back with us. My kindred hold no love for me any more. You will be in grave danger.'

'I'll be fine, Nin,' he assured the Delphinus ruler, as Candace joined her in the chariot. 'Give my love to my wife.' He stepped away from the transport, eager to see the women depart for home.

'Take good care, Noah. I'll send the chariot back to you,' Candace advised, fearful of the historian becoming lost in time.

Noah nodded in appreciation as he waved them farewell.

Maelgwn entered the vault beneath the Institute of Immortal History, and was not surprised to find the Governor, Vice-Governor and Tory already present. 'You thought of the chariots already. I suspected that you might have.'

Zabeel entered close behind his father and was momentarily relieved to find his relatives on the case. 'Have you had any luck tracking the Aten down?' He was desperate for some good news, as Floyd had yet to get the tracking system for the Aten up and running, and so the technologist had stayed on Lura to persevere with this quest.

Brian motioned to the empty space beside the high-tech chariot before them. 'Well, one of the chariots has gone somewhere, so I guess you could say we've made some progress.'

'Who has gone after Cordella?' Maelgwn was surprised to find his wife still present.

'Candace and Noah went after her.' Brian felt vexed by this fact, in retrospect. 'If I'd stalled her a couple of minutes, you could have gone.'

'How long have they been absent?' Zabeel implored, obviously worried out of his mind.

'They went a good couple of seconds before you got here.' Rhun stepped in to calm his younger half-brother. 'And I'll bet you that they're back within the count of twenty.'

Tory had to smile. She could tell Zabeel had started to count in his head and in so doing, he unconsciously relaxed a little — all her children had so much faith in their oldest brother that his word was almost gospel.

'See, what did I tell you?' Rhun announced as the chariot manifested and he won his bet. But Zabeel was already lost in an embrace with his wife, as was Brian. 'I would have brought the little woman if I'd known it was going to be this kind of an affair,' Rhun jested, turning back to his parents.

'Where's Noah?' Tory was alarmed by her dear friend's absence.

Candace left her husband to return to the chariot, and placing her hand upon it, it vanished back to Gibal's laboratory.

When she saw the chariot depart, Tory was relieved. 'So Noah is coming back?'

'Eventually.' Candace broke the news gently. 'We have reason to suspect our foe may intend to alter the past. How or when, we don't know. Noah has assumed Cordella's form to discover what the children of Dumuzi have in mind.'

'Your foe has a name ...' Cordella spoke up to enlighten them all, '... and his name is Viper. He found Dumuzi's secret stash of Orme and has been using it to maintain an immortal state.'

'But why should he have to maintain an immortal state?' Brian wondered. 'Once the gene is activated he should just remain immortal.'

'Not if his soul-mind has dark aspirations,' Maelgwn clarified and Cordella nodded to confirm this.

'Viper is searching for an incantation spell.' Cordella hesitated to say more as Viper's claims had sounded rather fantastic when he'd conveyed them to her.

Tory felt suddenly ill; in her gut she knew what the spell was for. 'Is this incantation used to summon an evil spirit?'

Cordella's emerald green eyes parted wide with horror. 'A crone he called it.'

'But Mahaud is no longer able to wield any power in the physical world,' Brian voiced his understanding of the situation, knowing what his sister feared.

'In the present that is true,' Tory mused, and then frowned. 'But in the past?' She shrugged. 'I think that could be problematic.'

'Problematic!' Brian boomed. 'If Mahaud latches onto an immortal, it will be a bloody disaster!'

'Viper is very smart.' Cordella's gaze fell on Tory. 'Much like Avery.'

'Like Avery?' Tory frowned. 'Why this comparison?'

Cordella appeared afraid to voice what she knew, but it had to be said. 'I believe Viper is a Nefilim-Falcon reincarnation of the pending Lord of the Otherworld.'

'What!' Tory gasped, her mind boggling at the implications of having two immortal incarnations of the same soul-mind running around — this was a cosmic first so far as she knew.

Maelgwn, however, was slowly nodding his head. 'This information explains a great many things.' He looked to Brian and Candace. 'I don't want to alarm you two, but I suspect that our foe may have already contacted your daughter, Fallon, disguised as my son.'

'Oh my Goddess!' Candace was horrified. 'Did he hurt her?'

'Well, no ...' Maelgwn proceeded cautiously. 'I have a feeling he might have taken a liking to her.' Brian was silently turning red with rage and Maelgwn was beginning to wish he hadn't mentioned it. 'I just thought I should make you aware.'

'And how long have you know about this?' Brian queried, supressing his urge to start yelling.

Maelgwn could see he was walking a razor's edge here. 'Up until a second ago I thought Avery might have been drunk and forgotten about their ...' He was going to say encounter, but thought better of it.

'Forgotten about their what?' Brian grabbed Maelgwn by the shirt. 'What happened?' Willing to know so desperately, Brian perceived telepathically what Avery had told Maelgwn. Brian, being one of the fourteen appointed guardians of the Logoi, could perceive the thoughts of anyone, whether they were wearing a thought-wave neutraliser or not.

'This Viper person tried to *seduce* my daughter! That's a little different to merely contacting her, don't you think?' When Brian saw he was distressing Candace he let go of his brother-in-law and regained a civil tone. 'How extreme was this seduction?'

Maelgwn smiled to relieve their concern. 'You have

raised a discerning and chaste daughter, have no fear of that. She declined his stronger advances.'

'Oh, thank god,' Candace breathed a sigh of relief. 'For a minute there I was having terrible visions of being grandmother to the Antichrist.'

'So why the interest in my daughter? To vex me?' Brian supposed.

'Not necessarily.' Tory offered her view. 'I think we all realise Avery is very fond of Fallon, even if he doesn't know it yet. If it turns out that she is his Chosen other and that Viper is a past-life incarnation of Avery, then … it stands to reason that Viper will be attracted to Fallon also.'

'Just wonderful!' Brian threw his hands in the air. 'How are we going to explain all this to my daughter?'

Candace bit her lip and drew a deep breath. 'Very delicately.'

You could have knocked Noah over with a feather when a half-caste Nefilim-Falcon male who was the very image of Avery entered his cell. It was a silent relief for the Sage, as now he understood the forecast of the Tablet of Destinies and that this was the leader of their adversaries — the pending Lord of the Otherworld was in the clear.

'Bring her,' he instructed the pair of Leonine-Nefilim males who had followed him through the cell door.

'Shall I blindfold the prisoner, Lord Viper?' queried the taller of the Leonine guards.

Lord, is it? Noah noted on the quiet.

'I don't think that shall be necessary.' Viper moved closer to Noah to stare down the captive. 'There's no way she can get back to her kin from here and I control her will.' Viper admired the NERGUZ control module that was clamped to his wrist. 'After we get where we're going, it won't matter how much she knows. She will become a devotee of the Dark Lodge, just like the rest of us.'

The young man's confidence would have been unnerving, but Noah knew his threats were no longer plausible.

'So,' Viper concluded, 'why miss the enjoyment of watching my great-aunt here strain her little brain as she attempts to figure out what the hell we are playing at, when she has no knowledge of Gaia's history.'

Noah lowered his eyes as if ashamed by the claim, suppressing his urge to grin. At least he knew he was dealing with Gaia's past now, not the distant future or some alternative dimension. And when it came to Gaia's history, there was nobody more knowledgeable than he — in the physical world, that is.

'Move it, auntie.' Viper shoved Noah into the possession of his guards who hauled the Sage all the way to a small five-man reconnaissance vessel.

If Viper was calling Cordella aunt he must be a grandson of Dumuzi, which explained why the traits of the Falcon kind featured more strongly in his appearance than the physical traits of his Nefilim grandfather.

It was a Falcon-Nefilim female named Gazelle who manned the pilot's seat of their craft.

'Why are we bringing the traitor?' The pilot appeared positively repulsed by the Delphinus leader's presence.

'My every decision has purpose, dear sister.' Viper motioned her back to her job. 'Have I ever given you cause to doubt my judgement?' he asked harshly.

To avoid an argument, Gazelle turned back to her controls.

Noah was not surprised to hear Viper refer to Gazelle as sister, as she resembled Lirathea as much as Viper did Avery.

Sparrowhawk's future bride, perhaps? Noah assessed her possible connection to the visions the Tablet had shown him. For as hard as Sparrowhawk had struggled to keep his deep affection for his sister, Lirathea, to himself, it had not escaped his tutor's notice. Noah knew this to be the cause of the rift between the new Falcon leader and his Otherworldly brother, Avery.

'Where are you taking me?' Noah appealed, with a tinge of desperation in his assumed female voice.

'I thought I ordered you not to speak?' Viper tapped the control module he wore on his wrist, fearing it to be faulty.

Noah had not considered this, and wondered what else his foe had forbid Cordella to do.

Viper approached and looked over the module Noah wore and, as all appeared in order, he cast her arm aside and then smacked Noah in the jaw. 'You be silent, bitch. You have lied to and betrayed your own kind, your very existence disgusts me. I have already told you all you need to know.'

Although Noah was immortal, a punch in the jaw still hurt. But better him than Cordella; he shuddered to think what Lura's Governess had already endured.

Noah watched as their craft descended through the atmosphere of the planet towards Europe. In his soul he knew they were headed for Britain, and ancient Gwynedd most likely. The man's heart froze with fear and yet soared with delight. The Dark Ages weren't named thus for no good reason. Evil thrived in this barbaric era of chaos and despotism. To every heroic legend there was an equally dark legend attached. And yet, if there was one destination in the whole of history that Noah desired to visit, it was the Dragon's birthplace and he pulled himself up when he realised he was willing it to be so.

It was a beautiful day in Central Park. Chailida had clear aquamarine sky for as far as the eye could see, and a warm wind danced through the gardens.

Fallon sat on a bench in the shade of a large tree, not really reading the book in her hands; the book was just an excuse to be left in peace for a while.

She'd never imagined one tiny encounter with Avery would cause such a huge fuss, but then, it hadn't even been Avery! The thought kept sending shock-waves through Fallon's body, as the memory of the encounter had been such a treasure to her of late that it was difficult to write it off as a violation. What was worse was that everybody seemed to know about it.

I shouldn't have shared the memory with Avery. To him nothing is sacred, she scolded herself, regarding Avery as the criminal in this affair. *He knew he hadn't seduced me and yet he let me believe he had. The man's ego is immeasurable!* She was silently fuming now, and nearly ripped the pages out of the book as she turned them. But as her thoughts turned to her mystery man, her anger dissipated. What had been his motive for the seduction? She was hard pressed to imagine what Avery would look like as a Nefilim-Falcon half-caste, but she amused herself for some time trying to form an image. She began to fancy that the pirate cum master thief, who was leading her father's council on a merry dance at present, had fallen madly in love with her and at the risk of being caught and arrested, he was pursuing her anyway.

'Hello, Fallon.'

The girl was startled from her daydreaming and was doubly floored when she looked over to find Avery seated beside her. But was it her old friend, or the impostor?

'I'm not talking to you,' she told him, looking back to her reading, as if her heart wasn't beating in her throat from the exhilaration of not knowing whether to flee, hit or kiss him.

'What have I done that is so awful?' he asked, gently brushing a hand against her cheek.

It was the impostor. Fallon's heart started doing gymnastics. Her father had practically ordered her to tell him at once if the fraud tried to make contact with her again — or even if Avery did for that matter. The council weren't taking any chances.

'It is not wise for us to be seen together.' Fallon slid down the bench away from him. 'Our parents know about our misadventure the night of graduation, and they're not very happy about it.' She knew she shouldn't be trying to warn him, but the way he looked at her and spoke to her so sweetly, she couldn't help but feel well disposed towards him.

'You told them?' he speculated, as if sensing she knew that he was not who he appeared to be.

'Avery told them,' she explained gently, afraid of scaring him off. 'I confronted him about the encounter. And, as Avery was otherwise detained with some wood nymph at the time, they figured out that I had been entertaining someone else.'

Viper raised both eyebrows as he quietly accepted that he'd been exposed, but was calm and unperturbed by the obstacle.

'I have known Avery all my life,' Fallon told him, 'and, although I have desired it, he has never regarded me the way you did that night.'

He bowed his head, a smile on his lips. 'He is a fool.'

Fallon shook her head and looked around to make sure they weren't being watched. 'I feel I am the one who is foolish ... advising my father's enemy.'

He appeared genuinely shocked that she knew who he was, but he did not ask her how she knew. 'And why would you ward me away from danger?'

Fallon's roving eyes came back to rest on her mystery man. 'To find out your motive.'

He sighed at the question; half amused, half bemused. 'You wouldn't believe me.'

'You sell me short.' She insisted upon a response.

'No, I don't,' he responded, rather adamant about

that. 'I would never sell you short, for I know what you are capable of.'

He said this with such devotion that Fallon's desire to discover the man behind the mask doubled. 'Then tell me. I promise I shall listen with an open mind.' She suddenly felt that she might be doing her father a service in befriending their foe and gaining a little insight.

He took a moment or two to pluck up his courage. 'The truth is, Fallon, I first met you in a dream.' He paused to assess her reaction — she did not appear doubtful, or convinced. 'It felt like no dream I have ever had before and it was recurring. It cast a spell over me that would last for days, and each time I had the dream, I was more and more compelled to seek you out.'

Fallon was following his wondrous tale with interest. 'But surely in the dream I was of your own breed? A Falcon incarnation of my soul-mind.' She pushed her esoteric understanding. It was only after she'd asked the question that she realised that it might be offensive to him. 'What I meant —'

Viper held up a hand to assure her an explanation was not necessary. 'You appeared just as you are.' His beautiful mauve eyes admired her intently and she wondered what colour his eyes truly were. 'I know that the fact that I am of different breeding to yourself must repulse you, but please believe that I meant you no offence that night. I did not intend to take such liberties with your body. You just looked so beautiful and I knew I'd ... never get the chance to be so close to you again.' His voiced trailed off and he stood as if preparing to depart.

'The memory of that night does not repulse me, even now that I know the truth. I feel it was either a miracle of emotion, or a very masterful act.' Her accusation cum confession gained her his full attention once more.

'I know you think I'm the bad guy, Fallon,' he appealed. 'But I can prove that that isn't true.' He turned away suddenly, overwhelmed by the task of making her see his side of the story. 'But that would require much trust on your behalf, trust I have not yet earned and have no time to earn.'

'You want me to accompany you somewhere, I take it?' Fallon enjoyed delighting him with her direct approach.

'It would be foolish of you to do that,' he cautioned. 'Perhaps we could go somewhere less public, to talk.'

Fallon took a moment to think about it. 'To our mountain top then.'

5

THE MASTER PLAN

Their small reconnaissance vessel spent days hovering over the ancient world of Gaia, cloaked from the sight of the planet's inhabitants, who went about their business oblivious to the space-age vessel observing them from above. Viper had his crew systematically scanning a large mountain range for human life forms. The pirate was searching for someone in particular.

Gazelle, the pilot, had been routinely complaining every couple of hours that their search was like trying to find a habitable planet in a galaxy, whereupon Viper would flatten her pessimism by reminding her that they had all the time in the world to find their target.

'I think I've got something.' The pilot startled her crewmates, all rather drowsy from lack of sleep — except Viper.

Their leader seemed never to tire, and Noah began to suspect that Viper had activated his immortality gene with gold Orme. Dark Orme would have cast a very distinct shadow over the pirate captain's person; Light Orme usually gave one a distinct glow, which was not apparent with Viper either. Noah suspected that his foe's malign intent was preventing the light of the gold Orme from empowering Viper to its full effect.

'What have you got?' Viper approached to view his sister's soft-light screen over her shoulder.

'A small warrior band, which includes one member approaching puberty, camped outside a cave,' she outlined, whereby her brother ruffled the soft plumage of the long quills on her head.

'This looks very promising. Zoom in the visual and pump up the volume. Let's hear what they're saying,' Viper instructed, more excited than Noah had ever seen him.

Noah couldn't see the screen from where he was sitting and was thankful that he would at least be able to hear.

'The translator doesn't recognise the language.' Gazelle was most perturbed.

'Shh!' Viper hissed, as his eyes glazed over to listen. 'I comprehend it.'

And so did Noah. It was the tongue of the ancient Britons, Brythanic.

'So, little prince, tell us what Cadfer be doing in there.' One of the larger warriors had taken hold of the youngest member of the party, hoping to scare some information out of the lad.

'Ask him thyself,' spat the boy. 'And remove thy hands from my person, or I shall have them severed from thy body.'

The warrior laughed at the young prince's threat, but became alarmed when the laughter of his colleagues tapered off abruptly. He turned to find Cadfer with his sword raised high. The warrior dropped the lad and withdrew his hands, barely fast enough to avoid the blade of his superior as he brought it down.

'Never touch my heir,' Cadfer threatened.

'Goddess, thee nearly took both my arms off.' The soldier drew his sword, in case he needed to defend himself further. 'There have been some fantastic stories flying around that claim thou art consorting with a witch.'

'And?' Cadfer prompted, as if this claim was not serious enough to warrant an explanation on its own.

'Thou dost not deny it then?' the warrior gasped, horrified.

'The dark path frightens thee, Mahon?' Cadfer queried, nonchalant.

'Such association be an unnatural sin against the Goddess.' The warrior looked to the rest of the men, noting they were spooked by his words.

'What dost thou think stealing the throne of Gwynedd from her appointed King will be, if not an offence?' Cadfer inquired, as his young heir edged his way around behind the defiant warrior.

'To defeat an opponent fairly be one thing, but to involve dark forces,' the man was horrified, 'will curse us all —'

The adolescent prince thrust his sword through Mahon and the huge warrior dropped to his knees, shocked by the blade protruding through his gullet and seeing his own blood spilling forth. 'Thee damned thyself by questioning my father's means,' the boy informed him, abruptly withdrawing his sword from the warrior's body whereupon Mahon dropped to the ground. 'Dost anyone else have any questions for my father?' The lad cast his eyes around at the astounded troops, who shook their heads in the negative, unable to believe such bloodlust in one so young.

'Caradoc certainly was a feisty little fellow,' mumbled Viper, 'a prince after my own heart.'

Noah had been racking his brains to recall who Cadfer had been, but as soon as Viper mentioned Caradoc, Maelgwn's bastard brother, it all came flooding back to him. The Sage knew precisely where they were — the Snowdon Ranges of Gwynedd in about 505 AD.

'This is the place,' Viper confirmed, much to his sister's relief. 'We'll wait for the soldiers to depart and then we'll go in.'

Noah had been fearing that Viper intended to slay Maelgwn in his youth and throw history into chaos, but an even greater dread beset the Sage when he realised Viper was here to seek Mahaud.

The sun was rising over the mountain peak on the far side of Kila, where Fallon and her mystery man had retreated to speak alone.

'Why did you steal the Aten and kidnap Cordella?' Fallon didn't beat around the bush once they arrived.

She refused to be blinded by her heart's desire before she assessed this man more closely.

'The only place I can hide from the Chosen is in time. Once Lahmu's more adept supporters, like Tory Alexander and her Dragon husband, are aware of my appearance, probably not even history will prevent them from finding me.'

'That's why you choose to appear as Avery,' Fallon realised, and this meant he was still as wary of her as she was of him. 'So I can never see you as you truly are.' She tried not to sound as disappointed as she felt.

Immediately his appearance began to transform. He sprouted quills covered in honey coloured plumage in place of Avery's platinum blond hair, and huge wings of the same colour unfolded from between his shoulder blades. His Nefilim ancestry was vaguely apparent in his features, as they were slightly more pixie-like than your average Falcon. His eyes were larger and more striking than Avery's, as they turned from violet to a vibrant shade of fiery amber.

He shrugged as she gazed at him, puzzled by his resolve and the risk he was taking.

''Tis the only way I shall ever know if I can trust you,' he stated calmly.

Fallon had never really considered being attracted to any other man but Avery, let alone a man of another breed. But find this pirate attractive Fallon did. He was more ruggedly handsome than his Homo sapiens counterpart and sported more of a warrior form. 'You appear just as Avery would if he were an angel.' She smiled to reassure him that she was pleased by the transformation and not repulsed, as he'd feared. 'And does my angel have a name?'

He smiled, set at ease by her flirtatious tone. 'My name isn't very angelic, I'm afraid ... I'm known as Viper.'

'Viper ... hmm!' She liked it. 'More of a fiery angel then, by the sound of it.'

'Definitely,' he confirmed with a nod.

'Do you want to tell me why you are so fired up against my father?' Fallon's tone softened as she became more serious.

'If you love your father, what I have to say will not be easy to hear,' he forewarned. 'My opinion of Lahmu is not very high.'

Although Fallon frowned, sure that Viper must have misunderstood her father somehow, she merely nodded for him to proceed.

He took Fallon back to the year of her birth, the same year the Nefilim had retreated from the physical world. He told of how Lahmu had been at a loss as to what to do with the children of Dumuzi, for, unbeknownst to Viper's kindred, the Chosen possessed the know-how to activate the dormant immortality gene passed into Viper's people by Dumuzi.

'Cordella was how I figured out the deception. I kidnapped her to question her. She told me about gold Orme and I found, in my grandfather's old chambers on board our vessel, Dumuzi's secret stash of the substance. But there was only enough left to free me from mortality.'

'But we met the night before Cordella and the Aten were kidnapped.' Fallon frowned, unsure if she wasn't following the story or if Viper was making up a fabrication and getting his details in a jumble.

'The Aten's time hopping ability has come in very useful,' he smiled.

'So it was you I met in the library at the Institute that day, and not Avery,' she concluded, feeling she was starting to piece the puzzle together.

'I've never been in a library in all my born days.' Viper chuckled at the notion. 'I'm afraid I don't know what you're talking about.'

'Oh,' Fallon found herself frowning again, 'that's odd.'

'The only thing I seek,' Viper jumped back to the subject of his cause, 'is justice for all of my kindred, which will be enough Orme to raise them all to their full immortal potential.'

'Well, I feel sure my father would not object to the advancement of your kind when it is your birthright, after all,' Fallon appealed, but Viper appeared far from convinced.

'Then why did he not tell us the truth in the first place?' he argued. 'Lahmu may as well have slaughtered us all twenty years ago, as not telling us is practically the same as murder, in that we suffer a mortal life until our death which in reality never has to be.'

'The last thing my father wants is another war.' Fallon knew that much. 'Let me plead your case to him. If I am wrong about Lahmu's resolve, and I'm not, then do what you must and I shall aid you. But if I am right, we'll both have all eternity to celebrate a peaceful resolution.'

'Well ...' Viper was actually considering it. 'You are his daughter. I suppose he might listen to an appeal from you.'

'I feel sure he will.' Fallon had grabbed both Viper's hands and before she'd realised it, she was kissing him to seal their deal.

Due to the seriousness of the developments of the past few days, Lahmu had decided to move the first meeting of his allied council forward. He wanted all the new members sworn in and functioning as a unit in order to combat the latest threat to the peace.

Tory decided to postpone her visit to Gaia until she saw her children assume their place in the council. Once this was done, her last commitment to the physical world was fulfilled.

Life's great purpose had been playing on her mind ever since Tory had resolved to return to the planet of her birth, for she had the most overwhelming premonition that she would not be returning to Kila for some time, if at all. Tory loved her adopted planet and was reluctant to return to Gaia, knowing how trashed the planet would seem by comparison with Kila. Perhaps the guilt of her neglect of her once home planet is what would persuade her to stay there? But whatever the reason turned out to be, Tory knew this premonition was her notice from the Logos to settle up her old life, as it was now time for Maelgwn and herself to move on. Raising their youngest three children in Chailida had been such an idyllic lifestyle these past twenty years, that, for the first time in their long lives, parenting and married life had almost seemed like an indulgence and for that Tory was most grateful to the Logos. But lately, she'd felt the divine at work upon her heart, urging her to pursue work of a higher and less self-indulgent nature. They'd had their time in the sun and now Maelgwn and herself were ready for a new challenge.

Maelgwn returned to their home at Central Park, having fetched Avery from the Otherworld to attend the meeting of Lahmu's council. Lahmu had arranged to have all his council members brought forth immediately to Government House in Chailida by members of the fourteen appointed guardians of the Logoi, who had the ability to teleport between star systems. Avery, who was the only exception to the rule, had sped himself forth to Government House and Tory was surprised to see her husband back at home, as he'd intended to meet her at the ceremony.

'You were right about not coming back to Kila, my love,' Maelgwn informed as he joined her in their bedroom, where Tory was dressing.

Although he'd startled her with his sudden appearance, Tory forgave him instantly, as Maelgwn was in such fine spirits, she didn't want to dampen his mood. 'Why so sure?'

'Because I've just been talking to the Master of our Soul Ray, who is tutoring Avery at present, and he told me our time here is at an end.' Maelgwn embraced his wonderstruck wife briefly and then let her go to pace out his excitement. 'Our personalities, mental bodies, astral bodies and physical bodies are all governed by different Rays, which is how you and I can differ in opinion although we are one soul-mind.' He ceased his excited pacing to emphasise: 'All the knowledge that the Sensor-sphere was trying to instill in me is beginning to make sense. At long last we've earned ourselves a promotion and are to evolve in the great scheme!'

'The Master of our Soul Ray?' Tory managed to squeeze out the first of the many questions his claim had inspired.

Maelgwn nodded enthusiastically, and taking hold of both her hands he urged her to be seated on the bed with him. 'The Lords of the Rays are the creating and sustaining energies that implement the will of the divine universal creator. These master entities project their thoughts and create a stream of energy, which, according to their differing aspects, plays upon all forms of life within this universal ring-pass-not.'

The ring-pass-not to which Maelgwn referred was the circumference of the multi-dimensional solar system, which marked the periphery of the influence that the central galactic sun had on the human soul-mind. Once a soul-mind reached a point where it realised the delusion of separateness induced by the lower planes of the Galactic and Solar systems, it gained contact with the higher mental realms of existence that was the abode of Dhyan Chohans, whose primary influence stemmed directly from the Cosmic Logos.

Tory was sort of following Maelgwn's explanation, but her husband had obviously had a great burst of awareness after speaking with the master being and she was struggling to keep up.

Her frown told Maelgwn that a more in-depth

explanation was necessary. 'All manifestation is of a seven-fold nature. The One Divine Creator manifests first as the three Major Rays, which the Christians once called the Father, Son and Holy Ghost. But in esoteric understanding, the three Major Rays are known as Will-Power, Love-Wisdom, and Activity-Adaptability. These three Major Rays along with the four Minor Rays of Art, Science, Religion and Transformation, make up the divine seven-fold nature of the Creator, also known as the Seven Rays before the throne of God. These seven aspects of the divine then relate to the seven planes of existence, the seven chakras of the subtle body and so forth.'

'And you spoke with which of these Masters?' Tory queried, still frowning.

'The Third Ray, Master Rakoczi, or the Master R. He is also the Mahachohan — the Lord of Civilisation at present. Which is why our soul is on his Ray,' Maelgwn rationalised. 'For he is in charge of bringing about the new civilisation for which all men wait. We have already served him well on Kila, Lura, Tarazean, Nugia, Karleashian and Numan. There is only one more planet to come of age —'

'Gaia.' Tory realised now why her future efforts must be concentrated on the planet of her birth.

'Now I'm making sense, aren't I?' Maelgwn grinned broadly and Tory did too.

Government House was a hive of activity as everyone prepared for the swearing-in ceremony and the first meeting of Lahmu's new council.

Fallon managed to locate her father in his office, jotting down some last-minute notes for his opening address. 'Father, I urgently need to speak with you.' The look her father gave her told Fallon that this was not a good time. 'What I have to say may have some bearing on the senate meeting,' she added. Brian relented and waved her forth.

'Quickly, sweetheart, I don't have much time.' He motioned her to a seat, but Fallon remained standing.

'Viper made contact with me again.' Her claim had her father on his feet immediately.

'What!' Brian headed around his desk to question his daughter more closely. He was under the impression that their foes were joyriding through time at present. If Viper had returned to the present day, then why hadn't Noah manifested to report yet?

'Now don't have a baby,' Fallon counselled him. 'He came in peace and departed the same way ... at no time was I in any danger.'

'That's a matter of opinion,' Brian frowned, still concerned. 'What did he want?'

'To explain his grievances. He knows about Orme, father, and that all his people have the birthright of immortality. Viper seeks enough Orme to save his people from mortality.'

'I feared as much.' Brian gave a heavy sigh.

'So?' Fallon prompted her father from his contemplation. 'Is there a problem?'

'Yes, there is a *serious* problem,' Brian enlightened her. 'These are not advanced souls. They would require much training and loving experience before Orme could benefit them permanently.'

'What do you mean, permanently?' Fallon didn't follow. 'Once you're immortal, you're immortal.'

'It doesn't work that way for souls of malicious intent,' Brian replied briefly, feeling pushed for time.

'But you don't know Viper, or his people, at all. On what do you base your judgement?' Fallon felt the heat of her anger and conviction welling in the pit of her stomach and reflecting in her cheeks.

'I base it on Cordella's first-hand summation,' Brian retorted rather harshly, annoyed that his daughter was defending the enemy.

Fallon was deeply perplexed by his response. 'But Viper still has Cordella in custody, doesn't he?'

Brian realised that to trust Noah's cover to his daughter would be very risky at present. 'Fallon, that's the end of it. You were supposed to report to me instantly if Viper made contact and you deliberately disobeyed me.'

'But, father, surely you don't want a war —'

'Goddamnit, child,' Brian roared. 'If Viper was any sort of an honest leader, he would have contacted me directly with his grievance and not broken the law. The next time this crook makes contact, you are not to discuss *anything* with him, is that clear! To do so is treason, Fallon,' he added in a more congenial tone of voice. 'Please understand ... I don't want to preside over my own daughter's trial.'

Fallon backed away from him, her eyes wide with horror. 'Very well, father, have it your way.' She turned and charged from the room, nearly bowling her mother over at the door.

'Heavens, Brian, what did you say to her?' Candace watched her daughter race away in tears.

'I want a guard with her at all times,' Brian instructed. 'That bastard grandson of Dumuzi's has been to see her again, and Goddess knows what information he has charmed out of her already!'

'Calm down.' Candace telepathically commanded the door closed. 'Tell me what happened?'

'He sent my daughter to plead that I grant his people immortality, to make me look like the bad guy in Fallon's eyes!' Brian threw his arms up in the air, exasperated. 'And I've played right into his hands, goddamnit!'

'So apologise to Fallon and stop acting like a baby.' Candace held both hands up in truce as she approached him and slid her arms around him for a hug. 'I feel sure she will willingly tell you everything she knows and co-operate with Viper's arrest, if only you make it clear to her that you are taking her seriously.'

Brian calmed as he gazed into his wife's deep brown eyes, absorbing her wise advice.

'Treat her like a naive little girl and Fallon will prove you wrong.'

'You're right,' Brian admitted. 'Fallon thought she was helping and I should've ... handled it better. I shall apologise. Like a grown-up,' he added, which made Candace smile. 'First thing after the meeting.'

Candace seconded his resolution with a kiss and then served him a large smile of support. 'I'll send a guard to keep an eye on Fallon in the meantime. Okay?'

Brian nodded and drew a deep breath to focus on this afternoon's proceedings. 'Now, let us figure a way to nail this guy. I want him away from our daughter.'

It was dawn in ancient Gwynedd, and as Noah stepped out of the spacecraft to find himself standing on history's soil he couldn't help but be overcome by wonder. Gaia's air had not a hint of pollution and, from where he stood amidst the Snowdon Ranges, not a hint of civilisation either.

'Come on, auntie.' Viper shoved Noah in the direction of the cave. 'Everything worth seeing is in there.'

As Noah followed the two Leonine crew members bearing green fluorescent torches into the cave, he secretly wished that he could ditch his responsibilities and do a little sightseeing in Gwynedd. Degannwy and Aberffraw, the strongholds of the Dragon's ancient empire, were close by here, although Maelgwn was only a boy of fifteen in this age — his father Caswallon was presently ruling. *Not for long.* The Sage dwelt on the claims he'd overheard Cadfer make the night before. Still, Noah knew that the young Prince Maelgwn was destined to cut short Cadfer's power and restore his father to the throne of Gwynedd — Maelgwn would thus earn his nickname 'the Dragon of the Isle'. The Sage wished he could feel so sure about the outcome of the current debacle in which he found himself embroiled.

Noah had never confronted the entity known as Mahaud. She was Tory and Maelgwn's arch-rival and had focused most of her activities around foiling their achievements. He wondered if the crone would see through his disguise? If the situation got out of hand, Noah knew he could will himself back to the chariot and withdraw to his rightful place in time. Safe in this knowledge, he felt confident about finally making the evil crone's acquaintance.

The foulest stench permeated their destination and got worse the deeper into the cave they ventured. The two Leonine warriors began vomiting, which added to the stench.

'Sorry, boss,' the taller guard appealed, dropping his torch and quickly retreating from the cave. The second guard handed Viper his torch and withdrew also.

'Christ almighty, it's only a smell!' Viper hollered after them.

'A very bad smell!' Gazelle empathised.

'You're not wimping out on me, too?' Viper made it clear by his tone that he'd be most disappointed if that were the case.

'Of course not,' she snapped, and retrieving the torch the guard had dropped, she strode ahead, pinching her nose. 'I can take it, and I'm *not* an immortal.'

'You will be,' Viper assured, 'if this meeting goes well.'

'I don't see how, when even you don't seem to be able to maintain an everlasting state of being,' Gazelle muttered under her breath.

It is your evil intent that binds you to mortality, Noah would have advised Viper had he been allowed to speak. Instead, he merely smiled, knowing that the Logos's means of rewarding the faithful was failsafe; a loving intent was the only antidote for Viper's problematic condition.

'I forbid you to hear,' Viper commanded Noah at once, but as the NERGUZ on Noah's wrist was not functioning, the pirate's order had no effect.

Gazelle's pace slowed and Viper approached to give her a whack across the back of the head. 'Such information is not for our prisoner's ears.' His sister didn't retaliate. In fact, she didn't even seem to be listening to him. Gazelle's sights were focused on the cave ahead and she seemed very apprehensive. 'What's the matter?' Viper questioned her.

'A forbidding energy.' she explained, obviously feeling a little silly in mentioning it.

Noah found it most interesting that Gazelle had picked up on the psychic energies of the place when she hadn't taken any Orme to enlighten her; perhaps this child of Dumuzi had Chosen potential underneath the hardened facade created by her tough upbringing.

'Well, what the hell kind of energy did you expect to be emanating from a crone ... love and sweetness?' Viper took the lead, dragging Noah along with him.

At the end of the cavern, stairs led down into a large, dark earthen chamber. Bats covered the ceiling and all sorts of reptilian predators slithered and crawled on the ground.

Obviously, being space-born children, Viper and Gazelle were not very familiar with wild animals of any sort.

'The ceiling is alive.' Gazelle, having descended the stairs into the chamber behind her brother and his prisoner, huddled close to them, realising she was not as brave as she thought she was.

'What the hell is that?' Viper queried rather loudly, sending the bats into a whirling frenzy.

Noah crouched low, wondering if this was why Cadfer conversed with the crone at night — the bats would be absent. Gazelle's scream was ceaseless until she'd driven all the flying creatures from the cave.

'Enough!' A booming unearthly voice hissed and four torches ignited in a circle formation before them.

Viper stood, and urged his petrified sister and his captive to stand straight also.

The firelight lit the cavern rather adequately and in front of each torch, outside the circle they formed, Noah spied four implements: a cauldron, a sword, a dark crystal and a twig, which Noah could only presume was a wand. The Sage knew that to step inside the circle would make them subject to the crone's will. Noah had to avoid penetrating her field at all costs. If the witch was operating at full strength, all psychic power drawn from the higher planes of existence would be rendered useless within the circle she'd cast. As the crone had obviously been feeding off Cadfer's selfish desires and ambitions, she was probably feeling fairly healthy at present. No sooner had Noah spied the dormant torches fixed on the walls of the cavern, than they ignited to form an outer circle that encompassed the entire chamber. Noah began to back up towards the stairs, pulling Viper along with him and the pirate wasn't resisting too hard. Noah desperately wanted to bestow his esoteric knowledge on the Falcon leader, and explain just how much danger they were already in — but that meant blowing his cover, which left the Sage only one option. He wrenched himself from Viper's grasp and willed himself back to the chariot.

'Going so soon?'

The gravelly strain of the crone's unearthly voice sent shivers down Noah's spine, for he realised his will had been overruled. He wondered if the crone was aiming her question directly at him, or whether she was referring to the seeming withdrawal of their entire party.

'I'd like to go.' Gazelle had seen enough to know she'd rather die than be associated with whatever belonged to that malign voice and the stench inside the cavern.

The cauldron was the implement closest to them. On the lid of the huge iron pot were two large bulges, which parted wide to reveal eyes with pupils of glowing red. The eyes assessed the three visitors very carefully.

'I haven't seen anything like you lot since before the Nefilim pissed off to wherever it was they came from. You're not from around these parts, or times, are you?'

Noah was horrified by her claim, as it was spoken in their modern tongue, which meant she was assessing them telepathically.

'My name is Viper, Mahaud.' Viper braved a step forward. 'And I come to you from the future, beyond your final demise, to offer you an opportunity to arise from the grave.'

'Oooh!' The eyes of the cauldron looked him over with relish. 'A pretty boy, too. Lucky me.'

'I have memorised your entire history here on Gaia and on the moon,' he persisted, in an effort to get the witch to take him seriously.

'Moon? How interesting.'

'Yes, that is where you are finally defeated,' Viper added, as the witch's tone was encouraging. 'But I believe we can alter that.'

How does Viper know all this? Noah wondered on the quiet, deeply affected by the horrifying conversation taking place.

The lid popped off the cauldron, startling everyone present. A heavy vapour of red and black began to ascend from the old iron pot and a dark figure, cloaked in red, took form. The black bony digits of the crone's rotting corpse protruded from the end of her sleeves and her pupils burned red from beneath the shadows inside her hood. The crone's vaporous body remained afloat over the cauldron, as she beckoned Viper closer.

'Tell me more, young prince.' She flirted with her new and exotic victim.

Viper proceeded to dazzle the crone, and indeed Noah, with his detailed accounts of all Mahaud's encounters with Maelgwn Gwynedd, Tory Alexander and their kindred. Had Viper been one of his history students, Noah would have been proud. Somehow, Viper had gained access to his chronicles, that much Noah was sure of. Then the Falcon pirate told of the crone's final demise at the hands of Gwyn ap Nudd and Tory Alexander, whereby Mahaud was banished into Density. Only a handful of the elite among the Chosen knew this tale. It had never been committed onto a chronicle to ensure that no one would know what had become of Mahaud, or that she'd even reared her ugly head again.

'This secondhand account of my death is sketchy at best. Are you sure you have it right ... I was banished to beyond the etheric realms of the Night Hunter?'

'The witness heard it from the Dragon himself. He speaks freely about the conquest when amongst close family members,' Viper replied and the crone began to chuckle to herself.

It must have been Cordella who told the last chapter of Mahaud's legend to Viper, Noah assessed on the quiet. Fortunately, dark Orme was not made mention of anywhere in the story, for Maelgwn would not let that secret slip, even to his family.

The crone went quiet for a time as she assessed all that had been said. 'You have done me a great service in delivering this information to me, Lord Viper, and thus I shall enlighten you to something.'

Oh, no ... Noah feared he'd been discovered and his cheeks burned in anticipation of being exposed by the crone.

'Yes?' Viper wondered what possible information this hag from the ancient world of a distant planet could have for him.

'You been having problems maintaining an immortal state,' she began.

'Yes, I have.' Viper was immediately excited by the topic. 'Do you know why?'

'You are a dark soul, Majesty. You have a dark heart, dark thoughts. I see in you the spirit of a Dark Lord, superior to any of the tyrants I have served throughout

117

the ages. The substance you are consuming to quicken your immortal state is attuned to cosmic light and love, and your dark nature is rejecting its aid. What you and your kindred need is a quickening agent that is black of substance.'

There could be no doubt in Noah's mind that he was the crone's source of information, she could not know about the dark Orme otherwise. He had hoped his adeptness at psychic self defence would shield his knowledge from the witch, but clearly the powers of darkness ruled in this place. He could feel the negative vibrations sucking the light from him, inducing fears he'd thought long departed from his soul — fears for his own wellbeing.

'Charichalum Orme ... is that what you're talking about?' Viper hazarded a guess. 'The substance they use to power the shield of the dead star, Anu?'

'Don't ask me,' Mahaud advised. 'I'm just passing on information I perceived from your prisoner.'

'What?' Viper turned to Cordella, his eyes ablaze with fury. 'How does she know all this?'

The crone suppressed her amusement. 'She is a he.'

'What?' Viper repeated, looking back to the witch, suspecting her of toying with him.

'His name is Noah Purcell. He's an historian and Sage of some repute in your age.'

'I know who Noah Purcell is,' Viper snapped, circling Noah now. 'Reveal yourself, prophet.' When nothing happened he gave his captive a whack in the jaw.

'You forbade her to hear,' Gazelle informed, suspecting that the witch might be lying.

'He can hear all right. Every word,' Mahaud assured.

'Show yourself *now*,' Viper threatened and when Noah complied, the Falcon leader was enraged beyond reason to see the famed historian whose chronicles he'd been studying. 'How long have you been in her place?' He belted the Sage when he did not reply. 'Only the Logos knows how much he's learned already!' Viper began to pace, panicked beyond reason.

'I know,' Mahaud boasted. 'He knows too much. But, it is no matter, as you will leave him here with me. His means of mobility through time is on board your ship, and once you take your ship out of this time zone, the prophet will be trapped in ancient Gwynedd.'

Viper didn't know whether to be excited by her proposal or not. 'But are you not coming back to the future with us?' he queried the crone, confused. Was she now rejecting his aid?

'And miss out on wreaking all the disaster you just described to me ... not likely!' Mahaud scoffed. 'The device you thought was restraining your prisoner is no longer functioning. If we allow him to leave my circle, he will vanish to warn our enemy of our plans. He would have done so before now, but I am restraining him and can hold him here so long as I remain. You must travel to some future time, between now and my demise, when I am not active in the material world. Summon me forth to you and I shall accompany you back to your rightful place in time.'

Noah hung his head for shame, realising he'd practically willed this scenario upon himself. He had wanted to stay and explore ancient Gwynedd and now his wish had been granted.

Viper, however, was most gratified by the crone's foresight and cunning. 'And how do I summon you forth, great queen of darkness?'

The crone was tickled pink by his flattery and she motioned to an old chest by the cavern wall, which opened. An ancient scroll rose from within and floated into Viper's possession. 'All you need to know is contained therein.'

The young lord smiled broadly as he admired his means to fulfil his ambitions. 'Well then, Mahaud, I shall be seeing you in the future.'

'I greatly look forward to our association and shall devise our strategy while I await our next meeting.' She pointed her crooked old finger in Noah's direction. 'Our little Sage has much he can teach me about our foe. I foresee a dark future ahead for us, Lord Viper.'

'I'm much obliged to you.' Viper took hold of his cowering sister's hand and led her towards the stairs.

'No, no … it is I who am obliged,' Mahaud assured.

'She means it,' Noah warned Viper. 'Mahaud will use you just as she has used every living thing she has ever come into contact with.'

'Of course she will, and I shall use her.' Viper shrugged. 'For that is what we villains do … we use each other.'

'Said like a true disciple of the Talas of Avichi.'

'Talas?' Noah had never heard the term before.

'Your beloved planes of awareness are known as Lokas,' Viper advised. 'Each Loka has a corresponding dark realm in Density and these worlds are known as Talas. Avichi is the name given to this group of sub-planes that constitute the eighth level of awareness and those below it. I believe you refer to them as Density.' Viper smiled at his own brilliance. 'You really ought to get better informed. I'm sure Mahaud will be more than happy to instil a sound knowledge of the dark path in you.' He waved Noah goodbye and bowed to the witch, before disappearing into the cave.

Noah summoned his strength as he turned back to the witch. *I am a rock*, he told himself. *I hear nothing, see nothing, taste nothing, smell nothing, feel nothing … I know nothing.* He wiped blank his mind and sat down to commence a deep meditation that he would stay submerged in until such time as he was freed from Mahaud's restraint. The young Maelgwn Gwynedd would be along presently to put a stop to the crone's mischief in Gwynedd.

The witch laughed heartily at Noah's defence. 'You cannot go five minutes without thinking of those you hold dear.'

Her words tempted Noah's memory to conjure images of those he loved. *Don't listen to her*, he commanded his mind to hold the images at bay. He had to find something else to concentrate on in order to block out her words. *What would a spiritual master do in my place?* He pondered the question but a second. *Pray.* But Noah didn't know any prayers. Then it dawned on him to recite 'The Great Invocation' that had been the creed of the Theosophical Society of nineteenth century Gaia, whose writings he greatly respected.

'From the point of Light
within the mind of God,
Let light stream forth
into the minds of men,
Let light descend on Earth.

From within the point of Love
within the heart of God,
Let love stream forth
into the hearts of men,
May Christ return to Earth.

From the centre
where the Will of God is known,
Let purpose guide the little wills of men,
the purpose which
the Masters know and serve.

From the centre
which we call the race of men,
Let the plan of Light and Love work out,
may it seal the door where evil dwells.
Let Light, Love and Power
restore the Plan
on Earth.'

The Sage felt empowered by the words and considered the piece he'd chosen as apt as any he could have thought of. But as he paused from his prayer to consider this, the witch's frustrated garble began registering in his brain once more.

'Listen to me, you pathetic excuse for —'

No, block her out. He ordered himself to concentrate on the Invocation, which he decided he would recite over and over until the Dragon arrived.

The events unfolding behind the scenes of Lahmu's first senate meeting with his new council of young bloods, were far more curious than the issues that were openly discussed.

Tory had been invited, along with Maelgwn and several other guests, to attend the meeting in an advisory capacity.

Lirathea shocked everyone when she arrived in rather extraordinary attire to be sworn into the senate — all trace of the college girl look had left her. Today she was dressed as a priestess — reminiscent of those women of the high spiritual orders of ancient Atlantis. Her dress was made of glimmering silver and fell from her neck to her toes. It was completely shapeless and unflattering to her young figure, with large long sleeves like those of a monk's habit.

What shocked Tory most was that Lirathea had shaved all her beautiful, long blonde hair off, and over her bald head her daughter wore a shimmering cowl that had a double layer of fabric so that Lirathea could veil her lovely face.

Needless to say Tory had a closed meeting with her daughter, just prior to the swearing-in ceremony.

'I am to represent the spirit world in the senate,' Lirathea began in her own defence, 'and must dedicate myself entirely to its service. I have thus resigned from the position as Head of the Mind Sciences in order to focus on honing my own skills for now. Mine will be a life of solitary study, mother. All the unnecessary distractions that a social life brings with it I must avoid at all costs.'

Tory had never understood the dedicated lives of priestesses and nuns, and had always thought the veiling of the face to be an extreme and sometimes detrimental practice. 'Who is it that you must hide from, Lirathea? Does this have something to do with a man?'

'No.' Lirathea denied Tory's assumption a little too quickly. 'But if I wish to be a solitary soul, it is hardly fitting that I risk attracting men with the glamour of physical beauty, therefore I renounce it.'

'And what of your Chosen other?' her mother queried, having heard this story before. 'He shall never be able to find you if you are hidden behind a veil all your life.'

'There will be no Chosen male born destined to be my lifetime companion,' she told her mother, seemingly at peace with the fact. 'For my soul-mind has already ascended beyond the ring-pass-not of the causal plane of existence, where the male and female aspect is again reunited. We then chose to return to the earth plane to aid and further the cause of the Logos, and having to choose a sex for physical manifestation, we chose a female body to promote the intuitive side of our nature.'

Obviously Lirathea had consulted her higher self on the issue, as Tory had never heard her daughter speak with such certainty about her destiny before. Tory had always wondered how those soul-minds took the solitary spiritual path and made a go of it. 'Is this the case with Avery, too?'

'No.' Lirathea was quite positive about this. 'His soul is a very spiritually adept one, but his male half has yet to learn commitment and his female half has yet to learn how to avoid being seduced by her own glamour.'

'You refer to Fallon,' Tory probed, and Lirathea nodded in response.

'They can each learn their life lesson from the other, but,' Lirathea gave a heavy sigh, 'I feel theirs will be a rocky road to romance.'

'You know about Avery's dark half then,' Tory supposed. 'The one known as Viper, who has attempted to seduce Fallon whilst masquerading as your brother.'

'A Falcon-Nefilim half-caste?' Lirathea raised both brows. 'Yes, I have seen him in visions, but I did not know he had tried to get close to Fallon. That could be very destructive for her relationship with Avery.'

'No kidding.' Her mother leaned back in her seat, worried and perplexed.

'All the Chosen have a dark half you know,' Lirathea informed Tory to break the silence, 'but few of these souls have had the opportunity to manifest into the physical world more than once.'

'Like Mahaud?' Tory posed and again her daughter nodded.

'The Dark Lords aren't permitted to reincarnate as we on the path of light do, but they can influence the actions and even steal the bodies of the darkly adept and the weak minded. They are especially powerful when they can gain control of one of their own soul-mind's reincarnations, because they feel more at home as it were.'

Tory gasped with fright and covered her mouth in an unconscious attempt to stop her thought being voiced. 'Could that be why Mahaud has focused her dark work around me? Could that horrid creature be the dark side of Maelgwn and myself?'

'That kind of information lay beyond the realms and grasp of my informants,' Lirathea stated. 'But I can tell you that I have an incarnation in manifestation at present, who has the potential to become a devotee of the Dark Lodge. She is the sister of Viper and the Chosen soul-mate of Sparrowhawk.'

Tory's jaw was dropping at this point, for this explained why Sparrowhawk and Lirathea had always been so close.

Lirathea knew what her mother was thinking. 'I had to know why I was so attracted to my brother, despite my will and conscience,' she confessed. 'I decided to do some past-life regression to find out if I had loved Sparrowhawk in another life.'

'And you discovered you actually loved him in every life including the present, but via another incarnation,' Tory summed up, her heart going out to her daughter.

'If not for my attraction to Sparrowhawk I now realise that I would never have been pushed to discover these hidden aspects behind the current conflict between the Lords of the Dark Lodge and the Great Brotherhood of Light. This knowledge inspired in me a revelation about my life and how I should lead it.'

Lirathea motioned to her appearance. 'Being born perfect is a curse, En Noah told me on my last day at the Institute. He said that I must do what I must without regret, and never feel sorry for knowing my own mind and the will of the Logos. Now I know what he meant when he said I had to save my energy for grander pursuits. I was sent to advise this world, but not to be of it, for I have another Chosen incarnation that shall do all the physical living in this age for me. My decision will not be easy for Sparrowhawk. He will misread my motives for taking to the veil. Still, I shall endeavour to do all within my power to steer his affection away from me and on to the path that will lead him to his true soul-mate in this day and age.'

Tory nodded to agree with her daughter's decision. This was not the first time one of her children had managed to amaze her with their enlightened reasoning and motivation. 'I am very happy that you have discovered your calling, my sweet, and I am so proud of you.' Her eyes suddenly welled with tears. 'You're all grown up.'

Lirathea embraced her mother and squeezed her tightly. 'I know your relief must be great. I have found my path and you can depart knowing that all shall fare well with me in the future.'

Tory pulled back to hold Lirathea at arm's length. 'You know that your father and I plan to leave Kila?'

'Why, of course,' she smiled. 'All the Masters are looking forward to the event with great anticipation. It is very important that you return to Gaia's aid. Both father and yourself still have much to learn from her.'

'Sorry, my girls,' Maelgwn entered the office, 'it's time.' He beckoned his wife and child to follow him to the senate chambers.

Although no one else in the room may have noticed how completely shattered Sparrowhawk was about Lirathea's nun-like appearance and her decision to spend her time outside the senate in isolation, Tory saw her Falcon son's pain and confusion.

Avery was in fine spirits, which almost mocked his younger brother's bewildered state. His fine mood departed rather abruptly, however, when he learned of his Falcon-Nefilim double, Viper, and of his visits to see Fallon.

Tory had never seen a man so vexed and jealous, although Avery chose to hide his true feelings for the girl by pretending to be more concerned about the fate of the planetary alliance. Still, Tory knew what was truly fueling her son's conviction to the cause of the senate this day.

An extensive search of the known galaxy had failed to turn up any sign of the craft frequented by Dumuzi's children these last twenty years.

As the children of Dumuzi were mainly space-born children who'd never had a planet of their own, they were unskilled and unfamiliar with the ways of earthbound civilisation and preferred life on their huge spacecraft. This seemed to verify Cordella's claim that all of Dumuzi's children were involved in the theft of the Aten and were supporting Viper in his attempt to contact the evil crone, Mahaud.

'I feel that a strong Chosen force must be sent to guard all the Orme Charichalum enterprises on Numan,' Lirathea advised. 'The spirit world is concerned by what could happen if the children of Dumuzi were to learn about the hidden applications of this substance. They must not be allowed to obtain Charichalum in its Orme state.'

Everyone present agreed.

'Who does the spirit world suggest I send to head our defence on Numan?' Lahmu queried his new spiritual advisor.

'Send Bast and Sparrowhawk,' Lirathea advised surely from behind her veil. 'Thais and his people should also double the guard of the Orme operations on Karleashian.'

'No!' Avery stood up to protest. 'I should go to Numan.'

'You have other commitments to attend to at present.' Lirathea was reminding him of his vow to the master tutoring him.

'I am hardly going to be able to concentrate on Otherworldly studies with so much adversity unfolding in the realm of matter,' Avery reasoned.

'You would defy the will of the Logos?' Lirathea queried, which promptly put a stop to his protest. Avery lowered himself to a seat, heeding her point. Lirathea held out her hand to her twin, and clutching his hand tightly she bethought him. *That which you wish to protect is still on Kila, anyway.*

Avery reclaimed his hand from his sister, not liking that she could clearly see the feelings that he was doing his best to deny existed.

'I need you stationed in the Otherworld, Avery,' Brian supported Lirathea, 'to report on any movement of the Aten through that realm.'

'I understand.' Avery tried not to sound annoyed about being stationed so far from the action.

'I also need to speak with you on another matter when the senate is adjourned,' Lahmu requested, with a smile that was not entirely inviting.

Avery knew he was about to be given the third degree about Fallon from her father, the most formidable warrior in the known universe. *Something to look forward to*. Avery nodded in assent to a drilling.

'The spirit world also recommends that representatives of the council be sent to Gaia to advise our kindred there.' Lirathea jumped to the next issue she saw to be a problem. 'I believe my parents have already been alerted to this calling by the Logos.'

All eyes in the senate turned to the ex-Governor and -Governess of Kila.

'It is true we have been made aware that a visit to Gaia is expected of us,' Tory began. 'Spiritually speaking, Gaia needs help. If our home planet remains alienated from the rest of our planetary alliance, we risk leaving her exposed to the dark influences that we are currently trying so hard to suppress.'

Nobody present seemed very keen to let the two most senior advisors of the alliance depart in the middle of a crisis.

'Did we not learn this lesson in ancient Gwynedd, during the Ossa debacle?' Tory drove home her point. 'By leaving the Saxons out of our alliance for the first twenty years, Mahaud was awarded the perfect opportunity to cast her dark influence over Mercia. The Tablet of Destinies has already named Gaia as the target most likely to be exploited should the Dark Lodge rear its ugly head at this time.'

'You're speaking as though a holy war is imminent,' Thais, the leader of the Centaur race, noted.

'It is not my intent to alarm anyone,' Tory emphasised. 'But better that we are prepared for the event, than to find ourselves faced with a catastrophe akin to the sinking of Atlantis once again.'

Having been on Gaia during the great deluge that claimed the greatest civilisation ever known on that planet, Thais nodded to second Tory's intention. 'Best cover all our bases.'

'Exactly,' Tory agreed, turning her sights on her brother, Brian. 'So unless Lahmu objects, Maelgwn and I intend to leave for Gaia immediately following this meeting.'

Brian had been ruling the alliance for twenty years without any aid from his sister and the Dragon, and yet still he was reluctant to lose their guidance. 'How long do you foresee your stay on Gaia will be?'

The big question. Tory looked at her husband who merely winked to encourage her to be honest. 'To make any real difference on Gaia, we suspect our move could be a permanent one.'

The announcement was met with great gasps and shocked mutterings, primarily from Tory and Maelgwn's six children, who were all present, including their eldest daughter, Rhiannon, who was head of KEPA, the Kila Environmental Protection Agency.

'Now that we have seen our children grow and assume their positions on this great council, Maelgwn and I have outlived our usefulness here on Kila.' Tory endeavoured to allay everyone's shock. 'To stay here would be nothing short of self indulgence for us.'

'But we shall see you again?' Sparrowhawk beat his siblings to the question.

The look of abandonment on Sparrowhawk's face was breaking Tory's heart, but she could make him no promises. 'We hope so.' Her son did not seem at all appeased by her answer, but bowed his head to accept their decision. She could empathise with her children, having felt the same rejection and loss when her parents had chosen to ascend to the causal realm of existence, along with her lifelong mentor, Taliesin Pen Beirdd. Tory's sights returned to Brian.

Obviously this move was deeply important to his sister, brother-in-law and the greater good. Tory and Maelgwn would never upset their family like this without just cause — the decision can't have been an easy one to make. 'I feel I speak for everyone when I say that your departure will be mourned by all within the planetary alliance for some time to come.' Brian became rather more emotional than usual, but realising personal sentiment was quite out of place in the parliament, he swallowed back his tears. 'However, it is not for me to question what the creator has decreed. You have my leave to pursue your quest as you see fit. May the Light of the Logos illuminate your path always.'

Under the large round conference table, Maelgwn gripped hold of Tory's hand and gave it an excited squeeze. Saying goodbye to their friends and family would not be easy, but to ignore the prompting of their soul would be impossible.

6

FREEING THE SPIRIT

Days passed, maybe weeks. It was hard to tell in trance, as he was. For a while Noah had thought that if he recited 'The Great Invocation' one more time he'd go insane. But persisting with his mental vigil to keep the crone's conniving chatter at bay, the Sage was now finding the words of the creed deeply comforting. While he remained tuned out, he did not have to contemplate the reptiles that kept crawling over his motionless body as they went about their daily routine.

'I know you wonder about the dark side, Sage.'

Mahaud sounded as if she was in close proximity to him. But as Noah's eyes were closed he couldn't be sure that she wasn't just toying with his perception.

'I know you have a thing for my Chosen female incarnation, Tory Alexander.'

Noah's eyes shot open to find the crone still hovering over the cauldron. He badly wanted to argue against her foul claim, but to do so would simply be bending to her will; thus he decided not to bother gracing her with a response. He closed his eyes and continued with his recitation.

'All the Chosen Ones have served the dark side in at least one lifetime and lost a small part of their higher self to the Dark Lodge. Light and darkness, good and evil, they must always coexist in balance. Without ignorance, greed, envy, anger, lust and fear to overcome, there would be no lessons, no point to existence. There would be no evolution, for want of a variety of stimuli to interact with.'

'Mankind's development is being hindered by the interference of the likes of you,' Noah argued, annoyed that she'd drawn him into her debate.

'Wrong, Sage boy. It is precisely my interference that quickens human development.'

He couldn't argue the point and the scholar hated that he was beginning to understand the crone's hypothesis. The panic in his heart caused a heat to rise in his body and he began to sweat under the duress of resisting her influence.

'So you see, scholar, that my dark purpose is just as important as your noble cause. We both serve the same almighty creator.'

'No!' Noah refused to concede this and a great rumble resounded through the cavern, then another and another — it sounded like the mountain that sheltered them was being rammed.

'That will be my next brush with destiny calling,' Mahaud commented, very calm about her impending defeat. But then, she could rest soundly knowing she would return to the realm of matter many times in the future.

Noah stood up as bits of rock crumbled from the walls and sharp stalagmites began to drop from the ceiling like huge daggers. The back wall of the cavern came crashing in, destroying one of the wall torches. This breached the crone's outer circle of influence and Noah was freed from her hold. A huge Dragon came crawling through the hole it had dug in the cavern wall and a small party of soldiers followed the huge creature into the cavern.

'Well done, Rufus.' A dark-haired teenage lad strode up to the beast to congratulate it. 'I told thee we could put thy destructive tendencies to good use.'

'Maelgwn,' Noah uttered under his breath, recognising the legend in the boy.

I feel all warm inside, the Dragon bethought his young male companion, in a sardonic tone. As Noah's psychic talent had been returned to him, he caught the Dragon's comment.

'At least thou art not being hunted by the men of Dumnonia.' Maelgwn advised the beast to look on the bright side.

Thee promised to get me back into the Otherworld. Thee did not say anything about a crusade.

'I'm sorry we got distracted, Rufus, but a few good deeds will make the Goddess look more fondly upon thy case.' The lad looked to the inner circle of torches, but there was no sign of the witch. He spotted Noah, but was not given the chance to address him.

'I was sorry to hear about thy mother, little prince.' Mahaud's spine chilling voice swept through the chamber. 'But then, she always was a bit of a slut.'

'I have destroyed thy source of substance, crone. I removed Cadfer's head from his shoulders and this fell off.' Maelgwn pulled a charm on a necklace from his pocket, and as he threw the item to the ground the Dragon torched it to a cinder with one small exhale. 'I shall take thy evil implements and bury them where no one will ever find them. Thou hast no more power here.'

'Easy come, easy go … there be more than one way to skin a Dragon,' Mahaud replied, her voice coming from nowhere in particular. 'Do and think what thou wilt, but I shall be seeing thee again, Maelgwn Gwynedd, and again … and again …' Her sinister voice and laughter trailed off into nothingness and all the torches in the cave went out.

As much as he would have liked to stay and get to know the young Maelgwn Gwynedd, Noah willed himself to the entrance to the cavern, as it was the only place in this region and age that Noah knew and could recognise.

Noah found himself confronted by an even larger force of soldiers, and an old, silvery-haired man who smiled broadly at the Sage's sudden appearance.

'A fellow druid,' the old Merlin assured the wary warriors who had witnessed Noah's miraculous manifestation in broad daylight. 'I shall take care of this.' He came forward and led Noah to where they might talk alone.

'Taliesin?' Noah whispered, guessing this man's identity.

'Are you looking for the High Merlin?' the Druid queried with some interest.

'As I am from the future and find myself stranded in this age,' Noah outlined his woes briefly, 'I believe Taliesin may be the only man alive who can help me. So, yes, I guess I am seeking him.'

'Your tongue and attire would indicate that you are telling the truth,' the Merlin acknowledged, raising his brow. 'And your aura tells me that you are not one of Mahaud's ilk.' The old man winked at Noah and then leaned closer. 'It is my guess that you are one of the Chosen.'

Noah gasped and smiled, relieved by all the explaining he wouldn't have to do. 'Then you are —'

The Merlin smiled and nodded, all traces of age fading from his appearance and within seconds, Noah recognised the Merlin, who had long since become an ascended master in the Sage's present age.

'Then you can help me?' Noah felt sure of deliverance.

'Perhaps.' Taliesin raised an eyebrow, seemingly intrigued. 'Our meeting is most fortuitous, as you can help me test a little theory for an enterprise that I've been musing upon.'

The Sage could not suppress his smile as he realised that he was to be the test subject for Tory Alexander's means to be brought back to the Dark Ages and begin the Dragon's line of the Chosen Ones. 'Would your theory have something to do with harnessing the universal energies that abide at marked ley line crossings on this planet, at certain times of the astrological year, for the purposes of time travel?'

Taliesin was rendered speechless for a second. 'You are indeed from the future,' he reasoned.

'Where your exploits are well documented, High Merlin.' Noah bowed to indicate his great respect for the Merlin's work, and Taliesin chuckled, rather tickled by the whole idea.

'The universe always provides.' The Merlin smothered his amusement when he spied the young Prince of Gwynedd traipsing up the hill towards them.

'I have loaded all of the crone's implements onto Rufus, High Merlin.' He eyed over the Merlin's strange companion and recognised him from the brief glimpse he'd had of Noah in the cave. 'Mahaud hast been vexing thee too, I presume?'

Noah was in ancient Gwynedd having a conversation with Maelgwn Gwynedd and Taliesin Pen Beirdd — he could barely contain his delight. 'Aye, Prince Maelgwn,' he replied, 'she is a thorn in the side of many.'

Noah knew Maelgwn was wary of the smile he wore, but he just couldn't wipe it from his face. He didn't know why he found the reality of Maelgwn as a teenager so amusing, but it was like witnessing a great lion reduced to a playful wide-eyed cub.

'So where to next, High Merlin? I think my Dragon be getting restless.' Maelgwn looked back to view his Dragon stomping about outside the cavern, showing little regard for the soldiers who were forced to flee out of the creature's path.

'I think we might be able to kill two birds with the one stone here.' Taliesin placed a hand on Noah's shoulder to assure him that he had their aid. 'Send your troops back to Gwynedd,' he instructed Maelgwn. 'We three and the Dragon will take it from here.'

The occult was thriving in early twenty-first century Gaia and thus it would be the perfect era to raise Mahaud from the sub-planes.

Assuming a human form, Viper went shopping in London. With so many antique dealers and stores that dealt in esoteric tools scattered about the city, Viper had no trouble in acquiring the four implements needed to summon Mahaud back to the physical world: a cauldron, a sword, a dark crystal and a wand. According to Mahaud's legend, the tools used for her summons did not have to be those that the crone had collected herself.

Mahaud's own collection of occult implements had been buried by Maelgwn Gwynedd soon after he defeated Cadfer. The evil tools were then found and used by the Saxon Warlord, Ossa, and were disposed of completely by Maelgwn's son, Rhun, a quarter of a century later.

But Mahaud's spirit was not banished back to her realm of origin after the Cadfer debacle and the crone had made an appearance in Gwynedd fifteen years after Maelgwn had buried her equipment, making herself at home in Powys in the service of Chiglas. This was an oversight that Myrddin corrected, with the help of Gwyn ap Nudd, when the crone followed Maelgwn and Tory to the late twentieth century.

However, the implements to be used for the crone's summons were all required to have served a dark purpose in the past. The sword must have drawn human blood; the stone must have been used for dark ritual or purpose in the past; the cauldron must have boiled the blood of the living; the wand must be crafted from a twig off a branch used to burn a living thing to death.

Viper avoided paying for any of his acquisitions by simply willing an item he desired back to the Aten. And when he returned to view his bounty, he felt very pleased with his efforts.

He'd managed to find a large double-terminated smokey quartz crystal, hanging from a chain, which had cursed all who had ever had the misfortune of wearing it — all its victims had died whilst wearing the stone. The legend went that with each death the stone had turned darker. Now, it was almost pitch black.

The cauldron he found had known a dark history with a child abductor, whose sick obsessions made the large iron pot very specific to Viper's requirements.

The fellow who was showing Viper the sword was unable to assure him that it had drawn human blood, so the pirate ran the salesman through just to be on the safe side.

Viper then hunted down a feral cat, made a bonfire and burned the animal alive. And, snapping a twig from the branch to which the cat was secured, he acquired the last of his tools.

Gazelle gaped at her brother's tales, sickened by them.

'What's the matter?' Viper slapped her shoulder in encouragement. 'You'd better find your stomach if you want to rule the galaxy.'

After her brush with the crone, Gazelle had already decided that she didn't want any part in unleashing Mahaud. She felt she had to say something to her twin brother, for he wouldn't listen to anyone else. 'I'll fight alongside you against the Chosen, Viper, but leading our people into the dark service of a witch was never the plan.'

'It was always the plan,' he retorted loudly. 'Only now, with Orme Charichalum, our immortality will be permanent.'

'The witch said that it would make *your* immortality permanent,' Gazelle clarified. 'She didn't say if it would work for the rest of us.'

'Of course it will work.' Viper scoffed at her reservation. 'We are bastards of Dumuzi born from the debauch.'

Gazelle bowed her head, not as proud of their family history as her brother was. She was tired of being abused by her kindred and pretending to be amused by their perverted and corrupt obsessions. How she envied Cordella, happily married to one of the leaders of Lahmu's council. The Delphinus Governess had appeared so radiant and content just prior to her abduction and Gazelle longed to know what such happiness felt like.

'Well, I see no need to delay.' Viper slapped his hands together and rubbed them vigorously. 'Ready the recon unit and let us go find ourselves a sacred site to defile.'

Gazelle nodded. What else could she do? She had no choice but to keep up her agreeable front. After a shot of gold Orme her brother's immortality was at full strength, and she knew he had the ability to read thoughts. Thankfully, he was not well practised in the psychic arts and so did not have full control of the talent. The problem for Viper in taking the light-giving substance was that it also sweetened his naturally dark nature, and thus he was not as suspicious and wary as he normally would be. This was the only reason he'd not discovered her aversion to his plans. Heaven help her if Viper got his hands on the immortality potion that Mahaud had suggested he use to quicken his dark potential; then there would be no stopping her brother, no end to the lengths Viper would go to in order to achieve his goals.

After saying their goodbyes to Tory and Maelgwn, neither Brian nor Avery were in the mood for an interrogation. The Governor surprised Avery by only requesting that Avery speak to Fallon.

'Viper has used Fallon's attraction to you to seduce her to his cause. He's hoping to turn her against me, and you.' Brian took a seat, and poured himself a much-needed drink. He was not a heavy drinker, but today he needed something to sooth his shattered sensibilities.

'I see the problem, Governor, and I will be happy to do as you request ...' Avery paused to frown.

'But?' Brian prompted his nephew to speak up.

'Well, the last time I spoke to Fallon she slapped my face,' Avery proffered, noting Brian's expression turn curious, 'so I doubt if she'd be any more receptive to my advice than your own, Governor.'

Brian chose not to pursue the issue of Avery's falling out with his daughter and swallowed his drink before speaking. 'Look, I'm not expecting miracles. Just stay with her until I finish instructing and saying my goodbyes to the rest of the delegates of the council. It's better than having a guard watching over her and she might open up to you.'

'All right.' Avery succumbed. 'I'll give it a bash.'

'That's a good lad.' Brian rose, pleased by the outcome of their little chat. 'I'll speak to Fallon myself in a couple of hours.'

Avery stood in front of Fallon's door, in retrospect considering that he would've preferred a drilling from Brian to the task he'd been given. He wasn't very good at sucking up to people, especially when he'd done nothing wrong. *I'll take that angle,* he decided on the quiet. *Now that Fallon knows it was Viper and not me who seduced her, then she has nothing to be angry at me for.*

Feeling more confident, Avery knocked. He gazed out over Central Park, which backed onto Government House, and was admiring the gardens when suddenly he found himself being yanked in the door.

'Are you nuts?' Fallon exclaimed as she closed the door of her apartment behind them and backed Avery up against the wall in the entrance foyer. 'Every major official of the alliance is in this building at present.'

Despite the confusion, Avery couldn't help but notice how very different Fallon looked today. She was attired in black skin-hugging attire. Her long, spiral curls were left loose, as they never had been, and bounced wildly about her upper body.

'I thought you'd never get here,' she uttered sweetly, and then kissed him with a passion.

After the shock wore off and the kiss rolled on, Avery reclaimed his mind to realise that Fallon thought he was Viper.

This kiss, which he was rather enjoying, was meant for his enemy and not himself.

'Wow,' Fallon emphasised as their lips parted, and she gave a shy smile.

'Indeed,' Avery agreed, his heart and mind racing. Should he make her aware of his identity?

'We should go. It's really not safe for you here.' Fallon took hold of his hands, whereupon Avery pulled her close and kissed her again.

Fallon was not holding back at all, and it broke Avery's heart to learn that he'd lost her devotion to another. Avery wanted to stop this encounter; he didn't want to know how far Fallon would take her affection. Her favour was most pleasing, arousing even, but her enthusiasm only heightened the case of treason against her. Simply by telling him that all the members of the senate were in the building at this time, Fallon was breaching the security of the alliance. *Please let this be merely a case of a young girl's romantic notions and naive curiosity getting the better of her. Please don't let Fallon be fully aware of the implications of her association with this man.*

'Fallon?'

They were startled from their embrace by the sound of Avery's own voice, and when Fallon stepped away from Avery to find Avery standing behind her, she moved clear of both of them. 'Oh shit,' she muttered. 'Which one is which?' Either way, she was in trouble.

'Give me your hand, Fallon,' the newcomer instructed. 'Quickly before he,' he motioned to the man she'd been kissing, 'exposes us.'

'No, Fallon,' Avery urged, 'he'll take you straight to your father.'

Fallon looked back to the newcomer, wary of him until he pulled a NERGUZ module from his pocket.

'To prevent them from following us,' he advised, 'just as we planned.'

'Avery?' Fallon looked at him, her face contorting with the disappointment she felt as she backed towards Viper. 'Why must you always toy with my emotions this way? Are my feelings just a joke to you?'

'I never toyed with your emotions in the first place. He did!' Avery waved a finger in the impostor's direction. 'And I am not the one about to betray everyone I ever cared about! Where do you get off kissing our enemy like that?'

'You couldn't possibly betray everyone you love, Avery,' Fallon retorted sharply. 'Because you are the only person you care about.' Fallon took the module from Viper.

'Don't, Fallon,' Avery warned. 'That module will also make you subject to Viper's will.'

'I know what a NERGUZ module does,' she snapped, tired of being treated like a naive child and despite Avery's caution she unclipped the module and attached it to her wrist.

'This is the control module,' Viper informed Avery as he handed Fallon the NERGUZ.

'See, I am not the fool you take me for.' Fallon took possession of the device.

'If you choose to trust this pirate over everyone who ever loved you, then you are a fool, Fallon.' Avery willed the module from Fallon's grasp, but before it had covered half the distance between them, Viper had willed it back to Fallon again. 'Remember what En Noah predicted,' Avery added, in a desperate appeal to get her to see reason.

'You had your chance, Pan man. Go find a willing wood nymph to toy with instead. I understand they quite enjoy torment.' Viper pulled Fallon close and she attached the control module to her wrist.

'Goodbye,' she said, and this word activated her NERGUZ as they vanished.

Avery tried willing himself after himself, which naturally didn't work. He needed to know what Viper looked like, and now that he'd been made aware that his enemy was part of his own soul-mind, a little past-life regression should solve that problem.

But first Avery had to convey this latest piece of bad news to Lahmu, which would be the icing on the cake of the Governor's already emotionally taxing day.

'This is definitely the place.' Viper strolled into the stone circle, which he'd seen numerous times in the chronicles of the Sage he'd left back in the Dark Age. 'Mahaud's implements were once buried under that tree.' He pointed to an ancient elder tree that stood outside the circle.

Gazelle gazed about at the beautiful lush countryside and the mysterious landmark in which they stood, feeling a little overawed. 'So, this is where Tory Alexander and Maelgwn Gwynedd first met?'

Viper had told her all the stories from the Chronicles he'd studied in the pursuit of information about Mahaud. Her brother had been sickened by all the good deeds and heroic adventures of the Chosen Ones, whereas Gazelle had found the legends rather romantic and inspiring.

'A most unfortunate occurrence for the Dark Lodge,' Viper lectured his sister with a stern look of concern on his face. 'Let's get those torches in place.' He looked to his helpers, who were all cousins, aunts or uncles of the Falcon, Leonine and Delphinus breeds. Every one of them had traces of their Nefilim roots in their appearance, which made them a race unto themselves. With Mahaud's aid, the children of Dumuzi would be a race to be reckoned with and they would thrive as rulers and not outcasts.

The already dismal day turned stormy as the ritual site was prepared.

Gazelle stood far away from the action, her face upturned to the sky to catch the light, drizzly rain that fell in a gentle, endless wave. She'd never experienced this kind of weather before: sandstorms, dust storms, meteor storms, yes, but a rainstorm, never. She wanted to go to Karleashian to experience such a climate, but as she'd always had precious little say in what she did, her dream had remained just a dream. Gazelle never imagined that she might actually get something out of this dreadful crusade of her brother's.

As the four torches were lit at the north, south, east and west end of the stone ring, the wind came up and the day grew even darker.

'Oi!' A middle-aged man approached the site, eyeing over the unusual costumes and elaborate make-up of the trespassers. 'What do you lot think you're doing? This site is not open to the public at this time of year.'

'Who are you, old man?' Viper queried.

'I am the custodian of this site.' He pulled a rifle from underneath his trench coat and, not liking Viper's tone, aimed it at the birdman. 'And I advise you and your friends to move on.' The custodian was startled as his gun left his possession and flew into the clutches of the man he'd threatened. 'How did you do that?'

'I'm a God,' Viper smiled, and shot the man dead with the rifle. 'Whoo-hoo!' he cried, surprised and exhilarated. 'Their weapons sure are loud.' The pirate wandered over and prodded the custodian with his foot. 'They sure do work, though.' Viper eyed over the rifle and decided he'd keep it. It would be a fine antique back home. He slung the weapon strap over his shoulder and, grabbing up the dead man, Viper dragged him into the circle. 'He'll do just fine ... save me hunting someone up.' He dropped the body and placed the crone's talisman around the dead man's neck. 'I suppose she would have preferred a living being, but ...' he shrugged '... we can't always have what we want.'

Viper ordered all his people beyond the radius of the circle. He joined his kindred and from beyond the crone's would-be grasp, the pirate recited the dark invocation.

Gazelle blocked her ears and turned away, as a dark seething red and black mist began to rise from the earth inside the circle.

The mist gathered over the dead body and entered it through every available orifice.

Viper's people gasped and took a step backwards as the dead man began to stir and rise. Their leader only smiled and held his ground, eager to speak with the crone.

When the man dragged himself to a standing position, he looked up, his eyes of glowing red inspiring another gasp from the onlookers.

'Is this body the best you could do, Viper ... it's dead!' The corpse ran a hand over its body and then held out fingers that dripped with red fluid. 'And bleeding.'

The unearthly voice of the crone, and her stench, did nothing to inspire confidence amongst those gathered, but Viper stood undaunted.

'Come, come ... I didn't cripple it or anything and besides, it's just a temporary arrangement,' Viper explained. 'I thought you might like to select the body you shall inhabit permanently, and I assume you want one in an immortal state? After seeing what has happened to your cohorts in the past, I am hardly stupid enough to offer up my person. You may select any of the Chosen for your purpose, and I shall fetch them for you.

But myself and my people are to be your students, Mahaud, not your puppets.'

'A thinking man.' The dead man's mouth curved to a grin. 'I knew you were of the elite the first time I laid eyes on you, Viper. You shall be a Lord of the Dark Lodge, the like of which mankind has not seen since our victory in Atlantis.'

'I am not familiar with that victory?' Viper frowned.

'Of course you're not ... the Chosen would never record one of our victories for reference. But I know all and intend to do a little publishing of my own.'

'The Dark Chronicles,' Viper smiled. 'That *is* inspiring.'

'But first we must fetch me a body.' The witch hobbled awkwardly towards him, as a dead vehicle was far heavier to uphold than a living one. 'And we must acquire the dark potion of immortality for you, your people and my new Chosen body.' As she reached the edge of the circle, Mahaud turned her carcass around to view the ritual site. 'I do like what you've done with the place ... a most pleasing ambience. Your tools were well selected.'

'I shall always do my worst for you, Mahaud, for as long as we agree,' Viper vowed, with a mischievously challenging grin on his face.

The crone nodded, understanding the threat. 'I believe you shall discover that we think so much alike ...' she stepped beyond the circle '... it's *scary*.'

At the same stone circle in Oxfordshire, back in the early sixth century, Taliesin sat in meditative consultation with the King Stone, which was further afield from the main circle of stones known as the King's Men.

Taliesin had willed Noah and himself forth from the Snowdon Ranges to this site beyond the borders of Prydyn and the young Prince of Gwynedd had flown the Dragon overland and caught up with them about an hour later.

Whilst the Merlin was quizzing the elemental who was the guardian of this site about the possibility of sending Noah to twenty-second century Gaia — or more specifically the year 2108AD — Taliesin had the prince digging a hole outside the circle in which to bury Mahaud's utensils.

Maelgwn seemed a mite disgruntled about the chore. The lad had tried ordering the Dragon to dig the hole, but the Otherworldly creature had insisted that, on an empty stomach, it couldn't possibly assist.

The Dragon had a taste for nefarious criminals and low-life human souls. The beast's digestive system was like a one-way ticket to the sub-planes; for any soul Rufus swallowed would never again incarnate. The crone, Mahaud, would have been very much to the Dragon's taste, but whilst she remained in a spirit form the beast could not touch her. None of the human souls present were evil enough to be of interest and so the Dragon remained hungry and at leisure.

'Can I help?' Noah offered his services to the grumbling lad.

Maelgwn stopped his furious shovelling. 'Who art thou, that the High Merlin would aid thee upon first meeting, friend?' The prince said 'friend' in a rather forced tone, as if undecided if this was the case.

'I am a friend to ye both in the future,' Noah replied simply. 'And I have come to be here in the course of my service to our mutual cause.'

Maelgwn wasn't too sure whether to take the claim literally or regard it as a prophecy. 'Then thou art a wiser man than I, to be aware of a cause to which I am ignorant.' The boy rose from his digging, sounding sceptical but not unfriendly.

'Live as many years as thou hast already and I promise all will be clear to thee by then,' Noah granted with a confident smile and motioned to the hole in the earth. 'May I?'

With curious nod, Maelgwn offered Noah the shield with which he'd been digging.

'No, thanks.' Noah held out a hand and, manifesting a steel-headed shovel, he commenced work.

Maelgwn was well used to the High Merlin manifesting the strangest objects at will, and so did not blink an eye when Noah did the same. 'A well crafted tool.' Maelgwn admired how efficiently the shovel did the job. 'May I try?'

'Surely.' Noah handed his tool over, gratified to have enthused the younger man into finishing the task.

'I just want this episode over with, so I can pursue a quiet life.' Maelgwn explained his disgruntled mood and Noah could relate to his reasons for dreaming of a monk's lot.

'Serenity stems from within and not from that which surrounds us.' Noah knew it was indeed Maelgwn's lot to go and study under the priests of the Roman faith for a time, but the young prince was also destined to return to

Gwynedd and become one of the most legendary Kings of his time. 'And what would become of Gwynedd in thy absence?' Noah posed. The bitter look on Maelgwn's face brought home the grim reality of the era that Noah was only passing through.

'Clearly, my *bastard* brother wants the throne far more than I do. So long as I am next in line to be King, there will be unrest in Gwynedd.' His jaw tightened a moment before he continued digging. 'I have saved my father's kingdom and released him from prison. And, without so much as a word of gratitude, he lectures me for involving myself with Otherworldly forces to subdue the threat.' Maelgwn took out his anger on the earth he was cutting into. 'I was not the one who picked the Merlin for my tutor; it was not my fault my mother insisted.'

'But,' Noah hesitated to mention the fact, 'I understand Caswallon lost his Queen in the uprising and must be grieving her loss —'

'I loved her far more than he ever did!' Maelgwn hollered in response, tears bursting from his eyes, which he quickly wiped away.

Maelgwn's adverse reaction stunned Noah and he suddenly felt terrible for churning up the lad's pain. The Sage was so used to discussing the affairs of the past in a clinical fashion that he knew he would have done better not to lecture. He was no great emotional counsellor as Tory Alexander was, but he found comfort in the fact that she would be along in fourteen or so years to alleviate the pain of this fine young man.

'Cadfer and his scum defiled my mother's dead body,'

Maelgwn uttered, full of hatred and disgust. 'I want no part in this world any more.' The prince's anger gave way to exhaustion, and he collapsed to sit on the side of the hole he'd dug. 'I am afraid I will never understand it or my kindred,' he mumbled, being haunted by the dreadful memories still so fresh in his mind.

The Sage crouched down beside the bemused prince to offer a little encouragement. 'But thou art one of the few who can change thy world for the better.'

The lad fixed him with a look that implied Noah's view was naive. 'I have seen enough horrors in the past few days to know that there is more evil in Gwynedd than good. To imagine that will change in my lifetime is a fool's dream, merlin, and I am no fool.' The lad's tears stopped as his resolve hardened. 'For all my efforts of late, what have I achieved?' Maelgwn got up, and deciding the hole was deep enough, he fetched the crone's utensils from his Dragon's back. 'The world be a sadder place for the loss of my mother.' He returned and cast the evil tools into the earth. '*Some change.*'

'It seems the summer solstice shall be our best chance of success,' Taliesin called ahead as he wandered over to join them.

As Maelgwn could not understand the language that Taliesin used to communicate with the stranger, he returned to shovelling dirt.

'I am sorry, High Merlin,' Noah apologised, 'but I could have told you that.'

'Good.' Taliesin sounded only semi-annoyed by the claim. 'Perhaps you can advise of the hour, as the Key Stone and myself seem to be in dispute.'

'Well,' Noah ventured, 'I understand the midnight hour has always served your purpose. I —'

'I knew it!' Taliesin smiled, gratified. 'Goes to show these earth elementals don't know everything,' he whispered aside to Noah and then resumed his normal tone of voice. 'The Key Stone thought midday, for extra power, but my argument was that midnight is for banishing magic and that's really our desire — to banish you to the future.'

'Indeed,' Noah agreed, not really knowing very much about ancient earth magic. 'So how long until the summer solstice?'

'Why, it's only a few days away,' Taliesin advised, seemingly delighted. 'Which makes your predicament all the more synchronous, don't you think? Here am I wanting to test my aptitude for wielding the ancient's technique for time travel and then the universe spits you forth to serve my end and I yours ... which does seem to confirm that I am adept enough in the eyes of the Masters to accomplish our aim.' The Merlin was smiling, until he noted something amiss. 'Where has the young Prince of Gwynedd gone?'

Maelgwn had completed the chore of burying the utensils and left the shovel alongside his finished task.

'Rufus, where did he go?' Taliesin queried the snoozing animal.

The Dragon opened one eye. *He didn't say.*

'Well, go fetch him back, we need to talk,' the Merlin instructed, a little annoyed by the hold-up.

Now I remember. The one thing he did mention was that he hast no intention of ever coming back. Rufus closed his eye once more.

'What!' Taliesin nearly had a pink fit. 'But with Sorcha dead, Caswallon will banish me from the court of Gwynedd. Without Maelgwn to report to me on court affairs, Gwynedd shall be doomed.' He paused to consider the kingdom falling into the hands of Caradoc and shuddered. 'I must speak with him at once.'

'He won't listen,' Noah informed, before Taliesin departed. 'But he will return to assume the throne and take up the old ways of his people once he grows disillusioned with Christian doctrine.'

'He's not going to study under those charlatans and ruin all my well-laid plans!' Taliesin vanished in a flurry.

Noah's head shrank into his shoulders. 'Perhaps I shouldn't have mentioned it.'

He recalled Maelgwn's reports of this era and that the High Merlin and himself had not parted on the best of terms. How wonderful it was for Noah to discover that he'd just sparked the quarrel that would keep the prince and the Merlin at odds for the next fifteen years.

7

GOING HOME

By the year 2108 all the lush green vegetation that had once surrounded the site of the King's Men stone circle in Oxfordshire had been reduced to dry, dirt by Gaia's erratic weather conditions. The Stones themselves seemed to be the only enduring landmarks in the vicinity. Even the elder tree that had grown over the witch's implements and endured through the ages had not managed to survive the twenty-first century. This was the case with almost all the planet's vegetation, due to over-exposure to the poisonous toxins humans had pumped into the atmosphere for so long and the many man-made disasters which occurred just prior to the great Gathering of Kings in the year 2037. Since then, all farming had been moved into biodome complexes outside the larger domed cities which were located above ground, underground, under the sea, in space and on Gaia's moon.

'Heavens,' Tory gasped, upon taking in the desolation of the site that held such sentimental value for her. 'I'd forgotten just how awful the destruction we'd left behind us truly was.'

'What do you mean?' Maelgwn pushed himself to sound positive. 'This is much improved ... at least the sky isn't black all the time now.' He placed an arm over his wife's shoulder and gave her a squeeze.

'Why on earth did you bring us to this location anyway? I thought we were headed to see Doc Alexander?' Tory looked up at her husband affectionately, thinking it might be a romantic gesture on his part, as this was the place where they'd first met.

Maelgwn shrugged boyishly, as if to say his choice of destination had not at all been influenced by their sentiments. 'I thought you might need to recoup your energies after all those farewells.'

Tory forced a smile and drew a deep breath to prevent herself from collapsing into tears again.

'Hey!' Maelgwn hugged her. 'All our long lives we've waited patiently for a time when there would just be you and me, and although I never seriously thought we could create this scenario for ourselves, here we are ... just the two of us.'

'And the problem of raising Gaia's consciousness ... let's not forget about that.' Tory pulled back, and with a sniffle, smiled sincerely. 'I just worry for our children and how they shall fare without us.'

'My love ...' Maelgwn drew a deep breath, knowing her doubts and thinking better of her for them. 'We were an inspiration to our people, but lately, you know as well as I that we have also been a crutch. They must learn to survive without us, to trust their own instincts and make their own mistakes. We cannot —'

Tory gently placed a hand to her husband's mouth to subdue his rambling and nodded. 'I know.'

Maelgwn kissed the hand that covered his mouth, and taking hold of her hand in both his own, kissed his wife's wrist, her shoulder, her neck, his soft caresses settling upon her lips.

The intimate attention was so welcome that Tory lost herself in the heights of emotion that he inspired within the humble vehicle that bound her soul and his to the realm of matter.

These two beings no longer needed to make love to invoke the sweet inspiration, calm and release that the physical act brought with it. Tory and Maelgwn were of one mind and one spirit these days; only their bodies had yet to merge on a permanent basis. Sex seemed an inferior substitute for the depth of union these two souls craved. Still, making love did manage to subdue their deeper yearning to a point. To a normal, happily married couple the idea that sexual relations were not an essential part of a relationship might seem odd, but to the spiritually advanced soul-mind a need of sex for sustenance meant that many physical world glamours were yet to be overcome. The glamours of personal magnetism, personal potency, devotion and the glamour of the physical body all thrived on such necessity. Tory and Maelgwn had progressed beyond relying on constant love and attention from another so that they might feel worthy within themselves. What made the couple feel most fulfilled these days was working together and channelling their combined energies into whatever given task was at hand.

Tory felt the light of the Logos filling her to overflowing whenever she was close to Maelgwn. Her eyes were closed as they indulged in the healing energy of their kiss; it lightened her heavy heart and filled her with a sense of excitement for the adventures that lay ahead.

The darkness behind Tory's eyes was growing intensely white, and when her eyelids parted they beheld a white light and mist spewing forth from the centre of the parched stone circle in which they stood. She gasped in confusion.

'Let's move,' Maelgwn suggested, racing beyond the ring and towing Tory along behind him.

'Thank goodness,' Tory commented as they reached a safe distance. 'Christ knows where we could've ended up.'

'I believe this is an arrival,' Maelgwn advised. 'You can tell that because the vortex of energy is spiralling outward. It's not being sucked inward, as it would be if it were a departure. Wait a minute!' Maelgwn cried out, appearing to have had a revelation. 'It didn't click until just this instant ... of course!' Maelgwn shook his head, as if attempting to get a grip on the extent of his epiphany. 'I haven't thought about this since I first met you and you claimed to be from the future. The only reason I even considered believing your story was

161

because I had once before met a man who'd claimed the same. I was fifteen years old at the time.'

'That was round about the time of Cadfer's uprising, wasn't it?' Tory assessed.

'I met the man from the future during the course of those events,' Maelgwn confirmed, looking Tory straight in the eye. 'And I do believe that man was Noah.'

'Noah!' Tory looked back to the phenomena unfolding close by. 'But ...?'

'Don't you see?' Maelgwn himself was only just coming to an understanding. 'That would explain why he has not returned to report to Brian about his mission. With the chariot he can cheat time and so would have certainly returned sooner. But he couldn't return if he'd been trapped in the Dark Age and had to rely on Taliesin's as yet unperfected grasp of the ancient methods of moving through time.'

'But how was Noah trapped?' Tory reasoned. 'He is very accomplished in the greater mysteries and psychic arts of defence —'

'Mahaud,' Maelgwn answered in a word. 'I met the man from the future when I went to retrieve her evil implements from a cave in the Snowdon Ranges. The Goddess had bid me to bury the crone's tools beyond the borders of Prydyn, in return for Otherworldly aid to take back my father's kingdom.'

'But are you sure it was Noah you saw?' Tory quizzed and her husband smiled.

'Now that I have made the connection ... I am sure.' He looked to the centre of the ring where the mist had cleared to reveal a lone body, unconscious on the ground. As the illumined mist cleared completely, he saw the strangely clad mystery man from his distant past in the Sage he knew so well. 'Taliesin's timing is impeccable, however coincidental.'

Tory followed Maelgwn to Noah's side, having had a thought that was not so amusing. 'This does seem to confirm that Viper got his audience with Mahaud.'

Maelgwn grimaced and nodded. 'But let us not jump to any wild conclusions before we've heard what our friend here has to say.' He slapped the Sage around the cheeks a few times, but achieved zero response.

The crone had taken up residence on the remote garbage level of the Aten's Star Chamber — the command centre for the huge mobile city. Her foul odour and that of the rotting corpse she inhabited was thus disguised and contained.

The smell didn't bother Viper. He thrived on the fact that he could withstand, and even enjoy, that which would drive most men to their knees and set them puking, or compel them to run for their lives. He'd noticed that whenever he entered the crone's space he felt an immediate affinity to the energy she generated. It was like coming home to mama.

Viper had murdered his own mother years ago for allowing him to be sexually abused all his life. Incest, child abuse, gang rape and orgies were all commonplace behaviour among the children of Dumuzi. That's what nurtured the dark nature of his people.

Mahaud was pure evil unrestrained by human morality; this Viper found very alluring. He aspired to be like her, for with such lack of conscience and such dark psychic power to wield, no one would get the better of him again.

'Bring me the woman who is the soul-mate of your Chosen incarnation,' Mahaud had advised, 'for, in sacrificing her to me, you shall be committing the ultimate crime against your Chosen self and the great plan of the Allied Logoi.'

Under hypnosis Viper explored the past lives Avery and himself had had in common. Viper discovered that he'd already met the Chosen incarnation of the female soul they had repeatedly married through the ages during his research mission at the Institute of Immortal History on Kila.

'You must seduce this woman, Viper.' The crone read his thoughts. 'But as your foe are already on guard, we must use your ship's unique advantage to our advantage … we head for the time zone just prior to your theft of this vessel, before our foe were alerted to a threat.'

How clever she was. Viper smiled broadly at the rotting old man in which the crone resided, concentrating on her eyes of glowing red that reflected the dark soul within. 'How shall I ever resist you once your soul-mind is in the body of my soul-mate?'

'You are a demon, Viper …' she lustfully admired the healthy young demi-god bewitched by her power, '… as sick and twisted as any I've known.'

'You have no idea how sick I can be.' He kissed the back of her cold, dead outstretched hand and then licked her palm.

'How about I let you prove your devotion to the cause?' She licked her dry, cracked lips with her corpse's rotting tongue, and grabbing hold of Viper she drew him close.

Tory was about the last person Noah had expected to greet him upon his arrival in the present, but the event was most pleasing to him. 'You are a wonder, Tory Alexander,' he mumbled, realising how groggy he felt when his words came out sounding rather slurred.

'Hey, that's my line.'

'Dragon!' Noah sat up to look about and spotting the large dark-haired, dark-eyed warrior, he scrambled up, excited to see him. 'I just left you in —'

'The Dark Age,' Maelgwn finished the sentence for him. 'I know, I was there. Still, I must confess that I only just made the connection myself.'

'You met Maelgwn as a lad?' Tory clarified, enchanted. 'I wish I'd been there.'

'I feel I owe you an apology,' Noah told Maelgwn, 'for enlightening Taliesin as to your intention to pursue a monk's life.'

Maelgwn slapped a hand down upon his old friend's shoulder and gave a hearty laugh. 'I did wonder at the time how the old wizard had discovered the details of what I'd planned, for I didn't take your claim to be from the future very seriously at the time. Still, it all turned out for the best, did it not?' He motioned to Tory, who'd been the second time traveller to visit Gwynedd in the Dark Age.

The response brought Noah's perception rocketing back to the present. 'Viper intends to team up with

Mahaud,' he spluttered out. 'The crone has given him the means.'

'We figured,' Maelgwn advised. 'You should report your findings to Lahmu at once.'

'Yes,' Noah nodded and then frowned as he hesitated to comply. 'How did you know exactly when I would return to the present, when even Taliesin couldn't predict an exact date or time within the desired year of my destination?'

'The Merlin will come to learn,' Tory intervened to remind Noah, who was obviously not thinking clearly, 'that the doorway through time only links from summer solstice to summer solstice of any given year.'

'I knew that.' Noah whipped himself verbally under his breath. 'In fact,' he realised, raising his voice, 'I told Taliesin as much.'

The bemused look upon the scholar's face made Tory laugh. 'It's one of those "what came first, the chicken or the egg" questions ... but fear not, I've created a few of those in my time travels.'

'I'm hooked already,' Noah admitted with a grin, but as his thoughts returned to seeking his Governor, another query sprang to mind and he frowned again. 'So, are you coming with me to report to the Governor?' Noah recalled that Maelgwn had made it sound as if he intended to stay put.

'Our meeting is pure coincidence,' the Dragon advised, considering it was rather nice that creation had allowed them this opportunity to say goodbye to an old and trusted friend.

'So, if you're not on Gaia to meet me, then why are you here?'

'We are taking the advice of a wise sage,' Tory informed him jovially, moving to take hold of her husband's arm. 'We are answering the call to Gaia's defence.'

'We have inspired our people to spiritual, mental and physical greatness,' Maelgwn continued, as their friend's mouth was gaping wide. 'We aspire to do the same here, so that Gaia, too, can join the interplanetary alliance and become part of the grander scheme.'

'Why do I feel like this is goodbye?' Noah could barely speak as his feelings were choking him.

Tory left her husband's side to hug their dear friend. 'You know goodbye is never really goodbye.'

'Yes. But then, I never thought that you'd be saying that to me.' Noah felt the pain of all those souls over the ages who had had to allow this amazing woman to vanish from their lives. He knew damn well he could find her with a thought, no matter where she resided in the universe, and yet, at the same time, he felt he might never see her again in this life. 'I don't understand this premonition of mine.' Noah pulled away from Tory, unable to prevent the teardrops from tumbling down his face. 'Are you planning to depart this world, Nin?' This was the only explanation Noah could conceive of.

'My dear, dear friend.' Tory wiped the tears from his face and, holding his head between her hands, she rested her forehead against his. 'I do not know what the universe has planned for us,' she whispered, her own emotion causing a mild suffocation. 'But I do know that

167

whatever destiny is given to us, on whatever level of awareness, it will always be entwined with thine.'

'Sorry, Maelgwn,' Noah apologised, in advance of kissing the man's wife and then squeezing her tight. 'I have so much to thank you for I barely know where to begin,' he mumbled through tears that were now free flowing.

'Me too.' Tory gasped for air and sniffled to regain some sort of composure.

'Aren't I taking this well?' Maelgwn spoke up, proud to have finally conquered his jealous streak.

'That you are.' Noah took the hint and let Tory go. 'I am going to miss you too, Dragon.'

'I very much doubt that you shall have the opportunity in the near future.' Maelgwn shook the Sage's hand. 'But I have faith that you will guide our people through this calamity and I have no qualms about leaving my kindred in your very capable hands.'

Noah exhaled deeply, both overawed by the compliment and horrified by the great expectations they had of him. 'I should go then,' he said, knowing that every second he delayed could be crucial. Noah looked from Maelgwn to Tory and then stepped back to where he could view them both. 'You are already sorely missed.'

'No need.' Tory shook her head to assure him. 'We shall always be close at hand.'

'And close at heart.' He placed a hand to his chest to pledge: 'God bless.' The great Sage struggled to repress his grief as he vanished from their midst.

Once Noah had gone Tory turned and took up both

her husband's hands. 'Thank you for allowing me the chance to say goodbye to him. I know —' she spoke up over his pending comment, 'that you are going to say that you fluked this instance, but deep down inside I know you suspected we'd find Noah here.'

'Maybe you're right.' Maelgwn gave himself the benefit of the doubt, deciding to allow his wife to think well of him.

'Of course she is right. Deep down we remember everything.'

Their attention was drawn to a slender middle-aged man dressed in a robe of violet and gold. Tory knew he was an Ascendant Master, as the mere sight of him filled her being with peace, love and hope. His hair was long, straight and dark, like Maelgwn's, although this man wore his longer and sported a tiny triangular beard on his chin. His eyes were soft blue and when the lord smiled he revealed the whitest, most perfect set of teeth that Tory had ever seen.

'Count, how wonderful to see you again.' Maelgwn greeted him warmly, bowing slightly to revere his presence.

'I thought we'd never finish all those goodbyes,' the lord commented, smiling warmly all the while. 'We have made far too many friends on the physical plane, which is why it has taken us so long to tear ourselves away from our involvement with matter.'

Tory was immediately infatuated with the way he spoke in the plural, reinforcing the idea that all are one. 'Is that why we are here on Gaia? To disengage ourselves from matter ... to ascend?'

'My dear Tory Alexander.' The Count held out his hands to her. 'What a joy you have been to me. Such bravery and compassion as I have seldom known in all my female lives.'

Tory took hold as requested, but bowed before the lord, feeling humbled by his beautiful ultraviolet aura.

'Only Maelgwn and yourself can answer your question, I'm afraid. I do not make your decisions, I just learn from them as you do,' he explained, urging her with a tug on her hands to rise. 'I am Master of your Soul Ray, but several of my colleagues govern other aspects of your manifestation in this life. You have a Personality Ray and Rays that govern your mental and astral bodies. Not to mention the Rays that influence the era and country of your birth, your planet and your solar system, your galaxy and so forth. This is how every incarnation of every soul-mind can create a completely individual experience. But, let us leave this forsaken part of the world and find more inspiring surroundings in which to take our repose and talk at greater length.'

As the master let go of one of her hands to take up one of her husband's, Tory thought she'd best speak up before they got sidetracked. 'What we really need is to speak with Doc Alexander.'

'Ah, yes, Cadwaladr,' the Count said. 'Melchizedek has been following his work on Gaia very closely.'

'Melchizedek?' Tory queried, trying not to sound rude or ignorant, although she felt both.

'Perhaps you know him better as the Sanat Kumara, the personality expression of the Silent Watcher whose consciousness is incarnated as the planetary Logos,' he explained.

'But I thought the planetary Logos, Gaia, was female?' Tory was confused.

'Indeed,' the Count conceded, 'but when dealing with the harsh reality of life on the planes of matter at this early stage of mankind's spiritual evolution, Gaia usually chooses to assume a male persona ... in the future that will change.'

'So you are taking us to meet Melchizedek?' Tory was intrigued by the notion.

'Eventually ... but first you must meet some of my Brotherhood,' the Count informed her. 'They are most eager to meet you both in person.'

'And we are eager to meet them,' Maelgwn assured before his wife could ask any more questions. 'Please lead us where you will, lord.'

After reporting the sad disappearance of Lahmu's daughter to him, Avery had been given leave to retire to a meditation chamber to familiarise himself with Viper's appearance and see if he couldn't learn more about the Falcon pirate's intentions.

Most of the Chosen didn't begin being tutored in past-life regression before the age of about eighteen years and were not permitted to regress alone before the age of twenty-five. Avery and his sister, having proved to be more psychically adept than any of the Chosen before them, were introduced to this technique at a younger age.

It was, therefore, rather a rude shock to Avery to be unable to conjure so much as a glimpse of his past life as

Viper. This failure found him seeking his sister, Lirathea, in the wilderness on the far side of Kila where the sun was just rising. Avery was on the same cliff top where all his problems had begun. Lirathea was seated in the Lotus position facing the sun, and was deep in meditation.

She wore a plain, shapeless robe of violet, drawn at the waist by a girdle woven in all the colours of the rainbow. The hood of her robe hung around her shoulders, exposing her bald scalp to the warm rays of morning.

'I still can't get used to seeing you shorn like that,' Avery commented to make Lirathea aware of his presence. When she did not break from her repose, Avery figured that his sister would continue to ignore him unless he came to the point. 'Why can't I view my past life as Viper?'

'It isn't a past life,' she spoke calmly and softly, moving nothing but her mouth. 'You and Viper are a split soul whose lives are unfolding simultaneously.'

'No, that's not done,' Avery protested. 'I am immortal. The incarnating soul stops here, with me.'

'When we agreed to hand over our physical bodies to Devas soon after birth, the Logos achieved quantum leaps of good to further the cause of light in creation. This then had to be counterbalanced with the cause of darkness. As the involvement of Devas in the physical realm had never been permitted before, the Dark Lodge of the Materialistic were also granted something by creation that had never been permitted before —'

'They allowed a damned soul to reincarnate,' Avery

concluded, positive that he was right. 'But why has this soul been allowed to inhabit one of my bodies?'

'Because if your angelic soul has been allowed to reside here in the physical, polarity demands that your demonic aspect be allowed the same opportunity.'

'Are you saying the dark soul that has incarnated was and is part of my own soul-mind?' Avery was repulsed by the notion and even a little insulted.

Lirathea nodded. 'In the course of a soul's evolution it must experience all aspects of creation, negative and positive, light and dark.'

'But your angelic soul had a stay here too!' Avery objected to being singled out and tested alone.

'And my dark aspect has also reincarnated,' she advised, opening her eyes and looking to her brother, 'only she is not as conceited as her brother, and shall not pose as great a problem as Viper is bound to.'

Avery placed both hands on his hips, dumbfounded for a second; it sounded to him like his sister was having a dig. 'Are you saying I am conceited?'

His reaction seemed to answer the question in Lirathea's opinion. 'It won't do you any good to take out your frustration on me. En Noah warned you this would happen, so you only have yourself to blame for the loss of your love.'

'I am not in love with Fallon!' Avery blew his stack, tired of hearing this unfounded accusation over and over.

'Beware when your words conflict with what is in your heart, for a great rivalry will be avoided by putting your ego aside and telling the truth.' Lirathea repeated their tutor's warning and stood. 'Well,' she emphasised, with a sardonic but happy tone, 'the great rivalry has been struck, Avery, so somewhere between now and graduation you have lied to someone about your feelings ... and when was that, exactly?'

Avery could only think of two instances where he'd been conscious of lying, and both times he'd been telling Fallon that he didn't find her attractive. The realisation caused him to bow his head in defeat. 'What mighty force causes someone to lie to themselves, sis? Why can't I just admit that she has bewitched me with her attention and now I can't bear to consider life without it?'

Lirathea could empathise with her brother, as she'd nearly glamoured herself into a big mistake, too. She'd been deluding herself into needing to be loved, whereas Avery had been fooling himself into believing he could do without it. 'Your reluctance is Viper's will holding sway over you. He would really much rather you stayed out of his way, and left Fallon's fate to his darkening and twisted discretion,' Lirathea informed her brother, knowing the fact would rile him.

'You think Viper has power over me?' Avery scoffed, choosing to be openly insulted instead of alarmed.

'I know he does. And even if his influence is unintentional, it can be powerful,' she warned. 'I know, because I am using my influence to guide my dark half towards the path of light ... I focus on sending her love and light every day.'

Avery cracked up; how could he take her seriously? 'You want me to devote love to Viper? I suppose you want me to wish him well too! May he be triumphant over us and spread his reign of horror throughout the galaxy!' He stopped raving when he noticed his sister's eyes were like daggers. This was a new look for her.

'Have you learned nothing from our parents?' Her look turned to bewilderment. 'The entire Interplanetary Chain Logoi is counting on you, Avery. Don't screw this up by being nonchalant. Viper has power over you because he's had it tough; his desire to succeed is strong. Underestimate him and he will show you up for the spoilt, well-to-do brat that you potentially are.'

Avery's head was bowed again. 'He already has exposed me as thus,' he admitted, feeling childish and very put in his place. 'So, would you be so kind as to advise your *loser* brother as to how he might rectify this catastrophe?'

'There is only one course of action for you,' Lirathea smiled, gratifed by his turnaround. 'You must win Fallon back.'

Avery rolled his head to one side, appearing pained. 'It is too late. Viper has taken her god knows where!'

Lirathea placed a hand on her brother's shoulder to calm him and waited until she had his full attention once more. 'It has been made known to me that Viper will raid one of our Orme production operations.'

'Which one?' Avery pressed for information. 'When?'

'I don't know,' she replied resolutely, prompting the disappointed Avery to back off. 'It will be soon though. I have foreseen Viper using Fallon to get into the facility, which gives you one last chance to set her straight about how you feel.'

'I don't like it when you say "last chance".'

Lirathea looked away to hide her dread, her voice dropping to little more than a whisper. 'I feel a terrible fate awaits Fallon if she does not come to her senses. Your love is very important to her.' The holy woman turned her violet eyes back to meet her brother's of identical colour. 'I cannot stress how vital it is that you make your true feelings known to her.'

'What terrible fate?' Avery was still caught up in that part of her claim. 'You know plenty that you're not telling me, don't you?'

'I can't see it,' Lirathea retorted sharply, perturbed about the fact. 'I have only felt its cold, bleak, guilt-ridden torture once, *briefly*, and I never want to feel it again.'

The look in her eyes told Avery not to doubt her word.

'Win her heart, Avery, it is the only thing that will save the day. And make sure Sparrowhawk is with you when you confront Viper,' she added as an afterthought.

'Why?' Avery frowned; he and his younger half-brother were anything but a team.

'The spirits tell me it will be beneficial to you both.' She shrugged, as if she knew no more.

'I don't see how?' Avery whined, resigning himself to obliging the spirit world's request.

'I was the cause of the rift between you and Sparrowhawk,' Lirathea pointed out, 'but now I have removed myself from society your reason for contention has dissipated, has it not? You two can no longer use me as an excuse not to get along.' Lirathea smiled a self-satisfied smile in conclusion and managed to coax a grin out of Avery as well.

'Perhaps this premonition of yours is trying to indicate that Viper's target will be Numan. That's where you've had Sparrowhawk posted,' Avery theorised.

Lirathea nodded to confirm that he could have a point. 'If anyone can head Viper off, you can. But you must not entertain any negativity during your quest ... if your heart is not full of love and good intentions for *all* involved then the Dark Lodge will have the upper hand and win the day.'

'I understand,' Avery acknowledged surely.

The Count brought Tory and Maelgwn forth to a narrow ravine that ran through a valley surrounded by pine tree covered mountains. The peace and natural beauty of the landscape captured their attention at once.

'What planet is this?' Maelgwn gazed up at the lovely blue sky that was littered with tiny white puffs of cloud. 'It is so reminiscent of the lost Gaia.'

The master paused from scaling the rough and uneven track that ran alongside a stream and turned back to look at Maelgwn. 'This is Gaia.'

Maelgwn smiled in disbelief at the Count's implication. 'Then, surely, this can't be present day Gaia. The sky is so clear here, the vegetation is pristine and the air is breathable.'

The Count shrugged. 'Nothing ails the environment of this particular site on the planet.'

'And where is this site located?' Tory queried, having been otherwise engaged perceiving the strong earth energies emanating towards a dwelling in the distance, which was situated overlooking the river.

'You are at Shigatse in the Himalayas,' the Count informed.

'Tibet,' Tory realised, quite overwhelmed by the fact. 'The roof of the world and the spiritual capital of Gaia. In all my travels I have never been drawn here.' She thought this odd, now, as most of the spiritual doctrine she'd read that corresponded with her own understanding of the cosmos had originated in this place.

'One is usually drawn here at the end of one's earthly travels,' the Count explained to Tory and then looked back at her husband to answer his query. 'The reason Shigatse has not been affected by the catastrophes that have plagued the rest of the planet is that the residents of this place will not allow it.' He smiled in closing and continued on his merry way.

As they approached the river, the dwelling came more clearly into view.

Of modest size, the structure appeared not unlike a temple shrine, with its beautiful Burmese-style turrets and tall marble columns supporting the roof on all sides.

The Count continued along the track past the shrine. Tory realised that the powerful energies she'd picked up on, passed through the structure and did not stop there, but flowed on to a destination further afield. From the outside of the little temple, Tory could see several people inside bowed to the ground in silent prayer before an altar that was strewn with fruits, flowers and other offerings and gifts.

'To whom do they give homage, Count?' Tory caught up to their guide to ask softly.

'Why, they give homage to the Masters we are here to see,' he informed and pointed to a bridge over a stream just up ahead. 'The houses where the Masters El Morya and Kuthumi dwell. We'll see them once we round the bend in the ravine just beyond the bridge.'

'And are they Ray Masters as you are, Count?' Maelgwn took hold of his wife's arm, enjoying their stroll in the mountains immensely.

'Indeed.' The Count smiled broadly exposing his gleaming white teeth to the daylight. 'These Masters are brothers and work very closely together. El Morya is the human manifestation or the Chohan of the First Ray of Will-Power. He is the destroyer and has had numerous human incarnations. One you might be aware of is Alexander the Great.'

Tory was stunned, knowing that this mighty leader had been one of her brother's incarnations. 'So my brother Brian is on Master El Morya's Soul Ray.'

'Yes, indeed, and has always been. As Lahmu, Brian was the destroyer of the Pantheon,' the Count explained. 'El Morya's brother, Kuthumi, is the Chohan of the second Ray of Love-Wisdom. As the Master Builder, you can see why he works so closely with El Morya.'

'Because after destruction there is always new growth and construction,' Maelgwn figured.

The Count nodded. 'One of Kuthumi's great incarnations was Pythagoras. Still, most of El Morya and Kuthumi's most vital and testing human incarnations were during the early Mayan and Lumerian periods, as they were needed to advance the human belief system and the consciousness of mankind. Kuthumi works very closely with the Christ consciousness, currently known as the Lord Maitreya.'

'So was Jesus Christ one of Maitreya's incarnations then?' Tory had to ask, she couldn't resist finding out more about the legend as she had never trusted the Bible's account.

'No,' the Count replied. 'But, it was the Lord Maitreya who heavily influenced Jesus for the last three years of that one's life leading up to the crucifixion. It was also the Christ consciousness who overshadowed Jesus during his time on the Cross, in order that he might endure the fourth initiation known as the Great Renunciation. He was the first human being who, in a marathon race of evolution, reached the enlightened state of Christ consciousness to become the way between humanity and the Father's home. Jesus has since taken the fifth and sixth initiations to become the Chohan of the Sixth Ray of Abstract Idealism or Devotion and prefers to be called Sananda these days.'

Tory and Maelgwn were both rather thoughtful after that information and so walked in silence over the bridge, digesting what the Count had said and greatly anticipating the introductions that were forthcoming.

On the other side of the bridge there was a beautifully paved path that ran off in both directions.

'This way.' The Count headed off up the hill. 'That which lies downhill is for Kuthumi to disclose to you, not I.'

Tory and Maelgwn hadn't thought to be curious about where the downhill path led, but now they were.

As they rounded the bend in the ravine two houses came into view. These dwellings were much more homely-looking than the pristine little place of homage down the way. Every aspect of their construction was rounded, domed or arched. The dwellings on Kila were built on the same architectural principles but the houses they beheld at present were more old-fashioned and had an oriental influence — if shrunk in size, the houses would be the perfect illustration of what Tory imagined an oriental pixie's dwelling might look like.

'Amazing,' Tory mumbled, referring not to the dwellings but to the convergence of earth energies that marked this spot as a ley-line crossing and a doorway to the Otherworld. 'This is the most powerful hotspot I have ever felt. It must be the grand central station of ley crossings.' The atmosphere of the place oozed tranquillity and peace, the like of which Tory had never felt in a conscious state.

'Not quite,' the Count granted, 'but Shigatse would be the major station next to grand central, Shamballa, which is very close by here.'

Maelgwn had no knowledge of such a place, but Tory had heard and read about the legends, long ago when she was a student. 'I was under the impression that Shamballa was just a myth?' She voiced her understanding.

'To the inept seeker,' the Count reasoned, 'it may as well be.'

A path led around to a tranquil garden courtyard at the rear of the house, where the Count invited Tory and Maelgwn to be seated.

'The tea is for you,' the master advised, motioning to a little table where an earthenware tea set was laid out on a tray, with two small bowl shaped cups at the ready and steam rising from the spout of the stout pot.

'I shall return.' The Count entered the house quietly.

'Tea then?' Tory did the honours.

'Definitely.' Maelgwn slouched in his seat and threw back his long dark hair from his face as if the act would clear his mind and help him get a grip on their circumstances. 'Why do you think we've been brought here?'

Tory finished pouring the tea and, handing Maelgwn's cup to him, she dropped her voice to a whisper. 'I'd say we're being recruited.'

'Yes,' Maelgwn agreed, 'but for what task?'

'I guess we're about to find out.' She held up her teacup and Maelgwn sat forward to clink her cup with his.

'This tea is very odd,' Tory decided upon taking several sips, each one having a different flavour. 'It seems to taste like anything you want it to taste like.'

Maelgwn seemed amused by her comment. 'I thought I was imagining things.'

Once they'd finished the cupful, both Tory and Maelgwn began to feel a change in their perception.

'Wow!' Tory put down the cup and gazed about at her surroundings. The colour of everything had intensified; in fact, all of her senses had sharpened. She felt suddenly detached from her physical surroundings and this inspired much joy and peace in her. 'That tea is very cleansing,' she commented, unable to wipe the smile from her face.

Maelgwn had his eyes closed and had slouched to a more comfortable seated position once more. 'Mmmm ...'

'Do not rise.'

Tory looked to the doorway to find that the Count and two other tall gentlemen had emerged, and startled by their presence she went to stand, as did Maelgwn, but hearing the instruction they'd just been given they remained seated and the three men joined them at the table.

Even before they were introduced, Tory could easily define which the Masters governed which Ray, for their attributes were clearly reflected in their assumed human forms.

El Morya was six foot six in height, with the deportment of a general. He spoke in short sharp sentences. His aura was one of overwhelming power and strength, and his commanding countenance invoked the deepest respect. His long, dark, wavy hair was mostly hidden by a white turban, which matched his long white shirt and loose-fitting trousers. A long wavy beard, neatly trimmed, covered a good part of the master's face, whose stern expression did not hide the enlightenment and gentleness that was reflected in his dark brown eyes.

Kuthumi was as tall and noble as his brother, but was of slighter build. His complexion was fairer than

El Morya's, and his golden-brown hair and beard softened his appearance. Out of his eyes of deep blue seemed to flow the love and wisdom of the ages. He was attired in much the same manner as his brother, only the heavier weave of the fabric was dark blue.

'We are aware that you both aspire to higher work.' Kuthumi got straight to the point, yet his expression was one of patience and he addressed the couple before him very kindly. 'We are in need of souls of your calibre at present, or we would not have called you back this soon.'

'Why the alarm, lord?' Maelgwn was naturally worried for his kindred.

'We are readying the agents of light for a dark event.' He forced a smile, not wanting to be the bearer of bad news.

'Has this event got something to do with the half-caste Nefilim rebel known as Viper?' Tory was guessing that it did.

'Viper is an agent for a leading exponent of the Dark Lodge on Gaia, and soon the dark cause will become Viper's cause and he will take up the quest with zeal.'

'What is the ultimate aim of the Dark Lodge?' Maelgwn asked the question, but both Tory and himself sat forward to hear the answer.

'To retard the evolution of humanity,' El Morya stated.

Kuthumi anticipated the next question and answered it. 'To guide mankind to reduce Gaia to a frozen moon, and the planet will be incapable of providing bodies for souls to inhabit ... evolution will be delayed by millions of years; to wipe away the culture of the ages and undo all that the Logoi have created, is the ultimate purpose of the Dark Lodge.'

'And Gaia is the best place to start glamouring humans into their own destruction.' This was what the Tablet of Destinies had told Tory.

Kuthumi nodded. 'Hence we need as many enlightened human soul-minds as possible to aid with the behind-the-scenes guidance of humankind.'

'We wish to be where we will be of greatest service to the Logos,' Tory assured the Masters, who all nodded, aware that her statement was true enough.

'We are proud of your devotion to the plan,' Kuthumi granted, 'but this decision is not one to be made blindly. Allow me to enlighten you both as to what would be expected should you choose to take a more causal role in the forthcoming events.' Kuthumi rose; the other two Masters remained seated. 'Accompany me,' he invited Tory and Maelgwn.

The couple obliged and trailed the master back down the side of the house to a track that led towards the bridge and beyond. Neither Tory nor Maelgwn had noticed that they no longer used their feet to advance, but rather they floated after Kuthumi, propelled forth by their will to know more.

On board the Aten, Fallon was not feeling very warmly welcomed. Not one of Viper's kindred to whom she was introduced seemed to have a nice word or kind look for her. Not that Fallon blamed them; after all, her father had deceived and cheated them of life eternal.

Viper's sister, Gazelle, threw Fallon off guard in that the half-caste Nefilim Falcon woman looked so much like Lirathea.

Gazelle's wings sported the same honey coloured plumage as Viper's, but where her brother's quills were short, the quills on Gazelle's head fell all the way down to her waist. Her large almond-shaped eyes were azure blue and were her only angelic feature. Suited up in tight fitting brown leather, Gazelle was far more warrior-like than her Chosen incarnation and her personality was as fierce as her appearance.

'The Chosen don't betray their own kind,' she stated with suspicion when introduced to Fallon. 'She's a spy, Viper.'

'Well, I trust her.' Viper struggled to remain civil with his sister.

'Do you trust her enough to tell her about our secret weapon?' In mentioning this, Gazelle taunted Fallon and vexed her brother at the same time.

'Fallon *is* our secret weapon,' Viper advised his sister, his look daring her to push the issue and incur his wrath later for her defiance. 'So, if you don't mind, we must retire to quieter quarters to devise our next move.' He took Fallon by the arm and guided her away from his troublesome sister.

'She will betray you.' Gazelle raised her voice to warn Viper, and then smiled confidently as she watched the Chosen traitor step onto a teleporter with her brother and vanish. 'And she won't be the only one.'

Gazelle suspected that once Fallon discovered that Viper was in lust with a vile rotting demon, the Chosen

One would return to her kindred to warn them and hopefully take the informant back to Kila with her. Gazelle wanted off this ship of fools before it was sucked into the dark depths of Density. Fallon was her ticket to a better life.

Viper was currently inhabiting the private chambers that had once belonged to the Nefilim Lord Marduk — the creator and father of the Chosen Ones. As with most quarters constructed for Nefilim occupation, the rooms were huge and sparsely furnished, with huge floor-to-ceiling windows that allowed for sweeping views of the vast expanse of space in which their vessel was adrift.

'I haven't spent a lot of time in space.' Fallon gazed out the window, trying to hide her nervousness at being alone with Viper at this moment.

'I have spent my whole lonely life here.' Viper came up behind Fallon and wrapping his arms about her waist, he began to kiss her neck.

He wanted her so badly. He wanted to smell her fear, hear her scream, see her bleed and taste her innocence before stealing it from her. He wanted to tie her up and torture her with every perverse act he'd ever endured as a child — and he would, once this Orme raid was over. And once he destroyed everything pure and wholesome about her, he would murder her. When Fallon suffered a mortal death, her immortality would kick in and Viper would make a gift of her immortal body to Mahaud. With the crone inhabiting Fallon's physical form, Viper and Mahaud planned to derive much pleasure from the eternal violation of the girl. To caress Fallon gently like this made Viper sick to his stomach; the only thing that made this seduction bearable was the knowledge that he was defiling the daughter of his enemy.

For some reason Viper's touch made Fallon shudder. 'It's cold in space,' she commented to hide her reaction and slipped away from him to conjure forth a jacket to put on. 'We haven't got any time to waste,' she advised Viper as she slid into the garment. 'We really should get cracking on a plan of attack.'

'You're not going to get all professional on me now, are you?' Viper pulled her close once more. He wanted her to give up her virginity to him voluntarily, just so he could see the look on her face after the Orme raid, when she discovered that he hated her guts.

'How am I to take your cause seriously, when it is clear you do not?' Fallon removed his hands from her behind. Beginning to feel a little pressured, she began to consider fleeing.

Inside, Viper was furious, but he couldn't risk losing her trust before he got his hands on the dark Orme. 'I couldn't have you thinking that I brought you here just for your expertise.' He backed off, and placing both hands behind his back Viper leaned over to give Fallon a peck on the cheek. 'Thanks for your help.'

Fallon found his schoolboy antics a bit extreme and so kissed his lips to reassure him. 'You're welcome.' With a smile, she let Viper go and slapping her hands together she took an official stance. 'Now, for a strategy.'

On the way to meet up with Bast and Sparrowhawk on Numan, Avery dropped by his Otherworldly office on

Gaia to pick up his messages from Templeton and make his apologies to the Count for being detained so long from his tuition.

Reports of the Aten have been coming in, young master. Templeton began his rundown on affairs. *It has been spotted moving through the ethers en route to ancient Gaia and was also reported visiting the early twenty-first century of this planet a couple of times. But the Aten is currently residing in your present day reality.*

'Templeton!' Avery was furious. 'Why wasn't I told this sooner?'

I was told you were in Lahmu's senate. The old willow tree sounded most defensive. *Uncontactable until otherwise informed, that was the impression I got.*

'I was finished with the senate ages ago,' Avery informed.

And I am expected to know this?

Avery bowed his head, conceding that the oversight was his own damn fault. Fallon's defection had his thoughts and guts in a knot, he should have checked in sooner.

You need not even make an appearance, Templeton continued to lecture. *All you have to do is drop me a thought.*

'All right, Templeton, I'm sorry,' Avery snapped, although it was intended to be an apology. 'Can we do anything to stop the Aten passing through our realms?'

Not unless you can remove the elestial smart rock from the drive system of the Aten, or dispense with every deposit of elestial crystal in the Otherworld. Templeton listed the options.

Otherworldly smart rocks came in all different varieties and each variety had different abilities.

The rock in question, Eli, has your ability to come and go between the material world and the etheric world at will. Because Eli is installed in the Aten the craft moves with him.

'Then why would destroying every elestial crystal deposit in the Otherworld prevent Eli from using the ethers to hop all over history?'

Eli tunes into the vibratory rate of his kindred in the Otherworld and thus achieves his safe passage through the ethers.

'And do all these smart rocks have the ability to manifest on the physical plane?' Avery queried.

No, young master, only those hunks that have been granted leave … Gwyn ap Nudd granted Eli the ability in order to aid the Lord Marduk.

'Did he now?' Avery was starting to become very angered by his mentor's convenient disappearance. 'Then surely I have the power to take the ability back.'

One would think so. Templeton's willow branches were bowed lower than usual, as he attempted to humble himself and avoid the brunt of the young lord's aggravation.

'One does not award a gift and then take it back.' The Count finally spoke up to draw Avery's frustration away from Templeton. 'How would you like it if I took the same ability away from you?'

Avery brought his surging emotions into check as he considered the master's point. 'I am not aiding the Dark Lodge,' he argued.

The Count smiled broadly at this. 'No, Avery, you

are a complete angel and would never abuse your authority here in the Otherworld.' The look of guilt on Avery's face said it all. 'And how do you know that Eli is not performing his function in the Aten under duress?'

Avery opened his mouth to argue, and finding he had no comeback, he sighed heavily instead. 'I am failing my initiation, aren't I?'

'You're young ... and the first human to take up this Otherworldly office,' the Count allowed. 'Still, being angry at others for your own shortcomings is not going to make your mistake go away.'

Avery held up a hand in truce. 'No offence, Count, but I seem to have had so many lectures lately, that I couldn't possibly absorb another.' Avery floated over to take a seat on a nearby rock.

'Fair enough,' the Count conceded. 'Let me see if I can be more constructive.' He glided over to be seated beside the young Lord of the Otherworld. 'I am going to do you the courtesy of just telling you straight ... a dark spirit is aiding your foe. You know it by the name of Mahaud.'

Avery was shocked into a standing position. 'How? *The Aten!*' he answered himself. 'Goddamnit! But how did Viper learn about Mahaud?'

'He disguised himself as you,' the Count enlightened. 'And then visited the Institute of Immortal History and did a little research.'

'Goddamnit!' Avery repeated as he began to float to and fro in a frustrated manner.

'Viper is going to need an immortal agent to play host to this spirit,' the Count suggested and seized Avery's full attention.

'Not Fallon, please!' the lad begged.

'It's a possibility,' the Count granted, 'but we cannot say for sure, as Viper's inspiration is drawn from the realms of Avichi which is beyond the comprehension of the Brotherhood of Light.'

A panic, unlike any he'd ever known, rocked Avery to the very core of his being. Anger and fear had always been strangers to him, but now that he'd made their acquaintance Avery seemed unable to shake their company and, compelled to fight them off, he lashed out. 'You could save her!' Avery knew the Count had the power and the know-how.

'If I take this test for you, then what will you learn?' came the master's calm response.

'Fallon's spiritual wellbeing is more important than any old test!' Avery stressed out. 'Please make my initiation something else, anything!'

The Count had to suppress a laugh. 'Your initiation was of your own design, Avery, not mine. Only you can stop the wheels that you have set into motion.'

'How?' he insisted.

The Count rose from his seat and floated over to place a hand on the lad's shoulder to calm him. 'Lirathea has already told you what you must do. And now that you know how high the stakes are, you have the conviction to achieve your goal. I hold no fear of that not being the case and neither should you.'

All the anger left Avery upon being touched by the master and he felt his attitude begin to improve and his confidence in his own abilities strengthen. 'Any other advice?'

'Your foe is seeking to steal the dark Orme,' the Count warned. 'They must not get hold of it.'

'But why?' Avery was confused. 'It is lethal to ingest. It kills not only the body but the soul as well.'

'Only in large doses,' the Count added. 'In small doses it just retards the soul, filling it with darkness and negativity.'

Avery had gone very pale. 'And it will grant immortality for those inclined towards the dark cause?'

'It will.'

'Then Viper could spawn a whole army of evil agents.' Avery was aghast. 'Does Lahmu know this?'

'Lahmu, and a select few others, who dealt with Mahaud last time she reared her ugly head.' The Count let Avery go upon feeling him ready to face the quest at hand.

Avery had not felt such clarity and confidence since the day he'd graduated and Viper began undermining his life. 'I should make haste to Lahmu to report and then go on to Numan to prepare.'

If Viper was after Orme Charichalum then Numan had to be his target.

'You are our front line of defence, Avery.' The Count smiled, confident that the forces of light would overcome. 'All the powers of creation go with you. Don't hesitate to seek our counsel or aid, should you need it.'

His attitude much improved, Avery bowed to the Count in gratitude. 'You have been of great aid already, my lord.'

8

INDEBTED

Past the little bridge the paved track rounded a
curve, and built into the cliff face was a stone
archway in which a door was set.

'Welcome to my museum,' Kuthumi bade Tory and
Maelgwn, and placing his hand on the door it vanished.

They entered a structure that was entirely lit by a
smooth crystal-like substance of which the walls, floors,
arched halls and domed ceilings were composed.

Inside was a vast system of subterranean halls,
chambers and antechambers that were filled with
artefacts, occult treasures and scriptures. Some of the
halls were entirely covered in ancient hieroglyphs, and
Tory recognised the language as ancient Sanskrit. The
glowing blue text was offset against the white
illuminated surface.

In the beginning, the causeless cause spat forth seven great waves of energy, which sped out in all directions into fathomless pure Space. When the points of these Rays condensed, hardened and materialised, atoms were formed. An atom is a dance of Rays in which is locked the spark of living fire. And with this spark, implanted in every atom, is the will to be a Sun.

'The secrets of the cosmos have been committed to these walls, as a reference for those human souls ready to advance upon their spiritual service,' Kuthumi advised Tory.

'It's beautiful,' she uttered, tracing a finger over the glowing text and feeling nothing but the smooth crystal surface. The text was not in any way written, printed or embossed; it was like a glowing blue gas that could not be felt or disturbed. 'It's almost as if the characters are formed from etheric substance.'

'The Otherworld has many advantages,' Kuthumi explained how the illusion was possible.

'The Otherworld?' Tory queried, noting that she was floating instead of standing. She looked closely at her hands and found she could actually see the frenzied motion of the atoms that composed her subtle body. 'This is an astral projection experience?' When the Count nodded, Tory was amazed at how oblivious she'd been to the fact. 'What was in that tea?'

Kuthumi laughed, delighted by her surprise. 'You left your physical forms under my brother's watchful eye and protection. The fact that you didn't notice your physical form missing is a very positive sign in this instance,' he assured Tory and Maelgwn. 'We thought we'd see how you liked functioning without your dense body, for if you are to fulfil your role in the forthcoming event, it will be beneficial for you to leave your Chosen forms behind.'

'Shame … I've grown rather attached to it.' Tory attempted humour. She no longer feared death and yet she felt a twinge of remorse at the idea of letting life go.

'We all give a heavy sigh at the thought of such sacrifice, but once the commitment is made you shall discover that the sacrifice is, in fact, the experience that you have just lived through,' the master encouraged. 'However, should you grow tired of the comparatively blissful life and liberation of the subjective world, there will always be a superior race developing a few thousand years from now into which you can incarnate and perform an objective role once more.'

'Any chance of you telling us what our role in the subjective world might be?' Maelgwn's curiosity was driving him insane.

'That is exactly what this excursion is all about. Please.' Kuthumi indicated that they should follow him further into the subterranean maze.

'You know what this reminds me of?' Tory posed to her husband as they trailed the master.

'Taliesin's Otherworldly labyrinth,' Maelgwn replied, having made the same observation himself.

'Taliesin was a Master of Time and so his collection was comprised of historical antiquities and technology,' Kuthumi granted. 'My interests tend more towards esoteric doctrine.' The hallway opened into a huge library with a high domed roof.

'Oh, my Goddess,' Maelgwn uttered upon sighting the collection, as he'd always been a keen scholar himself.

'This is most impressive.' Tory echoed her husband's appreciation. 'It's even bigger than Taliesin's library.'

'I have collected esoteric literature from every author in every dimension of this universe's development.' Kuthumi tried not to make this sound like a boast, though he was obviously proud of his efforts.

'Are Noah Purcell's *Chronicles of the Chosen Ones* here?' Tory couldn't help but test the master's boast.

'Both the fiction and non-fiction versions,' Kuthumi teased with a smile, immediately teleporting them to the section of the library where the texts were stored without even touching those he teleported.

'How can you have the fiction version of our history?' Tory frowned, as the master retrieved from a shelf a thick paperback novel and placed it in her hands. '*The Ancient Future.*' She read the title out loud. 'What's this?' She flipped it over and slowly turned pale as she read the blurb on the back cover, dumbstruck that it referred to her by name. She looked to Kuthumi for an explanation.

'Take your life story and relate it to someone in a dimension apart from your own and it becomes just a "thrilling Celtic fantasy that wreaks havoc with history".' The lord quoted the catchphrase on the front cover of the book. 'We do it all the time,' Kuthumi assured. 'King Arthur has been a muse to just about every historian cum fantasy writer that ever there was, and a few spiritualists as well.'

'But Arthur never existed?' Maelgwn argued.

'Not in the dimensions you have frequented, but in many other alternative realities he did become the legend that has inspired a million tales,' Kuthumi clarified. 'In the dimension that gave host to the late twentieth century existence from which Tory originally disappeared, none of what you have achieved in your current reality has taken place. A completely different inter-dimensional reality and evolution is unfolding there, and Tory Alexander no longer exists ... except in fiction.'

Tory quickly opened the front cover of the novel in her hand, to discover the date and place of publication. 'First published in Australia in 1996. That's three years after I vanished.'

'The author to whom you are to be a muse is a little hung up on the filmmaking business at present. It will take her higher self a few years to swing her round to writing a book.'

Tory read about the author in the front of the book.

Traci Harding was born and raised in Sydney. Her ultimate dream of making a high budget Australian science-fantasy film took her to England and Scotland where she visited the sacred sites and saw the fairy lights. This journey was her inspiration for *The Ancient Future*.

'Interesting,' said Tory at last. 'Does she ever get to make the feature film?'

'What do you think?' Kuthumi began handing Tory all manner of recorded software, disks, videos, thought recorders, some tiny plug thing and a pyramid crystal with a small chip inside it. 'As the ages go by the written legend will be adapted to many different formats and mediums.'

Maelgwn gave a chuckle, and Kuthumi and Tory turned to find him already absorbed in the novel. When the Dragon felt their eyes upon him he looked up to explain his distraction. 'She's really got your character pegged,' he taunted his wife playfully, before addressing Kuthumi. 'Can I borrow this?'

'By all means.' The master manifested another five books of the same thickness and piled them on Maelgwn. 'Here, have the whole series. You'll find this instance on page 199 of the last book.'

'Really?' Tory put all her software back on the shelf to sort through the books her husband held. When she found the third book of the second trilogy, Tory turned to the nominated page. 'It's true.' She read her response from the text.

'Of course it's true.' Kuthumi was amused, as Tory pointed to the dialogue of the book.

'You say that and then I say this.' She slammed the book shut. 'Best not get too caught up in that scenario ... I wouldn't want the book to get boring.'

'Ugh!' Maelgwn cringed after reading the blurb on the back of the second book of the first trilogy. 'This one is all about your quest to Atlantis, after I got yellow plague and screwed up my life in Gwynedd ... I think I'll skip that one.'

'Awesome covers,' Tory commented as she looked over the book her husband had rejected. 'So, who is this Traci Harding anyway?'

'She is an incarnation of yourself who is not so prone to adventure as you, but she does have a grand imagination and would not discount the fantastic details and events of your story.'

'So, how I am going to aid the event ahead by inspiring an author in a different reality?' Tory didn't understand the supposition.

'You have a karmic debt to repay to the inter-dimensional reality that you abandoned,' Kuthumi replied. 'Had you remained in your rightful dimension, you still would have become an agent of the Logos and had vast leaps in spiritual understanding, and the humans developing in that reality would have profited from your wisdom.' As Tory seemed sceptical about being referred to as wise, Kuthumi added, 'Wisdom is knowledge, gained by experience and implemented by love.'

Tory was touched by the definition. 'I can see what you're saying,' she warranted, 'but surely people will just write off the outlandish spiritual principles as fantasy.'

'Some will,' Kuthumi granted. 'But others will see glimmers of truth and inspiration in your tales. And then there will be those who dare to put your beliefs into practice. When they discover that they can create their own reality, perform miracles, bring out the best in people and heal their bodies through the power of the mind, then the reality that once spawned you will have benefited from your experience and knowledge.'

Tory smiled in a semi-vexed fashion. 'So, Jesus had to die on the Cross to pass his initiation, but all I have to do is pour my heart and soul out to some disillusioned film writer to achieve the same feat?'

'Hopefully, your fiction version of cosmic law won't cause as much trouble as many of the non-fiction texts have, like the Bible for example.' Kuthumi explained the logic of it. 'People are not so prone to change the details of fiction and they are not compelled to believe it and so will draw only as much truth from your story as they are prepared to believe at the time. The Master Djwhal Khul has offered to act as an advisor to you during your time as a muse. DK and the Count have a vested interest in the fusion of science and religious belief, and around the turn of the century in the reality you left behind this cause is to be furthered. Due to the esoteric nature of your adventures, I, the unifier of Eastern and Western thought, have also taken a personal interest in this cause. Your aid and role will be a very subtle one, but your tale will open the minds of many and thus further the cause of light in a dimension that is even more needy than this one. As every reality in every dimension leads to the house of the great creator, whether you aid evolution here or there is neither here nor there in the great scheme of things. The Count, as the Lord of Karma and the Lord of Time, feels this is a fair exchange for granting Taliesin's request to misplace you in time and create a breakaway dimension that has spiritually evolved more rapidly than most. The reality you created is to the great credit of you both, but the fact remains that Tory is indebted to the dimension that spawned her.'

'I am happy to repay that debt.' Tory reassured him that no further explanation was necessary.

'So what is to be my role?' Maelgwn tucked all the books under his arm.

'You are to be the inspiration of your sons during the event ahead.' The master clued Maelgwn in. 'The Count will serve as your advisor.'

Any other time, the news that they were to be separated would have saddened Maelgwn and Tory, thus they were both shocked to discover that they were not at all disturbed at the proposition. This confused the couple; were they falling out of love?

'Not at all.' Kuthumi addressed their unspoken concern. 'You have just transcended to a level of awareness whereby you have mastered your relationship with each other and are no longer glamoured by the fear of losing the love of your soul-mate. Mastering relationships and glamour are the first two esoteric initiations. The third initiation involving the mastery of direction, integration and science, you both passed with flying colours during the downfall of the Nefilim and the birth of the Immortal human races of the Delphinus, Falcon and Leonine peoples. Now, you approach the fourth initiation; the test which you will execute via a mental perspective only ... this is why you suddenly feel so emotionally detached. Once you have completed your service of selfless sacrifice, you shall be ready for the Great Renunciation and you shall again be joined as one. This glorious whole soul shall transcend the ring-pass-not of the lower triad of planes to which your soul has been bound for an eternity. At the causal level of creation you shall be reunited with your kindred among the host of Dhyan Chohans. They will welcome you home with open arms and bring you up to date on the progress of the great plan. The part you decide to play in evolution from then on will be for you to decide.'

Their bodies awash with excitement and awe, Tory and Maelgwn could do naught but smile for the longest time.

'So ... where do we start?' Maelgwn voiced his eagerness to roll with the program.

'Right here.' Kuthumi held his arms wide to imply his whole museum and teleported them back to the hallway of text that Tory had begun reading. 'You two have a bit of doctrine to absorb.'

Avery mentally announced his arrival to Lahmu. His appearance interrupted the meeting taking place in the Governor's private office — no matter what Lahmu was discussing the news Avery bore was more urgent.

'Avery! Praise the Logos!' Brian was in the lad's face before he'd fully manifested. 'We have learned that Viper plans to raise Mahaud.' The Governor motioned to Noah as his source.

'He has already raised the crone,' Avery corrected, much to the dismay of the Governor, En Noah, Rhun and Candace, who were also present. 'That's what I came to inform you.'

'And the sadist has my daughter!' Brian lashed out, although he diverted the outburst away from Avery.

'I have been made aware of the best course to pursue for Fallon's recovery.' Avery gave Brian some good news. 'I shall have her back in our fold before any harm befalls her ... I swear it.'

Brian's attention shot back to the lad and the frustration in his eyes hadn't ebbed any. 'Don't make me promises you can't keep,' Brian warned, 'not on this issue.'

'Lirathea will confirm that Viper plans to attack the Orme Charichalum stores on Numan very soon, and Fallon will be with him,' Avery vouched in his own defence.

'And what if my child is bewitched by then, or worse!' Brian struggled to keep the tears from escaping his eyes.

'Let me take the chariot and get her now,' Candace pleaded.

'Fallon is with Viper of her own free will.' Avery reminded her parents of the cold hard facts. 'I fear that I am the only one who stands a chance of changing her mind.'

'He's right.' Rhun stood to support his little brother's view. 'In a sense, Fallon has already been bewitched and unless that spell is broken, you don't stand a chance of keeping her away from Viper.'

'Or of keeping Viper away from her,' Brian fretted, for the Nefilim-Falcon demi-god knew what Fallon looked like and so could find her with a thought.

'I can hide her in the Otherworld,' Avery offered. 'A soul of Viper's calibre could never raise the vibratory rate of his atomic form high enough to seek her there.'

Some of the worry fell from the faces of the distraught parents.

'As I know what Viper looks like,' Noah offered what help he could, 'I can disguise myself as one of his kindred, teleport myself to him and see that no harm befalls Fallon before she reaches Numan. But, I shall have to take proper steps to ensure I am safe from the witch first. In the sixth century Selwyn made amulets to protect his people from the crone's influence. I shall do some regression and discover what was involved.'

'I shall go with Avery to Numan, and oversee the operation,' Rhun volunteered.

'But Sparrowhawk is already there.' Avery felt he could handle this operation alone. He couldn't stand to think of the sibling rivalry that would occur working with just one of his brothers, let alone the kind of brotherly friction that would arise from working with two of them.

'Well,' Rhun cocked an eye, pretending not to know what Avery's problem was, 'as Zabeel is headed to Numan while we speak, it looks as though we'll have all four sons of the Dragon on this mission.' He rubbed his hands together vigorously, greatly looking forward to seeing what kind of results their combined force would produce. 'And fear not Governor, Governess,' Rhun's demeanour became serious to address them, 'we will bring your daughter back, unharmed.'

Numan was a dark, cold dump of a planet. The landscape was black, the sky beyond the shield was the black expanses of space, and since Numan was the outermost planet of the Anu system, daytime here was as black as night. All the mining operations were underground. The Orme Charichalum production facilities were above ground in large shielded bases with artificially controlled environments.

Bast and Sparrowhawk were occupying the main office of the top-security vault complex. This was where the dark Orme was held for safekeeping until it was shipped off to the centre of the star system to power the dense black shield that harnessed the radiation of the dead sun.

Bast was bored out of her mind and Sparrowhawk wasn't helping the state of affairs any; he'd been pining over Lirathea becoming a monk ever since they'd left Kila. As Bast had informed him plainly that she was going to murder him if he brought the subject up again, Sparrowhawk had gone all quiet and broody.

'I don't know what you're worried about,' Bast scoffed, as she gazed out over the colourless base beyond the double shielded windows of the office. 'My sister has just run off with our enemy!'

'Even she's got a better chance at happiness and contentment than I have,' Sparrowhawk grumbled as he checked his weapons to make sure they were all in good working order.

'Oh ...' Bast growled with agitation. 'Do move on, Sparrow. If you could just get over yourself, you might be of some use to somebody.'

The door to the office opened, and in walked Rhun, Avery and Zabeel.

'Yee-ha!' Bast embraced the development, literally. 'Are you guys a sight for sore ears.' Nobody had to ask what she meant. 'What are you all doing here?'

'We think Viper is headed this way,' Rhun advised as he gave his cousin a squeeze. 'So we're your reinforcements.'

'Sweet!' Bast backed away to look all four brothers over, and what a handsome bunch they were. She considered it a great pity that the Dragon had not fathered a Leonine son. Her eyes came to rest on Avery. 'My sister is a fool.'

'No, Bast,' Avery insisted, 'I was the fool.'

Bast was accustomed to Avery supporting her when she was bad-mouthing her sister and she was a little taken off guard by his comeback.

'She's in a lot more danger than we thought, Bast, and I helped put her there.'

Bast had never seen Avery so serious, and the notion of losing her sister struck the fear of God into her heart. 'What's happened?'

Whilst Avery brought Bast and Sparrowhawk up to date with affairs, Rhun and Zabeel headed for the vault.

Rhun had the security guards lock Zabeel and himself inside the security safe, which was filled with row upon row of large crystal cylinders that had a reinforced Charichalum casing. With a wave of his hand, Rhun fried all the surveillance cameras inside the vault. 'We'll run a security recording,' he explained to Zabeel, who still looked confused.

'But how are we to keep a watch on the Orme inside the vault?' the Delphinus ruler posed. 'You're not going to suggest we keep a vigil, are you?'

'We don't need to watch the Orme stores, if they're not here,' Rhun enlightened, flashing a cheeky grin, which his far more serious younger brother returned. 'How are your teleportation abilities these days?'

'I'll go anywhere you go,' Zabeel assured.

'Then do as I do and follow me.' Rhun placed his hands on a Charichalum storage hanger that housed six of the dark Orme cylinders and then vanished with them.

'Holy moley.' Zabeel gazed over the thousands of such hangers in the vault. 'This is some ambitious plan you've had, bro.'

'Come on, keep up.' Rhun reappeared and took hold of another two racks.

Teleporting his load after his brother, Zabeel found himself in an identical vault to the one he'd just left. 'Where the hell are we?' He grabbed hold of Rhun before he disappeared again.

'Sorry, that's classified,' Rhun advised.

This second vault had been built upon Rhun's suggestion to Lahmu. At the time the dark Orme went into production for Anu's shield, they had known the potential dangers that the substance could pose to humankind and the Chosen Ones if it fell into the hands of someone with evil intent. This vault was just one of several security measures that had been devised as contingency plans should Charichalum Orme production be threatened or abused.

By the time they'd finished, Zabeel didn't know if he was coming or going. There had been a stage around the middle of their task when he wasn't sure which vault was which. It was a good thing Rhun was more focused, as they could've accidentally ended up with all the cylinders back in their original vault.

Rhun slapped a hand down on Zabeel's shoulder in

congratulations for a job well done. 'Now for the cylinders in the production facility.'

In the security office of the vault, Bast, Sparrowhawk and Avery had their eyes glued to the soft-light screens that monitored all the entrances to the building.

Rhun had just reported his deliberate destruction of the security surveillance in the vault itself, without offering up a reason. He'd instructed them to run old security recordings of the vault on the screens that usually monitored the area. The Vice-Governor had also advised that he was heading over to the production plant to batten down the hatches there.

'What the hell is he playing at?' Avery hated it that he couldn't demand that his older brother explain himself. 'Is this how a team operates?'

'Actually, it is,' Bast advised, whilst loading up the recordings Rhun had ordered. 'A team has a captain and the rest of the players take their directives from him. Unfortunately, Pan man, in this instance you're just one of the players.'

'Funny! I understood team work was several souls working in succinct harmony.'

'You want to apply that definition to the Dragon brothers.' Bast scoffed and laughed at the same time. 'Good luck.'

'Hey, hotshot.' Sparrow motioned his brother closer. 'You're approaching the security foyer with Fallon and a couple of the complex guards.'

'I'll alert Rhun,' Bast offered, knowing that given the choice Avery would not.

'If we must.' Avery assumed the appearance of his father, which shocked Sparrowhawk.

'Yeah, right, in your dreams maybe.' Sparrowhawk protested the tactic.

'Just so there is no confusion when Viper and I end up in the same place,' Avery justified.

'Viper is on his way.' En Noah appeared in their midst, in time to see Avery's transformation

'He has arrived, you might say.' Sparrowhawk updated their old mentor, directing his attention to the screen where Fallon's party was entering the foyer of the building.

'Where are Rhun and Zabeel?' Noah wanted to know.

'In the Orme production facility,' Avery responded, when a pouch on a long string was thrust into his hand. Noah gave one of these to Bast and Sparrowhawk as well.

'Put them on,' he instructed. 'They will shield you from the crone's influence. Keep your wits about you.' Noah looked at them each in turn and then vanished as abruptly as he'd arrived.

Rhun and Zabeel were down to the last dozen racks of cylinders, when Avery arrived on the scene.

'Need a hand?' Avery floated over to one of the racks, and placing his hand on a cylinder, he stared at the strange dark gas that was filled with glistening dark specks. Each cylinder had a long slim window in the outer Charichalum casing that allowed someone to gauge how full it was.

'You want to be useful ... now there's a switch.' Rhun gripped hold of a couple of racks. 'Follow me.'

But the Vice-Governor was delayed when Zabeel, who was closer to Avery, commented, 'Damn, little brother. Have you been bathing with the dead? You stink!' Zabeel grabbed his nose and took a couple of steps backwards.

When Rhun got a whiff of the vile odour, he recognised it at once. 'Mahaud.' A band was pulled over Rhun's head suddenly and he stopped centimetres short of elbowing Noah in the face. 'A thousand apologies, Noah.' Rhun recognised the amulet that was a means to ward off the crone.

Selwyn had given Rhun the same protective measure back in ancient Gwynedd, which Rhun had naively given to his would-be Queen for her protection. This chivalrous mistake had landed Rhun in a whole load of strife, so now when a wise man placed an amulet around his neck, that's where it stayed.

'Are you sure it's not Avery?' Zabeel had his sonic pulse blaster set for kill and aimed at the smelly impostor.

'Very sure,' both Rhun and Noah replied at once, whereupon Zabeel fired his weapon.

The crone did not attempt to flee and although thrown across the room by the impact of the bullet, she laughed as she transformed into the rotting human corpse in which she was currently residing. *You can't kill something that's already dead*, her multi-layered demon voice informed them as she raised the weight of the carcass up into the air. Eyes of glowing red peered at the

211

Chosen trio from the face of a dead man. *Soon it will take more than just a Druid's charm to protect you from us.*

When Bast, Sparrowhawk and the Dragon appeared in the foyer to meet their party, Fallon didn't blink an eyelid. The weapons Viper's force carried shot immortal strength chloroform, so although shamed, her kindred would not be harmed.

'I found her, father.' Viper thought he might have a chance of getting away with the masquerade, as Avery was not present.

'Well done, son.' Avery played along as he neared the impostor.

One of the female Falcon guards with Viper had captured Sparrowhawk's attention, for she was the spitting image of Lirathea and the discovery had him speechless. Fallon was partly blocking the warrioress from his view, but he could see that the beautiful guard was fiddling with something in her hands. Was it a weapon? Sparrowhawk reached for his own weapon, but enchanted as he was, he did not have the heart to fire at her.

When two shots sounded from behind her, Fallon expected her kindred to start dropping, but instead it was Viper who fell to the ground, and the other male guard. Then Fallon felt something dig into the small of her back.

'Lose the weapon, sister,' Gazelle advised.

Fallon looked back to her kin, who all had weapons pointed at her now. 'What are you doing? You're his sister. How can you betray Viper and your people like this?'

'How?' Gazelle scoffed. 'Because my brother is

shacking up with a demon from the sub-planes, that's how! And he's planning to use your body as a host for his sweetheart, ahead of dragging the souls of my kindred down into the sub-planes with him.'

'I don't believe you!' Fallon challenged, her emotions going into a seizure.

'It's true, Fallon,' the Dragon told her. 'He has raised Mahaud.'

At the sound of the crone's name Fallon took several steps away from Viper and discarded her weapon. 'Where is the witch now?' she asked, closing her eyes to endure the answer. 'Please don't say she's inside him.'

'No,' Gazelle stated frankly for everyone's benefit. 'Mahaud is inhabiting the rotting corpse of some twentieth century mortal from Gaia, who caught us resurrecting the demon. She has assumed Avery's form and is currently in your production facility stealing as much dark Orme as she can lay her hands on.'

'Dark Orme?' Fallon queried. 'Why would Viper be after dark Orme?'

'Christ, you're so gullible!' Bast threw her hands up in frustration.

'The witch told Viper Orme Charichalum was the only way the dark souls of Dumuzi's children could ever retain an immortal state of being,' Gazelle informed Fallon, feeling ashamed to be counted among the offspring of Dumuzi herself.

Suddenly the ground began to rumble, and all the glass windows across the front of the foyer smashed in turn. Everyone dropped to the ground as a mighty wind swept through the foyer and a mighty stench accompanied it. Mahaud manifested her rotting corpse of a host, and willed Viper's unconscious form to her. The unconscious guard also slid towards the crone. *Come, my pretty. You belong with us.* The crone motioned Fallon hither with a single decaying finger.

Fallon's legs went from beneath her and the next thing she knew she was flying towards the crone and screaming her lungs out.

Avery literally flew after Fallon and landing on top of her he willed them both to the Otherworld.

As the couple vanished Mahaud let out a deafening shrill, *Home, bitch!* The crone pointed her demon finger at Gazelle, who in turn looked to Sparrowhawk to plead, 'Please don't let her take me.' The hardened expression of a warrior slipped from the woman's face and the horror of a petrified child replaced it.

'It could be a trap.' Bast yelled her advice to Sparrowhawk over the crone's smelly storm.

Sparrowhawk looked back at Gazelle, who was battling fiercely against the crone's evil summons.

'I don't want to go to hell,' she appealed, tears of conviction spurting from her eyes. 'I'm dead meat, for sure.'

Sparrowhawk gripped hold of both her hands and pulled Gazelle to him, so that she might be protected by the charm he wore. 'One good turn deserves another.'

Bast came to stand between Sparrowhawk and Mahaud to aid him in protecting his captive; if this child of Dumuzi was telling the truth, it would be useful to pick the brain of their enemy's sister. 'Leave, Mahaud. You have no further business here,' Bast ordered.

Give that treacherous little whore to me, or I shall —

'Shall what?' Rhun appeared with Zabeel and Noah, who all stood opposing the crone.

I shall be forced to shoot you all to get to her, the crone finished, as the unconscious guard and Viper began firing their weapons. They got Rhun and Noah, who fell to the ground unconscious. Everyone else scampered for cover behind the large pillars that supported the foyer ceiling.

'Did she get at the Orme?' Bast asked Zabeel who was bailed up behind the same pillar with her.

'No.' Zabeel set her mind at ease.

Across the foyer behind another pillar were Sparrowhawk and his captive.

'I want to seek diplomatic immunity,' Gazelle whispered.

'I can grant you that,' Sparrow assured her, wanting to focus on her lovely face, but he was otherwise distracted keeping an eye on Mahaud's movements.

'Who are you, that you have such authority?' Gazelle tried not to sound scornful, but her protector appeared so young and not much older than she did.

'I am the newly appointed ruler of Tarazean,' he was pleased to be able to say for the first time ever.

'You're Sparrowhawk ... really?' She couldn't stop her voice from wavering with the awe she felt.

Gazelle had spent many a night fantasising about what the Dragon's Falcon son might look like. She had imagined that perhaps she might find true love with him and discover the happiness that Cordella had enjoyed since wedding the Dragon's Delphinus son, Zabeel.

'I thought you'd be fiercer looking,' she commented to hide her infatuation and delight.

'Sorry, I'm still working on looking official,' he joked, as Mahaud willed the unconscious guard and Viper around, trying to get a clear shot at her foe. 'What's in those bullets?' He fretted for the welfare of his brother and the Sage who were still down.

'Just immortal strength chloroform,' Gazelle informed. 'Fallon insisted that her kindred not be harmed during this attack.'

The unconscious guard unexpectedly ceased firing his weapon and Zabeel, the most telepathically adept soul still conscious, sensed the crone's fear at her loss of control.

'Enough, Mahaud!' Avery's voice resounded around the foyer, as he now floated high above the crone. 'Time to send you back to where the Night Hunter condemned you.'

The crone laughed off the threat. 'Save your energy, little novice, the Night Hunter you are not.'

'She's lying, Avery,' Zabeel yelled to his little brother, as he became conscious of Avery's doubt. 'She knows you are capable, she fears you.'

As Avery closed his eyes to call upon the Pan Ray to disperse the crone, she vanished from their midst, along with Viper and the unconscious guard.

'Damn it!' Avery floated down to ground level. Willing himself after the crone got him nowhere. 'Why can't I follow?'

'I do believe that the witch intended to return to Gaia's recent past,' Gazelle came out of hiding to inform him. 'Would that impede your will?'

Avery smiled as he recognised his sister in the stranger. Suddenly he realised why Lirathea had insisted that it was so important Sparrowhawk accompany him on this mission; Sparrowhawk's attraction to Avery's twin sister now made perfect sense. 'If that is the case, I should be able to locate the crone from the Otherworld.' He thought out loud for the Falcon woman's benefit. All the love and guidance Lirathea had been channelling this soul's way had obviously had the desired effect.

'Hold your horses, bro,' Rhun ordered as he came to and struggled to a seated position, feeling a little groggy. 'Our mission for today has been accomplished. Mahaud and Viper can't do any great damage without the dark Orme, and will be back for a second attempt.'

Avery was frustrated by his brother's demand for restraint, feeling it was ego based. Rhun just liked ordering him about. 'No, something isn't right, I can sense it.'

'Me, too.' Zabeel seconded Avery's view. 'My telepathic perception was that the witch was satisfied with today's misadventure.'

'She's deceiving you both.' Rhun waved off their concern, but then a thought occurred to him. 'Holy hell!'

'What?' Bast begged Rhun to voice his worry as she felt ill-at-ease also.

Rhun ignored the query, silently focusing on what a cylinder of Orme looked like. The next minute one of the cylinders manifested in front of him. 'Mahaud didn't have to steal the dark Orme. All the crone had to do was get a look at how we have the substance stored these days. Now all she has to do is will it forth whenever she requires it ... goddamnit!'

'Won't a PKA teleportation lock prevent her retrieving the canisters from the vault?' Bast suggested.

Rhun shook his head, frustrated by the event. 'It will only stop her from teleporting herself inside the vault. Damn, damn, damn!' Rhun was furious at himself and walked away so as not to direct his annoyance at anyone else. 'If only we'd dispensed with the cylinders sooner ... if Mahaud had never seen our storage process the PKA teleportation lock would have served some use.'

'I'm going after her,' Avery stated in a defiant manner.

'You're not going anywhere until we report this to Lahmu.' Avery was of the mind to debate the issue and Rhun knew it. 'If you are to defeat the crone now, you are going to need our help. You're not just battling one demon any more, but a whole race of them. Mahaud has never succeeded in taking over the body of a free immortal being, let alone one pumped full of dark Orme. We are all in very deep trouble, Avery. We have to stick together.'

As Rhun's appeal was heartfelt, Avery calmed and considered his point. Rhun had dealt with the crone before, which made him a greater authority on the witch than Avery was himself.

'He's right, Pan man.' Bast approached to beseech her friend to listen to reason. 'You've got a supreme team at your disposal, so for heaven's sake, utilise them! Don't allow your pride and ego to push you into rushing off unprepared.'

'If the crone has gone to the past, it's not like we can't catch her up at any time.' Zabeel made a further appeal.

Avery, considering that he had yet to make his peace with Fallon, gave up his protest with a nod. 'Strategy it is, then.'

In a beautiful Otherworldly glen, Fallon patiently waited for the Dragon to return as per his instruction. He'd assured her that she could breathe easy in the knowledge that she was beyond the reach of Mahaud or Viper here.

Fallon dangled her toes in the river, feeling at peace with herself for the first time since she'd become involved with Viper. Her attraction to him made her blood run cold now and her heart broke to think that Avery would surely despise her for having betrayed her kindred. 'How could I have been so, so ...?' Stupid, naive, wretched and blind all sprang to mind, but none of these words seemed to adequately capture how wrong she'd been.

I can see you averting a great calamity. En Noah's prophecy played on her mind. *But you must keep your heart and mind open to the higher purpose. Malice will confuse your perception for a time, making the right decision and course of action unclear.*

'How could I have failed to see the test, when it was *so* obvious? I love Avery,' she mumbled through her welling tears, knowing this had been the case all along. Her interest in Viper had only thrived on her futile attempt to make Avery jealous. 'Even Avery's lack of interest in me will never change that,' she realised, as her tears of disappointment and remorse dropped into the river and flowed away with it.

'You're wrong, Fallon.'

She turned to find the Dragon had returned.

'Avery loves you much more than he has let on.' He came to sit beside her.

Fallon brushed away her tears with a sniffle and shook her head. 'If he cares for me so much, then where was Avery today when the rest of our kindred came to my rescue?'

'He was right here.' The mirage of the Dragon faded away as Avery assumed his own form.

Fallon raised a fist to strike, but Avery blocked her intent by gripping hold of the offending limb. 'Another deception!' she accused, wanting to vent some of her own guilt back on him.

'The last deception,' he vowed, sincerely, ahead of kissing her to silence any further protest.

She struggled to resist his passionate outpouring at first, wanting to hold on to her anger, but having desired Avery for as long as she could remember, Fallon soon found herself swept along in the wave of emotion that his kiss inspired.

When they parted, Fallon was far calmer, albeit confused. 'I find it really sweet that you would lie to prevent me from running off again, but I promise there is no need —'

'Beware when your words conflict with what is in your heart, for a great rivalry will be avoided by putting your ego aside and telling the truth.' Avery quoted the prophecy En Noah had tried to warn him with. 'The only time I have lied since graduation, was when I denied that I found you alluring.' He stared deep into Fallon's eyes of piercing blue, so that she might know his confession was the truth. 'A fact that I have been denying for years.'

'Years?' Fallon uttered, bewildered. 'But why?'

'Because the lie kept me at liberty and gave me power over you,' he admitted. 'A power that I am now greatly ashamed of as my ego nearly cost us both, dearly.' Observing the look of betrayal on her face, he ventured to add, 'Or maybe my stupidity has already taken its ultimate toll? I will understand completely if your forgiveness is not forthcoming.'

The fear that had beset her body crumbled away, as Fallon's greatest wish was granted. 'I am the one who should be apologising, Avery.'

Avery could feel the tears of relief welling in his eyes and made no attempt to restrain them. He kissed her again and again, until their lips melted into a seemingly endless union.

'Is this your idea of protecting my daughter?'

Avery and Fallon were startled apart at the sound of Lahmu's voice.

'Father!' Fallon rose and rushed to embrace Brian, mumbling her apologies as she clung to him for dear life.

'It's all right, princess.' Brian hushed her to calm, rubbing her back and kissing her forehead to reinforce his claim. 'You're safe now.' He served Avery a nod of appreciation as the young Lord of the Otherworld was looking a mite concerned about being busted seducing the Governor's daughter.

In truth, Brian was well disposed towards having Avery as a son-in-law. 'Thank you,' Brian mouthed.

Avery simply bowed his head, gratified to have succeeded in the rescue as vowed.

9

FIRST CONTACT

As Tory and Maelgwn absorbed the last sentence of the glowing Sanskrit text from the last wall of Kuthumi's esoteric museum, the infrastructure of the learning facility became obscured by etheric light and their bodies felt suddenly constrained and cumbersome.

'There will be a short interlude in your tuition,' Kuthumi advised the couple, as they found their consciousness returned to their physical forms seated around the courtyard table of Master El Morya's home.

'How long have we been absent?' Tory queried El Morya, the Count and Kuthumi who were all still present. It had seemed like she'd been absorbing information for days, maybe weeks?

'No more than an hour has passed,' the Count replied with a smile, as time was his department. 'The etheric realms are very flexible that way.'

'We require you to accompany us to a more secure location,' Kuthumi requested.

'You seem to do a fine job of moving us about without our aid.' Maelgwn stated his observation and the lord nodded in acquiescence.

'Where we go now, you must enter of your own will,' he explained simply.

A gentle wind whipped passed Tory and Maelgwn. *Kalagiya*, it whispered as it passed around them several times. They understood it to mean 'come to Shamballa'.

'For choosing unification over separatism, nurture over exploitation, love over hatred, freedom for all over slavery, and selflessness over vanity,' Kuthumi summed up, 'come friends, seek your earthly repose in the outer court of our heavenly Father's abode.'

Tory called to mind what she had learned of Shamballa from the Sanskrit text she'd been studying. Shamballa was the seat of the Sanat Kamara, who was the Planetary Logos of Gaia, also known as Melchizedek, the Ancient of Days, the Silent Watcher and by many other names in different tongues and cultures. This mighty being was said to be incarnate in etheric form at a secret location in the Gobi Desert. Shamballa marked the spot where the will of the Sanat Kamara, or Melchizedek, was focused upon the planet and sent forth to carry out divine purpose.

Her revision was interrupted as Kuthumi stood and passed through the wooden tabletop to stand before

Tory and her husband. The master reached out and placed one palm against Maelgwn's forehead and the other palm over Tory's third eye area to instil in their minds a vision of their destination.

It was only as the master made physical contact, and Tory felt the true essence of unconditional love made manifest that flowed through him, that she fully realised the great honour that was being bestowed on her. Immediately, her eyes filled to overflowing with tears of inspiration and glancing aside she saw that Maelgwn had reacted in the same way; in all their years of blissful married life Tory had never seen her husband appear so happy and at peace.

A cathartic high followed which dragged Tory's perception from her husband's angelic face to a vision of a city composed entirely of light; it was adrift among a backdrop of stars, which rang true with what Tory had read of the sacred city of Shamballa.

The pinnacle of the stronghold reaches far into space. Being made of etheric substance, it exists on all planes of demonstration.

In Tory's vision the celestial city was diamond-like in shape and was situated within a pyramid formed of streams of fiery energies that originated from distant destinations in space. At the highest point of the tallest tower in the middle of the spectacular city all the incoming rays of energy fused into one stream which then split into three directions to form an etheric inverted steeple that extended all the way down to the surface of the earth.

Shamballa is on Gaia, too, in a hidden, secret valley.

225

Tory's consciousness followed the three streams down through the atmosphere and she found herself approaching a desert. She plummeted down towards the earth at great speed and as the ground rushed up to meet her, she changed course to surge across the open plains of the windblown Gobi Desert.

Gradually her momentum slowed and Tory found herself walking alone and barefoot across the barren ground; she was now dressed in long white robes that winnowed across her body and trailed behind her in the wind. Her feet seemed to have wings for they did not make contact with the earth on which she trod. And yet, her stride had great purpose as she rapidly approached a rolling range of barren snow-capped mountains.

The warrior of Light penetrates the four gates to Shamballa ... Loneliness being the threshold of the first ...

Tory was blinded by a memory from her time in Ancient Gwynedd. It was the day Taliesin had informed her of her immortal status and of how alone in time and space that fact had made her feel. At that time Tory had been led to believe that she was one of only a handful of Chosen Ones; she did not discover the extent of Marduk's escapades until decades afterward.

'I will see everybody die,' had been her first grievance.

'And reborn again,' Taliesin had pointed out a bright side.

Immortality had been too huge an idea for her to comprehend at once. Still, she had embraced her lonely plight willingly and bravely.

Her greatest and only comfort, then, had been knowing that Taliesin was immortal also. 'You will always be here?' she'd pleaded with, more than asked, the High Merlin.

'For some time yet,' he'd replied.

This instance, even more than her trip back to the Dark Age, had been a defining moment in her life — Taliesin had been always been there to support her at such times, before he'd ascended back to his soul source. Since then they'd had virtually no contact.

The second gate is Detachment ...

Tory's thoughts were turned to the birth of her twins, Avery and Lirathea. Their bodies had been commandeered by a couple of Deva changeling babies shortly after birth. Tory had mastered a state of detachment in order to gain a clear perspective on the seemingly horrendous events unfolding. She had even unwittingly willed death upon herself, the ultimate detachment, in order to glimpse Devachan to confirm the wellbeing of her children's souls.

It was only with this recollection of events that Tory remembered that Taliesin had been there at death's door to meet her and guide her back to the land of the living. This remembrance brought a tear to her eye; he was her guardian angel to be sure and she felt privileged at the honour of his tutelage and guidance.

The third gate is Isolated Unity ...

The recent indifference she'd felt upon discovering that Maelgwn was to aid their kin to victory without her came to mind. She'd felt numb to the news; she still loved her kindred but equally she loved all mankind.

Tory was in the world, but she no longer felt part of it. Not even the allure of her lover's touch could interest her in returning to physical world activity, hence it was clear that no earthly thrill would ever again evoke a response from her. She also realised that Maelgwn must feel the same way and it did not sadden her to know that she no longer enchanted him in a physical sense. Their physical relationship had been naught but a glamour anyway. As wonderful as their marriage had been, their attraction was but a means to keep the other interested and bound to the mutual cause of teaching the other the meaning of unconditional love. Now that they both understood this and felt an unconditional love for all things in creation, they could conquer greater concerns for the mutual benefit of all. Maelgwn and herself would always meet again and that was true of every soul she'd ever held dear. For, ultimately, they were all part of her super-consciousness and in this knowledge Tory felt great joy and liberation.

The fourth gate is Purity.

Her consciousness returned to the present and to the exhilaration of the wind rushing over her body.

The thought occurred that this might be the last time she would ever feel the physical effects of the elements at play upon her form; thus Tory opened herself completely to the experience, savouring it.

The constant, though gentle, resistance of the wind was in harmony with the pulsing ley-line energies that radiated outwards from the snowcapped mountains, urging her to stride against the tide of energy currents towards the wellspring. The golden sun's twinkling reflection on the imposing icecaps made them appear miraculously akin to the towers of the celestial city she'd just seen among the stars. The evening rays of the sun warmed her soul, and filled her with peace. She realised that all she wanted from existence now was to serve the great plan of the Logos, whose heart chakra manifested as the large ball of fire that hung low in the sky to one side of her — Tory's only will was to be part of the divine will.

These Four Gates are the foundation on which Shamballa is built. Three Doors lead the initiate deeper into the council chamber of the Sanat Kamara and with each door opened one of the three gifts of Shamballa is bestowed.

Greet the fiery angel that guards the outer chamber and enter the Door of Reason, whereupon you shall see things as they really are and receive the gift of Opportunity.

A great wall of fire erupted around the base of the mountain range. Tory was aware that extreme danger existed for anyone who attempted to confront this angel with a distorted mind or heart, but holding no fear or delusion, she did not waver from her course. From the monstrous force-field of fire confronting her, she felt only a beckoning warmth that washed through her like a cooling wave as she ventured to penetrate the wall of flame.

The barrier of fire vanished and Tory emerged triumphant to find that she was standing before the entrance to a cave.

Beyond the rocky region into which the cave extended, she could see the towering spirals of a jewelled city, peaking where the mountaintops had featured only moments ago. These towers were the receivers of the three rays that formed the inverted steeple that extended downwards from the celestial city beyond the atmosphere and reality of this world to encompass the sacred city on the surface of Gaia.

Within the beamed energy rays were impressions, knowledge and energies from older, more spiritually adept alien cultures which resided on planets on other planes of existence in the distant regions of space and in our own star system. Shamballa distributed this inspirational energy to the inhabitants of Gaia via the ley-line grid of the planet. How each inhabitant of the planet interpreted this energy determined whether or not the information benefited the cause of the Brothers of Light or the Dark Lodge of the Materialistic.

Tory could see the blue-white etheric streams of energy that she'd only ever felt before now shooting out into infinity in all directions.

'Welcome to the outer court of Shamballa.'

The greeting drew Tory's attention back towards the cave, where a master being now stood in the opening. Tory knew he was an ascended Master because he exuded the illumination of an enlightened being, akin to the other souls who belonged to the Brotherhood of Light.

'I am to guide your entry.'

Tory had never seen this master before, but she guessed his identity from the descriptions of the Masters she'd read in Kuthumi's library — the man's Tibetan appearance gave him away. 'You are the Master Djwhal Khul?' Kuthumi had mentioned that the

230

Tibetan had volunteered to act as an advisor during her time as a muse.

Tory approached the handsome middle-aged male who had short, snowy white hair and a well-trimmed moustache that turned down at the corners of his shapely mouth. Although the wrinkles around his almond-shaped crystal-blue eyes implied age, he appeared a young, healthy and virile man in all other respects.

'Please, call me DK.' He bowed slightly as if to say, 'At your service.'

'And you know all about me, I take it?'

'Oh, yes ... Tory Alexander.' He smiled as he pronounced her name proudly. 'I had quite a bit of involvement in your adventures, particularly in Atlantis, as esoteric healing has become my cause to promote. I am also well versed in Master Ray activity, past, present and future, as I am the Synthesis Chohan. I strive to achieve the perfect integration of all the Master Rays within each human soul-mind.'

The master's manner seemed so familiar that Tory felt immediately at ease in his company; he felt rather like an old friend. This notion tickled her inside and she got the distinct impression that DK was waiting for her to mention this.

'I had expected to find another ascended master awaiting me here today,' she ventured to say, whereupon the master burst into a huge smile and Tory's eyes narrowed. 'Taliesin?' She knew it was, for DK had begun to laugh. 'You've reinvented yourself since ascending. This is where you've been hiding out ... I should have known you'd never leave Gaia.'

'I couldn't stay away,' he admitted, suppressing a chuckle as he pointed out, 'but then, neither could you. I chose to come back here and spread the ageless wisdom wherever I could find a response. I preside over a large group of Tibetan lamas when I am not helping the Masters Kuthumi and El Morya with their work, although in the presence of these teachers I am but a novice.'

Tory's smile was so huge it pained her and yet she couldn't wipe it off her face. 'Has your female half, Seshut, come back to Gaia with you?'

'She is me, we are still one,' he explained. 'We choose to reflect a male personification as it is more suitable at this time, or at least it was at the time we returned to Gaia's cause in the form of DK.'

'My daughter, Lirathea, is a whole soul like you, but she has chosen a female personification.' Tory drew a parallel and DK nodded to confirm her reasoning.

'But I suggest that rather than trying to consider me as two different souls you once knew, just consider me as DK, whom you now know ... if that is pleasing to you?'

'That is pleasing to me,' she agreed, knowing that they would bump along together very well, just as they always had. 'So, you requested me as a student, DK?'

They began to walk into the cave, which was lit by the light exuding from her own form and even more so by the illumination DK's enlightened being was emitting.

'You are a hard worker and of great joy to the many entities that have had a hand in inspiring you,' he explained, taking her arm and wrapping it around his own. 'And, therefore, it is to my very great honour that you should keep choosing me as a tutor.'

His comeback made Tory laugh. 'So it's my fault you keep getting stuck with me, is that what you're saying?'

'To be sure,' he agreed, kindly. 'And I wouldn't have it any other way. However,' DK patted her arm to end their banter, 'back to more important matters.'

The cave ahead widened into a large cavern and the master motioned her to a spectacular pool of crystal that was forming in the middle of the great cavity. A glowing liquid substance, white in colour, oozed through the ceiling and slid down three uneven stalagmites that hung over the large round pool. Each stalagmite changed the colour of the glowing liquid before it dripped into the pool where three great mounds of crystal had formed; one was yellow, one blue and one red. At each pinnacle the colour was very defined, but in the pool the crystals had merged to create the full spectrum of the rainbow in glowing rock.

'This is without doubt the most beautiful piece of sculpture I have ever seen,' Tory uttered, as she rounded it.

'Sculpture, you say?' DK was impressed by her perception.

'I'm guessing that it is a work of art and not a natural formation?'

The master shrugged. 'It is, in fact, a bit of both. Can you tell me what it depicts?'

'To me ... it depicts the Solar Hierarchy.' Tory voiced her opinion and DK made no indication as to whether he agreed or not, which was very indicative of Taliesin.

'Why?'

'Well ...' Tory looked to the ceiling first. 'The source of this creation, the white glowing water, represents the Solar Logos, the source of all life. From the Logos shot forth the three Major Rays.' She pointed to the three stalagmites that transmuted the colour of the glowing water. 'These constitute the original sacred trinity. Red represents the destructive force of Master El Morya's Ray of Will-Power. Blue represents the healing power of Master Kuthumi's Ray of Love-Wisdom and the Yellow represents the Ray of Active Intelligence, the presiding master of which is ...' Tory squinted as she racked her brain. 'Ah yes,' she clicked her fingers as she recalled. 'The Master Rakoczi, of course. As the Head of this Ray the Master R is also the Mahachohan and The Lord of Civilisation. The three Major Rays extend down into the causal world,' she motioned to the three mounds of crystal, 'and merge with the four Minor Rays of Aspect to produce the Seven Rays of Life that create the physical realm.' Tory pointed to the sections of crystal beyond the mounds where patches of purple, indigo, orange and green stone had formed.

'Did I mention that you are a fast learner?' The Tibetan appeared very pleased by her analogy. 'But this is no ordinary piece of sculpture. Being composed of etheric substance it is designed to help you make contact with the subject you are to muse.'

'Whoa, really?' Tory looked deeper into the glowing rocks.

DK suppressed his urge to laugh. 'Your physical eyes will be useless to you, you must see via your third eye.'

234

He pointed to the middle of his brow. 'Come, sit, and I will guide you inwards.'

Once Tory sat and focused, with eyes closed, her etheric sight blazed into action and she was able to perceive the beautiful crystal sculpture before her with third eye vision.

Now the glowing water appeared positively ultra-luminous. Millions of atoms spinning at high speed composed the different forms inside the cavern — her own form included. Everything was drawing in light energy and emitting its own brightly coloured aura, the energy of which radiated out to touch everything else. Energy was radiating between herself and the Master DK, between herself and the pool, herself and the ground on which she sat. In this sacred place, all these energies were very positive and pleasing. It wasn't hard for Tory to see how a lot of bad energy got passed around in crowded cities, with so many people crammed in together and no nature to counteract the negativity.

Now look into the sculpture and ask the Logos to make its will known.

Tory heard the Master DK's voice in her mind and as per his instruction, she looked deep into the crystal to glimpse her new destiny. A vision erupted and consumed her consciousness and before she'd had the chance to realise what had happened, reality came to a standstill and Tory found herself floating over a large body of water amid a snow-covered highland countryside.

She looked down to view herself but it seemed only her consciousness was taking this trip. *Where am I?*

You're at the western end of Loch Ness, DK advised.

Tory looked around for the master.

I'm addressing your physical body, Tory, which is still seated beside me in the cave. DK put an end to her turning about. *I can see what you perceive. We can affect this place, but are not actually here … our will extends into our conscious perception, do you see?*

I understand. Tory began taking in the spectacular scenery. As it looked to be the middle of winter she was rather glad not to actually be present.

Do you see that car yonder?

There was only one car on the road that ran along the northern bank of the Loch. The little white car was heading west and judging from the make and style of the vehicle the year was somewhere in the late nineteen eighties or early nineteen nineties.

I see it, Tory confirmed.

Your subject is in the passenger seat, informed DK. *Let us catch up and take a look.*

With very little effort Tory willed her perception forth to the back seat of the car — never mind that it was full of luggage, she took up no space at all. She observed the young woman who she was to muse and saw a lot of herself in her subject.

She was in her mid-twenties, with shoulder length blonde hair, and although the colour didn't look natural, it suited her well. Obviously she was of smaller build than Tory, but it was hard to discern much about her subject's body, rugged up in clothes as it was and seated in a car. The writer looked a little under the weather as did her travelling companion, a dark-haired woman of roughly the same age and build as her subject.

So who is the driver? Tory quizzed DK.

She is your subject's best friend, he replied. *She will be editing your work, so you might want to do a little musing there as well.*

And how do I muse, exactly? Tory hadn't a clue where to start with this project.

Initially, a muse wishes to inspire, give their subject something to think about, something that will steer the subject towards the area of investigation that you wish her to pursue.

Tory had to think about this a second, as she could hardly send her subject on a trip back to the Dark Ages. Then she recalled the passage she'd read about the author in Kuthumi's library that described the writer being inspired to write *The Ancient Future* on her journey through Scotland. *It wasn't fairy lights she encountered in her travels, it was me,* Tory assumed, and as no response from DK was forthcoming, she asked, *I can do fairy lights?*

If your imagination and willpower is up to the challenge, I dare say you could, DK chuckled.

Tory willed herself beyond the car, which had turned off the Loch road and was heading over the highlands. The clouds were high in the sky but apart from being dark and ominous-looking, there was very little happening on the weather front.

In her imagination she conjured a mist that descended over the highland road and over the one tiny vehicle travelling along it. Inside the haze she envisaged countless tiny specks of light all flitting about in different directions, so as not to be mistaken for snow glistening in the headlights. As she witnessed her vision manifest around her, Tory rose up above the enchanted haze to view the extent of it. She wished the occupants of the car to feel all the excitement, sense of purpose and wonder that she felt upon setting out on this partnership.

I think they've probably had enough inspiration for the moment. DK advised her to end the spectacle.

Tory immediately dispersed the mist filled with lights, and with a second thought, she parted the clouds that had begun to rain in the distance and a huge rainbow stretched itself across the towering highland peaks.

The car pulled over to the side of the road and both the women climbed out of the car, looking around for the fleeting phenomenon, tears streaming down their faces as they beheld the most stupendous view imaginable.

From Tory's diminishing perspective she saw two tiny people and a car on the top of the world.

The crystal sculpture blurred out her perception of the Scottish Highlands in the late twentieth century and Tory opened her eyes. 'Now that's what I call an enchanting first impression. I think I'm going to like working with the subjective world.'

DK raised his brows to agree. 'You've most certainly got your subject motivated in the right direction ... a very good start indeed.'

PART 2

SIGNS

CHARACTER LIST

PART 2

Head of Ingram conglomerate	Hayden
Hayden Ingram's heir	Rainer
Leonine Impostor	Horace
Eli the Elestial	

THE WRITER'S GUIDES

Oversoul	Astarleia
Marriage guide	Hazel
Health guide	Frances
Detrimental spirit	Nictar
The Cat	Arthur
The Muse	Tory
The Agent's guide	Karmalina

ATLANTIS

Head Seer of the High Orders	Electra
Ruler of Usiqua	Prometheus
Prometheus' son	Deukalion
Murdered ruler of Atlantis	Agamemnon
Sorcerer	Aegisthus
Wife of Agamemnon	Clytemnestra
Exiled son of Agamemnon	Orestes
Six sisters of Electra and Orestes	Maia, Taygeta, Alcyone, Asterope, Celaeno, Merope
Prince of Tangier	Lugal
Spirit of Retribution	Uriel

Spirit of the Supreme Mysteries	Raziel
Viceroy to the Logos	Mikhail
Orion Lord of the Dark Lodge	Yahweh Aris
Nefilim God Allied to Aegisthus	Shamash
Nefilim God Allied to Prometheus	Enki

Prologue

Four years had passed since her trip to the UK and still the writer was no closer to seeing a film in production. She and her colleagues had done everything right: the budget, the breakdown, the proposal, and everyone they'd shown the project to had loved it. Yes, everyone definitely wanted to be involved, but when it came to writing cheques, everyone passed the buck. The distributor would get involved once a director was interested; the director would voice interest once some funding was raised. No big name director, no funding ... and round and round it went.

She hadn't written anything new in years, having been forced to go back to retail record sales to pay the bills. Working all day, every day, in a shopping mall for someone else's profit had killed her inspiration. She was fiendishly unhappy, despite a blissful marriage, and her soul was in such torment that she was getting sick all the time. Before her dream had started to slide, she'd been the happiest, most positive of souls and had never known a sick day in her life.

Her thoughts kept drifting back to her trip to the UK, to the mist filled with lights in the highlands and the amazing energy it had sent surging through her being, causing every muscle in her body to tremble and tears to stream uncontrollably from her eyes. She wished more than anything to recapture that awe inspiring feeling, but her world seemed too mundane now and she didn't know how to get the magic back, or if indeed it would ever come back. Maybe this was just the way reality was, and dreams didn't come true no matter how much you believed in yourself. She was losing faith in esoteric beliefs, like creating your own reality and healing the body with the power of the mind, as she seemed no longer able to bring these principles into play. Perhaps this was what growing up was all about ... coming to these kinds of realisations?

'Every dark cloud has a silver lining,' her mother always said. 'You must believe that what is happening is, for whatever reason, timely for your growth and therefore meant to be.'

But why would she put herself through this torture? Why, when she'd been so intimately involved in the film industry, had she failed to make her dream a reality? All she wanted to do was write for a living. How could everything have been going so right and then suddenly turn so wrong?

That magical moment in the highlands of Scotland had somehow marked a change in her destiny. There had been a lot of people who were very excited and keen to be involved in the film project before the trip, which is why she'd spent the money to go to the UK and further the project in the first place. Still, after she'd seen the fairy lights, all the hype around the film project had just dissipated, and the amazing coincidences and great contacts just stopped coming.

Another of her beliefs was that if things were going wrong in life, it was usually a good sign that you were going the wrong way or about to miss some important signpost. She already knew that she'd wandered off the track somewhere. The trouble was she couldn't seem to find her way back.

10

THE TROUBLE WITH MUSING

A symphony of vibrant pastel colour played upon the glittering celestial walls that formed the miraculous foyer in which Tory stood.

DK had brought her forth to this dwelling inside the outer court of the sacred city and although the area was huge they were the only occupants. The master had explained it to be a kind of quarantine area where the physical bodies of spiritual initiates could reside in peace, whilst working out any leftover karma they might have via subjective world service. This interlude as a spirit before making the Great Renunciation, gave the soon-to-be adepts some experience in subjective world mastery and protocol.

The architecture of this 'quarantine area' alone was completely unlike anything Tory had seen before, as it was built of thought matter and not physical matter; therefore, the laws of physics did not bind it. The walls curved all over the place. In one semi-circular area, stairs ran up both walls to meet at a platform in the middle, where an archway led to chambers. The unusual thing about the horseshoe shaped stairways was that the stairs had no definable supports — they rested on thin air. The sweet scent of a thousand flowers that always accompanied an Otherworldly mist, was prominent here as were the strong pulsing vibrations of a ley crossing. Uluru in Australia was a major ley crossing as well, but if Uluru marked the navel of the planet, Shamballa was the heart.

'We are in the Otherworld?' Tory asked, as her surroundings appeared denser than astral substance, but not as solid as physical world matter.

'This outer court of Shamballa resonates to a vibratory rate of the etheric world, yes,' DK granted.

The etheric world was the overall picture of cosmic space and acted as a matrix for all the seven planes of expression and their inhabitants. In Sanskrit, the mother goddess was named Matrix, meaning 'that which gives form'. The etheric world could support all manner of forms: physical, astral, mental, causal and beyond. Kuthumi's library, like Taliesin's labyrinth and the Sensor-sphere, were composed of physical matter in etheric space. This was the first mental structure Tory had ever encountered.

'Mental matter is very susceptible to thought forms,'

the master said, explaining the amazing architecture and artworks. 'Any thought forms!' he stressed lightheartedly. 'Which is why it is so important that only the pure of heart enter the sacred city.'

'Have the security measures here ever been breached?' Tory moved to admire a beautiful etheric sculpture of a robed man.

'They cannot be breached,' DK told her confidently. 'To the distorted heart, Shamballa does not exist. It cannot, as it would be beyond such a soul's capacity to raise their rate of vibration to a level which would allow them to perceive the sacred city, let alone enter it. Furthermore, Shamballa is destructive to all elements of separatism; the threat would destroy itself.'

'He's so beautiful,' Tory uttered, having come to a standstill before the statue.

'It's not surprising that you think so. That is the Lord Maitreya,' DK enlightened her.

'Christ,' Tory deduced from what she'd learned.

DK nodded and pointed out: 'Not to be confused with the Master Jesus.'

'Yes.' Tory confirmed her awareness of this. 'The Count already explained that little conundrum to me. I had spent my whole life convincing myself that the Master Jesus had been more of a hindrance than a help to mankind, but now I know otherwise.'

DK understood her reasoning. 'We can hardly blame the Masters for mankind's misinterpretation of spiritual doctrine. Most men only hear what suits them.'

Tory could have stood and stared at the statue all day, but DK reminded her of the quest at hand.

'Come.' The master headed towards the ethereal staircase. 'Rest your bones and let your mind do your bidding for a time.'

Upstairs and down a corridor, which featured ornate, fanned ceiling buttresses awash with undulating pastel colours, DK guided Tory to a chamber that was more dimly lit than the corridor or the foyer. The walls, ceiling and floor in the room were a mottled indigo and violet which exuded its own light. However, due to the dark colour scheme, it appeared to be night and it took Tory's eyes a few moments to adjust.

The only furnishings she could readily discern were two crystal beds situated in the centre of the round chamber. These were much like the healing cubicles of ancient Atlantis, only the composition of these beds was an etheric crystalline substance.

'Who is the other bed for?' Tory turned to ask DK and spotted the Count and Maelgwn entering the chamber behind them. This was the first time Tory had ever perceived her husband's aura and it glistened with light and vibrant rushes of colour. 'You look amazing.' Tory voiced her awe.

'You took the words right out of my mouth.' Maelgwn smiled and embraced her fondly for a time. 'You'll never guess who the Count was once.' Maelgwn left one arm about his wife and motioned to the master in question.

'You'll never guess who DK was,' Tory exclaimed, just as excited.

'Taliesin,' they both replied at once.

'How did you know?' Tory was surprised that Maelgwn had blown her punchline.

'Your father told me.' Maelgwn motioned to the Count again.

Tory looked at the Count, rather amazed by the news. 'Dad?'

'Oh, yes,' said the Count, winningly. 'In that reincarnation his soul-mind was primarily under my influence. The primary preoccupations of my Ray at that time were incantation, magic and ritual, and Myrddin was one of the greatest ritualists ever known. But enough of the past,' he decreed, as they were getting sidetracked. 'Let us get cracking on the future.' He gestured Tory and Maelgwn towards the etheric cubicles.

'Your bodies will remain here, but you can return to them at any time should you feel the need to consult one another, or should you find you need a break from subjective world experience,' the Count explained, as Tory and Maelgwn took a seat on separate beds.

The etheric crystal did not feel entirely solid beneath them. It felt very buoyant, like the water in a float tank but more solid in mass and dry.

'Should you need to consult with us, your advisors,' the Count continued, motioning to DK and himself, 'it is not necessary to return here and fetch your physical forms as we can see your etheric forms just as readily. As always, you can find us with a thought.'

Tory looked across to Maelgwn seated opposite her and he raised both brows to query: 'How about a kiss for good luck?'

'Luck is not a factor,' she grinned as she leaned across the void between the beds to meet his lips halfway.

'That is one physical world pleasure I will miss,' Maelgwn admitted as they parted.

'It is one all feel they shall miss,' DK advised, 'for any physical union between soul-mates is like sampling the divine nirvana of being a whole soul. However, there is no wantonness, desire or personal satisfaction attached to the ultimate union.'

'You certainly know how to motivate people,' Maelgwn warranted, sporting a huge smile as sat back onto his healing platform, and Tory did likewise.

'You are both now aware of your subjects and to join your charge you need only to wish it,' the Count explained as Tory and Maelgwn lay down, their eyes never leaving each other. 'The Logos will guide you forth to the appropriate time for contact, just as it was upon your initial contact. This time, however, your subtle bodies will accompany your consciousness, so that you have definition for the other guides influencing your subject.'

'My subject has other guides?' Tory was concerned by the news.

'Oh, yes indeed,' DK emphasised. 'Governing many different aspects of her life, health, marriage, career, friendships, not to mention the low-grade elemental beings that latch on.'

'Low-grade elementals?' Tory repeated the part that was of particular interest to her, although the Count saved DK a lengthy explanation.

'There will be an Oversoul, who will fill you in on all of this,' the Count advised as he and DK distanced themselves from their charges.

Maelgwn held a hand out to his wife and as she returned the gesture, the crystal cubicles on which they lay slid together to form one and the couple joined hands.

'Have you ever known two initiates to be as homesick for oneness as these two?' the Count commented to DK as they exited the chamber and sealed the door, leaving the room in complete silence.

'What an amazing day I've been having,' Maelgwn announced lightheartedly.

'You've made contact with our boys, haven't you?' Tory thought to inquire after their wellbeing. 'Are they in trouble?'

He squeezed her hand to reassure her. 'Nothing I can't muse them through. You just concentrate on your own subject, and let me know if you need my advice on anything.'

'I'm beside you all the way, if you should need me.'

'I will always need you.' With one more squeeze of her hand, Maelgwn let it go and rolled on his back to close his eyes and concentrate.

She knew he meant that he needed her in a spiritual sense, thanks to the duality of the male-female principle of their soul-mind. 'I wonder who we really are?' She knew Maelgwn was trying to concentrate but she couldn't resist musing the notion aloud. 'What master soul-mind will awake in the causal world once we are one again?'

Maelgwn smiled, having wondered the same thing himself. 'There is only one way we shall ever know.'

'I'm going,' Tory took the hint, and closing her eyes, she pictured her subject.

Tory found herself in a small but comfortable first floor apartment that appeared to be of the same period in the late twentieth century that Tory had originally left — it felt decidedly strange to be back to where she'd started.

Her subject was seated on the lounge watching television. In the physical world the writer would have believed herself alone in the room, but from where Tory stood there were quite a few entities floating about the woman she was to muse.

There was an old woman knitting, wearing nineteenth century clothing, who sat next to the writer on the modular lounge. A cat spirit was curled up on the subject's lap. A rather dubious looking entity of a dark, vaporous elemental nature, was hovering around the subject, changing forms as it babbled away to itself. 'Go on, have another cigarette, you know you want one. Or how about a drink? You haven't had a drink in ages!'

A kindly looking monk, who was sitting on the lounge on the far side of the subject, was making his own appeal. 'What you need is to have some dinner. You haven't had anything decent to eat all day.'

Above the subject's head a tiny ball of light was flitting about, but the most spectacular being in the room was a breathtakingly beautiful female spirit, with long flowing hair that was so white it sparkled silver. Her vaporous form was attired in long flowing robes of mauve and violet. She was lying high above the subject's head overseeing all that took place below.

It was this entity, which Tory assumed to be the Oversoul, who spotted the new arrival first.

'Ah, you must be the new muse ... thank heavens.' The beautiful being floated over and stood in front of Tory to greet her. 'The Master DK has been promising to deliver you to us for ages.' All the spirits present, bar the dubious elemental, looked Tory's way — the ball of light, floating above the subject's head, ceased all motion.

'So, you're the one who threw the big fairy light show.' The cat spirit jumped off the writer's lap and strolled over to join the conversation. 'What an inspiration that was! It intimidated the last muse so much that he went and found himself another subject to make feature films with. I've been tossing around an idea for a story myself, but the judge here,' he ticked his head towards the Oversoul, 'has ruled that it's not my department.'

Tory was a little taken aback to hear the unusual looking cat speak. She thought him unusual because of his ears, which folded forward, and his tail was shorter than most cats. 'What is your department?'

'To make our subject and her husband maternal,' the cat explained, 'for the benefit of the kid.' He nodded his head towards the tiny ball of light suspended in midair.

'Is that what it is?' Tory was delighted by the information.

'Arthur, a little silence please,' instructed the beauteous Oversoul. 'His last human incarnation didn't turn out very well,' the Oversoul explained.

'I was a stockbroker,' the cat butted in again. 'The stress killed me by the age of twenty-six.'

'So Arthur has been granted leave to pursue a cat's life for a while, in the company of a couple of human beings who will make him understand that life as a human is not always as stressful as his last incarnation was.'

'I'm not to be just any old tomcat mind ... I'm to be a pedigree Scottish Fold.' Arthur strutted around looking impressed with himself.

'You haven't been born as a cat yet, I take it?' Tory clarified.

'No, no.' The cat sat himself down. 'My soon-to-be owners will be moving house within the year, to the upstairs unit of an old federation house I've picked out. So, I'm waiting until after the move before I inspire them to come and get me. It's a good thing you've turned up now to muse my owner out of the rut she's in, as she isn't doing a whole lot to inspire me to go back to being a human so far.'

'I'm Astarleia.' The Oversoul recaptured Tory's attention and smiled warmly. 'I act as a kind of coordinator for all the guardians and advisors of this subject.'

'I'm Tory Alexander.' Tory returned the polite introduction before jumping back to a point of interest that the cat had raised. 'Our subject is in a rut?'

'I'm afraid so.' Astarleia looked back at their despondent charge. 'Since her last muse left, it's been very hard to keep her motivated about life in general. She tends to thrive when her imagination does.'

'It can't have been very long since I made first contact.' Tory strode over to take a seat on the coffee table, facing the subject.

'Four years.' Arthur jumped up on the table beside Tory.

'She's been uninspired for four years?!' Tory was most concerned by the news.

'I've been feeding her an outline of your story and dropping hints about what to research to prime her for your coming,' Astarleia added. 'But with working full-time in retail to earn a living, she's too exhausted to be interested in researching early British history, Celtic mythology and earth light phenomena.'

'Hello, dear, I'm Hazel,' said the old woman looking up from her knitting.

'Hazel is a good part of the reason that our subject has been happily married for nine years now,' Astarleia boasted on the old woman's behalf.

The old woman waved off the credit. 'I was married for close on sixty years myself.' She gave her credentials.

'My marriage was a very happy one too.' Tory thought she'd best not mention how long she'd been married for, which was somewhere in the vicinity of ninety years.

'Oh, my marriage was hell,' Hazel corrected. 'My husband wasn't anything like our subject's fellow. He's a real sweetie.' Hazel went back to her knitting.

'And this is Frances.' Astarleia introduced Tory to the monk, who nodded his head in greeting. 'He's been taking care of our subject's health.'

'I've arranged for her to start yoga soon.' Frances outlined the latest scheme he'd been working on.

'That's terrific,' Tory encouraged. 'So, her health is good.'

'Not lately,' Frances was sorry to say. 'But I am confident that it will improve greatly now that you are here.'

Tory frowned and looked to the dark annoying entity darting around their subject, blabbering over the top of their conversation. 'What is that thing?' Tory asked, as it seemed to be completely ignoring them.

'Nictar is a low-grade elemental who latched on to our subject when she took up smoking,' Astarleia advised Tory regretfully.

'And it just ignores you all?' Tory commented regarding his behaviour.

'It does not perceive us,' the Oversoul advised, 'as it is functioning on a lower etheric level than we are.'

'So our influence is more powerful,' Tory assumed.

'That entirely depends on the state of mind of our subject,' Astarleia concluded, whereupon all eyes turned back to their charge.

'Come on,' Nictar appealed. 'It must be ten minutes since you last had a smoke. You can probably fit several in before you get so hungry that you'll have to raise that lazy carcass off the lounge and fix yourself some food. With hubby away, why even bother? Just smoke away that hunger.'

The subject looked to the packet of cigarettes sitting on the coffee table in front of her.

'Oh, no, you don't.' Tory focused all her will on the subject. 'Now you listen to me, Traci Harding. You have to eat now, because after dinner we have some serious creating to do.'

'Yeah, good luck,' Arthur scoffed. 'The X-files is on next, she won't forego watching that.'

The subject placed a hand on her empty, rumbling belly and reluctantly decided to go feed herself.

Tory looked to the cat and grinned triumphantly.

'I'll believe in miracles when I see her start writing.' The cat spirit followed the subject to the kitchen.

'What are you doing?' The smoke-filled entity protested at being ignored and rushed through Arthur in pursuit of the subject. 'How about a smoke whilst you cook then?'

'Watch it, buddy.' The cat shook off the negative vibration that had moved through him and jumped up on the kitchen bench, out of the way.

'So ...' Tory turned to Astarleia, 'where do we write?'

'The office is up the hall,' the Oversoul advised, floating ahead to lead the way.

In the office was a computer, printer, telephone and fax, along with a couple of bookcases. One was full of reference books, the other with fiction novels, photo albums and files. There was also a large metal filing cabinet.

'What's in there?' Tory motioned sideways at it, as she began to peruse the reference books.

'Top drawer — electrical leads. Second draw — David's tour itineraries. Third draw —'

'Tour itineraries?' Tory queried with interest. 'Who is David?'

'Our subject's husband. He's a concert lighting director and has toured with just about every rock band known to man.' Astarleia sounded in awe of his achievements. 'He's somewhat of a technical whiz. Modern technology just astounds me,' she confessed. 'Let alone understanding how it works. He's destined for great things and is bound to be helpful to our cause.'

'I'd say so.' Tory smiled at the wonderstruck Oversoul and looked back to the books. 'He's going to design the jackets of our books.'

Astarleia was pleased by the news and surprised that Tory would be aware of such an event before she was. 'How do you know that?'

'Oh, an angel told me.' Tory's smile turned to a cheeky grin.

'The other two drawers are filled with files of paperwork, information and redrafts of Traci's film projects.' Astarleia got back to Tory's original query about the filing cabinet. 'I think that's why she avoids this room, as it reminds her of past failures.'

'Well, we'll not fail this time,' Tory assured the Oversoul. 'She's got a mighty fine collection of reference books here, some truly cosmic reading.' Tory looked to Astarleia, knowing this must be due to her influence.

'We do our best.' The Oversoul accepted the intended compliment graciously.

'Do any of these books make mention of Maelgwn of Gwynedd?'

'A couple of the Arthurian books do, but they are very obscure references,' Astarleia was sorry to say.

'Not to worry,' Tory stated confidently. 'We have a

whole chapter to write before we need to make reference to Maelgwn and his knights. She's already got a book on earth light phenomena, and that ought to serve as inspiration enough for the first big scene.'

'Do you really think you can get her writing tonight?' Astarleia wanted to believe it, but after the last four years of inaction she feared Tory was being a little ambitious.

'Yes, I do,' Tory said surely, as she schemed away in her head. 'And tomorrow she will be so inspired and eager to pursue the tale that she will go to the library and find the texts she needs to learn about Maelgwn.'

'But she has to work tomorrow?' Astarleia informed, not wanting to be a nuisance.

'Then we'll go to the library at lunchtime.' Tory shrugged off the problem and Astarleia burst into a huge smile.

'I'm so glad you've come, Tory,' said the Oversoul sincerely. 'I have a feeling you're going to be a very good muse and I am extremely thankful for your aid.'

Tory dragged herself away from her plotting to assure her new associate, 'It is I who am thankful to you, for giving me the means to work out my karmic debt to this dimension.'

The subject entered the office, crunching on a piece of grilled cheese on toast and began to peruse her non-fiction books.

'She's quite psychic this one,' Tory commented aside to Astarleia, who nodded.

'Thus the ease with which she perceives our suggestion. Still, she hasn't been this receptive in a while.' When their charge selected the earth light book from the shelf and sat down at the desk with it, Astarleia kissed Tory's cheek.

Tory was trying not to appear too stunned herself. 'Why not switch on the computer and bring up a blank file?' She moved in closer to egg their subject on. 'Just in case you want to take some notes.' Tory winked at Astarleia as the writer reached for the 'on' switch.

'Hey, the X-files is starting.' Arthur came romping up the hall to see where everyone had got to and was bowled over to find his soon-to-be owner in the office. 'Well, bugger me ... a miracle.'

'Shhh!' Tory and Astarleia stressed at once.

The writer hesitated from switching on the computer when she noted the haunting theme music of her favourite show wafting up the hallway. She closed the book and stood to leave.

'Forget the television,' Tory appealed. 'I'm offering you a trip to the Dark Ages, complete with handsome princes and knights, castles, dragons, Merlins, time travel and other Otherworldly mysteries.'

'Go on, write.' Arthur attempted to undo his interruption. 'It's only a repeat anyway.'

The writer sat down again, and licking her fingers in the wake of her cheese grill, she switched on the computer.

'Oh, haven't you given up on that ridiculous project yet?' Nictar appeared on the writer's shoulder. 'You got a D in English for Christ's sake. You're never going to be a writer.'

'Is there some way to dismiss that thing?' Tory

inquired, as she watched the writer rise and leave the room.

'The only way is to allow her to do as he wants,' Arthur replied. 'He's as quiet as a mouse when she's smoking.'

'Nictar telepathically perceives stimulation from our subject when she smokes, and he concentrates very hard to do so,' Astarleia clarified. 'The only other way to be rid of Nictar is if our subject stops smoking altogether and she's not very disposed towards that idea.'

The TV switched off and a haunting Celtic melody began to waft through the apartment.

'Now that's more like it,' Tory said with feeling. The melody created just the right mood for their tale.

The writer re-entered the office carrying an ashtray, cigarettes, lighter and a cup of tea, all of which she placed on the desk.

'Oh, for heaven's sake will you please have a smoke!' Nictar followed the writer back to the desk.

'Put us all out of our misery, will you, Trace,' Arthur insisted, jumping up onto the desk where he could check out the action.

'Arthur, we do not encourage her,' Astarleia scolded sweetly.

'I know.' The cat watched as the writer created a new file. 'But constant chatter makes me crazy!'

The writer, faced with a blank page, reached for a smoke and lit up. Nictar gave a satisfied sigh and shut up.

Frances and Hazel appeared in the office and were quietly delighted to see the new muse was on the case.

'All right then, let us work.' Tory manifested a copy of the not-yet-written novel in her hand and the book opened at her mental command. 'Chapter One, The Stones,' she read.

SC 1. EXT. SACRED STONE CIRCLE/ENGLAND. EVENING. The writer typed and then paused.

'Oh, no.' Tory had forgotten about this little snag.

'Listen to me, Traci, my sweet. This story has to be a book, not a film.' Astarleia intervened to assert her influence. 'No more waiting for other people to give the nod. If we write a book, our success rests entirely upon our own shoulders. It's high time you took control of your destiny ... fortune does favour the brave, after all.'

'What the hell,' the writer decided, deleting what she'd typed. 'Screenwriter, author, who cares,' she shrugged, 'as long as I'm getting paid for doing it.'

'That's the spirit!' Tory gave a cheer as the writer typed, Chapter One, and then paused. 'The Stones,' Tory prompted.

'But what Stones?' The writer looked at her reference books and pulled one off the shelf that detailed the sacred stone circles of Ancient Briton.

'Is the King's Men stone circle featured therein?' Tory asked the Oversoul.

'Yes.' With a wave of Astarleia's hand the book fell from the writer's grasp and landed open on the floor to the section that featured the said site.

After checking out the location of the King's Men stones in Oxfordshire on a map of the ancient world, the writer decided that the site would suit her tale well. She'd visited several stone circles whilst in the UK and knew well enough what the atmosphere of such sites felt like.

'Now to give my warrioress a name,' the writer

mumbled, reaching for a little booklet titled *What To Name the Baby*.

'Tory,' Astarleia advised her subject. 'Look under "T" names.'

'No, not Tori.' The writer picked up on the thought and rejected it. 'There's a chick on a TV soap called Tori and she gives me the shits.'

Tory laughed, familiar with the show her subject was talking about. 'Why not spell Tory with a Y then?'

The subject placed the book aside seeming rather pleased with this solution. 'Yes, with a Y. I like that, it's more masculine ... more befitting my character's warrioress nature.' The writer sat forward and placed her fingers on the keyboard to begin.

'As evening cast its shadow across the horizon ...' Tory began to relay her tale and all present fell silent to listen, bar Nictar.

'Any chance of another smoke?'

Six hours later, in the wee hours of morning, six pages of text scrolled past the writer's eyes and filled them with tears of relief. 'This is really good,' she decided, referring to how stimulated she felt, rather than to what she'd written, although that wasn't bad either. 'I want to keep going, but ...' She glanced at the clock on the wall that was telling her that she should have been in bed hours ago.

'Got any holidays owing at work?' Tory, who was still raring to go, questioned.

'I could probably get a couple of weeks off,' the subject posed, inspired by the idea only a moment. 'But I'd have to book them in advance,' she resolved sounding disappointed that she couldn't award her new story all of her time and energy straightaway.

'Then book your time off,' Tory urged enthusiastically. 'We have some serious researching that we can do until then.'

'A holiday and a research trip to the library, is exactly what the doctor ordered,' the writer decided, saving her work and switching off the computer for the night.

'I don't want to sound pessimistic, but I don't think two weeks off is going to make a dent in that doorstop of a novel you're holding.' Astarleia appeared concerned that the subject might get pushed too hard too quickly.

'I realise that,' Tory granted, 'but it will be a start. You and I will cook up a long-term solution in the interim which will satisfy everyone's concerns.'

Astarleia smiled, pleased that Tory was so easy to get along with. 'Come on then, let's get to work.'

'What do you mean? Isn't she going to bed?'

'Yes,' Astarleia concurred. 'But all of her other guides head off to arrange contacts and so forth when she sleeps, so this is the time when we muses of the spirit and the imagination get some of our best work done.'

'Does Nictar disappear too?' Tory prayed for relief from his constant nagging and negative attitude.

Astarleia nodded, fully appreciating Tory's disenchantment. 'She can't smoke in her sleep, so there's no point in him hanging around.'

'Thank heavens!' Tory emphasised, following the Oversoul into the bedroom. 'God is merciful, after all.'

II

ANGELS AND DEMONS

The four sons of the Dragon met with Lahmu, the Governess of Kila, En Noah, Bast and Lirathea for a closed meeting to decide what was to be done to combat Viper's latest threat to peace.

'Nothing and no one will be safe if that witch takes an immortal body and teams up with an army of immortal demons,' Brian stated, deeply concerned by their negligence of security, but rational and calm now that Fallon had been delivered home unharmed.

'Initially, it's Gaia they're after.' Noah was quite sure about that. 'If we can prevent Viper getting a stranglehold on that planet, he'll not have a chance to spread his chaos elsewhere.'

'I should head a task force and go to Gaia without delay,' Rhun insisted, eager to make amends for his last oversight.

'I am hoping your parents foresaw these events and that that is why they made their move to Gaia.' The Governor nodded to okay the mission. 'Name your team.'

Rhun was about to answer when he rethought his response and turned to his youngest sister. 'Tell me, Lirathea, who shall I need?'

Lirathea smothered her flattered smile. Her eldest brother had never taken her psychic aptitude very seriously, but now that the Governor relied on her word, obviously so did Rhun. 'Take your brothers, all of them, for strength,' she began. 'Fight as your foes may, the sons of Maelgwn Gwynedd will not be divided. Take Bast, for charm —'

'And me.' Fallon made her presence known to those in the closed meeting.

'What are you doing here?' Avery freaked. 'You're supposed to be hiding out in the Otherworld.'

Brian stood to agree with Avery, but was not given the chance to speak.

'Listen to me,' Fallon insisted. 'Viper may have wanted my body for the crone to inhabit, but I don't think the crone will want it once she realises that dark Orme does not have a lasting effect on my body.'

'Huh?' seemed to be the general consensus.

'If light Orme does not have a lasting effect on a dark heart then it stands to reason that the opposite is also true,' Fallon summed up, and everyone seemed amazed not to have considered this possibility. 'I also think,' she hastened to add whilst they were all still speechless, 'you should have Rebecca check out Viper's sister. Gazelle did good by us this day and I suspect that she may be more in tune with gold Orme than dark Orme. If so, there is a chance that Viper has the only truly dark heart amongst his people, or at least be one of very few.' She shrugged. 'Perhaps our problems are not so great as we think.' Once Fallon finished her rave, she looked around at everyone's stunned expressions.

'She's on the team.' Rhun awarded Fallon her due, as the rest of the room broke into a round of applause.

Fallon felt a bit self-conscious as she was not used to receiving accolades. 'It's just a theory,' she added demurely.

But it wasn't really her theory that they were applauding. It was the emergence of her full potential. 'It's a good theory,' her father granted, proud of her. 'Right then?' Brian brought the room back to order and turned his attention to Rhun. 'Anyone else?'

Rhun, in turn, looked to Lirathea.

'If Gazelle proves to be one of the righteous, she should also go with you.'

'Too dangerous,' Bast insisted. 'She could be a double agent, and as she is not one of the Chosen, she may prove fickle and betray us at a crucial moment.'

'That's unfair!' Sparrowhawk defended. 'She saved our butts back on Numan —'

'She was saving her own butt, Sparrow,' Bast argued.

'Rebecca will discover the truth.' Lirathea intervened in the dispute. 'And if Gazelle proves to be one of us, then we must make her one of the Chosen.'

Everyone gasped at this suggestion, although Sparrowhawk smiled as well.

'Light and dark Orme is the means which the Logos has given us to tell the righteous from the damned.' Lirathea put forth her view. 'The heart speaks for itself and cannot lie, therefore there should be no more withholding the everlasting life of gold Orme from any human who proves themselves worthy. If they turn against us, then their immortal state will be short-lived.'

Brian smiled, thankful to be beginning to understand the rules of the game they were playing. 'I shall handle the aspirants on a case by case basis,' Lahmu decided, looking from Lirathea to Sparrowhawk, who seemed particularly interested in the prisoner. 'Bring me Rebecca's findings on Viper's sister, Sparrowhawk, and then I shall decide what is to become of her.'

'Yes, Governor.' Sparrowhawk, thankful for his sister's intervention, looked to Lirathea, who winked at him. Suddenly he understood that the oracle had more than likely foreseen his meeting Gazelle, which explained Lirathea's withdrawal from him and public life.

'Meantime, Rhun,' Brian looked to his Vice-Governor, 'why don't you take the rest of your team and do a preliminary scout of Gaia? You should make contact with Doc Alexander and advise him of our concerns. If there's trouble brewing anywhere on the planet, he'll know about it, and where there's trouble you'll find our demon.'

'I shall touch base with the Otherworldly inhabitants there,' Avery proffered, 'and see what they know.'

Brian nodded to give him leave. 'Just you keep my daughter in your sight at all times and at the first sign of trouble you whip her back to the Otherworld, is that clear?' He got a nod in response from both Avery and Fallon.

'Let us to work, people.' Rhun inspired his team to action. 'Meet back here, this time tomorrow.' The Vice-Governor looked to Avery to make an appeal. 'That is, if the Pan man takes us to Gaia via his shortcut.'

'I suppose I could see my way clear to doing that.' Avery held out his hand to Fallon and she took hold.

They wandered over to join hands with the rest of their team and once the circle of five was complete, the group vanished.

As En Noah and the Governess moved in to have a close conversation with Lahmu, Lirathea turned to Sparrowhawk and took hold of his hand.

'I understand now —' Sparrow began to say, but Lirathea placed her fingers over his lips and silenced him.

'You don't know the half of it, Sparrow.' She smiled as she said this. 'And you don't need to. Gazelle is the woman you've been looking for. She's been badly hurt, but you shall mend her.' The oracle swallowed hard. 'She has no idea what love is, dear brother.' Lirathea let go of Sparrowhawk's hand and stepped away. 'Show her,' she advised and faded from sight.

The Falcon leader was emotionally confused by these events, but melted to a smile as he considered that he'd been given charge of the beautiful warrioress captive.

'Come, Sparrowhawk,' Noah requested once the young ruler was at leisure. 'I shall accompany you and Gazelle to see my good wife.'

'Sorry about the cuffs.' Sparrowhawk made conversation with the stony-faced warrioress who was his prisoner. In the lab next door, Noah and Rebecca ran tests on the tissue and blood samples they had taken from Viper's sister, and the Falcon leader had been left to guard her in the consultation room.

'I've been a prisoner all my life.' Gazelle shrugged, pretending not to be bothered. She did not look directly at Sparrowhawk as she spoke, however, which seemed to indicate a lack of self-esteem that was in conflict with her tough appearance. 'I feel safer here on Kila, in chains, than I ever did at liberty with my kindred.'

He looked up at Gazelle sitting on the bed from his seated position in a chair against the wall; Sparrowhawk couldn't help but feel for her, as he'd had such an idyllic childhood. 'Have you no fond memories of your childhood at all?'

Gazelle rolled her eyes, thinking it impossible to describe her past to such a well balanced, happy, polite, young man. 'I didn't have a childhood.' She took a stab at painting a picture for the lord. 'My fondest memory ...' she paused to take a breath and swallow her welling tears of anger, '... is when, at eight years of age, Viper murdered our mother for allowing us to be abused by anyone who made it worth her while. I watched him stab her, and I smiled with glee as the life blood flowed from her body.' She couldn't glance at the young Falcon ruler now. She didn't want to see the disgust and horror on his face.

Sparrowhawk died a thousand deaths in that moment, imagining what Gazelle's life to date had been like. It was too gut wrenching to entertain the notion for very long and yet this woman had lived such hell all her life. Suddenly, it wasn't hard to see why Viper had grown into such a monster. 'By what miracle are you still sane?' the warrior uttered. 'I am so sorry, Gazelle.'

Gazelle considered the honest remorse in his voice a rather odd reaction. This was not at all what she'd expected. 'It had nothing to do with you. Why should you be sorry?' Gazelle ventured a look in Sparrowhawk's direction and was touched by the sorrow that had overshadowed his handsome face.

'It is the responsibility of Lahmu's council to prevent such abuse,' he reasoned. 'I am part of that council and I —'

'Don't get all worked up about it.' Gazelle played down the hurt her plight had caused her. 'You're only new to the council, the way I hear it.'

Sparrowhawk nodded to concede she was correct, although it didn't make him feel any less guilty. 'I've been so wrapped up in my own petty pain that I forgot that others have woes far greater than my own ... woes that I should be doing something about!' he concluded, annoyed with himself. This was what En Noah's graduation prophecy had pointed to — forgetting the self and getting on with the job of making the universe a better place.

'Tell me about your pain.' Gazelle considered the request fair as she had just confided to him one of her darkest secrets.

Sparrowhawk shook his head and shrugged, shying away from the question. 'It is a mere trifle in comparison to what you have endured.' He dismissed the subject.

'Good.' Gazelle placed her hands on her hips to insist. 'Then you won't feel embarrassed when you tell me all about it ... or is the trust I have shared not mutual?'

'I trust you, Gazelle,' he was quick to assure her. 'It's just that —'

The door through to the lab vanished and Rebecca entered the consultation room, accompanied by En Noah.

'I have good news.' Rebecca looked at Gazelle and smiled broadly, although she approached Sparrowhawk and handed him the PKA orb thought recorder containing the report of her findings. 'Give this to Lahmu to consider, and I feel fairly confident of seeing Gazelle back in my lab within the hour to receive a dose of gold Orme.'

'You mean I'm not damned?' Gazelle was thunderstruck by the information.

'Quite the contrary.' Noah was happy to second his wife's opinion.

Gazelle had never known good fortune before and her pending initiation into the ranks of the Chosen Ones seemed too good to be true. 'But the witch said —'

'Mahaud lies,' Rebecca politely interrupted and approached the young woman to reassure her.

The Head of Genetic research on Kila seemed to float more than walk, and exuded such a healing energy that even Gazelle was aware of the lady's calming effect. The

Nefilim half-breed was so charmed by the red-skinned Rebecca, with large dark eyes and hair so long, black and smooth that it appeared like a sheet of silk, that Gazelle couldn't help but trust her. Trust had never been one of Gazelle's strong points, but the Chosen Ones inspired a faith in her that she had never had the chance to enjoy prior to contact with them. The Chosen seemed to Gazelle to be a race of angels manifest in the physical world and now she was being invited to become an angel too.

'I am one hundred and fifty percent positive that the light of the Cosmic Logoi shines through you. Your genes are far more receptive to gold Orme than its dark counterpart,' Rebecca claimed.

The hard-faced warrioress dared to smile. 'So, perhaps there are others among my kindred who are light beings as well?'

'That's what we're hoping,' Noah agreed.

'You still care what happens to your kindred, even after what they've put you through?' Sparrowhawk queried, as he stood to join the conversation.

'They're not all bad,' Gazelle defended, realising she'd planted the misconception in her guard's mind. 'Take your sister-in-law, Cordella, for example,' and found herself blushing, remembering how she'd envied Cordella's fairy tale romance and marriage to the ruler of Lura. Now Gazelle had been touched by one of the Dragon's sons also and just like magic, good things had begun to happen to her.

'We must deliver the righteous from the crone.' Sparrowhawk committed himself to Gazelle's cause and was surprised to see the joy fall from her face.

'And you would grant me and my people life everlasting, just like that?' She clicked her fingers.

'Lahmu has agreed to consider the fate of your people on a case by case basis,' Sparrowhawk answered. 'Lahmu's rulings will be based on the same simple tests you've undergone this day.'

'There is some compulsory schooling involved,' Rebecca let Gazelle know that there were conditions attached, 'which is mainly to help you hone the psychic skills that accompany immortality and get rid of all your negative belief patterns.' Rebecca paused, as their prisoner was looking a little shell-shocked.

'If Viper had only put our case to Lahmu in the first place ...' This thought made Gazelle seethe with frustration. They had raised that evil creature for nothing.

'I suspect that our council, unable to foresee these sad events, would not have been prepared to grant your request at the time,' Rebecca told the young woman as honestly as she knew how. 'But now Lahmu is prepared to allow it, proving that much good can come from a little evil.'

'Unfortunately, I have seen the flip-side of that coin.' Gazelle had an awful feeling that this beautiful dream was going to be snatched from her and she would descend into the nightmare once again. 'My brother is going to be more powerful than he was before and he will not forgive my betrayal.'

'Viper will be no stronger than any of the Chosen Ones, and, soon, yourself included,' Sparrowhawk pointed out and then smiled confidently to dismiss Gazelle's fear. 'We are more skilled at wielding our psychic talent and there are many more of us.' The Falcon ruler neared Gazelle and gently took hold of her hands. Gazelle seemed a little awkward about the event, but Sparrowhawk pretended not to notice. 'I will not let any harm befall you *ever* again ... believe it.'

Gazelle suppressed the embarrassed giggle that was welling in her throat; had any other man spoken to her so sweetly she would've spat in his face and called him a liar and a pervert. She was accustomed to playing the tough nut, needing no man's protection, for she had become her own protection. But the expression on the Falcon ruler's face made her frosty heart melt and go completely gooey. It touched her that this paragon of manhood would give a damn about a woman as wretched as she. 'I believe you, lord,' she managed to say graciously, without a hint of scepticism.

'I know what a big ask that is for you, Gazelle,' he said. 'But your blind faith will be rewarded.' He let go of her hands, and stepped away. 'And, please, call me Sparrowhawk ... unless of course you would like me to start calling you Nin, Lady or Madam, perhaps?'

Gazelle cringed at the selection. 'I'll take the first option, thanks.' She jumped down from the consultation bed. 'So, I'm off to meet the mighty Lahmu?' She drew a deep breath for courage. 'I'm up for it,' she bluffed.

'Of course you are,' Sparrowhawk encouraged, turning back to Noah to inquire, 'Are you coming, En?'

Noah smiled, amused by the question. 'Oh, I don't think Gazelle is in any great hurry to escape from you, Sparrowhawk. I'll await your return here.'

'Right you are.' Sparrowhawk waved, trying to smother the cheeky grin on his face, as all present were.

As Gazelle was not yet comfortable with teleportation or even holding hands with another to execute the task, Sparrowhawk had been walking her from place to place in Chailida. It also gave him a chance to show her around their fair city.

As the young couple departed, Rebecca took hold of her husband to give him a hug. 'That will be another wedding on the horizon for the Chosen Ones then.'

Noah had to admit, 'The Tablet of Destinies agrees with you there.'

The first person Maelgwn went to see after assuming his role as a muse was not one of his sons, but Doc Alexander — the Chosen guardian of Gaia. Doc's real name was Cadwaladr, he was Maelgwn's great, great, great grandson and he'd been the last of Maelgwn's line to rule as a King in ancient Gwynedd.

He found Doc in one of the many rooms of Taliesin's Otherworldly labyrinth, which Gaia's guardian and his wife, Vanora, had occupied since the rest of the Chosen Ones had departed for Kila. The couple had prospered here; Doc sat in conference with about twenty men and women, all of whom were sons and daughters. Among those gathered were the heads of the ICA (International Crisis Agency), the IFC (International Finance Corporation), UN, CIA, a few presidents and a handful of prime ministers as well. In fact, everyone present played a vital role in world development, being leaders in the fields of science, technology and so forth. Doc

Alexander had staged his death and dropped out of the public eye after seventy years of service and he now ran the whole show from the Otherworld via his descendants. Of course no one knew that all these world leaders were related, as they'd assumed different nationalities and personalities to suit the position they sought to secure. In the world view, the people and the press were happy that all these leaders cooperated so well.

After sitting in on a very interesting meeting, Maelgwn finally found himself alone with the secret world leader. 'Hello, Cadwaladr.'

Doc placed aside the virtual reality headset through which he'd started to view reports. He'd clearly heard his ancient name invoked but everyone on Gaia knew him as Doc Alexander, even his closest family. He ventured a guess at who was haunting him. 'Dragon? If you are here, feel free to show yourself.'

Maelgwn manifested his ghostly form on top of the long conference table at the opposite end to where Doc was seated. He was able to project an image of himself that Doc would recognise, because Taliesin's labyrinth was located in the etheric realm where all forms found expression including thought forms.

Doc had never known Maelgwn Gwynedd take a subtle form before. 'My word, Dragon, are you ascension bound?'

'I am,' Maelgwn verified, 'but I have a quest to perform beforehand and I am going to require your assistance to complete it.'

'Yes.' Doc stood, rather keen to learn more. 'I was just about to say the Count advised me that you would be paying me a visit. He said that your appearance would mark the beginning of the holy war that preceeds the Great Judgement and he recommended that I assist you in any way I can.'

This was all news to Maelgwn.

'So what has been going on out there in the big wide cosmos that I'm not aware of?' Doc, being largely influenced by the first Ray of Will-Power, liked to get straight to the point.

'I'm here to fill you in,' Maelgwn advised, 'before my sons arrive.'

Doc was well aware that Maelgwn's sons were all part of the intergalactic senate of Lahmu and thus he considered their pending arrival a very drastic measure that must have an equally drastic cause. 'I'm all ears.' Doc took a seat to get informed.

Lahmu decided to meet with Sparrowhawk and Gazelle in the senate chambers, as until he viewed Rebecca's report on the prisoner, he could not risk allowing Gazelle to enter any of the restricted areas of Government House, which was where his private office was located. Brian realised the large chamber was very impersonal and would be a rather overawing venue for Viper's sister's first meeting with him, so Brian made a point of dressing casual and seating himself at the side of the large round conference table that was closest to the door.

Sybil, the Secretary of State, announced the Falcon ruler's arrival and showed Sparrowhawk through to Lahmu. Gazelle was asked to be seated in the waiting room until summoned.

'I won't be long.' Sparrowhawk encouraged his charge to take a seat and relax, as he entered the council chamber and Sybil closed the door behind him.

'Hello there.' Sybil smiled as she introduced herself to the waiting female. 'I'm Sparrowhawk's sister-in-law ... I'm married to the Dragon's first son, Rhun —'

'Then you are Sybil,' Gazelle concluded, having taken an interest in the Dragon's family — she knew the whole family tree.

'Yes, that's right.' Sybil prevented her smile from broadening, for she knew why Gazelle had such a good knowledge of the Dragon's family. Besides being Secretary of State, Sybil was also a Seer, and had foreseen Gazelle's coming and involvement with Sparrowhawk.

'Are all of the Dragon's sons so ...' Gazelle's eyes drifted to the double doors through which Sparrowhawk had passed, as she tried to find a word that described all his fine qualities, '... chivalrous?'

Sybil laughed. 'It's in the genes ... their father, Maelgwn, was without doubt the most chivalrous man I've ever known and their mother, Tory, the most chivalrous female.'

Gazelle looked back to Sybil, her interest struck. 'Was, you say? You make it sound like they are deceased and I know that can't be?'

'No, not deceased,' Sybil assured, feeling she should be more careful with her casual comments. 'They have simply moved away from Kila to pursue missionary work elsewhere.'

'I see.' Gazelle nodded, noting that Sybil was careful not to mention where the famous couple had moved.

As Viper's sister, Gazelle could not be trusted with such information and that hurt.

Sybil picked up on this and sat down on the chair beside Gazelle's. 'After your meeting with Lahmu, I shall be able to speak with you more freely.'

Gazelle was touched that this woman, a stranger, would give two hoots about her feelings. 'That's completely understandable ... I'm surprised that my case has made it this far, this fast.'

'I know you can be trusted,' said Sybil, surely, gently nudging Gazelle's shoulder with her own. 'And moments from now Lahmu will make that official for all to know. Once that happens, there is not a Chosen soul alive that will doubt his word ... your past shall never again be held against you.'

Gazelle had not shed a tear for as long as she could remember and she swallowed hard to prevent herself from doing so now — she badly wanted to be accepted and trusted by these wonderful people. 'I trust you are right, Nin.' Gazelle had her first stab at positivity; being around the Chosen made one very aware of negative attitudes, for they seemed so out of place in the company of the Chosen Ones.

Sybil. Brian's voice came through the intercom pinned on the left shoulder of Sybil's robe. *Please send our guest on through.*

'It's time.' Sybil stood to show Gazelle in.

'What's Lahmu like? How should I act?' Gazelle started thinking of all the questions that she should have asked the secretary.

'It is imperative that you be yourself,' Sybil

advised, before rolling her eyes, 'because Lahmu certainly will be.'

Upon entering the large chamber, Gazelle did feel a little daunted, but Sparrowhawk was at her side in a second, wearing a huge smile of support.

'Gazelle, I'd like to introduce you to Lahmu, the Governor of Kila and the Head of the Intergalactic Senate.' Sparrowhawk motioned to a rather unassuming figure of a man, who rose from his seat at the conference table.

Lahmu sported a warrior form, but he was not at all the ominous figure that Gazelle had expected. Appearing to be in his early thirties, she knew the leader was much, much older than he looked, as were most of the Chosen. Lahmu was very attractive for a Homo sapiens, with his long blond hair neatly pulled back into a braid. This made his eyes, of a magnetic blue, all the more apparent — and the cute dimple on his chin. Lahmu stood shorter than Gazelle and it felt funny to be looking down upon the legend as he shook her hand, when she'd expected it would be the other way around.

'Gazelle,' he greeted her warmly, 'you would not believe how many of my prayers were answered when you came to the defence of my kindred on Numan.'

The girl was literally stunned speechless by his confession. It was so unexpected; she had suspected a judgement not a compliment.

'My daughter was returned to me unharmed. I have been supplied a means to divine the righteous ones among your kindred and Sparrowhawk here looks cheerier than he has in ages.' Brian let go of his guest's hand and winked at his dignitary, who was trying not to look embarrassed.

Gazelle rarely smiled and yet she found her mouth stretched to aching point; the leader of the known universe was hinting at matching her up with Superman. *I must be dreaming,* she decided on the quiet.

Lahmu's attention suddenly swung back to her, and as if having read her mind he pinched Gazelle in the top of the arm.

'Ouch!' She rubbed her arm; she was definitely awake. 'What was that for?' Gazelle wondered if he had read her thoughts.

'Ah, you do speak?' Brian jibed informally and made her smile again.

Lahmu was so odd for an intergalactic leader. His personality was more like a court jester — the intelligent kind, not the fool. 'Majesty, I —'

When Lahmu laughed at the first word that came out of her mouth, Gazelle became self-conscious and clammed up.

'Forgive me.' Brian calmed himself. 'My kindred are a disrespectful bunch and thus I am unaccustomed to being venerated so highly.' He clarified his thoughtless outburst. 'Please feel free to call me Governor, as you are hereby granted residency on Kila.'

Tears sprang from Gazelle's eyes as the emotion of true joy choked her for the first time. 'I'm a citizen!' she spluttered, brushing away the offending droplets quickly.

'Obviously you will be required to vow allegiance to my senate.' Brian returned to his seat at the conference table. 'Then, not only will you be a citizen, but I have granted you your own apartment on Chailida's central Isle of Parliament. You shall work for me until you find another vocation you feel more compelled towards.' Brian was tempted to glance at Sparrowhawk but managed to refrain.

Gazelle covered her gaping mouth, having never felt so overwhelmed by generosity.

'Not that you'll have much time to enjoy your new abode, as you'll be accompanying Sparrowhawk and his brothers, and my daughters, on their forthcoming mission.' When Brian noted tears tumbling down Gazelle's face and over the fingers that covered her mouth, he raised both brows to concede. 'It's a scary thought I'll grant you, but I think you're tough enough to cope.' The comment was intended to make her laugh, but she only cried more, shaking her head slowly and laughing between sobs.

'Are you all right?' Sparrowhawk inquired, keeping his distance to prevent making her feel awkward. He materialised a handkerchief and gave it to Gazelle, who couldn't seem to decide whether to laugh or cry.

'You are all so polite and considerate and welcoming.' Gazelle drew a deep breath and managed to prevent her voice from wavering, although her body had begun to tremble and she couldn't control it. 'I am not used to such kindness and it seems to be having a very odd effect on me.'

Brian had forgotten this girl was only mortal. 'When is the last time you ate or slept?'

Gazelle thought about it and then shrugged. She was too tired to recall.

Brian picked up the orb containing Gazelle's case files and his authority to activate her immortal gene and tossed it to Sparrowhawk. 'See to it that Gazelle gets something to eat en route to see Rebecca, and after her immortality is taken care of, show Gazelle to her new apartment, where she can relax a little before you're both due to meet with Rhun. We can run through her vows to the senate before you leave tomorrow.'

'I shall make sure we report to you a little early then, Governor.' Sparrowhawk was delighted to have Lahmu's permission to be at liberty with Gazelle for the rest of the day; a day that would turn out to be the most important of her life.

'I can't thank you enough for this opportunity to better myself,' Gazelle sniffled, knowing this wasn't one hundredth of what she wanted to say. Lahmu was granting her immortality and a life worth living along with it.

'There is no need to better what is already perfect, Gazelle,' Brian assured her, which only served to inspire the girl to tears once again. 'Lunchtime.' He prompted Sparrowhawk to go get the girl fed.

When Rhun, Zabeel and Bast arrived in Doc's conference room, they found Doc Alexander alone and absorbed in the transmissions he was viewing inside the sleek headgear he wore; this encompassed his eyes and connected to a set of sensor-gloves.

'Cadwaladr?' Rhun called for his great great grandson's attention and Doc removed the VR unit from his head.

'Ah, Rhun, I've been expecting you.' Doc rose to greet his guests. 'This must be the Dragon's second son, Zabeel.' Doc shook the Delphinus leader's hand, after he'd shaken Rhun's. 'And this must be Bast.' Doc looked at her and bowed his head graciously. 'My sources are correct, you are very lovely.'

'Well, just tell me who your sources are, and I'll pay them more money?' Bast always asked the most pertinent questions as subtly as possible.

'The powers that be are very interested in your quest here and I have been advised to bring you up to date with a little problem we've been having here on earth … and on the moon for that matter,' Doc admitted.

'What kind of a problem?' Rhun's curiosity was struck. 'Advised by whom?'

'I told you, higher forces.' Doc insisted on leaving it at that. 'As for the problem, it is an uprising.'

'In what country?' Rhun needed specifics.

'In all countries,' Doc was sad to advise. 'The cause of the anarchy is a satanic cult aimed at teenagers, that encourages them to blame their parents for their misfortunes and knock them off if so inclined. Since a cyber-metal band called 'Bloodlust' started the movement, teenagers have stopped committing suicide and have starting committing murder.'

'Killing their parents?' Rhun squeaked, horrified.

Doc nodded. 'Such instances have risen 200 per cent in five years.'

'A cyber-metal band?' Zabeel cocked an eye, looking rather worried by the images of large battalions of technological monsters that were brewing in his head.

'Relax.' Rhun slapped a hand down on his brother's shoulder. 'Cyber-metal is a form of music ... right?' He passed the ball back to Doc.

'Murder-metal music performed by the artists in a VR space.' Doc waved his hand at a blank wall that lit up to project a 2D image of the recording he'd taken off the VR network. 'This is a sample of what you can expect if you hang out at the "Bloodlust" VR site.'

The music sounded like a high-speed collision that just went on and on forever, and the images were of band members involved in every vile, bloodthirsty, perverted and debauched act imaginable. The lyrics went something to the effect of:

My parents made me what I am.
They fucked the world; they don't give a damn.
The ozone got punctured, now we live in a dome.
I call my computer home.

I got screwed, now do I lie?
My parents deserve to die!

Rhun covered Bast's eyes. It was nothing he hadn't seen before in one battle or another, but as tough as Bast was he felt the explicit images too much for her mental consumption. As Bast didn't protest, Rhun figured she appreciated the gesture. Zabeel, who was ninety years old by human standards and had lived half his life with pirates, wasn't looking too impressed either.

'Your teenagers like this?' Zabeel queried, wondering

what kind of a planet Gaia was, as he'd never actually been here before.

'It's all just graphics in a VR space.' Doc threw up his hands, frustrated. 'Graphics are so realistic these days that you can create anything you can conceive of and make it appear true to life in VR space.'

'Graphic is right,' Zabeel emphasised.

'Unfortunately, murder is only a crime when someone is actually killed; sexual exploitation is only considered thus if a human being is actually exploited. What you see here are just pixels on a screen.' Doc pointed out the trouble they'd been having getting the site banned. 'We've given it an R rating: censoring access to the site via the children's VR Network, but all kids need is a password and they're into the adult network. They've got lawyers from hell this band —'

'Hey,' Zabeel pointed to the screen, 'the lead screecher of "Bloodlust" looks just like Avery ... well, it looks like Avery had he never washed or had a haircut.'

'Oh no,' mumbled Rhun as he realised Zabeel was right; this could pose all sorts of problems. 'Well, at least we've found Viper. Your higher powers have told you about him, I take it?' Rhun's attention shifted to Doc.

'Just today,' Doc confirmed, waving his hand at the wall, and the image changed to that of a satellite picture of a biodome city. Rhun let Bast know it was safe to look. 'The Bloodlust cult has come to occupy a biodome city. Although, when a large and respected company, the Ingram Corporation, applied for the construction grant we had no idea that the city would go to the demons, as it were.'

It was considered the height of fashion in the demon-dome to wear items of clothing that your murdered parents were wearing at the time you murdered them. It was also considered very chic to have any scars, that your parents might have inflicted on you, showing. Needless to say the Bloodlust dress sense was very tatty, stained and smelly. Hair was worn as long and matted as possible, and woven throughout was everything from weapons to condoms to drug-taking implements. Drug and alcohol abuse ran rampant, although the crime rate was exceedingly low. Anyone convicted of a crime against the state in the demon-dome itself was banished for life and having been a resident in the Bloodlust dome, in the next biodome city you'd be arrested out of hand. Thus people fled to the demon-dome to escape all manner of crimes and offences, not just those favoured by Bloodlust — any sinner was welcome.

All Rhun could feel was sadness. It was devastating to see so much hatred and violence in people so young, for hardly any of Viper's die-hard devotees appeared to be over twenty years of age. 'So when did the Ingram Corp make the application?'

'About sixty years ago,' Doc recalled.

'Sixty years ago!' Rhun exclaimed.

'Viper has fled back into time,' Avery arrived on the scene to tell everyone what they'd just discovered themselves. Fallon was with him, as per Lahmu's instruction.

Doc nodded to the new arrivals. He knew the male was Gwyn ap Nudd's apprentice; the Night Hunter himself had introduced them long ago. 'It all came together this morning when your —' Doc stumbled over his slip of the tongue. 'That is ... my sources informed me —'

'You were going to say, your ... something? Our what?' Rhun became very suspicious suddenly, and like a hawk seeking prey he began scanning the empty space in the room. 'Your *father* was perhaps what you meant to say?' Rhun suggested a little louder than necessary, suspecting that his father was close at hand. He could sense his presence.

'Well, I do know how you hate me treading on your toes.' Maelgwn manifested his subtle body in plain view of the gathering, although he kept his distance.

All present gasped at the Dragon's new celestial appearance.

'Father, where is the rest of you?' Rhun demanded to know.

'In a safe place,' Maelgwn assured. 'I am to have a subjective role in this event, so you can rest assured that I won't be stepping on your toes from now on ... not literally in any case.' He made light of what must have been shocking news to his children.

Rhun felt the way he had the day his father had departed this world and Rhun had been left with the daunting task of assuming the throne of Gwynedd. 'But you never hinted at being dissatisfied with earthly life?' He tried not to sound as bewildered as he felt.

'It was precisely my complete and utter satisfaction with life that has brought your mother and myself to this resolution,' Maelgwn pointed out, knowing the fact was obvious.

'I never wanted you out of my life,' Rhun protested, having not spent as much leisure time with his father and mother as he would have liked to.

'Me either!' Avery added his appeal.

'That makes three of us,' Zabeel objected also, not liking the idea of being parentless again.

'That's good,' Maelgwn answered nonchalantly. 'Because, until we shut down Bloodlust and stop Viper poisoning the minds of the young people of this planet, I am going to be your muse.'

'Huh?' replied all of his sons in unison, a perplexed look upon their faces.

'That means,' Maelgwn clarified, 'that when you hear my voice in your head telling you to do something, you do it ... if you know what's good for you.' He threatened them in jest and managed to raise half-cocked smiles from all three boys. 'You've proven quite good at it so far, I must admit, except for you, Rhun. You need to be more aware.'

'So far?' Rhun was on the defensive again. 'What do you mean, so far?'

Maelgwn's free-floating apparition vanished and reappeared behind Avery whereupon he uttered, 'Assume my form so that there is no confusion when you confront Viper.' He disappeared again and then manifested behind Zabeel. 'What is that horrible smell?' Again Maelgwn vanished and finally materialised behind Rhun. 'Don't let Mahaud get a look at the Orme.' Maelgwn smiled at their shocked expressions before relocating himself back where he started. '*Déjà vu*, anyone?'

'I see,' said Rhun, rather disgruntled that he'd not proven as perceptive as his younger brothers had. 'I shall do better,' he proffered, not wanting to be out of sorts with his father when he was so close to losing contact with him for good. 'I am grateful for your efforts.' Rhun looked back to Doc and apologised for the interruption. 'You were saying that you made the connection between Bloodlust and Viper this morning, and ...?'

Doc explained that they thought Viper had fled back into time in order to establish all the contacts he had in the present day. He had the ownership and rule of one of the grandest and most technologically advanced biodome cities on the planet. 'Viper seems to have as many connections in high places as I do,' Doc announced, wishing that he was exaggerating. 'And all who side with him are individuals that my people always have trouble dealing with.'

'There is something I don't understand,' Rhun frowned, perplexed. 'If Viper went back in time, then how come he didn't create a breakaway dimension, as mother did when she went back to the Dark Age?'

'With Mahaud to advise him,' Doc speculated, 'Viper might have carefully avoided changing the past whilst setting himself up for the present. He could have had his people kill, and assume the identities of, top politicians, businessmen and lawyers who were loners, and many in these professions end up alone due to their commitment to the job. If these impostors then stuck by the decisions, changes and events that shaped the life of their victim, causality might still be intact. Viper could have specifically planned events around not causing a breakaway dimension before he reached the year from which he originally stemmed, thereby ensuring that he had a firm support base here on Gaia before any of the Chosen Ones knew about it. Perhaps Bloodlust were a cult that did emerge at this time and Viper and his people have just assumed control?'

'Viper could have a lot of kindred by now,' Avery wagered. 'They must have multiplied somewhat in seventy years.'

'Seventy years!' Rhun was even more shocked by this estimation. 'That lands Viper's people here on Gaia precisely at the time the Chosen Ones migrated to Kila.'

'Exactly.' Avery made it known that he'd already worked that one out.

'How do you know what year Viper fled to?' Rhun made the query sound like curiosity, but he did hate being upstaged.

'I've just been speaking with Eli's family,' Avery advised.

'Eli?' Rhun quizzed, as the name was not familiar.

'The large elestial crystal that powers the Aten's time drive system.' Avery filled him in. 'Apparently, Viper threatened to detonate the Aten's self-destruct mechanism if Eli didn't take them where and when they wanted to go. Eli, having become rather attached to physical world existence, and being physically built into the Aten to allow the crystal to drag the space station from one time zone and dimension to another along with him, had no choice but to agree. Still, Eli telepathically conveyed Viper's movements en route through time to his kindred deposit as he passed through etheric space, and thus I feel obliged to rescue the poor mineral. This information has only just come to hand due to the recent alert I issued to the dwellers of the Otherworld advising them that I was seeking information on the Aten.'

Rhun stood staring at Avery as if he'd been speaking double-Dutch. 'So you've been talking to rocks?'

'Rock elementals, rather, that assume the form of rocks on the lower levels of awareness.' Fallon was delighted to be able to explain and Avery nodded his head to agree with her definition. 'They were really very lovely,' she stated for the record, 'once I got over the initial shock of their size.'

Avery, feeling that summed up that topic, smiled broadly at Rhun and awaited his word.

'You can pilfer the Aten once you lead our task force back to the last century. If anything happens to you before we make the trip back to the past, we'll have a much harder time trying to stop Viper from this point in time.' Rhun glanced sideways at his father to see if he agreed with the strategy and as he said nothing at all, Rhun assumed his reasoning was sound. 'Before we collect the rest of the team, however, I suggest we pay Viper's demon-dome a visit and see if we can learn anything that might help us shut him down once we get back to the past.'

'Not a good idea,' Maelgwn advised. 'Viper's people will be able to spot you the same way you shall be able to spot them ... your aura will give you away. Dark Orme casts a shadow over its initiates that can be psychically perceived, and the Chosen's light aura will just as easily be spotted by anyone of the Dark Lodge.'

'You don't need to move from where you are to familiarise yourselves with the demon-dome.' Doc waved his hand at the screen.

There were mobile cameras that flew all over the rogue demon city and you could access the visuals via the Bloodlust website on the internet, which was now a supernet that was lightning fast and powerful, thanks to a network that ran on a photon optic linking system.

'I also have files on Viper's conglomerate and his key political supporters,' Doc added. 'But the Dragon and myself believe that the key to stopping this disaster from unfolding lies with these two men.' Doc pointed to the screen that displayed two still-frame images. 'Hayden Ingram and his son, Rainer.

'Hayden Ingram was the chairman of the conglomerate that made the original application for construction. His son, Rainer, inherited his father's empire some forty years later. Rainer brought his associates out of the biodome project after his father's death, allegedly from natural causes, but the finding was highly contested. Hayden had just announced his intention to sell his controlling interest in the biodome, when his perfectly good heart gave out on him. At age forty, Rainer then became one of the Bloodlust cult's biggest and oldest supporters.'

'That explains how the cult moved into the Ingram biodome,' Rhun acknowledged. 'But which era are we to target?'

'We considered trying to prevent the construction of the Ingram dome,' Doc advised, 'but having looked over the application there was no reasonable objection to fight the construction. From a legal standpoint I couldn't see us winning.'

'So we prevent old man Ingram's death.' Zabeel jumped the gun, being telepathically sensitive, to conclude.

Doc gave a firm nod. 'Precisely.'

12

MATRIX OF MIRACLES

At the end of two weeks off, the writer had her first five chapters and had made huge leeway with her research.

It had been like a beautiful dream, waking early every morning, making a cup of tea and sitting straight down in front of the computer to be whisked away to the Dark Age. Tory, Maelgwn, Brockwell and all the other characters felt like old mates now and the writer delighted in each and every minute she spent in their company.

You would think that this writer would be overflowing with joy and pride from her achievement, but she wasn't. Tomorrow the beautiful dream was to end and the only time she'd get to visit her friends in ancient Gwynedd would be on the odd weekend she got off and the nights when she wasn't left completely brain-dead from her day in the mall.

Her guides all feared that their charge was heading for a nervous breakdown. They observed as the writer sobbed uncontrollably into her husband's sweater; the man was doing his best to understand.

'Look, I don't think we can do without your wage altogether, so you can't quit your job yet,' her husband reasoned and the writer whined, disturbed by the fact. 'But perhaps you could look around for a casual or part-time job ... whatever you earn will suffice.'

'That's it!' Tory and Astarleia resolved at once.

'You think?' The writer considered this a fair compromise and, although she couldn't dedicate all her time to writing her tale, she could at least dedicate more of her time to it. 'I'll start job hunting.' She resolved with a sniffle to be more cheery and gave her lover a huge hug for his continued support of her writing career, even though it had never earned them a cent.

'I'll submit our request to the matrix and see what I can arrange,' Astarleia advised the other guides.

'The matrix?' Tory queried.

'Yes. You might know it better as the etheric web — that's how we Oversouls keep in touch and arrange meetings, contacts, chance encounters and so forth for our charges,' Astarleia enlightened. 'Thus, miracles can happen if the will of one's charge is sufficient to dispose another interested Oversoul and its charge to step in and help. At other times fate steps in to meet our requests and something beneficial will happen by chance rather than arrangement. We'll just have to wait and see what eventuates.'

The next day when the writer trudged into work, she managed to look pleased to be there, safe in the knowledge that it would not be for long.

Since she'd started writing about Tory Alexander, the character seemed to have integrated herself into the writer's own personality. An inner strength and knowing now drove her and she found herself daring to trust in the universe once again. She would create the reality she wanted for herself if she did not fear or doubt her own power to do so. She had decided not to hand in her resignation at work until she found a new job, but she would get the paper early Wednesday morning and start hunting.

Upon arrival in the staff room, located right behind the record counter, the writer found the manageress in a bit of a tizz.

'Our casual just quit,' she explained.

The news was like a gift from heaven and the writer could hear a crowd of voices in her head crying, 'Yes! Take the job!' Four hours a day, five days a week, sounded pretty damn fine.

The concerned look on the manageress's face had tripled. 'Well, I don't see what you're smiling about.'

The writer thought she'd best explain her amusement. 'I want the job,' she said, but what she was thinking was, *The universe works swiftly, I must be on the right track.*

The people at work thought she was nuts, throwing in a full-time position to go part-time when work was so hard to come by. Her family and friends even found it difficult to fathom her new spurt of enthusiasm for writing. She never went out any more and, although the writer didn't mind the odd interruption in her writing time, once she was in writing mode it was hard to get her to emerge. Visits from people, and telephone calls, went on without the writer really heeding what was transpiring, for she was entranced by the Dark Ages. Everyone close to her was very supportive. Still, some feared that, like the five years she'd dedicated to film writing, naught would come of all her efforts.

'What are you going to do with the manuscript once you've finished writing it?' a friend asked one day, eager to help her form a strategy. 'Will you send it to a publisher?'

The writer shrugged, having not given this much thought, but as her belief in the supernatural world grew daily, she replied, 'By the time I am finished writing this, the right person to aid it to publication will come along.'

'But haven't you even considered who you'd like to publish it?' Her friend obviously thought that the writer's faith was a little naive.

The writer turned to peruse her reference books and finding that most of them bore the HarperCollins logo, she made her decision. 'HarperCollins would be good. If they're good enough for my references, that's good enough for me.'

And that's all the planning on that front that the writer intended to do. She would leave the minor details to the universe to sort out.

* * *

Consorting was a more apt way to describe what those concerned with the writer's little universe were up to.

Tory was learning all about six degrees of separation: that via mutual connections, only six people separate you from any other person on the planet — the same applied to Oversouls and guides.

Astarleia and Tory had managed to track down the Oversoul of the literary agent they felt would best represent their charge. The agent was the most reclusive and influential to be found on this side of the planet, so arranging a chance meeting was not going to be easy. And before they could start scheming, the Oversoul in question had to feel kindly disposed towards the writer before the agent in her charge would feel the same.

The Oversoul they sought to impress was a beautiful dark-haired gypsy called Karmalina, tracked down via the Oversoul of an actress friend of the writer's mother, who happened to know an author who was already in the agent's huge stable of talent.

In the first instance, Karmalina visited Tory and Astarleia at their charge's house, to observe the young writer at work, before deciding whether or not to plot her a path to the literary agent whose interests Karmalina safeguarded.

'A formal introduction,' Karmalina decided, after hours of observation. 'But a meeting with my charge is still a way off. And will require a few leaps of faith for your girl,' she stipulated.

'Thank you so much,' Tory said happily — scoring

an agent would mean one of her major hurdles was out of the way.

'What must we do?' Astarleia prompted the fiery Oversoul, all dressed in shimmering red, black, purple and white.

'When the manuscript is complete, your charge will give a copy to her mother, who will pass it on to her actress friend. She, in turn, will like the manuscript and suggest to her author friend that *he* show it to his agent.' Karmalina held her arms out wide as if to imply she would take it from there. 'However, the author friend is not going to know your girl from a bar of soap, and that's where this mission is going to require a little effort on your aspirant's part. For there will be made known to her an opportunity to meet this author, and if your girl manages to impress him, she'll get her break and her manuscript will be passed on to my charge for perusal. I can't guarantee my charge will take your girl on board, but at least she'll get a look in ... fair enough?'

'Very fair,' Astarleia nodded. 'You've been most gracious.'

'She seems like a good kid.' Karmalina glanced back to the writer, still buried in her work. 'I hope I see you all again soon.' She waved and vanished to attend to her own charge.

'So that's how it works,' Tory mused now that they were at leisure. 'We can arrange these opportunities to occur for our charge, but it's up to her to seize the moment.'

'Exactly,' Astarleia confirmed and Tory exhaled heavily as she considered.

'Geez, I must have had my guides working overtime during my life,' she concluded, and gave Astarleia something to chuckle about.

'They still are,' Astarleia agreed.

It took one year to complete the manuscript that was, at present, simply titled *The Dark Age*. Tory was a little concerned as the title wasn't the one that the book would be published under, but Astarleia assured her that somewhere along the road to publication their writer would be encouraged to rethink the title. Once the writer's mind was open to a change, it would not be hard to suggest the destined title. At present, however, the writer felt that every word of her manuscript was etched in stone, including the title, so there was no point trying to persuade her into changing anything until the publisher's editing process started.

The writer's best friend had been doing a fine job of tidying up the manuscript and had been just as open to Tory's guidance as the writer had been. With every review of the text, 'The Dark Age' got closer and closer to reading as Tory knew it eventually would. This initial editing process would take another year to complete, as their charge couldn't spell, was dyslexic, and had never been very good at English. Thus, the poor best friend had her hands full trying to explain why the story wasn't flowing as well as it should and why useless bits of researched information had to go.

This was where musing was not an exact science, for although Tory conveyed the story to her charge, the writer had her own free will and thus would wander off on little creative tangents. These would later be addressed and corrected by editors who would bring the story back to its pure form, as per the completed version of the tale that Kuthumi had given Tory as a reference.

During the course of writing *The Dark Age* the writer had a few strange experiences of note. One that happened constantly was that words would pop into her sentences that she didn't even know the meaning of and, after referring to a dictionary, the writer would discover the word was in the perfect context. The same kind of strange coincidences had occurred during her researching sessions. For example, placing Taliesin's Otherworldly abode at Lynn Cerrig Bach. The writer had known this location was the last stand of the druids against the Romans — as good a place as any to stick a temple, the writer thought. Then, later on, when the writer was researching something else, she chanced across a story about an excavation team who had started digging statues of the Goddess out of the ground at Lynn Cerrig Bach and the statues dated to the same time as the temple in her story ... weird! Still, as the character Miles said in the story, a little bit of Tory's magic rubbed off on all she touched and it seemed that her creator was no exception.

Now that the story was complete, the writer made a gift of a copy of her manuscript to every member of her family — her mother included. Her mother, after reading the story and finding it thoroughly enjoyable, asked her best friend, who was an actress, to read it.

'I don't know if I am just biased, or if this story is really as good as I think it is,' their charge's mother explained upon passing it to her friend, who promised to read the manuscript and offer her professional opinion.

In two days' time the actress was on the phone to the writer singing her praises of the story. 'I have a very good friend who is an author,' she explained to the writer, 'and although I doubt he has time to read your story, I believe he will take my word for it and pass it on to his agent if he feels you are worth his recommendation. I am taking him to the opening of the Sydney Spring Festival of New Music, and as so many people you know are going to be there, why don't you come down and meet him?'

And that was how the writer found herself at the promotional reception standing on the balcony overlooking Sydney. She was very nervous about meeting a real author and had no idea what she was going to say to him, not having read any of his books. The author had also written for TV, so she did stand a slim hope of not appearing to be completely ignorant, for she was familiar with this aspect of his work.

She was sucking hard on a cigarette, trying to reclaim her nerves, when she spotted her mother's actress friend through the large glass windows, entering the reception with a couple of male friends in tow — one of whom she assumed was the author she was here to meet.

This was one of those defining moments in her life; the writer could feel destiny urging her to put out the cigarette, swallow her fear, walk inside, and introduce herself. 'Well, here goes everything,' she mumbled, losing the smoke and, taking a deep breath to rouse her courage, she did as her instincts prompted.

At least she was spared the embarrassment of introducing herself. Her mother's friend gave her a sterling recommendation to the renowned author, before leaving them alone to talk.

'So you're the one who wrote this amazing manuscript I've been hearing about?' asked the distinguished-looking gentleman politely, although the writer could plainly see that he wasn't really very interested and she didn't blame him — she must have seemed to be like a starstruck kid to the man.

'I am.' She grabbed a drink from a passing waiter's tray.

'So, tell me, what is your manuscript about?' He scanned the crowd for someone he could wave over to spare him having to hear a long and drawn-out synopsis.

'It's about a female martial arts expert who gets transported by a merlin back to the Dark Ages to aid him to change the course of British history,' she spat out, hoping the subject matter would interest him.

'Really?' He looked at her, obviously a little intrigued.

'Yes,' she replied enthusiastically, trying to think of something intelligent to say. 'I find the concept of simultaneous time very interesting.'

The author chuckled. 'Simultaneous time ... what is that?' He was suddenly content to pursue the conversation.

The writer went on to explain her theories on time travel, reincarnation, karma, dimension jumping and so forth, and was surprised to find she was really enjoying herself.

'Goodness,' the author stated in high spirits, once she had finished. 'I have enough trouble keeping track of day one, day two, or day three in my scripts, let alone all the jumping backwards and forwards through time you're talking about.'

The writer's heart was doing backflips. She had made a good impression on him and his flattery, and interest in her — a total nobody — made a mighty impression on her too.

'When you have finished editing, I could send your script to my agent,' he offered and the writer needed to use all of her restraint not to start jumping up and down screaming praises to the universe there and then. 'Now, my agent won't contact you unless she likes it,' he warned in advance. He then suggested that if the writer wanted to know what was happening with the manuscript she could chase it up through the mutual friend who'd introduced them. 'Still, my agent doesn't usually waste much time,' he assured her. 'If she likes the manuscript, you'll know fairly quickly.'

The manuscript left the writer's possession looking like a medieval fairy tale.

There was a standard format for the layout of manuscripts — double-spacing, plain font, printed on one side of the page only. However, being a non-conformist and appalled at the thought of her story looking standard in any way, the writer completely disregarded the normal protocol. This manuscript had to enchant upon sight.

Ornate borders surrounded the text on the title page, reference pages, and each new chapter page. She had even been mused into creating a couple of maps, the like of which she'd sketched up for her own reference. As she had yet to master the paths function of the PhotoShop program on her computer, the writer's husband got roped into doing the graphic layouts of the floor plans of Aberffraw and Degannwy, the two main strongholds of her story.

Much like the character Tory Alexander, the writer was not a very ritualised kind of girl. Still, having observed how well Tory's little ceremony for the elements had served her in the story, the writer performed the same kind of ritual in her lounge room to ask the spirits of nature to bless her book with success.

The casting of her circle was not quite as easy as it would have been had the writer not had a young kitten sticking his little nose into everything. She tried locking Arthur out in the sunroom, but his meows of protest were not conducive to the mood she was trying to create. When she let him back in, he seemed to have comprehended his predicament, as he jumped up onto the lounge and settled himself down to let his owner get on with her summons.

What Tory and the other guides could see, that the writer could not, was all the tiny beings who gathered around her during the ceremony.

Tiny winged fairies of the air known as Sylphs, emerged from the smoke of the incense burning to the east of the writer and her manuscript. Fiery Salamanders danced in the flames of the candles burning in the south, whilst fish-like Undines splashed about in the golden goblet, filled with water, in the west. Gnomes popped their heads out from the flowers and soil in the planter pot that the writer had placed in the north to represent the earth aspect of nature. All the elementals present took the writer's request very seriously, once she had offered each elemental group an appropriate gift.

We recognise the creativity of this aspirant and her work, one of the fiery elementals said. *Those who resonate to our influence of valour and courage will read this work and adore it and remain loyal to the creator and her future works.* The being cast a little ball of flame upon the manuscript in the centre of the circle. The flaming orb burst into tiny sparks of yellow, red and orange before making contact with the work, and these tiny lights then sprinkled themselves over the manuscript. Once the object to be blessed had absorbed the offering, it appeared to take on a slight etheric glow.

Next a Sylph, composed of nothing more than the sweet-smelling smoke of the incense, offered the blessings of the element of air. *May your desires for this work come to fruition with the greatest of speed. Good communications will bless you. Adaptability and constant learning will make future works come together with greater ease.* The little winged being looked at Tory and gave her a wink. Then the Sylph moulded a ball of smoke and blew it towards the manuscript, where it spun itself into a whirlpool spiralling down into the work, whereupon its etheric glow increased.

A small merman hung his upper body over the top of the goblet of water, as if he was in a swimming pool and very much enjoying his swim. *Your work shall inspire the understanding and depth of emotion in all those souls receptive to the greater mysteries, yourself included.* He splashed water over the manuscript, and each droplet produced a glistening bubble that vanished upon contact with the work and boosted the etheric field yet again.

A little gnome, who was still admiring the golden earring and coin that the writer had stuck in the soil as an offering, plonked himself down on the coin as if to guard it and said, *If you continue to work as hard as you have been, much acquisition and wealth will come from your passion and thus your wish to be a full-time writer will be granted within the next three years.* The ugly little man cast a pile of dust towards the manuscript and each granule turned into a tiny fairy light that settled and sank into the enchanted work, now illumined with the blessings of all four elements.

The writer thanked the beings for their consideration and dismissed them to go about their normal business. Perhaps her little ritual was rather silly and childish, and yet she felt empowered for her efforts and even more confident of success. 'I have done my very best for this story. The success of it I now entrust to the universe,' she announced, sliding it into a large envelope for postage.

'Have no fear, my sweet,' Astarleia assured the writer on behalf of all her guides. 'The situation is under control.'

The writer and her husband celebrated their tenth wedding anniversary a few days later, and they were on their way out to dinner when she got THE CALL.

What the writer had discovered in the past few days was how renowned the agent reading her manuscript was, which made the event of the agent making contact so soon all the more heartstopping.

My agent won't contact you unless she likes it.

The author's comment flashed through the young writer's brain as the agent introduced herself and they chatted briefly about their mutual friends.

'Listen, my sweet,' said the agent, becoming more businesslike. 'I've just read part one of your manuscript, and if the rest of the story is as good as this, you've got yourself an agent.'

Oh, my God! the writer cried inside, speechless with delighted shock — all she could manage to squeeze out was a gasp with a joyful whimper at the end. She heard the cheering of the voices that softly aided her when writing, and, in fact, advised her at all times, above the sound of her own erratic triumphant thoughts. 'Thank you soooooo much.' The writer's brain and tongue finally connected.

'My pleasure,' the agent assured graciously, before going on to request two more copies of the manuscript to send off to potential publishers.

By the time the writer got off the phone she was floating on air and her husband, who'd been eavesdropping on the conversation, was walking around the lounge room with his fist clenched in delight, cheering, 'Yes! Yes! Yes!' He grabbed up his wife and twirled her around a few times. 'You did it, babe! Good for you!'

'Good for us!' the writer corrected, without knowing

just how right she was about that, given that her husband was just about to lend his interest in 3D graphic art to design the cover artwork for her book.

It had all been arranged with his muse, a technologist from the future whom Tory had yet to meet. She had been introduced to the writer's husband's Oversoul, Lenny, who was a charismatic onboard systems engineer on a bomber plane that went down in World War Two, although Lenny maintained that the events surrounding his demise had been beyond his control.

The guides of different charges didn't perceive each other on a regular basis; they usually only interacted when working or scheming together. The writer and her husband had some guides in common, such as Hazel. The tiny ball of light who represented the couple's future child also took to flying about its father's person when he was in the writer's vicinity, but otherwise hovered close to the mother's form.

As the guides watched their charges in the throes of a loving embrace, the old woman, Hazel, who was in charge of marital affairs, came to stand between Tory and Astarleia to express her pride in their efforts of late.

'Best anniversary present ever, ladies,' Hazel stated for the record — this development promised to make everyone's job a whole lot easier.

'Can we please go to dinner now? There is drinking and smoking to be done.' Nictar prompted the couple to make a move; there was nothing the deviate entity loved more than a good celebration.

* * *

Tory was impressed that her charge was eager to start researching the second book of the trilogy before they'd even sold the first one. They had received a couple of rejections from publishers who claimed to have loved the book, but having just taken on new fantasy writers, felt they must decline her work at this time. The knock-backs didn't faze the writer any as her manuscript was currently being looked at by HarperCollins.

As soon as her agent had told her of this development, the writer recalled her off-the-cuff comment to a friend suggesting that this publisher was her choice. The writer took her agent's note, highlighted the publisher's name, and stuck it up on her pinboard along with all the pictures of places and faces which had helped inspire her story. Was the universe really listening — only time would tell?

Karmalina was delighted when she arrived and found the young writer and her guides already hard at work on the sequel. 'Congratulations, ladies, your writer has just become a published author.'

'So the powers-that-be at HarperCollins agreed?' Astarleia gathered, as the publisher's Oversouls were the only ones Karmalina had been requested to approach — as per their charge's desire.

Karmalina burst into a huge smile as she nodded in confirmation and then frowned, as there was a condition. 'But they're going to make you cut sixty pages —'

'Oh, thank God! Yes, please,' Tory pleaded in desperation. 'Are they going to make us rethink the title too?'

'They are.' Karmalina was impressed that Tory knew of this.

Tory closed the book from which she was reading to her charge and raised the cover so that Karmalina might view it. 'This is the second book of the first trilogy ... I have connections in high places,' she explained, and the beautiful etheric gypsy gasped.

'You're one of those cross-dimensional autobiographical muses,' Karmalina surmised, 'like King Arthur and Obe One Kenobi!'

Tory recalled Kuthumi mentioning something to this effect. 'I owe a karmic debt to this, the dimension of my origin,' Tory outlined her understanding of the situation.

'Why didn't you say so in the first place?' The fiery Oversoul chuckled with delight as she pressed her hands together. 'Which of the Masters do I have to thank for sending you our way?'

'Ah ... Kuthumi and DK,' Tory answered to the best of her knowledge.

'Fabulous!' Karmalina clapped her hands, delighted by the information. 'So we can expect a good serve of esoteric doctrine, science and healing from your future works?'

'All those topics played a major role in my life,' Tory conceded, pleased to be in Karmalina's obvious favour.

'I look forward to reading all about it,' she assured with a wave and took her leave. 'Keep up the good work.'

Tory looked to Astarleia in the wake of the gypsy's departure. 'Star Wars was a true story?'

'In a galaxy far, far away,' Astarleia concurred.

'Wow, I wish I'd visited there.' Tory imagined what it would be like. 'I think I would have made a fantastic Jedi Knight. They never did have any female Jedi, did they?' She was rather put out by this oversight.

'I believe they will in future,' Astarleia said to appease the muse.

Tory dismissed her little fantasy as she realised her charge had paused from her reading and was daydreaming out the long, slender windows inset in the double French doors at the end of her office. 'Research,' Tory reminded the writer, who snapped out of her daze and went back to reading. 'Karmalina certainly seemed pleased to learn that I am a cross-dimensional muse.' Tory was curious to learn why.

'Naturally, as such muses are considered the choice ones,' Astarleia enlightened her. 'See, you're not an artist, you're not making the story up as you go, so you're more likely to succeed in finishing your work. Also, you are from another dimension and are bound to bring new concepts and ideas with you into this world. And that's not to mention that to be at a level to cross dimensions in the first place, a soul-mind must have the support of the Master Rays, which is always a good sign for success.'

Tory could see why Karmalina was so joyous, but she wasn't sure all the reasons were completely justified. 'I don't know the ending,' she confessed, only just this moment realising this to be the case.

What do you mean, you don't know the ending? Arthur, who'd been napping on the lounge beside the writer's desk, gave a disgruntled meow.

'Well ...' Tory thought back to Kuthumi's library,

when he'd advised the page number of the final book that this moment was recorded on. 'As far as my story is concerned, we are currently residing around the middle of book six. So how could I possibly know the ending, when it has yet to come to pass in my reality?'

Astarleia seemed to be following, but Arthur placed both paws over his face, perplexed.

'I don't know what's happening with my kindred or Maelgwn ...' Tory was about to fly into a mad panic when Astarleia reminded her of something.

'The books!' The Oversoul tapped the book in Tory's hand. 'You can read what happens to your kindred. And besides, who knows what will have eventuated when time catches up to itself in the story? I mean you have at least four and a half books to convey to our charge before we reach this instance in time.'

'You're right. I can also read what happens to me!' Tory realised, of the mind to manifest a copy of the sixth book, but Astarleia was shaking her head.

'I wouldn't do that here, unless you want the last part of book six mysteriously manifesting at the beginning of book two.'

'Point taken,' Tory conceded.

'Between books perhaps,' Astarleia suggested, 'or maybe you could take a leave of absence between trilogies to catch up with your kindred?'

Yeah! Arthur meowed. *Then maybe some of us other guides might get to try our hand at writing.*

'Are you planning on leaving the land of the living so soon, Arthur?' Tory quizzed, as the cat stretched out on the lounge. 'You've only just arrived.'

I knew this was a whirlwind gig when I took it. I've got to be outta here by the time the kid arrives, Arthur meowed in response

'Shh, puss.' The writer urged the cat to keep its meows to itself. 'I can't concentrate.'

As the music that accompanied the nightly news was heard coming from the lounge, Arthur raised himself to go and reposition himself on the lounge in front of the television. 'Later, ladies.' Arthur meowed back at them and drew the writer's attention.

'Wouldn't want to miss the stock market news, hey Arthur?' The writer shook her head, amused. She'd often caught Arthur watching the financial market news. He was the strangest cat she'd ever come across and the sweetest too. Both she and her husband loved him dearly and spoilt him rotten.

'A whirlwind gig?' Tory turned to Astarleia to question.

Astarleia looked rather sad suddenly. 'He has a rare disease that is pretty well exclusive to his breed. It's his cute, flat face and nose that are the problem ... he can't drink water without getting it up his nostrils. It's too difficult to see the waterline, which is why he prefers milk. Still, his intestines are not getting flushed properly and this indulgence will kill him by the time your first trilogy is complete.'

'That's tragic.' Tory would have felt for the animal had she not been functioning purely from a mental aspect at present.

Astarleia nodded to agree. 'He likes it here, and he'll want to hang around for a while when his time with this couple has ended. Thus, I've decided to let him have a crack at that book he's been wanting to write ... between your trilogies perhaps?'

Tory looked a little horrified by this notion, wanting to complete her mission as quickly as possible so that she might move on to higher realms and work.

Astarleia noted this, but she also knew things about their charge's future that Tory didn't. 'We'll see how it all pans out, shall we?'

13

CONNECTIONS OF CONSEQUENCE

The sunrise over the city of Chailida was an incredible sight and seemed all the more wondrous when Gazelle considered that this was her first morning of eternal life. Born a space child, it was rare that Gazelle ever witnessed dawn on the surface of a planet and yet here she was viewing the sunrise from her own apartment in the newest and most exciting settlement in the galaxy. She was one of the Chosen Ones now and having been made familiar with the vows she was to make to Lahmu and his senate this day, she felt honoured and grateful — her life finally had a good purpose.

It was hard not to think about Sparrowhawk.

Gazelle had never dwelt on anyone as much, in all her born days, as she had on the Dragon's Falcon son in just this past day or two. She'd never met a man who made her feel attractive or special and she'd certainly never entertained the desire to let a man get close to her.

Gazelle ran her hands gently over her leather-clad form, dead to all touch for as long as she could remember. The thought of Sparrowhawk touching her like this caused the body beneath her hands to tingle and then tremble in delighted anticipation. *It's not going to happen*, she told herself in all seriousness and her delight ended. *Why would he want this used dishrag of a body?* The thought made her want to cry, for although she was far from being a virgin, Gazelle had never given her body willingly to anyone and now that she did feel disposed towards the love of another she felt unworthy of him.

'I thought you might need a pep talk by now.'

Gazelle sniffled back her tears as she turned from the sunrise to face the lounge room of her apartment, and found a Homo sapiens incarnation of herself holding out a handkerchief to her. 'Who ... who?'

'Who am I?' Lirathea helped out the tongue-tied Falcon female. 'I am Lirathea, the representative of the spirit world on Lahmu's council, and the second daughter of the Dragon,' she explained, whereupon Gazelle's eyes broadened all the wider.

'But ... but, that would mean ...'

It was a good thing Lirathea was telepathic as it saved a lot of guesswork. 'Up until recently, Sparrowhawk has been habouring a secret love ...' Lirathea began the tale she was here to tell and it gained her Gazelle's complete attention. 'He kept his feelings secret because the object of his desire was forbidden to him, being that I was his sister and of a different human breed to himself.' Lirathea saw the burst of awareness that the information gave Gazelle reflected in her face. 'So you see, there is absolutely no need for you to weep. Your greatest aspiration is, in fact, the answer to Sparrowhawk's prayers, and mine.' She urged Gazelle to finally take the handkerchief and she did, although her tears had ceased to flow.

'You were the cause of the woes of which he spoke?' Gazelle gathered, her mouth curving to a smile as she wiped the escaping tears from her face. 'No wonder he was hesitant to discuss the issue with me.' Then the Falcon woman gasped as it came to her that their brothers bore the same striking resemblance that she and Lirathea did. 'You're Avery's twin, aren't you?' Gazelle paused to ponder how strange this all was. 'Is there a reason for the uncanny coincidences in our appearance?'

'That explanation is going to be a little overwhelming.' Lirathea floated to a seat. 'Are you sure you're ready to know?'

'After a lifetime of lies, all these truths are rather refreshing.' Gazelle took a seat to hear Lirathea speak.

When Sparrowhawk arrived to collect Gazelle for her first briefing with Lahmu, he was rather alarmed to find Lirathea huddled in close conversation with the new object of his desire. 'What are you doing here?'

He attempted to cover his horror by sounding merely surprised to see Lirathea.

'Oh, I had a few things I needed to discuss with our new recruit.' Lirathea stood to make her departure.

'What kind of things?' He ventured to pry.

Lirathea found his distress delightful. 'You're so cute when you're flustered,' she commented playfully, looking to Gazelle for her opinion, 'isn't he?'

'I've never seen him flustered before,' Gazelle commented, feeling quite privileged to be privy to his secret and thus able to join in on his sister's teasing. In Gazelle's opinion, however, Sparrowhawk was gorgeous all the time, but she lacked the confidence to say so in this instance.

'I'm not flustered,' Sparrowhawk insisted. 'Why should I be flustered by the prospect of you two meeting?' he queried, making his unease all the more obvious. Still, the sideways glance and smile that the two women served each other seemed to confirm the Falcon male's dread and thus he appealed to Lirathea. 'You told her?'

'Nothing ...' his sister smiled, 'that isn't true.' She vanished.

Sparrowhawk wanted to die where he stood. 'That's my family for you. Always popping in when you least expect them.'

Gazelle smiled in an attempt to alleviate his discomfort. She rose and wandered back to gaze out the large window that overlooked the city. 'Then I hope they do so to me often,' she granted, 'as that was without doubt the most amazing conversation I've ever had. I've never spoken with an oracle before.' She explained why she felt overawed. 'Probably because I never imagined that there was anything in my future worth knowing about.'

'And were you pleasantly surprised by what my sister had to say?' Sparrowhawk just couldn't resist finding out about their topic of conversation.

Gazelle picked up on this and found it amusing. 'Beyond my wildest dreams,' she teased, unable to contain her welling urge to smile, which caused Sparrowhawk to smile also. He wandered over to join her in admiring the view, and Gazelle became more intent upon the scenery as the moment threatened to become intimate.

Sparrowhawk stared at the view in silence for a time, while he roused the courage to ask, 'Was I in your future?'

Gazelle looked at Sparrowhawk, stunned by the candour of his question — his eyes remained focused on the horizon, however. She didn't feel right discussing what Lirathea had told her about Sparrowhawk and why he might be disposed towards her. Gazelle wouldn't believe he held feelings for her until he confessed as much himself. 'Well, you did just help me achieve immortal life,' she commented diplomatically. 'So I was kind of hoping you'd be around to share some of it with me.' She looked down to avoid eye contact with him. 'Truth be known, Sparrowhawk, you're the only friend I've got, or have ever had for that matter.' She sniffled back her welling tears, becoming annoyed at herself. 'Shit, now I'm crying again. What is it about you? I've never shed a tear and yet you manage to get me going every time I see you.'

'Hey.' Sparrowhawk gripped tight both her shoulders. 'Spiritually and emotionally you're purging a lot of rubbish right now, a few tears are to be expected.'

'I'm sorry,' she let her emotions flow, 'I'm not normally like this.'

'Really?' Sparrowhawk's tone implied that this went without saying. 'What are you normally like then?'

'Well, actually,' Gazelle sniffled and gave half a laugh, 'I'm usually a right little bitch,' she confessed. 'Tough as guts.'

'Then I think I prefer you this way.' Sparrowhawk risked pulling her close to give her a hug and his timing proved good as Gazelle did not pull away, but continued to sob and chuckle against his chest.

'I think my normal self will prove of more benefit to Lahmu somehow.' She responded at last, feeling torn between the warmth and comfort of Sparrowhawk's embrace and her natural impulse to push him away. Instead, she just eased away from him. 'Speaking of whom.'

Sparrowhawk backed up a step. There was so much he wanted to say to Gazelle, but she was not yet ready to hear it. 'Time for your first lesson in teleportation then.' He dispersed the uncomfortable mood with the cheer of his statement.

'So, we are agreed?' Rhun pushed Brian and Candace to commit to his request, but they appeared none too keen to concede his point. 'It has to be done, you know it does.' He appealed to them to see reason. 'It's not anything I haven't endured myself.'

Brian gave a nod, placing his hand over the intercom pinned to the front of his suit to telepathically request that his secretary send in the rest of Rhun's team. 'Make it snappy,' Brian requested, his voice going hoarse on him.

'Fear not.' Rhun drew his pulse laser and set it to kill as his four brothers, both Lahmu's daughters and the Falcon-Nefilim defector entered the Governor's office and came to stand in a neat semicircle facing Lahmu.

'Good day all —' Brian had not even finished his greeting before Rhun opened fire and shot dead his entire team.

'Christ!' Candace freaked. 'Where did you learn to shoot like that?' She rushed over to greet her daughters as they returned to the land of the living.

'I've been practising my mind control,' Rhun boasted, appearing pleased to have downed the full team before they'd even known what hit them.

'Well, what did you kill Zabeel for?' Brian felt a little uncomfortable with the impromptu massacre. 'Zabeel assumed his immortal state twenty years ago!'

'Oops,' Rhun uttered, ahead of making a dash to Zabeel's side to apologise.

'What the hell?' his Delphinus brother moaned, as he recovered first, and Rhun aided him to a seated position. He would have thumped his older brother, but Zabeel only had the energy to give Rhun a shove. 'You shot me?'

'Sorry, bro, I guess I got carried away. I clean forgot you'd already assumed an immortal state.' Rhun cringed as he awaited his brother's response.

'That hurt!' Zabeel emphasised.

'I know, I'm sorry! Here,' Rhun handed him the gun. 'Kill me if it will make you feel any better.'

'No,' Zabeel refused. 'That would just make *you* feel better.'

'Give me the gun, I'll shoot him.' Avery was up on his feet and fuming. 'Zabeel is right, that hurt! Why did you do that?'

'So that on this forthcoming mission to the past, you won't get sick or tortured as a mortal could.' Candace rose from reassuring her girls to explain to Avery their reasons for the shock move.

'Well, you could have warned us,' Avery barked, leaning down to aid Fallon back to her feet.

Rhun shook his head. 'I was warned beforehand and, believe me, the wait for your death blow is worse than death itself. It's all over now, be grateful.'

Avery unexpectedly willed the weapon from Rhun's grasp to his own and promptly shot his older brother. 'Yeah, thanks so much,' Avery mocked as his brother fell to the floor.

'Do you feel better now?' Candace scolded, taking the weapon from Avery.

'I would if he'd stay that way.' His eyes remained glued on his brother.

'That's an awful thing to say ... to do!' Sparrowhawk emphasised. 'He just did us all a favour.'

'He did?' queried Gazelle, raising both eyebrows as she held her throbbing head. 'And I thought my kin were ruthless.'

'Avery, you are the one out of line.' Lahmu spoke to quiet the riot. 'That comment and your actions could be construed as sedition. Rhun is the Vice-Governor of Kila.'

'And what do you call shooting dead half of your senate?' Avery challenged.

Lahmu approached Avery and glared at him. 'A mission imperative,' he stated firmly. 'Would you be saying such things about me had I pulled the trigger?'

Avery backed down, heeding Brian's point. 'No, Lahmu, I would not ... but then you have a far better sense of team play than my brother does.'

Brian understood Avery's complaint, as Rhun was a bit of a one-man band at times, but then so was Avery. 'Nonetheless, you owe Rhun an apology when he comes around.'

Avery appeared reluctant.

'If being subordinate to your brother's command is going to be a problem, you are a risk to this mission, Avery,' Brian clarified.

Avery resented Rhun's style of command, but he took comfort in the fact that once they returned to the past he would be pursuing his own mission apart from Rhun, to free the crystal Eli from the Aten. 'I would never act contrary to your representative's instruction, Lahmu.'

'Good.' Brian accepted his assurance. 'I need a unified team for this task, as so much depends on the outcome.'

'Damn, that does hurt,' Rhun grumbled as Sparrowhawk and Zabeel helped him up. 'Thanks so much for reminding me,' he commented in Avery's direction, sounding as though he didn't really blame him.

'I apologise,' Avery stated for Lahmu's benefit. 'I got carried away.' He used the same excuse Rhun had used to Zabeel and shrugged, forcing a smile. 'No hard feelings.'

'Of course not.' Rhun mimicked Avery's dry tone. 'What are brothers for?' In reality, Rhun would probably have booted him off the team if Avery had not been their means to return to the past.

In order to return their team to Gaia in the year that that planet had known as 2088AD — the year of Hayden Ingram's reported suicide — Avery had enlisted the help of Eli's elestial crystal relatives. They resided in the Otherworld.

The year of destination was also known on Kila as 50AC (fifty years After Colonisation), which was the year before Avery, and most of their team, were even born.

The rare time-savvy elestial crystals existed on a planet in an old quadruple-star system to be found on the innermost reaches of the etheric body of the galaxy that Gaia's astronomers had named the Milky Way.

It was a seemingly dead planet with no atmosphere to which Avery teleported each member of their task force, but the multi-coloured suns shone brightly in the distant reaches of the dark sky. As did the many suns of the neighbouring star systems, which were situated much closer together than the outer star systems with which Rhun and his team were more familiar. The combined light of the suns and stars illuminated the planet's surface to the same intensity as bright moonlight.

Once Avery had ferried everyone forth, he took a seat on a rock to recharge his batteries.

'Well, Pan man,' Bast commented, gazing out over the vast canyon before them. 'I have to tell you I expected a destination that was a little more awe inspiring than this.'

'The sky is amazing,' Sparrowhawk voiced his appreciation as he gazed up at the colourful array of suns.

'I like the zero atmosphere.' Zabeel did a backflip and chuckled as he did so. 'It's like being in water without being wet.'

'We are still only residing on the physical plane of this planet,' Fallon advised in Avery's defence, as she'd been to visit the elestial crystals before. 'The Otherworldly realm here is far more aesthetically pleasing.'

'Okay, I'm good.' Avery gave himself a shake before closing his eyes to focus on his next task.

'What's he doing?' Gazelle whispered her query in Sparrowhawk's ear so as not to disturb Avery.

'He's creating a gateway to the Otherworld, through which we may all pass,' he whispered in response.

'Whoa,' Gazelle mouthed silently as she observed a great body of light-filled mist rising out of the deep crevices in the canyon.

As Rhun observed his little brother absorbed in his silent summons, he too couldn't help but be impressed by the extent of Avery's abilities. He would be Lord of the Otherworld before too long, and Rhun conceded that Avery deserved to be awarded the same respect that he'd once given the Night Hunter.

The mist rose up out of the canyon and spilled over the edges to where the warriors stood. The sweet smelling celestial vapour rolled on over their party and continued to engulf the planet, and as it did the stony ground began to glow with myriad pale pastel colours.

'Good heavens, this is mad!' Gazelle chuckled nervously, having never witnessed anything like it.

'Best get used to it, as your Chosen studies will bring you to realms Otherworldly quite a bit,' Sparrowhawk was delighted to tell her.

Avery rose up into the air to make an appeal to the canyon, which was glowing with rainbow-hued etheric light patches. 'Oh, great elestials, I beg your counsel.'

'This is where things get really spectacular,' Fallon advised her teammates in a low-key whisper.

The great peaks of crystal rock, separated by huge crevices, began to move and then to rise. As they arose, the huge entities unfolded into bright glowing crystal forms, that although rugged and rock-like in appearance, resembled human shapes. They had heads with faces and mouths to speak, arms to wave about, and legs that melded into the floor of the glowing misty cavern. In all cases their primary colour was white, although veins of two or more differently coloured crystals ran through their forms; the variety of colours was what gave each of the crystal identities its own character.

He begs our counsel. One of the largest rocks thought projected his opinion for all to hear. *That makes for a nice change from the Night Hunter's approach of ordering us about all the time.*

Yes, indeed. May you rule ever long, little human, replied another of the massive formations in a voice that was more feminine.

All the huge rocklike creatures gave a massive cheer and by thumping their fists on the ground they gave Rhun's team a quick thrill as the earth literally shook beneath them.

'I thank you all for the vote of confidence,' Avery told the huge creatures as he glided in to get amongst them. 'I have come to claim the favour I requested at our last meeting.'

Just name the event and a year where you wish to join Gaia's civilisation, young lord, said the main male spokesperson for a deposit streaked with crystal veins of black and blue.

You do intend to save our Eli from himself, don't you, lord? said a female elestial streaked with crystal deposits of pink and yellow.

'Lahmu and his Vice,' Avery motioned back to Rhun, who took a bow, 'have given their consent for me to do so upon my return to the year 2088AD Gaia time.'

That was not one of Gaia's best years, the male elestial cringed in recollection. *Sure we couldn't interest you in somewhere, or when, else?*

'No, this year is very specific to our needs; we have to prevent a certain man's death,' Avery explained.

But you shall surely cause a breakaway dimension to erupt, the female instructed. *Preventing deaths, births, marriages and significant events always does.*

'I realise this,' Avery replied, 'but by so doing I hope

to entrap someone in that breakaway dimension and thus keep him safely away from my own.'

This would be a person of dark character, I take it? the female elestial assumed.

As Avery had learned that the best way to understand his realm was to listen to the advice of the locals, he chose not to cut the elestial's curiosity short. 'The dark character is Viper,' he replied simply, whereupon a grumble was heard from all the entities of rock who were listening to the conversation and they shook their heads, most displeased.

Pardon my saying so, lord, the female elestial ventured. *It is true that he shall be locked out of your present reality, but the same awful future will still erupt in that other dimension, unhindered by your kindred.*

'So,' Rhun summed up from the sidelines, 'what you are saying is that it is all right for us to prevent Hayden Ingram's death, provided that we also hinder Viper's dark aspirations so that he cannot make a huge impact on the causality of any dimension.' The Vice-Governor of Kila paused to mull over this theory a second and then frowned, perturbed. 'But what if one instance cancels out the other and causes the two dimensions to converge back into one?'

All dimensions merge into one eventually. He's pretty smart, this one, the male elestial commented of Rhun to Avery.

'He likes to think so,' Avery conceded, folding his arms.

As you will have deflected Viper's influence in the past, your situation in the present will still be much easier to deal with, the huge rock formation advised Rhun, who nodded to acknowledge his point.

'So, you will help us?' Avery gathered.

The elestial crystals were amused by the question, but it was the male spokesman who explained their delight. *We are bound to do your will, young master, just as we are bound to advise you. All the wonders of the Otherworld are at your disposal.*

The huge crystal deposit lowered himself to a crouched position and his back flattened, forming into a large round crystal plateau. His outstretched arm reached to the canyon ridge, where the rest of Avery's team stood, and formed a long flat walkway that led to the plateau.

All aboard, the female elestial encouraged Avery's people, and then remarked as she watched the tiny humans wander down the walkway. *Some of you will certainly stand out in a crowd, where you're bound.*

Rhun looked over his Delphinus brother, his Falcon brother, their new Nefilim-Falcon friend, and Bast, the Leonine. 'She's right.' He hit himself for nearly forgetting. 'You guys and girls are going to have to assume a Homo sapiens form for this mission.'

Sparrowhawk, Bast and Zabeel all complied at once, without even pausing from their stride down the walkway, for they'd been taught the technique during the course of their schooling with En Noah. The living organic fibre from which their suits were made adjusted itself to fit their new forms.

'Oh, yeah!' Bast looked from Zabeel to Sparrowhawk to Rhun. 'You three are definitely brothers,' she commented, as in human form their similarities were far more striking. Avery was the odd brother out in not having their father's dark, dead-straight hair.

Gazelle came to a standstill, however, having never attempted a feat of transformation before. 'Um?' She panicked, feeling useless for holding the proceedings up. 'I have no such training,' she reminded them.

'It's easy.' Sparrowhawk encouraged her to relax. 'You just have to will the transformation, that is all.'

'What?' She gazed at him perplexed. 'I didn't even know what free will was until a few days ago.' She defended her reluctance to try. 'I can't even imagine what I would look like as a Homo sap—' Her protest ceased when she realised this wasn't true. She closed her eyes and focused on her memory of Lirathea.

Rhun had to smile when he saw the look on Sparrowhawk's face when Gazelle transformed into their sister.

'I think I would prefer to have hair.' Gazelle smiled as she ran a hand over her bald scalp, amazed by her own achievement.

'Lirathea had hair not so long ago,' Sparrowhawk informed, taking hold of Gazelle's hand to send her a mental image.

Moments later, platinum-blonde strands of fine, straight baby-soft hair sprang from her head and quickly extended over her shoulders and down her back, stopping once the tips reached her waist.

'How's that?' Gazelle asked softly, her voice almost letting her down as Sparrowhawk's adoring gaze cast a spell over her.

'Very good.' Rhun moved them both along, wondering if it was going to be difficult to keep Sparrowhawk's mind on the job.

It was weird having no wings; it felt liberating in a way. Gazelle could still sense her extra appendages, but she stroked her shoulder blades to find they were indeed missing. As her hand passed through the void, her touch gave naught but a mild tingling impact in her vanished body parts. Gazelle very much liked her disguise. It made her feel like a new person and more akin to the angelic oracle to whom the identity belonged.

Avery lowered himself down to join Sparrowhawk on the walkway, just as stunned by Gazelle's transformation. 'I don't ever recall our sister's hips swinging quite like that,' he commented, as they both watched Gazelle striding down the walkway ahead of them.

'No,' Sparrowhawk agreed with a grin. 'This is definitely a new look for her.'

The party were instructed to stand on the periphery of the round plateau and they watched as the centre of the solid crystal structure turned to glowing vapour. This began to swirl inwards in an anti-clockwise direction. As the whirlpool increased in speed the porthole to the past opened wide.

'Now this is really something,' Gazelle mumbled; today was proving to be a real eye opener. She had thought that her brother's crone's abilities were amazing, however dark, but the Chosen certainly had their ways and means as well.

In you all go, the female elestial announced their flight. *We recommend feet first.*

Gazelle's wonder dispersed abruptly when she witnessed Zabeel, Avery, Fallon and Bast run and take a flying leap into the void. 'Oh no.' She moved away. 'Not this little black bird, no way!'

'We'll do it together, hey?' Sparrowhawk suggested, but Gazelle backed up, refusing to give him her hand. He looked to Rhun for assistance.

'She can't stay behind, we need her,' Rhun advised, ticking his head towards the void and giving his younger brother a firm nod of encouragement.

Sparrowhawk caught Rhun's meaning and with a shrug of apology to Gazelle, he bundled her over his shoulder and went charging towards the swirling mystic porthole.

'Where is my free will now?' Gazelle thumped her porter's back in protest and wailed as they jumped into oblivion.

Rhun smiled, pleased by the prospect of doing a little time exploration. 'It's been too long,' he decided, taking a running jump and somersaulting into the porthole. 'Yeehaaaaa!'

Maelgwn was waiting for his sons and their female team members on arrival at their destination in 2088AD. All his people were amazed to find themselves standing on the top of a building without having sensed the slightest impact from their fall through time. None of the team were aware of their etheric colleague's presence, for Maelgwn's current form held no sway in the physical world; having left all his physical world matter back in the outer realm of Shamballa, he could only play a subjective role here.

Maelgwn?

He distinctly heard his name called and was delighted to recognise the caller. *Tory?* He willed to see her and her etheric form manifested before him. His presence became known to her also. 'Could you have repaid your karmic debt so soon?'

Tory shook her head and smiled broadly, pleased to see him. Having read to her charge about Maelgwn for three years, she'd become rather homesick to see her other half. For even though her astral body of emotion was not in use at the moment, intellectually she missed Maelgwn's company. 'I've just finished relaying the first trilogy and I've been booted out by a cat who aspires to be an author. Whilst my charge has a baby, builds a house and shifts residence, her Oversoul suggested it might be best if I took a year off and returned to do the second trilogy when all the chaos has died down. It also gave me the opportunity to come and investigate the ending to our story. I don't feel right learning what happens from the books Kuthumi gave me, as I like to think that we do have some choice and influence over what is about to occur.'

'I know what you mean,' Maelgwn said. 'I've been avoiding reading the last book of the second trilogy for that very reason.'

'So, what have I missed?' Tory sought an update.

'You'll be hanging around to help me for a bit then?' Maelgwn was gratified by the idea, having missed her company too. Without her, he had no one to bounce ideas off, as he didn't like to trouble the Count with unimportant decisions.

'If you don't mind me tagging along and taking a few notes?' Tory inquired, feeling that Maelgwn was genuinely keen on the idea.

'It's always a pleasure,' he bowed graciously to confirm, but by the time he came back to vertical, Tory's attention had already reverted to their boys.

'My little heroes.' She wandered among her children and was enchanted by Zabeel and Sparrowhawk's Homo sapiens appearance. 'There's no mistaking they're your boys.' Then Tory turned to view Lirathea and could see the etheric double of a Falcon woman underneath. 'Sparrowhawk found Viper's sister.' Tory clapped her hands together, delighted; she'd been informed of this eventuality by Lirathea.

Maelgwn was observing Avery flying about in midair in an attempt get a look at the name on the front of the building in order to check that they'd reached their desired destination. 'While this lot get over their wonder and figure out where they are, allow me to fill you in on what's been happening.'

'Please do.' Tory drifted back to her husband's side to get the full story.

14

THE DEFENCE OF
THE CHAIR

From this great height the biodome city held no great wonder for the guys and gals from Kila, as the look of it was similar to some of the shielded cities on Numan and Tarazean, but this archaic substitute was nowhere near as spectacular.

Avery returned from his flight to land on the top of the building where his team awaited his report. 'We're right where we want to be, on top of the Ingram Building.'

Rhun frowned, as he'd not given his brother leave to go investigate. 'That's good to know, Avery, but you'd best not fly about on Gaia like that. Somebody is bound to see you and if they do, our cover will be blown.'

'I'll be careful,' Avery retorted. 'And anyway, if

anyone were to catch me, I could simply glamour them into forgetting.'

'Not if you're not aware of being seen.' Rhun pressed his argument. 'This is not the Dark Ages. The technology here is pretty advanced and you can bet that the security surveillance is pretty efficient as well ... try glamouring a camera.'

'What we really need to confirm,' Bast burst into the middle of their brotherly dispute, 'is today's date.' The hour was clearly defined by a huge digital clock on the side of a nearby building which read 12.34.

Rhun pondered the best way of checking the date and, having lived on Gaia earlier this century, his first thought was to find a newspaper. He approached the edge of the tallest building in the city, and gazing down on the main street far below he spotted a newspaper stand on the corner. 'Some things never change,' he mumbled to himself.

Cars no longer congested the streets of the cities on Gaia; all traffic was directed through enclosed superhighways underground. Those who wished to take in the city sights as they travelled could walk or catch the electric monorail that ran through the city, four levels above the street. This system guarded against poisonous fumes leaking into the biodome's sensitive air supply, which gave the citizens and all the plant and animal life a beautiful breathable environment, free of toxins and radiation from the outside world.

'Avery, I need you.' Rhun waved his brother over, as Avery was the most efficient at getting about unseen, thanks to his Otherworldly glamour.

Avery was stunned by his brother's sudden change in attitude. 'Need me,' he echoed as he wandered over, placing a hand on his heart to suggest that the shock was too much.

'You see that little stand on the corner over there.' Rhun pointed and Avery nodded. 'That's got to be a newspaper stand. I want you to go down there and ask the proprietor for today's paper.' Rhun manifested some cash and shoved it into his brother's hand, and then had another thought as he observed the clothing of his team. 'Ask him if he has any unisex fashion magazines, while you're at it.' Rhun then proceeded to project himself around the roof of the building, looking for the best place for Avery to descend to ground level.

As none of Rhun's team had ever been in this city before they couldn't simply will themselves forth. Rhun had taken the liberty of familiarising himself with the appearance of Ingram's private office, so that part of their quest would not prove a problem — he had acquired personal memories of the room from Doc Alexander.

The newspaper stand was within their sight, but the streets below were crammed with people and chances were that Avery would be seen manifesting if he teleported himself forth.

On the ground floor, along one side of the building, was a colourful array of decorative awnings, which Rhun suspected were shopfronts. 'Project yourself onto the top of the awning and then jump to street level from there.

'Got you,' Avery confirmed as he removed his weapons, eager to get amongst the people below.

Rhun grabbed hold of his brother to prevent his departure and clarify his orders. 'Come straight back.'

Avery assisted his brother to release him and then vanished. This sent all his teammates rushing to the edge to monitor his progress.

After touchdown on the awning, Avery stuck his head over the edge to take a look at the passing traffic to make sure he didn't land on anyone. Spying a group of young women approaching, he did a somersault and landed in their path. The ladies gave a shocked squeal, followed by excited giggles when Avery served the gaggle of young women a wink and a smile. 'A thousand apologies, ladies.'

'Wow, scuba man.' The most attractive of the girls stepped forward to confront Avery, who appeared to her to be wearing some kind of wetsuit. 'You have the most incredible eyes.'

'Why, thank you.' He accepted the compliment. They were forced to move along by the oncoming hordes. 'Yours are very pretty also.'

'What I mean to say is, I've never seen anyone with eyes that colour.' The young woman was completely charmed. Still, one of her girlfriends was displeased.

'Where do you get off, jumping from shop awnings in front of people like that?' the friend frowned.

Avery shrugged, as he came up with a simple explanation. 'It was a dare.'

'I think you're very daring.' The pretty woman took hold of Avery's arm to walk with him across the open part of the thoroughfare.

'Yeah.' The suspicious friend elaborated on her train of thought. 'We could have just pulled out a gun and shot you.'

'I am not afraid of death,' he retorted casually, which impressed the rest of the girls all the more.

'What the hell is he doing?' Rhun queried in a tone that implied he should have known better than to send Avery anywhere there were young females.

'That's what I'd like to know.' Fallon was quietly fuming.

'Avery can't help the fact that he's good looking,' Bast defended, having been blessed with beauty herself. 'Women are going to fall at his feet whether he's attached or not.'

'He could just as easily have avoided those girls,' Rhun argued, and Fallon gave a huff to agree with their commander on that point. 'It is Avery's choice how he uses his alluring quality.'

'That would be the pot calling the kettle black, wouldn't it?' Zabeel scoffed at Rhun's gall. 'I think the real reason you resent Avery so much is because he's too much like you! Coupled with the fact that he's more psychically gifted than the rest of us put together.'

Bast and Sparrowhawk applauded the theory.

'Maybe the reason he chatted up those girls,' Zabeel continued, 'was to enable him stroll across the plaza without looking suspicious ... it's called blending in with the locals.'

'All right.' Rhun granted that he might have misjudged the motive for Avery's shenanigans. 'Sorry,

Fallon,' he apologised for working her into a tizz. 'I know Avery is very fond of you and would never betray your trust.'

Fallon wasn't too positive about that, but she forced a smile in appreciation for the reassurance.

They watched as the gaggle of young women escorted Avery back to the awning, but he didn't appear to be carrying the paper and the magazine Rhun had ordered.

'Wasn't I specific enough?' Rhun muttered under his breath, and although he was a little agitated, he decided to reserve judgement until after he'd heard Avery's explanation.

Avery gave the pretty girl some cash, ahead of jumping up to grip the awning and swing his body back up and over the large canvas.

Avery manifested in front of his brother and handed him a small handheld device that had a viewing screen, a scroll button and zoom function, along with a couple of disks. 'They don't have the trees to waste on paper production these days. Everything is on disk.' He took one and shoved it in the top of the viewing mechanism. 'Those girls were very helpful.'

'I'll bet they were.' Fallon folded her arms, making her objection clear.

'A thousand apologies, darling heart,' Avery walked over and gave Fallon a kiss and a squeeze, 'but unfortunately, I'm not very good at chatting up men.'

Fallon gave an unsure smile, wanting to believe that his flirtations were just business. Avery took hold of both her shoulders to look her straight in the eye.

'You're the woman I'm going to marry. I shall remain true to you alone from this day forth, for so long as we both exist,' he impressed on her, whereupon all their teammates played up their shock at the surprise announcement.

'Is that a proposal, Pan man?' Bast, despite her differences with her sister, was amazed and overjoyed that Fallon had finally caught the elusive love of her life.

Fallon looked at Avery, suppressing her welling excitement until she heard his response.

'Why the hell not?' Avery decided, going down on one knee before Fallon. He manifested a ring inset with glistening Otherworldly stones, and held the token treasure up to her in offering. 'Would you do me, and all the inhabitants of the Otherworld, the very great honour of becoming my wife and their Queen?'

'Oh Avery ...' Fallon melted to her knees and kissed him. 'Yes.'

As Gazelle gasped back her welling emotions, all eyes turned her way. 'I'm sorry,' she wheezed with a sniffle, 'but I've never seen anything so romantic in all my born days.'

Bast conjured a handkerchief from the ethers, as she was standing closer to Gazelle than Sparrowhawk was. She handed the item to their newest team member with a sure smile. 'Hang around this lot long enough and you'll get used to it.'

Gazelle was surprised that Bast no longer seemed suspicious of her, but rather was downright friendly. Lahmu's word had had a positive effect on all of the

Chosen; their attitude towards her had altered, just as Sybil said it would. She felt suddenly trusted and accepted, which was enough to reduce her to tears once more.

'Today's the day, people,' Rhun advised as he finished reading the headlines. 'And I think I know why Viper picked today to knock Hayden Ingram off.' Rhun turned the viewer to face his audience and the headline read: 'Ingram to sell controlling interest in biodome. 'We've got two hours to prepare.'

Since Hayden Ingram had put his biodome shares on the market, he'd tripled the security on his private offices in the Ingram building. These rooms were the only place where he felt protected any more.

There had been several attempts on his life recently and the latest bout of death threats had spooked Hayden more than usual. For these had been found in places that only his son, close friends and personal bodyguards had access to. Each threat took the form of a hex and came in a box that usually contained something decomposing, be it a severed human body part or a small dead animal, and a voodoo doll, made to resemble Hayden, with pins and knives stuck through it. Sometimes there was even a poisonous snake, spider or scorpion inside. Normally such things were just water off a duck's back to this sharp businessman, but a growing suspicion that his son might somehow be involved was undermining his usual confidence.

Rainer had changed lately. As a teenager he'd been a loving and supportive son to Hayden, especially after the loss of his wife — Rainer's mother. But since his boy had turned twenty-one he'd become a little too keen on running the family business. In fact, Rainer had really been stepping on his father's toes, by arranging business dealings without his father's knowledge. When Hayden had tried to pull his son into line, Rainer's attitude towards Hayden chilled considerably. He went from being a bright and positive lad to a dark and moody character in the span of just a few weeks.

Now Hayden feared that Rainer was conspiring to have him murdered — or at least to force him into hiding or a mental asylum — so that Rainer could collect his inheritance and assume full control of Ingram's business dealings. Rainer had been none too keen on the idea of Ingram selling its controlling interest in the biodome and had argued the decision with Hayden ever since he'd suggested it at the board meeting. But now the fact was public knowledge there was nothing to be done about it. Hayden would sell and would only breathe easier once he had. He'd seriously considered writing his son out of his will, but having spent his whole life building a business empire to pass on to his boy, Hayden couldn't help but consider that his whole life would then seem something of a farce if he did.

All the large curtains in his office were drawn closed in an attempt to keep the outside world out. And to keep out the inhabitants of the biodome which was about to have a change in management.

The hourly news updates on the several television screens on Hayden's office wall were all leading with the Ingram story. None of the stations had managed to capture any film of him this morning, so they ran old footage. Even Rainer was keeping a low profile today.

With a soothing chime, the face of Hayden Ingram's lovely young secretary came up on the monitor on his desk. 'Your son and the rest of the board members are here to see you, Sir,' she announced, appearing a little overwhelmed. 'They're showing themselves in.' She shrugged apologetically.

'That's fine, Cindy.' Hayden didn't want an all-in brawl erupting. 'Tell security to let them through.'

Rainer came barging into his father's office, followed by the rest of the board members. 'The board have rethought their decision on the sale of our stake in the biodome,' Rainer took centre stage to oppose his father, 'and have unanimously voted against this sale.'

'Well, as the Chairman, don't you think I should have been present at the meeting?' Hayden remained seated to address the onslaught. He found it rather miraculous that Rainer had managed to suddenly convince all the company directors that the sale was a bad idea. Still, in the end, it was Hayden's money and he had final say.

'All those in favour of selling Ingram's interest in this city, raise your hands?' Rainer asked the directors and not one hand went up for the count. He turned his attention back to his father to appeal. 'If you would just hear what I have to say, father, I could convince you.'

'I'm sure you could.' Hayden was just as eager as his son was for them to speak together. No death threat was going to stop him from doing exactly as he saw fit with his own fortune. This time, Rainer had gone too far.

'If you gentlemen would be so kind ...' Rainer prompted the board members to retreat and, as though under some sort of spell, everybody left without saying a word. Rainer had been doing all the talking.

'Look, son, I know you see me as an old man with one foot in the grave, but I am not dead yet!' Hayden stood to voice his disapproval. 'Where did this sudden cut-throat desire to succeed come from?'

'You used to listen to my advice,' Rainer retorted, holding out his hand. A futuristic-looking handgun appeared out of thin air.

'You can't be serious,' his father scoffed, despite the magic trick. 'This room is monitored ... security will burst in here at any minute.'

'I don't think so.' Rainer grinned confidently. 'You know my friends have a way with computer systems, especially if they have access codes.'

Inwardly, Hayden was starting to panic, as security was obviously slow to respond. 'So, what is it you want me to do, Rainer?'

'Die,' Rainer requested, aiming the space-age weapon at his father. 'Heart attack,' he stated as his preference.

The sound of a weapon firing nearly gave the older Ingram heart failure, but it was his son who was hit when a light bullet shot forth from behind the thick curtains and stunned Rainer into a statue. Hayden breathed a sigh of relief, believing that his security had been on it after all, although their defensive measures were certainly something new. Then three unknown male persons emerged from behind the curtains of his supposedly impenetrable office. When one of the strangers began shooting at the video surveillance cameras in the office, the tycoon ducked for cover, and the gunman managed to take out every one of the cameras.

Hayden slowly raised himself from behind the desk. 'Who *are* you people?'

'I don't see why we had to wait here,' Bast grumbled at her lot as a female. She and Gazelle had been left to guard the roof, whilst Rhun, Sparrowhawk and Zabeel had gone to rescue Hayden Ingram. Avery and Fallon had gone to see if they could release Eli the elestial from the Aten before Viper got a whiff of their presence here and nicked off into the future.

'We were left behind in case anything goes wrong during the rescue.' Gazelle repeated their commander's reasoning. 'We have to have a plan and a team B.'

'I meant, why couldn't one of the men have stayed here, and I go on the mission?' Bast clarified her grievance. 'I never get to do any of the fun stuff.'

'Oh, I don't know,' Gazelle considered; she had a gun that shot golden Orme filled darts in one hand and her photon blaster in the other. 'The way I see it, we are the frontline of defence. If Viper did teleport himself down to Gaia's surface to find out what's going on in Ingram's office, he'd probably land here, on the roof.'

'You know me so well.' Viper's response startled both girls to an about-face, and in that blink of an eye Bast managed to draw and join Gazelle as she aimed at Viper. Their better judgement told the women to hold their fire, however, as a wall of Viper's people confronted them with their weapons drawn and aimed in their direction. 'This is an unexpected surprise. Fancy seeing Nugia's ruler, the Princess Bast, and my treacherous sister, *here*. I can see your ugly mush behind that pretty persona you're wearing, Gazelle.'

'I'm not a princess.' Bast drew his attention away from his sister, as she still feared Viper. Bast did not.

'Oh, but you fancy yourself as a princess all right,' Viper accused. 'But you won't once my lot get finished with you. You'll feel every bit the filthy little slut that you potentially are.' Viper faced the palms of his hands together and then slowly drew them apart — a dark ball of electrically charged energy erupted in between. Viper cast it at Bast and she vanished.

Gazelle wanted to fire at Viper so badly, but she knew she would not live to depart and warn the others. The new weapons carried by her kindred no doubt shot dark Orme darts — two hits and there would be no bringing her back to the land of the living, as her soul would be trapped in the sub-planes forever. 'What have you done with Bast?' Gazelle demanded instead.

'You really care about your new little group of friends, don't you?' He smiled, delighted that she now had a weakness to exploit. 'I've just sent the royal lioness on the road to her darkest destiny,' Viper taunted. 'I have a few associates who are in need of a little pussy.'

'Don't you dare harm her.' Gazelle was suddenly angered beyond belief; she would not allow the souls of the Chosen to be tarnished by the horrors she had known.

'That's a girl,' Viper encouraged her. 'Hate me, I know you want to.'

Gazelle recognised her brother's game, but she'd grown stronger since she'd seen him last and would not buy into it. With her heart racing in her chest, she conjured an image of her commander and vanished from Viper's sight.

'Well, I'll be damned,' Viper snarled, annoyed and secretly jealous. 'They made her one of them.'

Once Rhun had shot out all the surveillance cameras, he turned his attention back to the horrified tycoon. 'Just think of us as your personal bodyguards, Hayden.'

'But I have personal bodyguards! Have you been spying on my son? Who sent you?' Hayden spat out a couple of the numerous questions he wanted answered.

'Doc Alexander,' Rhun advised.

'But Doc Alexander is dead!' Hayden refuted the claim.

'Don't believe everything you read in the papers.' Rhun encouraged him to give them the benefit of the doubt.

'But even if Doc is still alive how did he know about my situation?' Hayden thought back to the 2020s and Doc's involvement with the holy man, Cadfan, who had made many accurate predictions. Perhaps the old diplomat had some new prophet in tow? Doc was almost considered a saint in this day and age and Hayden came to the conclusion that if his life wasn't safe in Doc's hands, he couldn't be protected.

'This isn't your son.' Rhun thought Hayden might appreciate being informed of this fact.

'What do you mean? Of course he's my son.' Hayden looked at the lad frozen stock-still in the middle of the room. 'I think I know my own boy when I see him.'

Rhun raised both eyebrows in question, and then transformed his persona to appear like Rainer. 'Still so sure about that, are you?'

Hayden gasped, recognising his son's voice. 'Who are you people? What are you?' The old man didn't know what to think.

'The truth is, Hayden,' Rhun transformed back to his true form, 'we are from the future.' He handed the tycoon a disk that was compatible with the computer systems of this day and age. Doc had recorded some of the information he'd collected on the demon dome's future — starting with the reports of Hayden's death. 'This might answer some of your questions as to why your preservation is so important.'

As Hayden sat down to view the information on the disk, Zabeel noticed their prisoner blink and so hit him with a stun bullet again. He stood observing the Leonine who was hidden inside the guise of Rainer, noting the dark aura that emanated from him — there was no doubt he was one of Viper's people.

Rhun conjured up a NERGUZ module and placed it around the prisoner's wrist. 'Contained,' he announced and the word locked the module onto his prisoner and bound him to do Rhun's bidding. This was one of the old modules, designed by Gibal for Marduk in order that renegade immortals could be controlled. The more recent version of the device allowed the subject to maintain their psychokinetic abilities and their free will, which would prove too great a risk on this mission. This older module was the same as those Viper had laid his hands on, and Rhun could only figure that the pirate had duplicated the technology by accessing the Lord Gibal's old files pertaining to the device, from the technologist's last laboratory located on board the Aten. 'You are not to remember anything said pertaining to Hayden or Rainer Ingram, their company, Viper, Mahaud, Lahmu or his senate. All the names of people and places you encounter or hear, will remain unknown to you. Do not leave my sight.' Rhun gave his final instruction.

Hayden was riveted to his computer until the presentation ended. He wanted to believe that these people were frauds and that the presentation he'd just seen was a well-constructed hoax, but in his heart he knew that God had just spared him from death for a very good reason. 'If this man is not my son,' the thought came as a great relief to him, and yet at the same time it caused a stabbing panic in his chest, 'where is Rainer? Is he still alive?'

'Let us find out.' Rhun turned to his prisoner. 'Please assume your true form and tell me your name.'

'My name is Horace.' The Leonine pirate manifested before Hayden and the shock cast the old tycoon back into his seat.

'Is this the product of genetic engineering in the future?'

'This race and many others are the product of the distant past,' Rhun explained politely. 'They were whisked away from Gaia before the great deluge. It was only Homo sapiens that were left to drown.'

'Whisked away by whom?' Hayden ventured to ask.

'A race of beings who no longer exist in the physical universe, and thus you need not concern yourself with them,' Rhun informed him.

'Well, actually,' Sparrowhawk corrected, 'if we've just gone back twenty years then you'd still be in the process of freeing the human races from Nefilim rule.'

'The Nefilim?' Hayden gasped, being a well-read man. 'As in the Bible?'

'Yes,' Rhun granted. 'Thank you, Sparrowhawk, for confusing the issue. Now,' his sights returned to their Leonine friend, 'tell us, Horace. Where is Rainer Ingram?'

'I don't know what Viper's done with him,' Horace replied.

'Who is this ... Viper?' Hayden demanded to know.

'We suspect he is the lead singer of Bloodlust,' Rhun said. 'However, as that band will not come to prominence until fifteen years from now, only Satan knows whose persona Viper is hiding behind at present.'

'Viper remains on the Aten,' advised the Leonine. 'He is studying the dark laws of nature under the tutelage of a witch, who has possessed the body of one of our more foul-minded females. Viper oversees his plans for Gaia from space and sends forth agents to do his bidding here on the surface.'

'Agents like you,' Rhun prompted.

'Viper's will is strong,' the Leonine defended; the NERGUZ prevented him from lying. 'I was compelled by Viper to follow him down the dark path to immortality and this is my service to the Prince of Darkness who gave me immortal life.'

'And all of your people have proven susceptible to dark Orme?' Rhun prayed they had not.

'There is only a handful of us who seem to generate enough evil intent and resentment to maintain this immortality. Everyone else has to be re-injected,' Horace concluded.

This was good news for their mission indeed. 'And which group do you fall into, Horace?'

'I am one of the handful,' he smiled, proud of the fact. 'My hatred made me whole again.' The Leonine gripped hold of his private parts. 'Keeps me whole.'

The Dragon's sons all looked at each other a second. 'We won't go there,' Rhun decided and his brothers both agreed.

The shock of the day's developments might have aged Hayden twenty years, but he suddenly felt filled with a great sense of purpose, the like of which he'd not felt since his boy had turned on him. Now Hayden knew that his son had not rebelled, but was being held hostage somewhere — or *worse* — he realised his boy needed him. 'Will you help me bring these demons to justice and find my son?'

'That is the whole reason why we came to your rescue, Hayden,' Rhun confirmed, sensing the hope rising in the tycoon. 'We shall find Rainer, hold no fear of that. But you must come with us, now. If Viper's people do have control of the systems in this building, they're bound to have been watching this office via those surveillance cameras I shot out, and they'll be sending some people to find out what's going on in here.'

'What have I got to lose?' Hayden answered, checking his watch. 'I should have died twenty minutes ago, so I guess destiny has freed up my schedule.'

As Gazelle manifested before Rhun, she locked a NERGUZ around her wrist. 'Viper's on the roof, we have to *leave*.'

'Where is Bast?' Rhun queried, as everyone present gathered in a circle and held hands.

'Viper has grown in power ... he did something to her and she vanished. I don't know where.' Gazelle struggled with the words to explain what she'd witnessed. 'Please, we must *leave*.'

'Lynn Cerrig Bach,' Rhun uttered, as he envisioned the entrance to Taliesin's Otherworldly abode, currently being inhabited by Doc Alexander.

Avery and Fallon had visited the Aten's Star Chamber before.

The shiny black floor reflected the stars, shining through the clear dome encompassing the entire chamber, which was so huge that one could not see the outside walls from the centre — the sea of stars just faded into black nothingness in all directions. A huge crystal chair marked the centre of the chamber; it sat atop a perfectly round set of stairs. These allowed access from any direction as the throne could rotate a full three hundred and sixty degrees. This crystal throne represented the head of the elestial crystal they were here to free.

As suspected, Avery and Fallon found the Star Chamber empty.

This was the heart of the time drive system of the Aten, and as Viper was not time hopping at present, it stood to reason that this control centre would not be in use. As Viper had no idea that Lahmu had sent a task force back into Gaia's past, the thief had not bothered to have the time throne guarded.

Avery scaled the stairs and took a seat on the crystal throne, placing both his hands face down on the solid arms to communicate with it. *Awaken Eli, the elestial, I have come to set you free.*

Fallon, who was standing at the base of the stairs, was given quite a start when the floor on which she stood began to retract carrying her with it, and the full form of the crystal arose to tower before her.

Young master, thank heavens you have come. I have been trapped … blackmailed!

'I know,' replied Avery, 'so let us get you out of here as quickly as possible. What must I do?'

Just will me free of the Aten, lord, Eli instructed eagerly.

A moment later the metal bonds that riveted the huge crystal to the ship withdrew and Eli was released from his nightmare.

Oh, thank you, lord, thank you, Eli stressed. *I know I have caused you much grief, thus your mercy is all the more appreciated.*

Avery flew back down to the floor, waving off the crystal's gratitude, when suddenly he was possessed by a vision of Bast fighting off many attackers. 'I think Bast is on the Aten,' he advised, sensing that she was close at hand.

'Yes, I feel her too.' Fallon seconded Avery's hunch.

'Eli take Fallon back to the Otherworld with you. I want both of you to wait for me at the Night Hunter's office,' he instructed, and the huge crystal swept Fallon up in his massive hand before she had the chance to protest.

'No! I'm coming with you,' she insisted, trying to break loose of Eli's grasp.

'I'll come for you soon, I promise.' Avery waved as Eli vanished with his fiancée and then focused his will on finding Bast.

Avery found himself in the master living quarters located beneath the Star Chamber. These chambers now seemed more like a public hotel than the private abode of a God.

There were several men of Leonine-Nefilim descent lying unconscious on the floor about him and Bast was showing off her psychic know-how and warrioress skills on the half a dozen men still conscious. Avery considered aiding her to fight off her attackers, but she seemed to be enjoying herself and so he waited in the wings until she'd downed the last man standing with a kick to his jaw.

'Did I say that I never get to do any of the fun stuff? Shame on me.' She taunted the moaning males around her, as Avery applauded her display.

'Why are you here?' Avery approached her to inquire.

'Viper has a new magic trick.' Bast shrugged. 'He sent me here. I suppose this lot were meant to intimidate me.' She cast her eyes over the carpet of bodies around them.

'They may have taken dark Orme, but their psychic and fighting skills are very underdeveloped.'

The exit door in the chamber opened and Lirathea floated into the room. Only it was not Lirathea who was wearing her body today, for underneath the facade was the dark, rotting presence of Mahaud, with eyes glowing as red as hot coals.

The problem was that Avery couldn't discern at this distance if the crone was projecting the persona of his sister, or if the witch had snatched his sister's physical body. 'You want me to believe that you could comfortably exist inside Lirathea's light-filled form,' he scoffed.

Maelgwn and Tory, having seen their other three sons safely to Lynn Cerrig Bach, had popped in to check on Avery's progress on the Aten and were horrified to see Mahaud sporting their daughter's body.

'Well,' replied the witch in her choir of guttural voices, 'she gave it up of her own free will, so I'm comfortable enough with the arrangement.' She slid her hands down over Lirathea's much admired form. 'What a shame your Falcon brother isn't here, eh?' She blew Avery a kiss as she massaged between her legs with both her hands, moaning with delight.

Bast, who was admittedly shocked by the witch's foul implications, looked Avery's way to find him fuming and having never seen him lose his cool, she gripped hold of him to prevent him doing anything rash. 'She's just baiting you.'

'I haven't been a virgin for eons.' The witch laughed at Avery's dismay. 'Never mind, Viper will just have to do the honours.'

Avery cut loose from Bast's hold, of the mind to attack the witch.

It's only a vehicle, Avery.

Lirathea? Avery calmed to communicate with her.

The witch can do me no true harm as I am immortal in body and soul. Mahaud may have my body right now, but my soul is standing right beside you.

'Lirathea?' Maelgwn willed to see their daughter, as did Tory. This latest development warranted an explanation.

Lirathea made her etheric form visible to her parents. 'Not now, father.' Her attention returned to Mahaud and her brother. 'I want you to leave, Avery,' she implored him.

'Still, it's not your sister that I am really after,' Mahaud advised.

'Wait, Avery.' Maelgwn overruled Lirathea's order. 'Let's see what she's up to.'

'I know what she's up to.' Lirathea overruled her father. 'Avery, leave!'

Avery found the argument in his head between his father and sister most disconcerting.

'If you tell me where that mother of yours is hiding out, I could let you have your sister's body back,' Mahaud proposed. 'Bear in mind that she has not yet died a mortal death and still feels in the mortal way.' The witch produced a handheld electric prod and held the live end to her breast a moment.

Lirathea shrieked as she felt the impact and Avery heard her pained cry echo through his mind.

Tory and Maelgwn rushed to Lirathea's side, helpless to ease her suffering.

'Tell her to nominate a place and I shall leave my vacated body there for her,' Tory advised her son.

Mother? Avery was nearly shocked into querying her presence aloud. *When did you arrive?*

'If Lirathea is harmed in any way the deal is off.' Tory kept Avery focused. 'Please tell her.'

'No, mother,' Lirathea objected. 'Only whilst your body rests in the outer court of Shamballa can you fulfil your quest for the Masters as a muse. If Mahaud takes over your body you shall be bound to the same time and dimension that she occupies.'

'Will Mahaud take my body?' Maelgwn requested Avery to ask.

'Then, in order to fuck him I'd have to fuck myself,' the witch laughed at the suggestion. 'I want Tory Alexander and then that playmate of hers will be my toy boy, anyway. Your father owes me and I intend to see that he pays.'

'My father will see right through you, Mahaud,' Avery stated, very sure about that.

'Where I intend to take him, my sweet, the Dragon won't care.' Again she chuckled, obviously impressed by her secret designs.

'Sounds like we're in for a real treat.' Maelgwn looked to his wife to check her resolve.

'Arrange a place, Avery,' Tory instructed her son. 'Then you and Bast meet us back at Taliesin's. I have a few ideas to toss about.'

In the entrance foyer to Taliesin's labyrinth, Rhun and party were relieved beyond belief to have Bast returned to them safely and Gazelle was astounded that Bast had flattened her brother's feline thugs.

Rhun, however, was greatly alarmed to learn his youngest sister had relinquished her body to Mahaud.

'What the hell were you thinking?' He directed the query at his sister's etheric form, which had manifested alongside those of his parents.

It was the only way I could find out what the witch was up to, Lirathea explained to everyone.

'And what have you discovered?' Rhun awarded her the benefit of the doubt.

I know why Mahaud wants mother's body so badly. Lirathea looked at her mother, sorry to say it: *She is a past-life incarnation of you that never returned to your higher self.*

'I don't believe it,' uttered En Noah, whom no one had noticed arrive on the scene.

'What are you doing here?' Rhun queried, hoping nothing else had gone wrong at home.

'I had to pick up the chariot I left on the Aten, to ensure Viper didn't find it.' The Sage waved off the explanation, and approached the spirit forms present, remaining focused on Tory. 'Mahaud called you her Chosen incarnation, but I did not want to believe her.'

Tory was emotionally detached from the situation and so could consider the news rationally, without feeling insulted, disgusted, guilty or horrified. 'How did I become so wretched?'

Only you can find that out, Lirathea told her mother. *And if you do, we can truly put an end to Mahaud, by going back in time and making sure she never comes to exist in the first place.*

'Ancient time travel.' Rhun rubbed his hands together, very keen on the idea. 'Now that's what I call an adventure.'

'But why is stealing the body of her own incarnation so important to Mahaud?' Sparrowhawk posed, curious.

Because it would be like regaining control of her own body, Tory replied, having already had this conversation with Lirathea, to whom she returned her attention. *How did you find out about this?*

Mahaud confided in Viper and told him about her desire to steal your body. Lirathea turned Maelgwn's way and delivered the news as gently as possible. *Mahaud claimed that father set her on the dark path when he deserted her.*

I would never desert you, Maelgwn told his wife, with certainty.

Tory nodded, knowing he spoke the truth. *Something went horribly amiss somewhere.*

'It does seem to explain why Mahaud is so dark on the Dragon, however,' Noah conceded.

Do you have any idea at what period in history this sad episode unfolded? Tory inquired of her daughter.

No, Lirathea was sorry to say. *Although I did find out one piece of information that could prove helpful. Mahaud was the name given to this entity by Shamash when he cursed her, as it means 'mighty battle maid'. But before her terrible trial took place she was known as Electra, which means 'shining, brilliant'.*

'Electra was also the name of one of the seven holy daughters of Atlantis,' Noah added for everyone's information. 'She did not escape the sinking of the continent as she became caught up in the murder of the

365

ruler of Chailidocean. Her sisters went on to establish great races of people all over the new lands beyond their submerged continent. The faintest star in the Pleiades is named after Electra, for it was her prophecy that saved the life of her sisters and indeed the spiritual wellbeing of mankind.'

Tory was absolutely stunned by Noah's claim. *If we are talking about the same Electra, then how was her character so grievously altered as to become Mahaud? I must get close to her and find out,* Tory resolved and began formulating a plan. *There must be a way to reverse my immortality, so that when Mahaud enters my body, she won't pose such a threat.*

She'll shoot you full of dark Orme and try and turn you to her path. Maelgwn could see their eternal life together slipping further and further away.

I am not afraid to face whatever it is she's running away from, Tory told him in all honesty, *for clearly we cannot hope to ascend before we reclaim this missing part of ourselves. There must be a way for me to get back in control of my body and trap Mahaud in there with me.*

Gazelle, unused to dealing with the witch, was appalled by the idea. 'Why would you want to do that?'

So as to probe her memory and discover the exact time and place her tragedy unfolded. Tory looked to Rhun. *So that you can go save her. Us,* she added as an afterthought. Tory could not simply do a past-life regression, as Mahaud had never returned to their higher self. Therefore, via regression she could not recollect the details of this lifetime. *With Mahuad out of existence, Viper's position in our home dimension and time will be weakened considerably.*

'And hopefully, that will aid Gaia's future too,' Doc advised, having viewed the information his future self had sent back for Hayden Ingram to view.

Hayden, who was standing beside Doc, nodded meekly to agree with the theory, although due to the Otherworldly spirits with whom they were conversing and the nature of the conversation, the business tycoon could not bring himself to speak.

Tory suddenly gasped, excited by a theory she was considering. *If Mahaud can give a physical being a charm that allows her to control their will, and if I were to be wearing such a charm on my person when she enters my body —*

'Then she,' Noah cut in, excited by the theory, 'as the occupant of the body, would be forced to do your bidding.' He nodded, thinking this a sound basis for a plan.

But doesn't the wearer of such a charm have to willingly accept the amulet and put it on? Maelgwn queried.

I will, Tory assured, *right before I vacate my body.*

Maelgwn frowned, not as certain the trick would work.

'I know what you're saying,' Noah granted Maelgwn his point, 'but perhaps we can devise a spell that will enable Tory to put her body under a kind a self-induced hypnosis.' Everyone looked at Noah and grinned, impressed by his suggestion; even Maelgwn raised his brow.

'Better still, I shall be the hypnotist,' Maelgwn informed them.

* * *

The crone had advised Avery that she wanted Tory's body left at the King's Men stone circle.

Noah carried out his mission to retrieve the chariot from the Aten without incident. He then brought the time hopping transport to Doc's Otherworldly abode in 2108AD Gaia time, as that was where Tory and Maelgwn's physical forms still resided in the outer Court of Shamballa. Noah would then provide the couple the means to join their kindred in the past. Everyone else from Kila awaited Tory and Maelgwn's return in Doc's Otherworldly labyrinth in the year 2088AD Gaia time.

Since she was being detoured from musing duties, Tory thought she'd best explain herself to her guardian in this affair, the Master DK. Meanwhile, Maelgwn would seek out the Count to explain their intentions. Tory also wished to question DK on the matter of switching off her immortal gene. She knew this was possible with dark Orme, as they had rendered the Nefilim goddess Aya mortal thus, but would such an act be frowned upon by her Logos and his minions, who had gone to such pains to make her one of the Chosen by filling her being with divine light?

Tory's etheric spirit joined the Master Djwhal Khul on a grassy mountainside on the borders of Tibet, overlooking the Lamasery over which DK resided as Abbot.

'Greetings, Tory Alexander.' He acknowledged her arrival before turning to address her. 'You have made a discovery.'

Yes I have, she admitted, *although not a very pleasant one, I'm afraid.*

He smiled to reassure her. 'Only by experiencing all-that-is do we truly come to understand and emulate the Logos. If you think something is unpleasant or a waste of energy, that is a judgement and the divine never judges.'

I believe Mahaud may have sprung from something one of my incarnations did during the fall of Atlantis. Tory got straight to the point.

'And now that it seems Armageddon is again upon you, you think there might be a connection?' The way DK asked the question, it seemed as if he knew there was.

Is there? Tory hadn't even conceived of this premise. *I thought that the time of the Gathering was the event that Armageddon predicted.*

'The battle of Armageddon is waged within each and every being during every thought of each and every lifetime. For within the righteous ones is the memory of an ancient anger and hatred that you bore for those who once had power over you, and still do have control over humanity to a large extent.'

Are you talking about the Nefilim? Tory had a funny feeling that he wasn't.

'No,' DK advised in all seriousness. 'I'm talking about the Dark Lodge of the Materialistic. The Lords of the Dark Face, the Men in Black.'

Tory gasped with shock as the connection between the Dark Lodge of old Atlantis and a secret agency that was rumoured to exist on modern day Gaia was made known to her.

'I advise you not to jump to any conclusions about these beings, for that would be a judgement,' DK warned. 'It is up to you to bring about a shift in the sands of time yet again, safe in the knowledge that you have learned much from the Nefilim debacle. When an entity next comes to you voicing hatred and a desire to control your life, what shall be your response? What interaction on your behalf will change the tides of time and evolution?'

Love? Tory ventured.

'And non-judgement,' DK added in reminder, and Tory nodded, believing she understood his point. 'Dwell on your warrior past, Tory Alexander. Every time you saw good people and nations destroyed by the hatred and greed of a jealous, greedy, warlike race, did you not think ... here they go again? When will they ever learn? Why must they destroy in this manner?' DK emphasised the frustration of such instances and Tory found herself nodding in agreement with the master. Then DK smiled, having led her into a trap. 'If you did ask these questions, you were judging your fellow man who, like you, is struggling to learn as you are learning. The souls of these warlike peoples stem from the Orion system. These beings struggle to understand love. The only way they can express their attraction is through war and conquering. Still, they are you, as much as your soul-mate is you. You will just be one with your soul-mate sooner, that is all.'

Tory's eyes were again wide with wonder. Although she knew how the human body had been perfected she'd never pondered where the soul-minds had originated. She'd certainly never considered that the differing attitudes, and levels of awareness, of mankind's races was due to their soul-minds originating in different star systems. *And from what planet did my soul group derive?*

'I believe you already know the answer to that question,' DK teased and Tory's jaw dropped a moment before she voiced her guess.

From the Pleiades?

'Originally,' DK nodded. 'But the remnants of that civilisation only exists on the causal plane of awareness these days. You've also incarnated on other planets, some in this very solar system.' As Tory fell quiet, pondering all that had been said, DK continued: 'It is a wise move to regress to a mortal body to face your alter-ego. This will be considered by the Logos as a great act of courage and sacrifice.'

Tory caught the master's meaning, for she had been told that the fourth initiation of Shamballa involved sacrifice. *This is to be my crucifixion.* Now she understood DK's explanation of Armageddon.

'The gift of sacrifice is harmony,' DK offered his viewpoint, having endured the initiation his student was about to face, 'and beyond this trial, the second door of Shamballa that leads to the central city, will open to you and grant you its gift of enlightenment.'

Tory smiled sincerely, thankful for DK's inspiration and then went straight-faced as she considered her next move. *So I must take the dark Orme,* she assumed.

'Heavens, no.' DK faked a stressed tone, to imply how severe he thought the suggestion to be. 'The Water of Life shall grant your desire.'

The Water of Life? Tory frowned. *Wasn't that the ancient's name for gold Orme?*

'No, no, you're confusing it with the Fountain of Eternal Youth,' DK corrected. 'There are three sacred

371

fountains that flow in Shamballa, the third being the Fountain of Rejuvenation, the waters of which you've been refreshed by in the past.' He nudged her memory. 'The Water of Life will deactivate the immortal gene in your body without exposing you to the dark side of creation — as Orme Charichalum would — and allow Mahaud more command over you.' DK handed her a tiny phial containing a glowing blue substance. 'Do what you must, with the blessing of the Logos.'

Tory accepted the instrument of her physical death from the master, seeing it for the great treasure it was — her ticket to the ultimate union. *And what of my musing responsibilities?*

'They can wait,' DK told her calmly. 'Time is an illusion, after all.'

Willing herself forth to her physical form, Tory woke in her body as if she'd merely been dreaming her time as a muse, and yet the phial DK had given her was in her hand. Her head felt too heavy to move, but Tory adjusted to being earthbound quickly and rolled over to see Maelgwn sitting on the far side of the Tablet on which they'd lain together. In his hand was a phial of the same glowing blue substance, which he held up in cheers to her before swallowing the liquid down. 'No!' Tory leapt up in an attempt to stop him drinking the potion, but she was too late. 'There is no need for you to suffer too.'

'You don't go anywhere without me.' He forced out the words through gritted teeth as the great weight of his mortality came over him. When the pain stopped increasing, Maelgwn looked up at Tory, who was hugging him close in an attempt to comfort his transition. 'Am I old?' he asked, fearful that he now appeared his age, which was well over a hundred years.

Tory chuckled at his fear. 'You don't look a day over thirty.'

'Really?' He sounded surprised, daring to sit up straight and stretch his aching bones. 'It sure feels like I'm a hundred.'

Tory grinned at his moaning as she had not heard him whine so in a long time. She then took a deep breath to rouse her own courage. 'We're going to die, you know?'

'I know,' Maelgwn replied. 'And you know the only thing that perturbs me about us departing this world?' He took Tory by the hand.

Tory's emotions suddenly caused her eyes to flood with tears, for she did know his grievance. 'Your lovely person shall perish and I shall never again hold you, or touch you.' Tory stole the opportunity to do so now.

'Aye,' Maelgwn squeezed her in return, 'but then I take comfort in knowledge that, when it is all over, I shall have your soul to embrace.'

15

INSIDE THE ALTER EGO

At Doc's Otherworldly abode in the past, Rhun, Zabeel and Bast were utilising their free time to question their prisoner about Viper and the whereabouts of Hayden Ingram's son. Unfortunately, Horace didn't know much.

'Why were you chosen to impersonate Rainer?' Rhun queried, having gotten nowhere with his other questions.

'Just lucky, I guess,' Horace replied with a good serve of cynicism, before stating what he knew. 'Viper is assured that I will stay faithful to his dark cause. Dark Orme keeps me whole only so long as I am in the service of the Dark Lodge.'

'Yes, you said that before.' Zabeel recalled they'd decided not to pursue the issue. Still, it did seem pertinent. 'Please explain.'

'Viper called me to his cause as a mortal.' Horace glanced at Bast, the only female present, and then returned his gaze to Rhun and Zabeel. 'He had some of his thugs remove my privates and rather than be a sexless freak among freaks, I chose to take the dark Orme and serve the cause of the crone. The dark Orme made me whole again.' Horace smiled at the agonised expressions on his captors' faces. He then looked to Bast, who appeared discomforted by his gaze now. 'How about helping me test the new equipment, sweetheart? You're not one of mine, but you'll do.' He stuck out his tongue and began wiggling it in her direction.

'You'd have to earn it, my lovely,' she teased, in a seductive tone. Bast neared Horace and straddled the seat in which he sat to sit upon his lap. 'And so far, you've not done me any favours.'

As Horace raised his hands to touch Bast, Rhun forbade the prisoner his intent, so the Leonine continued to communicate his desire with his free moving tongue.

Bast gripped both sides of the prisoner's face firmly and stared deep into his eyes that were glazed by a dark shadow. 'Don't delude yourself, my friend. You are the victim in this scenario. There is no point in trying to deflect your fear onto me as that won't aid your cause. We are here to help you.'

'I don't want to be helped,' he replied coldly.

'Then you shall never truly be whole,' Bast concluded and climbed off him.

The prisoner was obviously stunned by Bast's approach and as she seemed to have caught him off guard rather nicely, Rhun handed over the prisoner's NERGUZ control module to her. 'I'll leave him in your very capable hands, Bast.'

'Bast!' exclaimed the prisoner, his mood darkening again, for the module had removed what little untrained psychic ability he had. To Horace, Bast appeared to be a Homo sapiens and he'd not suspected her to be the leader of the Leonine people whom he despised with a vengeance.

'Very good,' Bast told Rhun, ignoring the prisoner. 'Good luck with the exchange.'

As soon as Rhun and Zabeel departed, Bast assumed her true form and turned back to the prisoner. 'I am Bast, so state your grievance, Horace.'

'My injury was your fault!' Horace spoke through gritted teeth.

'Was it now?' Bast couldn't imagine how he'd reached this conclusion. 'How so?'

'Am I, and my kind, not every bit as much a Leonine as you are?' he prompted.

'Yes, Horace,' she replied reasonably.

'Then why is it that you rule on Nugia and I was outcast and condemned to a life amongst butchers and whores!' He demanded an answer.

'Your people chose to remain segregated from the rest of the tribes, Horace. Lahmu offered you sanctuary on any of the planets he rules, bar Numan,' she pointed out.

Horace burst into tears and shook his head. 'And how would we have been looked upon by the citizens of Nugia? It's all right for *you* ... *you* are one of the *Chosen Ones*, bringing the traits of that mighty race to your people. But I carry the Nefilim gene pool within me, the essence of the greatest known oppressors of mankind!'

'The Nefilim had their good points, too, like intelligence for example —'

'Nobody wants to know about a relationship with an Antichrist!' He cut her off. 'And especially not one who is no longer even capable of consummating a relationship.'

'That is your own impression of yourself, Horace. Cordella and Gazelle have faced the truth about themselves and made good of their lives,' Bast reminded him firmly, but with compassion. 'So don't give me that outcast crap. You isolated yourself, just as you are doing now, as we speak. The way of the righteous is to trust —'

'The way of the righteous will reduce me to half a man,' Horace snarled.

'That's where you are wrong! Become whole in spirit and mind, and the body will surely follow,' Bast argued. 'Joining the ranks of the Chosen will make you whole, just as surely as the Dark Path, but you must let go of all the anger and resentment, the desire to control and repress —'

'And what is this you are doing to me, if it is not control and repression? Are you trusting me?' As his tears of pent-up anger flowed freely, Horace felt his heart lightening and his private parts shrinking away. 'I hate you,' he yelled, not quite as passionately as he would have liked, as he was weakening to her influence.

Bast noted his appearance physically ageing, which was a positive sign, as it meant the effect that dark Orme had over his heart was lessening. 'Soon I will be able to award you such trust,' Bast assured him, 'but there is still much darkness in you.'

'So why don't you shoot me with the good stuff and sweeten me to your cause, bitch?'

Bast slowly shook her head. 'It wouldn't have a lasting effect. You'd return to the dark path eventually and then we'd be right back where we started. Only you can reverse your selfish cause to a selfless one.'

'Look, I don't know where Rainer Hayden is, so why don't you just leave me the fuck alone?' he suggested rudely, concerned that he would not be able to resist her beauty, her patience and caring.

'It's not Rainer we are looking for any more, is it, Horace?' She grabbed a seat and straddled it, to lean on the back and concentrate on the prisoner. 'Let us discuss where you went.'

When Noah arrived in the past with Tory and Maelgwn, their family and friends were thrilled to see them. All of the Dragon's sons lined up to give their parents a squeeze and although the lads did not realise it would be the last time they would hold their parents thus, Tory and Maelgwn were making the most of the moment.

When the family reunion had calmed down, Rhun, who was rather good at hypnotism, guided his father in putting Tory under.

'When next I say the word "confide", you shall fall into a deep trance. Your body and mind will be subject to my will alone until such time as I bid you go in peace.' Maelgwn outlined their arrangement. 'Nod if you understand.'

A sigh of relief was heard from all those present as Tory nodded her head. Satisfied, Maelgwn clicked his fingers and his wife awoke.

'You didn't make me impersonate a duck, did you?' she joked as she regained her perspective.

'Tempting,' Maelgwn smiled, 'but no.'

'So you and I are right to proceed?' Tory concluded as she rose from her seat.

'We are going with you,' Rhun insisted on behalf of all his brothers.

'No need.' Doc came forward and placed a chain bearing a medallion around the Dragon's neck. 'Concealed in the pendant is a mike and camera. We can view the event from here. If anything goes wrong, you can all be there in the blink of an eye.'

'We don't want to put the crone off by having a large force present,' Maelgwn explained, examining the pendant that was a replica of the Dragon medallion he'd once worn in ancient Gwynedd.

'But psychic phenomena always interferes with electronic transmissions.' Rhun became rather edgy, as he sensed there was something his parents weren't telling him.

Doc shook his head. 'We won't have that problem with Taliesin's equipment,' he assured. 'It's still way ahead of its time.'

Maelgwn could tell that Rhun still wasn't comfortable with the plan. 'I need to speak with Mahaud alone,' he said, to justify their decision.

Rhun knew his mother had regressed to a mortal being for the sake of the mission and although she still radiated the light of a divine being she had the weary look of a mortal about her — his father, too. 'You're not immortal any more, are you, father?'

'No,' he replied simply, and all his boys were plainly horrified by the news.

'You won't have a hope in hell if Viper turns up.' Rhun knew he was stating the obvious, but what were his parents thinking of?

'Thanks for the vote of confidence.' Maelgwn brushed off his son's concern with humour. 'May I remind you that I fought several major battles before I was immortal, two of which involved Mahaud.'

'And may I remind you that your second confrontation with her killed you!' Rhun insisted that his father take the threat more seriously.

'And yet here I am,' Maelgwn concluded in good cheer, and seeing Rhun's annoyance he resolved to be more serious. 'I have a feeling Mahaud will be keeping this exchange to herself. I doubt she has told Viper of how powerful she expects to become with the acquisition of your mother's form. Your mission to the past is of vital importance. Once you know the date, destination and details of Electra's plight, I want you to go back to her aid, no matter what events are unfolding here in the present. Your mission to the past will alter everything here, so there is no point in worrying about us. Understand?'

Rhun nodded to concede the validity of his father's reasoning.

Noah approached and gave Maelgwn a talisman. 'Once Tory's spirit has abandoned her form, place this charm around Tory's waist, where it will not been seen. Once Mahaud has entered Tory's body, this talisman will bind her spirit to the mortal form and prevent her departing the body ... just in case Mahaud discovers Tory's depleted state before you have the chance to command her into a trance. King Solomon swore by the amulet's power.'

'Then that's good enough for me,' Maelgwn granted. 'I thank you for your pains in research.'

'Research has always been a pleasure in Taliesin's library,' Noah admitted, feeling no thanks were required. 'I await your speedy return.' The smile of the Sage faded, for Noah had that awful premonition again as he bid Maelgwn and Tory farewell. He foresaw that he would never again shake the Dragon's hand or sit in wondrous discussion of the greater mysteries with the woman who had changed his life. The knowledge caused a great sadness to well in his throat and heart, but for the sake of their relatives present, Noah merely waved the couple goodbye as Doc teleported them to the prearranged place of exchange. *You are my greatest friends and inspiration*, he thought, although he knew that having forfeited their Chosen abilities Tory and Maelgwn would not hear him. *I shall miss you as long as I live.*

Doc had transported the couple to a spot within walking distance of the meeting place, although it was out of view of the stone circle.

They ensured that they arrived early for the exchange, to give Tory the chance to vacate her body. She already had Noah's talisman hidden beneath her attire. All Maelgwn had to do was fasten it around her waist once Tory's spirit had left her form.

'Power to you,' said Doc and immediately vanished to avoid being spotted and raising suspicions, for anyone in the know would wonder why the couple needed another of the Chosen kind to teleport them to their destination.

Tory sat down to prepare to vacate her physical form and Maelgwn knelt down beside her to provide a pillow for her head — he would carry her soulless body the rest of the way.

'Well ...' She drew a deep breath and savoured her last few moments of being able to experience with her physical senses — the sound of the wind rushing over the barren plains; the smell of the warm, dusty air; the feeling of great expectation and an aching in her heart; the sight of Maelgwn's loving face and the taste of his kiss. 'I've truly loved this life,' she told him, 'thanks for sharing it with me.'

'The best is yet to come,' he told her, and as a tear threatened to escape his eye Maelgwn held her close and kissed her repeatedly.

Tory smiled as she eased herself away from her beloved, a little tearful herself, but pushed for time. 'I'll see you *out there*.' She rolled her eyes to refer to invisible space and then laid down to chant her soul out of her body.

It is done, Maelgwn heard Tory advise in his thoughts, at which time he fastened Noah's charm around her waist and then gathered her body up into his arms.

Across country Maelgwn carried his wife's limp form. He knew that everyone, themselves included, would greatly profit from their sacrifice. Then it struck him as a little selfish to consider what they were doing as a sacrifice, for they had to take responsibility for the advent of Mahaud. If they could reconcile the renegade incarnation with their higher self, then they would be simply undoing the karma that they had originally created. Maelgwn had to admit he was curious to learn about the role he'd played in Electra's undoing.

When he reached the King's Men stones Maelgwn noticed that the implements of dark magic had been positioned in front of torches that marked the four cardinal points. The torches were not alight at present, but still Maelgwn was not fool enough to enter the circle. He lay Tory's body down well away from the stones.

Mahaud, in the form of Lirathea, manifested in the centre of the circle. 'I want that inside the circle, pretty boy,' she advised in a choir of satanic voices.

The dark cloud cover that eternally covered this part of the world began to twirl into a turbulent vortex above the witch.

'You have the power to drag it in, surely?' Maelgwn proffered. 'Lirathea's body for Tory's, that was the deal. I was not part of the bargain and so I have no intention of entering your sphere.'

'It is no surprise to me that you would readily exchange your love to save your own skin ... nothing really changes, now does it, Dragon? Have it your way.'

Mahaud willed Tory's body to rise and as it sped past Maelgwn he gripped an arm. 'Not so fast. I want Lirathea within arm's reach when you depart.'

'I've been tricked by you before.' The witch raised her hand and zapped Maelgwn with lightning shot from her fingertips. He let Tory go and as her body entered the witch's circle the torches burst into flame. 'No more favours.'

Damn, thought Maelgwn, unsure if the witch's circle of fire would prevent him from triggering the hypnotic suggestion they'd implanted in Tory's brain.

It will be all right, whispered Tory, and Maelgwn trusted her word.

The black and red mist of Mahaud's spirit streamed out of his daughter's mouth, nose and ears and into Tory's body.

As soon as her form was vacated, Lirathea took control of her body and finding it rather heavy after her time as a spirit, she stumbled several times in her attempt to reach the circle's circumference. She tried willing herself out of there, but inside the witch's circle she had no power.

'Where do you think you're going?' Mahaud raised Tory's arm and drew Lirathea back towards her.

A big wind arose from nowhere and blew out the torches, whereupon the witch lost all power over Lirathea.

Will yourself to your brothers this instant, Tory instructed her daughter, who vanished.

'What's going on?' Mahaud snarled as she re-ignited her torches, somewhat annoyed to have lost her other captive.

'You may have possession of my wife's body, but her spirit is free to do as it pleases,' Maelgwn stated in a provocative tone, as he realised Tory was responsible for freeing Lirathea.

'Not for long,' Mahaud claimed confidently. 'I know a few unfriendly spirits who shall see to her.'

Again a wind arose to extinguish the torches and Maelgwn stepped into the circle. '*Confide* in me,' Maelgwn urged the crone, whereupon she fell immediately into a trance. 'I want to talk about Electra.'

'Electra?' Mahaud hissed as the four torches burst into flame once more and startled Maelgwn.

Apologies, that was me, Tory bethought her husband. *Now we have the circle fortified with our energies, it is safe to proceed.*

'Sit.' Maelgwn bade his subject do as he did. Tory's form took a seat on the ground in front of him. 'Who was Electra? I want the date, by the modern calendar, of when she perished?'

'Electra was the second daughter of Agamemnon, the last true ruler of Atlantis,' Mahaud replied, and although her numerous devilish voices sounded rather sedated, her eyes of burning red coals were daunting. 'The demise of the last small portion of the great island continent of Atlantis coincided with Electra's damnation. They both perished on the summer solstice of 9564BC.'

Viper had worked himself into a complete state. He was being thwarted on every front.

The time hopping crystal had been stolen from the Star Chamber. Bast had flattened his immortal warriors and vanished. His agent on Gaia, who had been doing such a fine job of impersonating Rainer Ingram, had been kidnapped, although Viper had sent another agent to the surface to take Horace's place. They may not have killed Hayden Ingram, but his disappearance was working to their advantage just as well, because the sale of the biodome had been prevented. But the disaster that most concerned Viper was that of Mahaud vanishing, along with the body of the oracle, Lirathea, which Viper had aided the witch to seize.

Mahaud had claimed that if she couldn't have Tory Alexander's body, or the body of Lahmu's daughter, then she would settle on destroying the angelic soul of the Dragon's youngest daughter. Viper had wondered why the crone persisted in possessing the bodies of the Chosen Ones, when their light filled body only caused her hardship in having to reverse the process and fill it with darkness. He'd suggested to the crone that the body of one of his Dark Ones would complement her nature more readily, to which Mahaud had replied: 'There is nothing so wretchedly pleasing as to corrupt the soul of the incorruptible.'

Now Viper was beginning to suspect that Mahaud had an ulterior motive for seizing the body of the Dragon's daughter. And as Mahaud hadn't mentioned her additional reasons to him, Viper naturally assumed that the crone was out to betray him.

Mahaud and Viper had created a room of summons, where they could call upon the knowledge and power of the Lords of the Materialistic. On the floor, they inset a Charichalum hex mark engraved with ancient symbols of the Dark Lodge. In the centre of this circle was a screen, where the secret symbol of any fallen lord could be projected. The spirit was forced to answer the call and support the cause of whomever summoned it forth.

Viper was of the mind to perform such a summons and find out what the witch was up to, but he discovered the evil utensils required for his conjuring were missing, just like Mahaud.

'Now I've got you,' he mumbled, pleased by this discovery. He'd expected the crone to pull a stunt like this later rather than sooner, but never mind, Viper had placed a homing device beneath the huge cauldron, just in case. 'Dick me, would you, witch? We'll see about that.'

Viper took one of his reconnaissance vessels to track down the cauldron that was pinpointed on the surface of Gaia.

'I should have known.' Viper observed the King's Men stone circle in close up on one of his vessel's soft-light screens. As the Dragon was having a civil conversation with Tory Alexander, who had clearly been claimed by Mahaud, it was quite obvious to Viper that the witch had got herself in a spot of bother.

'Do you want us to blast the site, Lord Viper?' asked his tactician, who had targeted the site with their ship's missile launcher.

'Presently.' Viper placed his hand on the PKA control plate and issued his command to turn up the volume of the conversation he was viewing on the screen.

'My lord, our thrusters will be churning up the cloud around us,' his pilot advised. 'Our presence probably won't go unheeded for long.'

'I have them in my sights,' Viper pointed out. 'At the first sign of suspicion, we shall blast the Dragon, his spouse and that treacherous witch into the next life. Until then, shut up the lot of you ... listen and learn.'

In the room of hexagons in Taliesin's Otherworldly labyrinth, Rhun's team stood observing the situation unfolding at the King's Men stones.

Lirathea's narrow escape from the witch had had them all alarmed for a moment, but the Dragon's sons were greatly relieved when their sister joined them at their Otherworldly hideout.

'How are they doing?' Lirathea hugged Avery, Sparrowhawk and Zabeel briefly, then made for the screen.

'Fine,' Avery assured her. 'Now,' he added to imply they had been worried for a second there.

'Shhh!' Rhun urged them all. 'I need to hear this.'

'I'd like Mahaud to move aside a moment and allow me to speak with Electra directly.' Maelgwn continued his discourse with the lost soul inhabiting his wife's body. 'Can you speak with me, Electra?'

'I have nothing to say to you,' replied the subject in Tory's own voice, although she spoke in the language of the ancient Atlanteans.

This utterance caused butterflies to begin fluttering in the pit of Maelgwn's stomach; it was as if her voice, coupled with this dialect, triggered some deeper recognition in him. For, although he was no longer immortal, Maelgwn still recalled the ancient dialect very well. 'So you recognise me?'

'Yes, I recognise you.'

As she glared deep into his eyes, Maelgwn noted that the deep red eyes of the crone had faded and been replaced by Tory's own violet ones.

'Your face has been scorched upon my memory,' she said with deep malice. 'I shall never forget you, Prometheus.'

'Prometheus?' Maelgwn uttered the name and was blinded by a vision of a red skinned people laying siege to the city of the golden gates.

He, Prometheus, of the fair skinned race of tall Atlanteans that ruled Atlantis, was leading the attack. *If you find the sorcerer kill him!* Prometheus yelled as he charged over the innermost bridge that led to the palace and the high temple of Chailidocean.

'I recall a battle ... against a sorcerer.' Maelgwn relayed.

'That would be Aegisthus, who, with a little help from me and a lot of help from my mother, was my father's murderer.' Electra hung her head as she recalled the shameful circumstance.

'Why did you aid the murder of your father,' Maelgwn probed gently, 'when it so obviously grieves you?'

'I did not know that my father was to be cursed with the summons of my design,' she shot back at Maelgwn in her own defence. 'I was plagued by nightmares for years, because I was foolish enough to trust my own mother.'

'What were your nightmares about?' He skirted around the subject.

'The destruction of my civilisation,' she replied, raising her eyes to look Maelgwn in the eye once more. 'I foresaw fire, flood, war, death ... and you.'

'Tell me what happened,' he entreated her.

The subject looked Maelgwn over as if trying to assess whether he was serious. 'This world has never known such a time of upheaval, wretchedness and strife. Why do you want to go back there?'

'I need to remember,' he advised gently. 'We both do.'

'Even when the rest of humanity has politely chosen to forget?' Electra scoffed. 'Why should we?'

'Because we can then help the rest of humanity to remember, before history repeats itself,' Maelgwn encouraged.

Electra considered his request, and even though she was obliged to do his will, she was still hesitant to recall the period in question. 'History will not repeat itself, not to the same extent of horror. The human soul-mind, on the whole, has evolved somewhat in the last ten thousand years. Atlantis marked the halfway point in the evolution of the human soul-mind on this planet; at that time, matter held full sway in the physical realm. Human consciousness had fully descended into the physical ... in other words it had gone as low as it could go in the cosmic scheme of things and this was reflected in the self-indulgent, egotistical and materialistic nature of many of the people who lived just prior to the last great deluge.'

Maelgwn nodded his understanding, urging her to continue.

'Although my father's murder triggered the native rebellion, the siege on Chailidocean that you recall was the beginning of the end for Atlantis.' Electra bit her lip as she pondered where to begin her tale. 'The prophetic dream I'd glimpsed in bits and pieces since the day my father was murdered, was finally channelled in its entirety a handful of days before the siege.'

'A ball of fire grows daily in the sky, reflecting the anger of the native tribes. When the fire in the sky grows larger than the sun and lights your city with its brilliance half the night, the dark races will merge into a united force that will storm this city, and your desire to hold it will bury it in myth.'

Following visions of the events the spirit predicted, Electra found herself standing in a light beam that faded into darkness in every direction. Her six sisters clung to her for fear, asking her what to do. 'They must leave,' the spirit whispered to Electra, using her voice, and as her sisters rushed away from her, Electra turned to confront the sorcerer who had murdered her father. He stood in the shadows beyond her light, and was illuminated by the magic energies that danced between his fingers. 'You and I shall wait,' Electra advised. 'We can go to hell together.'

'No.' A beautiful, dark-haired man who stood to her right, reached out to her. 'You have done nothing wrong.'

'Who wants to be saved?'

She turned left to see her brother, Orestes, circling a beautiful maiden, with whom he was obviously enchanted. Electra glanced back to the sorcerer, who smiled, seemingly gratified by her brother's preoccupation with the unknown maiden. Then her gaze fell upon the handsome stranger holding out his helping hand to her.

'Come,' he urged her with his outstretched hand.

'When the fireball passes over Chailidocean, Gaia will shake furiously and be cast into darkness.'

The voice of the spirit blinded Electra with images of destruction once more.

'Filled to overflowing with divine inspiration, mankind has chosen to follow the influence of the Dark Lodge by using sacred knowledge for selfish purposes. Thus no scholar of sorcery will survive to record the tales of the great civilisations that shall be no more. Lands will rupture and fire shall consume those kingdoms not engulfed by the ocean's backlash. Every cradle of civilisation will Gaia cast off into the waters fed by her tears. The great Mother will enter a time of mourning, for herself and for the terrible scars that will be buried deep within the subconscious of her peoples forevermore. Humanity will be returned to the wilds of nature, to be humbled by Gaia. The Black League will prevail. Only a handful shall remember the divine secrets through the wretched eras to come. These guardians will remain in hiding until such time as the Logos sees fit to entrust mankind with cosmic knowledge and grant the species a second chance at planetary evolution. This is the promise of Uriel, the Prince of Retribution and the humble servant of the Logos.'

The harsh male characteristics departed Electra's

voice and her head dropped forward until her spirit gained control of her form and she raised herself upright.

'Take her away,' Electra heard the sorcerer command. Aegisthus always had her head covered with a hood before he had her brought forth from her imprisonment in the High Temple to foretell events for him. He may have been a mighty sorcerer, but he feared the spirits Electra had access to.

Aegisthus did not have the pure qualities required to channel the angels of the Logos, nor did he know the sacred seals, chants, perfumes and ritual offerings that would allow him to persuade or command the higher angels to his service. The sorcerer had to rely on low-grade elementals to do his dirty work for him. He'd attracted these to his service by sacrificing animals and humans via torturous ritual. Every macabre murder enriched the vitality of these semiconscious vampire-like creations of sorcery. The low-grade elementals would then render the sorcerer service in exchange for this strengthening of their presence in the physical world.

Electra smiled to herself as she was led away by two of the sorcerer's guards. 'Your days are numbered, Aegisthus.'

'As are yours, little princess,' he replied. 'A virgin sacrifice should please my Otherworldly pets no end.'

He made this same threat every time he saw her, but the truth was that Aegisthus would not dare to harm her, lest he anger the spirits of the Logos who used Electra as a channel and confidante. 'Embrace the one true God, Aegisthus, or —'

'I am a god!' he roared. 'As powerful as any of the Nefilim.'

'The Nefilim are not gods,' Electra commented back to him. 'They, like you, just like to think they are.' Again she smiled to herself as she left the sorcerer fuming. It was her small way of avenging her father and she endeavoured to rile Aegisthus at every given opportunity.

'Clytemnestra!' Aegisthus called forth Electra's mother, now that the virgin oracle had departed. 'Prometheus and Orestes are rallying a force.'

'You don't know that it was Prometheus that Electra saw in her vision. She didn't mention him by name,' Clytemnestra advised him wisely, as she was bound to do, thanks to a beautiful jewelled necklace that she'd accepted from the sorcerer as a gift. This is how she had been enchanted into betraying her whole family to please a man that she now despised. The charm prevented her from openly expressing her feelings; she was cursed to be forever amiable to her captor.

'But Prometheus is harbouring your son in the snowy, mountainous region of his kingdom, and is no doubt in sympathy with Orestes's cause to overthrow me,' the sorcerer argued.

'Well, perhaps you shouldn't have sent your Otherworldly pets to dismember Prometheus's wife,' Clytemnestra commented, and then added quickly to appease her master: 'Electra also mentioned a maiden with whom Orestes would become enchanted.'

Aegisthus frowned. 'It is Prometheus we need to enchant. If he ruins Electra she'll be useless as a channel.'

'But by betraying her vows of chastity to the Logos, Electra would lose the favour of the spirits who protect her and you could make good your threat to feed her to your bloodthirsty pets,' Clytemnestra pointed out, hating herself for her quick, reasoning mind and her greed in accepting Aegisthus's gift all that time ago. Already her husband was dead, her son banished and her daughters imprisoned. She had thought things couldn't get any worse, but she was wrong. 'And as far as this enchanting maiden goes, why take any risks with the power of her beauty? You are friendly with some of the Nefilim lords who have the know-how to create for you the perfect female for the job. The only thing my son loves more than battle is seeking his pleasure in the female form.'

'Yes.' Aegisthus rubbed his hands together, his mind ticking over with possibilities. 'I see what you are driving at.'

'And what of the spirit's prediction of ruin for Atlantis?' Clytemnestra wondered how the evil magician planned to combat that threat.

'Ha!' he scoffed. 'The spirit also said that the Dark Lodge would prevail, and I am the leading exponent,' the sorcerer boasted.

'Electra said the Black League,' Clytemnestra pointed out.

'The Black League, the Dark Lodge, same difference,' the sorcerer snapped.

The Dark Lodge was the name that had been given to the order of lords who studied the dark arts of sorcery under Aegisthus. His grandfather, Shu Sar Alaric, who was the first son of the renowned Shu Sar Absalom, had founded this secret order. When Alaric came to rule Atlantis he despised the High Orders of Helio (the male aspect of the Logos) and Heliona (the female aspect of the Logos) for the secrecy of their doctrine, ritual and purpose. The resident High Priestess at the time Alaric came to rule refused to bend to the new Shu Sar's demands to be taught the sacred ways of her order. Alaric banished her and all of her order, including the Nefilim prophet and teacher, Shu Micah. The temples of learning once dedicated to the different gods in the service of the Logos — deities representing the divine qualities and knowledge of the Master Rays — were reduced to government institutions committed solely to the cause of increasing the size of the Atlantean kingdom. Some of Alaric's own brothers opposed the changes and they died defending the ideals of their father and lost the kingdoms that had been their birthright in the process. There was no stopping Alaric once he'd discovered sorcery and only those who were in the Dark Lodge knew who had instructed the Shu Sar Alaric in the dark arts.

Dark sorcery thrived in Atlantis under Alaric's rule and throughout the reign of the son who succeeded him. The Dark Lodge of the Materialistic came into being and then anyone who did not agree with the Shu Sar became a live sacrifice to feed the elementals that were in the service of the Dark Lodge. Many people fled Atlantis to the native kingdoms beyond Alaric's rule. For young men, women, children and babies, Atlantis became a dangerous place. The innocent were prized as sacrifices for their life force was most invigorating to the evil elementals, who in turn could grant the sorcerers' ever greater power. This incredible loss of young blood accounted for the huge reduction in numbers of the tall, fair Atlantean people that the native tribes referred to as the Titans. But something became apparent over the two thousand years of blood, lust and greed that followed: the more wretched, bloodthirsty and desire-driven that mankind became, the quicker their physical forms began to age. Absalom had ruled for thousands of years, Alaric ruled for little more than one thousand, and his first son died having only ruled for eight hundred years. The age expectancy of all the Titans reduced in accord with their ruler and their common acceptance of his low values, practices and ambitions. Aegisthus's cousin, Agamemnon, was the next to succeed to the throne, but he was more of a warrior than a conjurer. Whilst Agamemnon was off conquering the native kingdoms with his bare hands, Aegisthus, head of the Dark Lodge and Agamemnon's own cousin, began his takeover bid for rulership.

For thousands of years the virgins of the High Temple were bred purely to be sacrificed for the cause of the Dark Lodge and to be used by the strictly male members of the order for pleasure. All the women had proven useless as seers since the High Priestess and her students had been banished. Until the advent of Electra and her sisters. All seven daughters of the Shu Sar Agamemnon had been proven to have psychic ability, but none so much as Electra, his second born.

Electra had proved from a young age that she'd been granted the ability to speak with the greatest spirits in the service of the Logos. The spirit Mikhail instructed her of each spirit's function and how they might be summoned. Electra was also educated in the functions of all the lesser spirits and given the know-how to have power over them so as to direct them towards the positive service of mankind. She was warned against the ways of the Dark Lodge by her spiritual advisors and made to vow never to disclose her knowledge of spiritual doctrine to any soul bar her sisters.

Agamemnon never entered the Dark Lodge and was quietly wary of the order. He allowed his daughters to form a separate female order apart from the daughters who served the Dark Lodge and thus his daughters became Agamemnon's own personal seers. However, Agamemnon did not heed his daughter's prophecy to lay down his arms, and make peace with his fellow nations before he lost his own.

The Dark Lodge was now greatly feared throughout the known world — especially after Aegisthus had single-handedly seized the most prized city of them all. And, as any graduate of the order could conquer entire kingdoms with their conjuring and enchantments just as easily as any other, Aegisthus's territory was expanding rapidly.

'Now, don't try and distract me,' Aegisthus warned Clytemnestra, knowing that this was the only form of defence that his curse had left the woman. He admired her cunning and enjoyed doing battle with it. 'I must communicate with some of my Nefilim associates at once.' He turned and left his conjuring tower.

Hurry Orestes. Clytemnestra willed with all her

heart for her son to attack and reclaim his birthright from Aegisthus, even though she knew that Orestes would surely kill her for the part she'd played in his father's murder. It was as the spirit had said: her people had become infatuated with material wealth, and the jewelled necklace around her neck was proof of her own selfish desires. But her daughters were not guilty of this crime. They had spent their lives in the service of the Logos and did not deserve to be condemned with the rest of their nation. *Save them, my son, and I shall die a happy woman.*

Once returned to the High Temple that now only sheltered herself and her six sisters, Electra made haste to the circular platform located in the middle of the once spectacular abode of worship.

Aegisthus had ordered his elemental forces to strip the jewels from the High Temple to decorate the conjuring tower of the Dark Lodge, which stood high upon a mountain peak overlooking Chailidocean from the west.

The oracle's sisters had been anxiously awaiting Electra's return. 'Did you discover anything?' Maia, their eldest sister, queried as all the women trailed Electra to the middle of the temple.

'The escape we've been planning is very close now, but a safe destination still eludes me,' Electra uttered in an aside to her sisters, while she marked out the sacred seal of the spirit whose services she wished to employ. She used a large chalk rock that left a very definite mark on the timber floor, but it would be easy to wash away.

'Have your senses taken flight?' Maia gripped hold of Electra's hand to stop her completing the symbol. 'What if Aegisthus comes —'

'He has other matters to attend to at present,' Electra informed her sister and carried on regardless. 'I must act quickly while he is distracted.'

'Orestes is going to attack Chailidocean then?' Taygeta assumed.

'I have seen it,' Electra confirmed, to her sisters' great relief. She then gave her youngest sister, Celaeno, the list of herbs that she required to call forth the spirit of the Supreme Mysteries.

Maia was even more horrified, as this was the last entity they needed the sorcerer gaining access to. 'I hope you know what you are doing.'

'I shall explain all once I am done.' Electra stepped up onto the circular platform and faced the centre, giving the mental command that retracted the dome overhead. Two shafts of light fell at opposing angles across the platform: one beam was cast by the afternoon sun, the other due to the flaming orb in the sky that had been drawing ever closer for as long as they'd been alive. The young oracle focused her attention inward and began the chant that summoned Raziel.

After a time a loud clap of thunder was heard and the two shafts of light miraculously began to merge into one centred beam that was so bright the sisters could no longer see beyond it to the brilliant blue afternoon sky. A winged figure was seen to descend slowly down the shaft of celestial light and land on the platform before Electra. The oracle immediately fell on one knee before the great spirit and her sisters did likewise.

The huge, glistening being folded his mighty wings away and held up a hand to gesture. 'Greetings, friends. How can I aid?'

'Welcome, Raziel. I thank you for responding to my call,' Electra began, keeping her eyes diverted from the being's face. He was a prince among spirits and to meet the gaze of such a powerful being would drive her mortal brain beyond sanity. She was able to recognise the spirit by his voice, his robes and the golden book he carried, which contained the secrets to the mysteries of the universe and the fifteen hundred keys to unlock those mysteries. 'I seek to know if the Black League and the Dark Lodge are the same order?'

'No, my friend, they are not,' the spirit replied. 'The Black League is an underground society formed by the Pleiadeans to oversee intergalactic intelligence here on Gaia.'

'You mean there are beings from other planets among us besides those of the Nefilim kind?' Electra wasn't too sure what the spirit was inferring.

'Every being has developed through a series of evolutions on different planets in other star systems on various planes of awareness,' Raziel explained. 'As the Nefilim made it their business to perfect the human form, other interstellar races made it their business to contribute to human soul-mind evolution by incarnating into the human race. Or they simply assume a human form in order to live amongst the inhabitants

401

of this planet and influence the development of mankind in both constructive and destructive ways.'

'Are you saying I could be from another planet?' Electra ventured to ask and the angel was heard to chuckle.

'Your soul-mind came to this planet from the evolutionary cycle of Venus, which took place eons before this planet became habitable. The Venusians were the result of the interbreeding of the Pleiadean and Sirian settlements on that planet. As you are a Titan in this incarnation, it means that you have Vegan blood in your veins, for they were the original Titans, who stood twenty-five feet tall on average. They made their contribution to your gene pool long ago.'

'How does the Black League fit in?' Electra attempted to get the pieces of the puzzle to fall into place.

'Those interstellar intelligences who have not incarnated into human soul-mind evolution maintain their original forms and oversee the development of mankind from their secret bases adrift in deep space and their secret cities deep within the Earth. The Black League is in council at present. I could show you, if you wish it?'

Raziel's casual offer sent shock waves through Electra's body. 'I would be greatly honoured.' She bowed lower in gratitude. The spirit held out a hand to Electra and she was consumed by his celestial radiance.

One day's march from Chailidocean, and the army, composed of the various native tribes of Atlantis, had tripled in number since Prometheus and Orestes had begun their journey north from Usiqua.

The red skinned son of the Shu Sar Absalom, Jerram, had once ruled Usiqua, but Absalom's descendants had been done out of their rulership and lives during Shu Sar Alaric's rule. Turan, Alaric's twin brother, had been sent to rule the native tribes in Usiqua following Jerram's execution. Alaric had expected the native people to rebel against their new leader and his family, and do the Shu Sar out of the trouble of having to dispose of his brother himself. But the peoples of Usiqua came to love their new ruler and his wife, Temperance, once High Priestess of Chailidocean. Alaric tried many times to correct his grave error, but every attempt to make war on Usiqua failed miserably. Turan and his family had come into the favour of some of the Nefilim, who supplied him with the technology to protect his kingdom against the armies of Chailidocean. In addition, Temperance sought the guidance of the Logos in devising a means to deflect any evil spirits cast at their kingdom by the Dark Lodge. This protection had served their descendants well, until the day Turan's great grandson, Prometheus, took his wife beyond the borders of their kingdom on a diplomatic errand. After thousands of years Alaric's vengeance found an outlet, when his grandson, Aegisthus, seized the opportunity to send his demons to dismember Prometheus's first and only wife.

Prometheus stood on the main deck of his largest hovercraft, observing all the native peoples of Atlantis converging to join their convoy from the east and west, in all manner of flying and land transports, riding on large animals and walking on foot.

'Surely this is the mightiest army this continent has ever seen,' commented Orestes, clapping his hands, pleased by the turnout and confident of victory.

Prometheus nodded to agree with Orestes, finding the numbers rather disturbing; controlling such a mixed bag of warriors was going to be difficult. 'I don't see any of our brother, Atlas's, official forces among them?'

The Titans of the royal line all called themselves brothers, be they cousins, uncles, or in-laws, as they were all directly descended from the Shu Sar Absalom. Orestes and Prometheus were actually only distant cousins and Atlas was equally as distant a relative.

'Did you really expect to see Atlas get involved in this?' Orestes asked. 'The dark lands of Hyperborea are far removed from Aegisthus's threat. And as Atlas has sorcerers among his people to combat the Dark Lodge if they do manage to extend their reign that far, Atlas probably feels this serves us right for trusting the Logos and not utilising these new dark forces that have come into play in our land.'

Every time the Dark Lodge and their creatures were mentioned, Prometheus was tortured by the vision of the blood-drenched chamber in which he had found his wife's remains. Not one piece of her had been left intact; Prometheus's healers were forced to identify the body from the blood and shredded tissue left dripping from the walls. This hadn't been an unprovoked attack, Prometheus realised. It had been Aegisthus's way of objecting to Usiqua harbouring Orestes. Prometheus had

had no intention of making war on Chailidocean before his wife's death, but now avenging her horrid end was all that he lived for. 'In that case, Atlas is as responsible for my wife's death as the sorcerer who gave the command to kill her,' he concluded.

'If my mother and sister had not betrayed my father, all of this would have been avoided.' Orestes started to quietly fume, as he did every time he thought about his father's betrayal. 'They will pay for the havoc they've unleashed.'

'But was it not your sister, Electra, who smuggled you out of the city and saved you from certain death at the hands of Aegisthus?' Prometheus queried and Orestes nodded, his scowl remaining constant. 'Why would she conspire to kill the Shu Sar and then go to so much trouble to spare his heir, Orestes? It makes no sense at all. If she was for the sorcerer, Electra would have left you to be slaughtered.'

One of Prometheus's advisors entered to request an audience with the two military leaders on behalf of a prince who had travelled from beyond the ocean east of Atlantis to speak with them. Both Prometheus and Orestes were most intrigued by the announcement and gave their permission to show the leader in.

The black skinned warrior was tall by native standards, although he still stood a good foot shorter than Prometheus and Orestes. The black prince was painted and dressed ornately, as was the way of his people, and bowed before the men he'd travelled so far to see.

Prometheus's advisor stayed to translate the conversation for his Shar. 'Greetings, Prometheus,' he interpreted the words of the visitor. 'I am Lugal, ruler of the city of Tangier. My apologies for disrupting your preparations for war, but I bring a warning to you from our mutual ally, the Nefilim Lord Enki.' The translator's eyes opened wide as he looked to his Shar, interested to hear the response.

Prometheus was a little shocked himself, for he had not had any direct contact with the Nefilim though he knew his forefathers had. 'I am grateful for your journey,' Prometheus said in welcome, keeping an open mind. 'What is the message?'

Lugal came forward and handed Prometheus a thought band recorder. The Titan accepted the gift, not knowing what to make of the sleek metallic band. The prince, noting the Titan's confused expression, had a quiet word with the translator, motioning to his forehead as he spoke.

'He advises that you should place it around your forehead, my Shar.'

Prometheus, eager to hear the message, moved to comply, but Orestes snatched the item from his friend.

'How do we know Lugal is telling the truth?' Orestes demanded. 'This could inflict pain, madness or death for all we know.'

The translator filled the prince in on Orestes's concerns before Prometheus could prevent it; he didn't wish to offend the prince, who by all appearances was going way out of his way to aid them.

The visitor launched into a long spiel, which the translator quickly interpreted to the Shars.

'My capital is named after the most beautiful

woman who ever lived. Her name was Tangis ... she was my wife.'

Prometheus's heart immediately went out to the prince, realising that Lugal, too, had lost his wife.

'Tangis was travelling back from Antilla by sea when a sorcerer came to my city and demanded that I surrender my lands to Aegisthus, ruler of Chailidocean, lest my wife's boat perish in a storm.'

'I had no idea Aegisthus's ambitions had spread so far,' Orestes commented, more disposed towards the stranger as he took a seat to hear him out.

'I did not take the threat seriously,' the translator continued his task, 'and even if I had done, I would not have agreed to betray my people without a fight.'

The prince paused for a moment, revering a memory, and then continued his account.

'So, fight we did. My people died horrible deaths. I lost my wife, my family and my lands.'

'And yet you live?' Orestes commented. Prometheus found the implication of the question most offensive; fortunately, Lugal did not.

'The Master Enki rescued me and quelled my fire for revenge. He told me that I need not concern myself avenging my wife, as the destruction of the sorcerers of Atlantis had already been arranged by a greater power.'

'Us, right?' Orestes flattered himself.

The prince slowly shook his head. 'You must leave this continent at once, if you wish to live.'

'This *continent?*' Prometheus looked at the band in his hands, concerned for Usiqua, as it shared the landmass with two other kingdoms of Atlantis.

Cintrala and its capital, Chailidocean, Aegisthus had thieved. The kingdom to the far north of the continent, Portea, was ruled from its capital Menocea by Menoetius. Menoetius was a first cousin and close ally of Atlas, who ruled the land beyond the great sea that bordered Portea. Atlas's kingdom was known as Hyperborea — it was also known as the Dark Land, for the distant north of this landmass spent six months of the year in darkness. Menoetius did not oppose Aegisthus's dark lords when they'd come calling in at Portea and had thus managed to maintain his position and lands which he now ruled with one of the dark lords at his side.

Even Orestes was silent as Prometheus raised the thought band recorder belonging to the ancient Nefilim lord and placed it on his forehead.

16

IN THE LEAGUE OF GODS

The enormous majestic chamber was not entirely solid in structure: the walls, floor and ceiling, in fact everything within sight, seemed to be composed of brightly coloured, semi-translucent light matter. *We are in the spirit realm?* Electra bethought her guide.

This is the ethereal world that exists between planes and dimensions, Raziel advised.

Electra understood that only her conscious perception had accompanied the spirit to this place ... her body she'd left back in the High Temple. She turned in circles, taking in the beings that sat at the huge, circular conference table over which she hovered — this featured a speaking platform in the centre. At one section of the table sat strange hairless beings, with black slanted eyes, and bodies and heads much larger than their spindly little arms and short little legs. Some of these beings were very tall (twice Electra's Titan height of seven feet), and they were bluish in colour. The representatives seated opposite them exhibited the same alien features, but they were shorter even than the native tribes of Atlantis and their skin had a greyish tinge. The rest of the assembly was a surprise to the oracle. *Why, most of them are human ... sort of.* She noted some variation in skin and hair colour, height and radiance, but these lofty beings were all readily recognisable as human — although they appeared more like angels minus the wings.

Don't be deceived by appearances, for those you perceive as human have assumed a humanlike form for communication purposes. Or they have incarnated into human soul-mind evolution and then ascended back towards the Logos maintaining that form, Raziel told her. *A body is only a fleeting collection of atoms drawn together around a monad, that is the divine-spiritual life atom, in order that it might interact with matter and express itself in the physical world. The expression of myself that I show to you is not at all like my true form, but it is acceptable to you. All the beings you see here have made important contributions to mankind ... physically, mentally, psychically, emotionally or spiritually. For this is the senate of the Brotherhood of Light, who are dedicated to the development of the human soul-mind.*

Then why are they called the Black League? This puzzled Electra. *This name does seem to confuse the issue.*

410

And what is confusion? It really means co-fusion with all-that-is? When you are at one with all-that-is and do not judge, you will see both positive and negative as beneficial to evolution. You cannot have creation without both polarities. You cannot know the divine without having experienced both polarities. You judge the word black to mean evil and of low order, when it is, in fact, all things mysterious. It is from the darkness of the womb that you emerge into the physical world, and thus black represents female energy. Out of the darkened depths of the cosmic void sprang this universe that you are yet to understand. Humans fear what they do not understand, that which is beyond their control, and this is where your misconception and fear about blackness and darkness comes from. The Black League formed with the desire to promote the path to inner wisdom in more warlike and vengeful intelligences who were integrating themselves into human consciousness. Beings such as those from Orion which have been incarnating into the human race since before the golden age of Atlantis. Raziel was about to point out the obvious, when Electra guessed.

So these Orions are the force behind the Dark Lodge.

Indeed, granted the spirit. *They desire to conquer your land and your people, just as they desired to conquer your spiritual ancestors, the Pleiadeans, in their last evolution, long ago in another star system.*

But what became of their own planets? Electra wondered why this interstellar soul war was now being played out on Gaia.

What warlike soul is ever content with what it has? The warrior's purpose is to conquer, and many planets have been destroyed in the struggle. The souls that escaped migrated to

411

colonies they had already established on Maldek, a planet that is now just an asteroid belt. That is, one planet away from you towards the outer rim of your star system.

So, the Orions followed the Pleiadeans to this star system, Electra assumed.

And continued the great War of Heaven.

But how do the Nefilim fit into all this? Electra wondered. *Do they know about these alien souls waging war over the human beings whose bodies they perfected on this planet?*

And on other planets in this system too, Raziel added. *Only a chosen few of the Nefilim are advanced enough to have been contacted by the White Brotherhood. The Nefilim are represented by the hooded figure.*

Electra noted the hooded character, who did not sit at the conference table, but stood in the background quietly observing the proceedings.

Ironically, it suits the purposes of the Orions to suppress the knowledge of their presence and work on earth. The more debauched souls among the Nefilim are, with the advent of the Sorcerers of the Dark Lodge, only just beginning to understand the potential of the vengeful soul group that have integrated themselves into human consciousness. This is why, every so often, the Nefilim are baffled when they find themselves confronted with a human soul-mind who is more advanced than they are, for these individuals are the great leaders of previous interstellar races who have come to lead humankind with their experience. You are one of these old souls, Electra. That is why you are so psychically gifted and why even the greatest exponents of the Dark Lodge fear you. For you have the power to instruct the spirits of the Logos, including Uriel, who holds the key to the bottomless pit of Abaddon.

The destructor. Electra choked on the thought. *Did this great leader I once was have a name?*

Between yourself and your male counterpart, you have been, and will be, several great leaders, known by many different names in many different dimensions —'

My male counterpart? As she asked the question, she had a fleeting vision of the tall, dark-haired Titan she had been seeing in her dreams.

He is you.

The spirit startled her with the claim, but Electra's attention was diverted to below where one of the seven angel-like men floated up onto the speaking platform to address the assembly.

'My news is grave,' announced the speaker who, Raziel advised, was known as the Master El Morya. 'The Orions have chosen to hold the Black League to ransom. They take full responsibility for setting the approaching asteroid on a collision course with Gaia and they will divert the threat away from the planet once we have agreed not to oppose their invasion of the civilised world.'

This is how Maldek was destroyed and many worlds before it. One of the tall blue beings floated to a standing position, using thought projection to express his view, for he had no mouth. *Let us not make the mistake of allowing this world to be destroyed by resisting the demands of the Dark Lodge yet again. I feel we must try giving them the power they have fought so long to win. Perhaps then they shall cease to fight, and work in co-operation with us.*

413

I agree, one of the short grey beings floated up into the air. *Nothing can be achieved without a globe that will sustain human life. We all know the eons of effort that go into making a planet habitable. To start evolution all over again from scratch will set the divine plan back even further than ten thousand years under the influence of the Orion consciousness will.*

'Then warn those dear to you,' El Morya instructed. 'Direct them to the great underground civilisations to the far north and north-east where the survivors of past deluges have fled, for only in these sanctuaries shall the coming strife pass unheeded.'

A destination for my sisters, Electra thought on the quiet.

It is unfortunate that the second great outpouring of Shamballa energy into mankind will now further the cause of darkness. The tall blue being sounded disappointed. *We've worked so hard, ever since the initial outpouring of universal consciousness into man, to create a being able to sustain divine life force. Our kindred souls already committed to the human reincarnation loop are going to forget everything we have taught them and, indeed, they will forget their ancestry and their involvement in the divine plan.*

'Polarity demands this phase of evolution be played out at some time. Better now than later. The Dark Lodge of the Materialistic presently holds sway with well over half the earth's surface dwellers,' El Morya pointed out. 'We cannot ignore the will of the people. In time they will grow tired of earthly pleasures, riches and pain, and will seek their cosmic roots. Then we shall answer their call for knowledge and they will resume the path towards the spiritual advancement of Gaia.'

Will Gaia approve of our decision to retreat? the Pleiadean wondered.

'The decision will be most disappointing to those concerned,' El Morya conceded, 'but clearly humanity is not ready to take the quantum leap with Gaia into fourth density. We can only hope that a quantum leap backwards will make her peoples twice as keen to progress by the time of the next Shamballa outpouring.'

Prometheus removed the thought recorder, and the look on his face was one of utter bewilderment.

'What did it say?' Orestes harassed, having been waiting patiently for his friend to absorb the communication.

'I cannot do as the Lord Master Enki asks.' Prometheus turned to Lugal, still overawed by the request the ascended Nefilim lord had made of him.

His translator did his job and came back with Lugal's response. 'Then you shall die.'

'I realise that,' Prometheus conceded. 'However, I shall have this communication delivered into the hands of my son, Deukalion, and he shall build this "Ark" and fill it with all species of animal and plant, just as the Master Enki requests.'

When the translator gave Lugal this message, the prince smiled broadly and spoke to Prometheus's advisor, who relayed Lugal's response: 'Then your seed shall live on.'

'What is an Ark?' Orestes could not be silent any longer. 'Why are you going to die? Will I die?' he squeaked in conclusion.

Prometheus looked at the man he considered his brother and placed a hand on his shoulder. 'Not if you take this communication to Deukalion immediately and aid him with the project.' Prometheus held out the thought band recorder to his young friend.

'I see.' Orestes eyed the band over and then took a step away. 'I want to destroy Aegisthus just as much as you do.' He resisted the option Prometheus gave him, even though it would spare his life.

'There is no point in both of us getting killed doing it.' Prometheus offered the recorder once again.

'And what if it needs our combined talents to thwart the sorcerer?' Orestes took another step away. 'And besides, I have my treacherous mother and sister to deal with. Send a good man back to your son, Prometheus, someone with family to save.' He decided to forego the safe path.

Although Prometheus thought his younger friend foolish, he admired his determination and commitment. 'You should go with my messenger.' Prometheus went to hand Lugal back the thought recorder, but the prince moved away and declined.

'I return home now,' Lugal advised Prometheus via the translator. 'I have completed my task for the Nefilim lord who spared my life and I now intend to stand on the top of the tallest mountain, of what was once my kingdom, and witness this continent sink beneath the waves, along with my wife's murderer. May the Logos be merciful to you all.' The prince turned and departed.

'What in the name of the Logos was predicted in that communication?' Orestes wasn't entirely sure he wanted to know. 'The new sun that grows in the sky must have something to do with it. I could really use one of the great astrologers from Absalom's time right now.'

'It is not a sun,' Prometheus advised him. 'It's a chunk of metal, rock and ice that is nearly the size of Atlantis. And it's not getting bigger, it's getting closer.'

Orestes's jaw dropped as he considered what this meant to their mission. 'How close is it?'

'Less than one moon cycle,' Prometheus responded, still deeply shocked himself.

Orestes nodded, considering this might be ample time to invade Chailidocean, avenge his father and make a getaway to some far off land. 'So, if a small planet is going to drop out of the sky and destroy Atlantis and everything in it, then why are we going to attempt to destroy the sorcerers?'

'Even if we tell them the world is coming to an end, this force you see around us is not going to turn back without the satisfaction of a war,' Prometheus stated honestly. 'I shall not abandon those I have inspired to rebel against the Dark Lodge. And quite apart from all that, the only way I shall rest easy in my grave is if I see that demon, Aegisthus, perish with my own eyes.'

'Ah, yes.' Orestes seconded the notion. 'And what a glorious sight that will be.'

Prometheus cocked an eye to urge Orestes to consider the safe option. 'Worth dying for?'

Ostestes grinned, hungry for revenge. 'Twice over.'

'And so the invasion of Chailidocean went ahead,' Maelgwn assumed.

'But I was prepared for it,' Electra continued. 'There was one secret about the High Temple that always eluded the Dark Lodge and that was the underground passage that led to the Mount Duranki Plateau. The plateau was in plain sight of the city for all people of pure heart to see it, yet to those of the Dark Lodge naught could be seen but the precarious rocky terrain of uninhabitable mountain peaks.'

'I understand,' Maelgwn said. 'There was a place that passed in and out of physical existence in this way later in history; it was known as Avalon. Some people could find their way to it, others would get lost in the mist. And Shamballa is an illusory place to the dark of heart.'

'I was advised by the spirits to lead my sisters to the Mount Duranki Plateau the moment the invasion commenced. I was assured that they would be rescued by members of the White Brotherhood and taken to a safe haven.'

'And you did not go with them?' Maelgwn wondered why.

Electra shook her head and suppressed a non-amused smile. 'I was not innocent. I had the guilt of my father's betrayal hanging over my head. Thus, I went to await my brother's justice at the grave of my father.'

By the time the attacking force had penetrated the inner island, Aegisthus and his sorcerers had retreated to their Dark Lodge which was fortified by a supernatural electromagnetic field that could not be penetrated by any living thing. The dark wizard had Clytemnestra with him, although his adepts had been unable to locate the seven daughters of Agamemnon.

Electra found it hard to suppress a smile as she considered how irate the sorcerer would be to lose her services for, without Electra, Aegisthus had no link to the divine, no link to the truth. Now the sorcerer would have to rely on low-grade elementals for information, and they rarely bothered with little details like getting their facts straight ... and due to the demented substance from which they were made, they were also compulsive liars. There were spells that could bind these spirits to tell the truth, but having limited knowledge of the physical world, and therefore no concept of history, space or time, elementals were known to get a bit confused when attempting to predict future events.

She knelt in prayer before the memorial to her father; Agamemnon had no grave, his person had been incinerated by a ritual spell of summons that Electra had concocted herself.

Her mother had come to her with a private request. Clytemnestra claimed that Aegisthus had been trying to seduce her in Agamemnon's absence and had threatened to seize the kingdom. Her mother had made it clear how desperate she was to be rid of the sorcerer's threats and begged Electra to use her knowledge of the spirit realm to find a spirit who would dispose of the sorcerer and rid them of his evil presence. Feeling that it was to the benefit of their people, Electra agreed to find such a spirit and to devise the ritual that would command the spirit to carry out any task that Clytemnestra asked of it.

Electra had been made aware long before, by her most trusted spiritual guide, Mikhail, of a group of spirits known as the Fallen Ones. Mikhail had described these Fallen Ones as more involved in the physical world than those of his ilk, and thus they were more readily available to be of service to humans. Electra had been given a silver ring to protect her from the glamour of the Fallen Ones, also known as the Lords of Darkness, should they ever appear to her and attempt to tempt her to their cause.

Using the ring for protection, Electra put out a psychic request to make contact with one of the fallen. Electra found herself confronted by a spirit who answered to the name of Power. Electra had imagined that a fallen angel would be as ugly as the divine spirits were beautiful, but to the contrary Power was very physically attractive and had an alluring energy. He agreed to help Electra and dictated to her the summons that Clytemnestra could recite to bring him forth for her instruction. Electra had asked Power what he required in return for his service and he'd insisted that such service brought its own rewards.

Only now did Electra realise the full implications of what Power had meant. When Clytemnestra instructed Power to dispose of Agamemnon instead of Aegisthus, chaos descended on the nation. Electra had lost her silver ring of protection to Aegisthus, who now also knew the ritual to call forth Power. Fortunately, Power was not as well disposed towards serving Aegisthus, as there was little point in corrupting the already corrupted; the dark spirit was not proving as useful an ally as the sorcerer had expected. The ring only protected the wearer from the fallen — it didn't grant any power over them.

Electra and her sisters had placed the small memorial to their father inside the high temple walls, for the sorcerer wouldn't allow a public place of remembrance to be constructed. However, he allowed the daughters of Agamemnon a small shrine where they could privately grieve their loss.

Electra remained on her knees, but turned herself around to face the troops she heard entering the temple. Orestes was at the head of the force and was accompanied by the tall, handsome man from her visions. *He is you*, she recalled what Raziel had said of him.

Her brother drew his laser sword as he approached and extended the deadly blade. 'Where are my sisters?' Orestes demanded to know, before making himself clearer. 'The ones that remained faithful to our father?'

'They have fled the impending crisis for a far off land,' Electra advised.

'You know about the crisis?' Prometheus interrupted and Electra nodded.

'Don't change the subject.' Orestes came up behind Electra, and placing his foot on her shoulder he urged her to lean forward in preparation to lose her head. 'You have been found guilty of acting as an accomplice in the unholy murder of our father, the Shu Sar Agamemnon. Have you anything to say for yourself, before your head and body are parted?'

Electra and Orestes had always been very close. It killed her inside to know that he bore her so much malice, although she did not blame him.

As Prometheus observed Orestes raise his sword, he wondered how his friend could bring himself to end the life of such an angel. She knelt here, head bowed, accepting her fate.

'I'll assume your silence is an admission of guilt,' Orestes warned her.

Electra was not listening. She was ready to leave this wretched existence and join her beautiful spirits in their realms.

From above Electra perceived a bright beam of light fall upon her. Mikhail, the Viceroy of the Logos, descended to protect her by enfolding her with his wings. Electra had never looked Mikhail in the face, but she knew him by his warrior-like metal armour.

'May the Logos have mercy on your soul, Electra.' Orestes slashed downwards with the beam of his weapon, but the fatal strike was deflected by Prometheus's weapon. 'Stay out of this, my friend,' Orestes cautioned, perturbed that his ally would interrupt. 'This is none of your affair.'

'Look at her.' Prometheus urged Orestes to open his eyes. 'Can you not see the light radiating from her being? This is not the face of a traitor.' What Prometheus wasn't saying was how much of his wife he saw in this woman.

Orestes had never met Prometheus's wife, for Prometheus had been on a diplomatic errand with her at the same time as Orestes's request for asylum in Usiqua had reached him. Prometheus had granted the request from afar; the ruler's wife was murdered before they returned to their kingdom.

Orestes looked at his sister for the first time since he'd entered. She did look like an angel, and she had saved his life once. 'Curses!' he snarled, as his will to kill her flew right out the door. 'All right then,' he seethed, feeling it was Prometheus's fault that he'd lost the nerve to avenge his father. 'I'll spare her life for you, Prometheus. But as I want nothing further to do with her, I make of her a gift to you, to do with as you see fit.'

Put on the spot, Prometheus was stupefied for a moment. 'I feel sure Electra has an explanation for what happened. Perhaps if you'd hear her side of the story you will not be so eager to be rid of the only kindred you have left.'

Orestes looked to Electra, who had her eyes bowed reverently. 'Well, dear sister, let us hear what you have to say,' he asked again, sounding exasperated with giving her a second chance.

Tell him you were deceived, the spirit protecting Electra advised.

Usually, Electra always followed divine advice. 'I used my knowledge for a dark purpose, and even though that purpose backfired on me it does not make my crime any less severe.'

'See,' Orestes rounded on Prometheus. 'She admits her guilt and is prepared to die for her crime.'

'And she will soon enough, without you adding another soul to your conscience.' Prometheus reminded his friend of the disaster to come. 'You have said that Electra holds sway with the spirit world. She might be our only chance to seek our justice before the universe wreaks its own.'

'And what if Electra is working for Aegisthus, as our mother is?' Orestes argued. 'We cannot risk it.'

'The spirits claim that mother is under a spell that Aegisthus concocted.' Electra pleaded her mother's case. 'None of her betrayal of her kindred was of her own choosing. She accepted a jewelled necklace from the sorcerer and from then on was bound to do his will.'

'So you did not know you were aiding in the plan to kill your father when Clytemnestra asked you for a spell of summons?' Prometheus put forward.

'I should never have relinquished such power to a novice.' Electra insisted on accepting blame. 'In allowing mother to shield me from any part in a murder, I shirked my responsibility to the Logos and thus my own throat was destined to be cut.'

'Your will is my command.' Orestes raised his weapon once again.

Prometheus raised a hand to again stop the execution. 'Do you know how the Dark Lodge can be destroyed, Electra?'

'I understand it will be destroyed without any aid from us,' she replied.

How odd it was that this stranger was so determined to defend her. But when Electra remembered what Raziel had said about Prometheus, she realised that on a cosmic level he was trying to save his own skin. Still, it would not serve him. If she died now, she would amend for the life she aided to take and leave this world a pure soul totally devoted to the Logos. The tall, handsome stranger's defence of her was deeply stirring to her blood and she feared being distracted from her devotion to the Logos if she was granted the opportunity to know him better.

'Kill me, Orestes,' she requested calmly, although there was an underlying panic in her voice. 'My life is owed.' *Please, Mikhail, withdraw my protection, and greet my soul upon death's release*. She knew the spirit was the cause of her brother's procrastination.

Time stood still. Every movement, every sound, was suspended, but only Electra perceived what had happened. Mikhail floated back to where Electra might view him.

Look at me, Electra, the spirit requested. *Behold my face*.

The oracle raised her eyes to view the face of the free floating entity addressing her and gasped as she noted the resemblance between the tall handsome stranger and the divine spirit. 'You are Prometheus?' She frowned, as she further considered what Raziel had said about him. 'You are me?'

The essential spiritual essence behind your soul-mind was carried down into evolution by my fallen counterpart, Mikhail confirmed. *Thus, within you lies the potential for my evolution and the evolution of all our forms on every level of awareness between my home plane of demonstration and yours*.

'Is Power our fallen counterpart?' Electra assumed this was why the fallen spirit had answered her summons, and yet Power had not borne the same physical resemblance that Mikhail shared with Prometheus.

No, he responded simply, not wanting to get off track. *Death would be the easy way out for you at this time*, the spirit advised. *The Logos still has services for you to perform in his name. As horrendous as your life has been of late, this is nothing compared to what lies in store for you, Electra ... there is much darkness ahead.*

'Darkness?' Electra recalled what she had recently learned about the subject. 'I cannot know the divine without having experienced both polarities,' she said, a little hesitantly.

What you are being offered is a speedy path to spiritual advancement via extreme torment. Should you choose to die now your soul will evolve as it otherwise would have, but your greatest aspiration, to serve the Logos at a subjective level, will be much slower in coming to fruition.

'Am I to open myself to the dark path or resist it?' Electra begged for more information, on the verge of tears, for she knew this trial was the will of the Logos.

You will be subject to it. Whether you become its victim, ally or master, will be completely up to you. But polarity demands your understanding of the darkness if you aspire to higher spiritual work.

'You understand darkness thus?' Electra wondered what the point to all this was.

No, Mikhail conceded humbly. *Only my fallen aspect understands darkness, and it understands the void very well. At the end of this great round of evolution my fallen aspect shall return to me and I shall understand all that it has learned in its travels.*

'Merciful heavens,' Electra sobbed. 'I dare not refuse this gift and yet I fear acceptance.' Her life as a holy oracle had been a very sheltered one and she suspected that her protection was about to be removed. 'This is goodbye then, Mikhail?' Her voice nearly fled her.

The beautiful being nodded. *The only spirit of high order who may answer your call henceforth shall be Uriel.*

'It is he who holds the key to the pit of Abaddon.' Electra found the strength to accept her place in the divine plan. 'I am the humble servant of the Logos.' She stood and walked away from her brother's glowing blade and then turned to bow to Mikhail. 'I will the divine will.'

Mikhail smiled, proud of her. *Thy will be done.*

The spirit vanished and Electra's world came to life once more.

Both Prometheus and Orestes were stunned to find Electra standing instead of kneeling, and in an entirely different spot.

'How did you do that?' Orestes protested after his sword fell on thin air.

'I believe I shall be of some service to you yet,' she informed her brother and his companion. 'Lock me up if that will ease your mind, but you need me alive.'

Orestes was sceptical. 'Why should I listen to you?'

'With the pending destruction of one half of the planet looming, what have you to lose?' Electra made her own appeal to his good sense.

In truth, Orestes was far more in awe of his sister's mysterious ways than he was letting on. 'Lock her up,' he ordered after some consideration.

Prometheus was a little disturbed by the decision. 'Make sure she is unharmed,' he added to Orestes's instruction to the guards. 'Any man that defies that instruction will answer to me.'

The ruler of Usiqua had been certain that his heart had died along with his wife. And yet, as he watched

Electra being led away, he felt an ember spark to life and warm his soul. *This is not my beloved back from the grave.* He cautioned himself against encouraging that misconception, but Electra was so like his wife, Prometheus couldn't help but feel kindly disposed towards her.

She was the most beautiful creature Aegisthus had ever seen. 'This is superb work, my Lord Shamash. She is beyond my expectations.' The sorcerer was very tempted not to use the maiden to distract Orestes from seeking revenge and instead keep her for himself.

'She is a human clone of my sister, Inanna, who is still the fairest female in the entire universe.' The Nefilim lord had a self-satisfied smile on his face, but it was not Aegisthus's praise that had him in such fine spirits. 'I call my creation Pandora, meaning "all gifts", both good and bad.' Shamash's grin grew. 'As is the case with my sister.'

Aegisthus clapped his hands together, delighted. He did have one question, however. 'What is the story with the vase she's holding?'

'Ah.' Shamash had wondered when the sorcerer was going to ask. 'That is a little magic spell of my own design,' he boasted, delighting in the worried look on the sorcerer's face.

'I didn't know the Nefilim bothered with magic.' Aegisthus made his craft sound inferior to the Nefilim's gift of psychic ability, although he knew magic could render psychic power useless, which is why the sorcerer dared to have dealings with the Nefilim in the first place.

'Most of the Nefilim don't bother with it.' Shamash teased the sorcerer by saying little on the subject. 'Under hypnosis I have suggested to our beauty that she is not to open the vase until she has bedded Orestes. Once she has charmed away his heart she will open the vase and her warped aspect will take her over.' Shamash finished outlining how well he'd completed his end of the bargain. 'You can't be too careful with humans. Sometimes their heart can sway them off course, but not our little woman.'

Aegisthus, having heard Shamash's explanation of the magic spell, was much relieved to discover that it was nothing more than subliminal suggestion and not really magic at all. 'You have met all my requirements and then some, lord. Now may we discuss your price for this service?'

Shamash walked around the entranced female that represented his half of the bargain. 'I want the maiden, Electra,' he announced, knowing that Aegisthus would object.

Aegisthus was tempted, but he refrained from protest and thought about how to sweeten the deal for his Lodge. 'There is certain information that I would have out of her first.' The sorcerer stated his condition.

'Would you have to torture this information out of Electra?' Shamash sounded well disposed towards the idea.

'Oh, most certainly,' Aegisthus assured.

'Agreed then,' Shamash granted. 'You have my permission to use every means at your disposal to extract the information you require from her.' This arrangement suited Shamash's plans very well.

'Rely on me, lord,' Aegisthus vowed. 'I am well versed in such methods.'

Shamash nodded, knowing that this twisted mortal soul was telling the truth. 'I propose that we introduce Orestes to Pandora and then suggest an exchange ... our seductress for Electra. And to save risking your own mortal skin, Aegisthus, I shall put the proposition to Orestes on your behalf.'

Aegisthus despised how Shamash always managed to remind him of his mortality. 'You are too kind, my lord, but I fear there may be one snag with our plan —'

'I told you, Aegisthus,' Shamash hated to repeat himself, 'that ball of fire will pass Gaia by and you will retain your kingdoms once Orestes is out of the way.'

'I believe you, my lord,' Aegisthus assured, although he knew damn well that Shamash was lying. 'The problem is that the oracle foretold that Prometheus will come to her defence.'

'Ah yes, Prometheus.' Shamash had to suppress his smile for fear of appearing smug. 'Have no fear, I have a deterrent that will take care of his devotion. I shall away to Orestes, and bring back Electra for your interrogation.'

When the Nefilim lord had departed along with his beautiful living statue, Aegisthus screwed up his face in disgust. Did Shamash take him for some sort of idiot? 'As far as Shamash knows, Atlantis will be destroyed. In fact, I'd say he is counting on it. Still, thanks to you, Yahweh Aris, I have information that he does not.' Aegisthus turned and bowed in gratitude to his ally, who removed his spell of invisibility.

Yahweh Aris was the Overlord of the Orions and he claimed to be older than the planet they were currently residing on. Yahweh was a title that was given to him as a leader of his people, much like the title Shu Sar referred to the leader of Atlantis. Aris was very tall indeed, a good four feet taller than the Titan in his company, and this also made the Orion taller than any of the Nefilim. Some of Aris's race had incarnated into human consciousness — Aegisthus was one of these incarnations. Up until now their activities had been confined to the peoples of the dark land that Atlas ruled, Hyperborea. Originally, only a few souls belonging to the Orion consciousness had been able to weasel their way into the Atlantean nation where Pleiadean and Sirian soul-minds were developing rapidly and prospering in peace in a pleasing climate.

The Shu Sar Alaric had started the Orion invasion of the continent and his descendants ensured their stronghold was maintained. Soon their consciousness would invade the greatest empire on earth and Aris planned to incarnate as the next world leader. It had been under Aris's influence that the Shu Sar Alaric had formed the Dark Lodge, and the Orion warlord had been the source of Alaric's knowledge of the dark arts. The Nefilim may have been the undisputed masters of genetic engineering, but the Orions had perfected many techniques for harnessing elemental forces.

They had also learned to tap into the ley line grid of the planet, using the information channelled through the etheric matrix to develop science and technology which would benefit the cause of the Dark Lodge of the

Materialistic. This information was known only by the Grand Masters of the Dark Lodge of whom Aegisthus was one, although the sorcerer was wrong in assuming he was the only Grand Master on the planet at this time.

'Now that the Brotherhood of Light have agreed not to interfere with our invasion of this continent, we will redirect the asteroid away from your kingdom,' promised the being with dragon-like features.

The Orions were human in form but not appearance. They could shape-shift to assume a human personification and they were also known to assume the form of a Dragon.

'Whatever serves our cause, my master,' Aegisthus humbled himself before his mentor. 'But what shall we do about Shamash?'

'When he delivers Electra back to you and we discover the name of the Prince of Darkness and the symbol that will bind him to our service, we need not concern ourselves with even the entire Nefilim Pantheon. For we shall have at our disposal the only force that holds more sway in the physical world than the Logos that gave it life.'

17

AN APPETITE FOR DESTRUCTION

Alone in her cell, Electra was plagued by visions of the torment and torture that was in store for her. Rape, mutilation, humiliation, sickness, filthy conditions and evil entities unlike anything she'd ever dared to imagine lay in her immediate future.

'I've changed my mind,' Electra wept. The swift death that her brother would have dealt her looked awfully appealing now. 'I don't want to be a victim. I could have died a noble death.'

Her cell door vanished and she feared that it would be Aegisthus who entered but to her great relief it was Prometheus.

He eyed over her detention cell. It was clean, dry

and dimly lit, and although it had no windows, it was an acceptable containment place for a prisoner of Electra's stature. The oracle was huddled on the stone block supplied for sleeping, with both her arms wrapped around her knees. 'You are under no threat of death any longer,' Prometheus assured Electra, having caught her last utterance.

'The spirit world disagrees with you, my Shar.' Electra collected her shattered sensibilities and managed calm speech. 'I'm afraid a truly horrid death awaits me here.' She gazed at the floor, a hopeless look upon her face.

'Then I shall take you away from here,' Prometheus offered gallantly.

'After you destroy Aegisthus or before?' Electra questioned flatly, for she already knew the answer.

'There are no words to describe the state in which his creatures left my wife's mutilated body,' Prometheus explained. 'I must see to it that she is avenged.'

'I understand.' Electra smiled meekly, resigning herself to a horrible end.

'No, listen to me, Electra,' Prometheus insisted, seating himself on the stone slab in front of her. 'I intend to make good our escape. Back in Usiqua my son is building a vessel, a design supplied by the Nefilim Lord Enki, that will survive the forthcoming deluge.'

His sweet sentiment almost roused a smile from her, but not quite. 'Why should you care what happens to me, Prometheus?' Electra knew why he was compelled to aid her. She just wanted to know what Prometheus thought his motivation was. The question took some of the wind out of his sails and Prometheus seemed to be having trouble finding the words. 'I remind you of her, don't I?'

Prometheus looked up to catch the oracle's intrigued gaze. He nodded, thankful to be avoiding a lengthy explanation. 'Yes ... very much so. It is like meeting her all over again.'

Prometheus was a good twenty years older than Electra, but as the Titans of Atlantis still lived for hundreds of years, he appeared no older than she did.

'So you find me desirable, Prometheus?' Electra suddenly conceived of one way of thwarting the sorcerer. The Dark Lodge would come for her, but she would not be a virgin. An innocent no longer, and cut off from her spirit world contacts, Electra would be virtually useless to the sorcerers as a sacrifice or seer.

It had been some time since Prometheus's wife was murdered and having missed her, Prometheus took little prompting to accept Electra's favours. The oracle was truly not expecting the earth to move during the encounter, but in a funny way it did. She was glad that she did not go to her death having never experienced such intimacy with another human being. No matter what lay ahead she could remember this brief, blissful interlude.

'I haven't felt this way in so long.' Prometheus kissed her head as she lay peacefully at his side.

'I haven't felt this way *ever*.' Electra stated the obvious, with a chuckle, and her amusement took Prometheus's breath away.

'You have her laugh, too.' He sat up straight, struggling with a decision. 'Only a fool would risk losing love again to avenge a love lost. What is the point, when the Logos intends to punish the guilty anyway?'

Electra sat up also, her eyes welling with tears of hope. 'You mean ...'

Prometheus gripped her hand. 'Let us flee this place, this instant.' He kissed away the questioning look of relief on her face. 'I never thought to find love again in this world and I shall fight to the death to see you safely away from here.'

'You have no idea what this means to me,' she mumbled through her tears, as she kissed him three times over.

'Best save it,' Prometheus advised, reluctantly. 'Time is of the essence.'

In the corridor, troops awaited them, and advised that Prometheus and Electra had been requested to join Orestes in the Chailidocean room of court.

Electra's glimmer of hope flickered out abruptly, for she felt her tribulation was at hand. *The Logos won't let me flee.* She wept silent tears as she was led to her doom. *I chose this.* It was so unfair that she had made her decision before she had felt earthly love. Now she would have opted for a life with Prometheus gladly! Why had she not stuck with her brother's decision in the first place? Why was she so determined to destroy herself? Had her father been a saint, then maybe her remorse would have been justified. But the truth was he was a warring tyrant every bit as bad as Aegisthus. She could hardly believe that she had allowed her guilt to convince her that her life was worth so little.

'Do not weep.' Prometheus held her firmly as they walked, to reassure her. 'This is but a minor delay.'

Electra nodded, but try as she did, she could not stop shaking.

Prometheus stopped, turning Electra to face him and look into his eyes. 'I swear by the Logos that I shall not allow any harm to come to you. You shall be leaving Chailidocean with me this day.'

She closed her eyes, so wanting to believe him. Dwelling on her future for a moment, the horrid scenes of torture from her visions were still prominent, but through this image bled another and she could see herself fleeing the city with Prometheus. This meant that the possibility had been opened to her. 'I believe you, my Shar.' Her heart fluttered with new hope and with a smile, she ceased to shake.

They entered the room of court to find a Nefilim lord and the beautiful maiden who Electra had foreseen would enchant her brother. The oracle began to shake once more.

'Look, Prometheus.' Orestes motioned to the beautiful maiden at his side, who appeared rather smitten with the young Shar. 'Aegisthus has sent me an exchange for my treacherous sister ... have you ever seen a peace offering that was so lovely?'

'An exchange?' Prometheus was immediately worried. 'You can't accept,' he warned.

''Tis the same as accepting a gift,' Electra warned, knowing that Prometheus was right. 'Remember what happened to mother.'

'But this is not a piece of jewellery.' Orestes ignored her.

'No,' Prometheus warranted, 'although at some point in the near future I'm sure that you plan to put her on, as it were. Be careful, Orestes. Women are your weakness and Aegisthus knows it.'

'Look who's talking,' Orestes scoffed. 'You were incited to civil war for love.'

'But this is an obvious trap.' Prometheus was feeling desperate.

'Well, the way I see it, I can either spend my last days on this earth attempting to reclaim my kingdom from the sorcerer, both of which are destined to be destroyed anyway. Or, I can take this beautiful creature and attempt to outrun this disaster,' Orestes resolved. 'Now which option do you think is more attractive?'

Prometheus couldn't believe what was happening. What had happened to all his young friend's conviction? 'So my wife died for nothing? And what of your people?'

'Most have done what I plan to do, they have fled.' Orestes's eyes remained intent upon his new plaything, whose hands he raised and caressed with his lips. 'And don't act so high and mighty about our cause, Prometheus ... you and Electra were off to combat the sorcerer when my guards found you, is that right?' Orestes looked at his ally and his guilty look said it all. 'I thought so.' He grinned, having made his point, and looked back to Pandora.

Prometheus's eyes turned to the unknown lord,

whose height and pixie-like features identified him as Nefilim. 'And who might you be, lord?'

'He is the Lord Shamash.' Orestes spoke up. 'He's here to collect Electra.'

'No!' both Prometheus and Electra protested at once.

'You gave her to me,' Prometheus reminded his ally, 'thus she is no longer yours to exchange.'

'And you gave her back to me,' Orestes argued. 'Or was it you who locked her in a cell, hmm?'

'I won't allow it.' Prometheus drew his laser sword and extended the blade.

The Lord Shamash chuckled heartily at the heroic gesture and, although his mouth was not moving, Electra feared that the Nefilim was telepathically communicating with her would-be saviour. When Prometheus nodded, Electra became concerned. 'What is he saying, Prometheus?'

Prometheus' eyes opened wide, as if a dagger of fear had pierced his heart.

'Please don't listen to him.' Electra openly began to sob once more, as Prometheus closed his eyes, holstered his weapon, turned and walked away from her.

'Prometheus? Prometheus!' Electra wept, horrified by what his departure meant. 'You swore to me,' she yelled after him.

'Oh, dear me,' Shamash commented as he approached the oracle. 'Have we given away the prize already?'

'What do you want with me?' Electra brushed the disappointment of her betrayal from her face and turned to confront the huge, glowing figure of a god.

'I am just the messenger,' Shamash assured her, and as he clamped a hand down on her shoulder, Electra's world disappeared in a flash of etheric light.

'Dragon? Are you listening to me?'

Maelgwn heard Electra ask the question although she sounded far away. His eyes were wide open, but it was not the King's Men stone circle in Oxfordshire around him now. Maelgwn was still in Orestes's room of court, confronting the question of why he'd abandoned Electra.

'I won't allow it.' He drew his laser sword and extended the blade in Shamash's direction. The scene was realer than real; all Maelgwn's senses were functioning and on overload as they picked up on the peculiarities of his new circumstance.

'Dragon, what is it?' Electra requested to be filled in. *'Why are you shaking?'*

'I must know what Shamash said,' Maelgwn stammered. His own voice sounded distant to him and it was drowned out by the Nefilim lord's hearty chuckle that mocked Prometheus's heroic gesture.

Before you do anything you might regret, allow me to let you in on a little secret I've discovered.

The lord did not move his mouth and Prometheus heard his voice inside his head. He looked at Electra, who was frowning, confused by the silence.

No, she cannot hear me, for this little secret is to remain between you and I.

Prometheus nodded and Electra's concern mounted.

'What is he saying, Prometheus?' Electra begged to know.

I know of a certain little Shar of Usiqua who is working on a project for a rogue relative of mine.

Prometheus' eyes opened wide, fear gripped his being.

'Please don't listen to him,' Electra sobbed.

If you do not make a silent and peaceful about-face and return home, with your forces, I shall drop a bomb on Usiqua this day that will render the entire kingdom uninhabitable. Nothing will survive. I remind you that the protection awarded your kingdom by Enki protects it from attack by Chailidocean forces and technology. Mortal man has not possessed the technology to threaten your mountainous kingdom to date, but I do, Prometheus, so don't tempt me.

Prometheus knew that such a fate awaited his kingdom in any case, but his son needed time to finish the vessel he was working on and load it. He had no choice. It was Electra or his family and Prometheus knew what his wife would have expected him to do. He closed his eyes and prayed for forgiveness, as he holstered his weapon, turned and walked away.

'Prometheus? Prometheus ...!'

Maelgwn fell to his knees as the vision dissolved and his own sight brought him back to his current situation. He had abandoned Electra in her hour of need, and the fact choked him with regret. 'I ... I, I cannot express how —'

'Save it,' Electra said flatly, unmoved by his remorse and distress. 'It won't change anything.' She paused from her tutorial, lost as to how to find words to relay the next part of her tale. 'What the Dark Lords did to me —' she began, but choked on the thought.

Maelgwn could plainly see how distraught the memory made her and he leaned closer to suggest they skip the gory details. When the gory details suddenly manifested on his wife's body, he was shocked into falling backwards. 'Oh, my lord.'

'The result of my stay in the Dark Lodge,' Electra stated, feeling a picture would save her a thousand words. She floated up into the air and turned around so that Maelgwn might be given the full picture.

Maelgwn would have said her naked body was all skin and bone, but she had sustained so many cuts, bruises, sores and burns that he could barely see any skin. Her toenails and fingernails had all been removed along with a few toes and fingers. Her hair had fallen, or been ripped, out of her head, all bar a few tufts and her beautiful face was battered and scarred beyond all recognition. The most prominent scar was a large, round, intricate seal that had been carved into her belly.

'Dear Goddess of mercy,' Rhun mumbled, echoing the horror of all witnessing the transmission from inside Doc's Otherworldly headquarters. 'What Mahaud has done in revenge over the years almost seems reasonable.' He'd always despised the crone for her crimes against his family and yet now he realised she was family. It was gut wrenching to imagine how the beautiful Electra had been reduced to this state in just a few days.

'Hah, hah,' Viper laughed out loud as he viewed the witch's wounds. 'Silly old slut! Serves you right.' He blew a raspberry at the screen on which he viewed her.

'Enough with the drama.' He waved an arm about in protest. 'Get on with the story. Did you raise the Prince of Darkness or not?'

When Electra noted Maelgwn staring at the seal carved into the skin of her belly, she explained, 'I am proud of this wound, as it was the only one I inflicted on myself.' She held her rotting hand over the huge symbol. 'This is how I defeated Aegisthus,' she stated proudly, but with regret, 'and damned myself.'

'Will you explain?' Maelgwn requested gently.

'Have you not enchanted this body to do your bidding?' Electra didn't see that she had a choice. She resumed Tory's form and floated back down to a seat in front of Maelgwn.

'If I didn't need to know, I wouldn't ask.'

Electra seemed impervious to his assurance, and after he had seen Prometheus abandon her as he had, Maelgwn wasn't surprised.

'I believe I was exposed to several days of physical torture and sorcery before Aegisthus asked me to name the leader of the Fallen Ones otherwise known as the Prince of Darkness.'

'Satan?' Maelgwn queried. 'Abaddon?' He had a second guess.

'Satan is the name given to the Lord of Darkness in an opposing aspect. Abaddon is his name when he assumes the role of the destroyer,' Electra explained. 'But the name that is most true to the devil himself is Lucifer, meaning he who gives light. I met him once,' she boasted casually, 'but I shan't get ahead of myself. In any case, it didn't matter which of the mighty spirit's names I gave the sorcerer, the Prince of Darkness was locked away and I knew he would be unable to respond. Then Aegisthus got wise to me, having had a discussion with Power who informed him that a certain spirit held the key to Abaddon's pit and that only I could summon the keymaster.'

'Power has revealed to me the seal to command the Prince of Darkness. Now all I need is for you to set him free,' Aegisthus prompted from his crouched position in front of the oracle. He feared that the prisoner's senses may have completely taken leave, and so he prodded her a few times to see if he could raise a response. 'Given up the fight, Electra? Well, I shall have you perform that summons, so don't go anywhere just yet.'

Electra knew the flaming orb must be due to impact on Gaia soon. It was the only thought that kept her uncooperative. Soon death would come and snatch her from this nightmare. 'You're a dead man anyway,' she mumbled. 'We're all dead.'

'Oh, that's right,' Aegisthus announced cheerily. 'Being in a cell you wouldn't have noticed that the orb has changed course and is now headed away from Gaia.'

Electra had a seizure of fear as she recalled some of what was said during the meeting of the Brotherhood of Light. *The Orions take full responsibility for setting the approaching asteroid on a collision course with Gaia and they will divert the threat away from the planet once we have agreed not to oppose their invasion of the civilised world.* The Brotherhood had agreed and Electra had overlooked the consequences of their decision to give the Orions a free reign. She'd been clinging to a misconception and her stupidity and circumstances made her incredibly angry. Electra screamed out her frustration and just kept on screaming.

The sorcerer was pleased by the reaction. She was weakening, and upon his return visit she would be ready to do his bidding.

When she had screamed and cried away what little strength she had left, Electra realised all her faith in the Logos had fled along with her other hope in the asteroid. The almighty was not going to punish the wicked after all. The Dark Lodge with their sorcery could keep her barely alive like this indefinitely, and they would, just to keep pumping her for information. She couldn't imagine what the future of the human race would be like if the Dark Lodge harnessed the powers of the Dark Lord to further their own cause. 'I must not release Abaddon into their charge.' She strained to think of a way out, but she had no energy, no will. 'I don't want to be a victim.' She hung her head, wishing death would come.

What if you could seize all power from the Dark Lodge, and safely release the destroyer to finish them off?

The presence of the Nefilim lord manifested in the dim cell and blinded Electra.

'How?' She questioned the means before the motive, shielding her eyes with her hand and squinting whilst her eyes adjusted to the Nefilim lord's lustre.

'I have learned the Dark Lodge's ultimate seal, the one used to summon forth all the elementals in their power. You are a channel,' he suggested. 'If you drew this seal on your person you could summon all their evil entities unto you and hold them captive, so that they could not answer the call to service of the Dark Lodge when you direct the Prince of Darkness to wreak his vengeance upon them.'

If Shamash did know the details of such a seal, it would grant her the ability to summon forth the elementals that were aiding the Dark Lodge, but the seal would need to be drawn in fresh blood to attract them to her trap. If she died before she released the evil beings from her hold, they would remain attached to her soul and she would be damned to their realms of existence. 'And what do you stand to gain from all this?' Electra knew the Nefilim couldn't be trusted. 'I was under the impression that Aegisthus was your ally?'

'That mortal halfwit and his wizards are growing far too greedy for my liking.' Shamash outlined his motives. 'They are already moving into territories who pay homage to me and, quite frankly, I think it high time they were taught a lesson.' Shamash sent Electra a mental picture of the all-powerful seal and then tossed her a low output laser knife that was not powerful enough to end her life, but was an ample tool with which to burn through her skin's surface and draw blood. 'Aegisthus will return soon so I shall depart. I leave the fate of the world in your frail little hands.'

Electra had tried summoning the fallen spirit whom Mikhail had said would make himself known to her if she decided to live, but the spirit world had been silent since her capture.

'I have no choice, either I do this or the Dark Lodge shall,' she uttered, feeling that this was why the Logos had wanted her to live, as she was the last chance the righteous had for retribution. Electra pulled her naked, battered body up against a wall and gritting her teeth, she began to carve the seal on her gut.

When she had completed every detail of the motif, she lay herself out on the hard, cold stone floor, opening her arms wide.

'Enter all creatures
bound to this seal,
grant me your obedience
and power to wield.'

The atmosphere inside her cell became turbulent with activity, as one by one hideous spirits appeared above her before they ploughed their way into her body. Once all had entered her being, her breathing resounded with the growling of many disgruntled demons.

Very good, Electra heard Shamash say as he appeared suddenly before her, holding out his hand towards her heart. 'All their power shall now be mine.'

She felt her ribs pried open and then a great tug at her chest. The last thing Electra saw was her heart still beating as Shamash clutched it in his hand.

'Come when I call you, Mahaud,' Shamash advised his dying victim, 'and we shall strike a deal whereby we all get what we want.'

As a great darkness and density closed in on her, the creatures to whom she was attached began growling and snarling in protest. Her spirit did not take flight once separated from her body but rather, it felt weighted, restrained, suffocated of thought, and she felt herself being dragged into a thick bog of dammed energy.

The next time she became aware of anything else but her fear-filled struggle to surface from the thick sea of hysteria in which she was embroiled, a voice called through the deafening din of the sub-planes.

Mahaud, I summon you forth!

A mental picture of a symbol carved of flesh and blood presented itself to her soul-mind and broke the drought of thought she had been experiencing.

I am Mahaud, her soul-mind was able to respond. At last she was breaking free.

A great lightness swept over her and she found herself floating before the Lord Shamash. The numerous growls, snarls and howls that were emanating from her being seemed to indicate that all her beastly elementals were still in tow. After their little stint in Density together, her demons felt like old chums now; it was comforting to know she had them on side.

'What took so long?' she thought and her beasts spoke her mind for her.

'I came straight here and summoned you forth,' Shamash assured. 'We are in space and so shall not be disturbed.'

'Awfully brave of you, if I may say so,' Mahaud commented coolly, seeing how the Nefilim lord regarded her damned being with a sense of reserve. He feared her newfound power and that too was comforting.

'You idiot!' her numerous voices growled. 'By killing me you've bound me to these elementals indefinitely!'

'Now, now.' He urged her not to try and rebel. 'The seal over which you are hovering binds your beasts to obedience, and you, being bound to them as you have pointed out, will endure their punishment if you do not behave and show a little respect for he who created you.'

She tried to lash out and found herself being drawn into oblivion once more. 'NO,' her beings cried, 'anything but that!' The great weight on her spirit lightened and her state of alarm ebbed.

'Wonderful,' Shamash announced. 'Now that we have that sorted out, I assume you still wish to lavish your revenge on those who destroyed your kindred ... so, let's make a deal.'

'We are listening, lord.' She humbled herself before the Nefilim. She despised being told what to do, but there were others she hated more than her new master. She would grin and bear him ... for now.

When the Otherworldly shield that had been protecting the Dark Lodge from attack vanished, the lodge was overrun by a diehard force of natives who were still keeping vigil in Chailidocean, waiting for an opportunity to take their grievances out on the order.

Aegisthus had been on his way back to see Electra when the invasion started. The sorcerer had not run anywhere in eons, but he scampered for his life down to the dungeon and locked himself in with his hostage.

The sight of Electra's gutted body chilled Aegisthus to the bone, not because it repulsed him, but because only the Nefilim made so clean a kill. The same deed done by elemental forces was decidedly more messy. In fact, Electra's heart had been ripped out so efficiently that the bottom portion of the seal carved on the oracle's gut was still clearly definable. Upon recognising this seal the sorcerer figured out what had happened to his creatures, and this information provided him with a means to summon them back to his service.

Quickly he pulled a drawing stone from his pocket and began depicting the seal on the stone floor. The sound of the native hordes destroying everything in their path was drawing closer and urged him to draw quickly.

'Too late, Aegisthus.'

The sight of the hideous etheric world beasts attached to a vaporous human form sent the sorcerer scampering backwards.

'I kept telling you that you were a dead man, but you wouldn't believe me.' She gloated over her impending kill, feeling herself strengthened by his fear. 'How does it feel to know that you've spent your whole life perfecting the instrument of your death?' She reared up ready to strike.

'Wait!' Aegisthus screamed. 'Without me you shall be bound to my pets forever ... is that what you want?' The sorcerer was pleased when the demon backed up to consider his question. 'I know how to separate your spirit from their influence,' he added, to hasten the decision, but his tactic backfired.

What he really meant to say was that he could separate his pets from her influence. 'Oh, I don't know ...

I kind of like my new companions,' she teased, stroking the heads of the numerous creatures who protruded from her form. 'They make me feel safe,' she advised, 'safe, from people like *you*.' She startled the sorcerer as she moved in close and chuckled at his fright. 'I know how Prometheus's wife was killed.' She leered over her victim, the claws and jaws of all her beastly elementals opening wide. 'Care for a demonstration?'

The silver ring of protection that Aegisthus had stolen from Electra with Clytemnestra's help was not on his person and Mahaud did not bother searching for it. It would be buried along with the rest of this wretched civilisation.

In the thick coating of blood that now covered the floor of the dungeon, she willed the seal of Uriel to take form. 'The time of judgement is nigh. Regent of the Sun who is the spirit of political reform and holder of the Key to Hades, I command thee, release Abbadon!'

A moment later Mahaud found herself floating in the centre of the Mt Duranki Plateau confronted by a radiant spirit. Uriel appeared brighter to her perception than ever before and she could make out little more of him than the scroll he held in one hand and the open flame that danced upon his other hand. These were his defining signs.

Your plight has sealed the breach, the spirit told Mahaud. *The gate is open. Let Abbadon teach his lesson to humankind.*

Mahaud felt a great tremor deep within her. Distant at first, a feeling of great expectation quickly rose to the surface of her being, and as the feeling rose it changed to one of liberation. The powerful force reached the surface of her manifestation and burst forth from her. The first burst of energy shot directly upwards towards the sky. Then a steady flow of energy ensued and distributed itself via hundreds of streams of light that shot out across the world in every direction via the ley-grid.

The distress call from the Dark Lodge in Chailidocean couldn't have come at a worse time for Yahweh Aris. His largest space vessel had been hit by an unknown light anomaly and it had adversely affected the navigation and tracking systems of the electromagnetic laser light weapon which the Orions had used several times to redirect the asteroid threatening Gaia.

'Why are we repositioning to fire?' Aris demanded an answer from his crew.

The head technician could only shrug. 'None of the control panels will respond, Yahweh Aris ... somebody is overriding the entire system.'

'That's not possible!' the Dragon leader seethed. 'The Black League wouldn't dare to try something like this!'

'Our primary weapon has locked on target, Yahweh,' his tactician fretted. 'There's nothing I can do to stop it firing.' His fingers raced over the control pad but there was no response.

As the laser fired, Yahweh Aris began to quietly seethe. 'Tens of thousands of years' planning, ruined.'

Immediately following the missile's release, all control panels returned to normal.

'Will the impact send the asteroid into Gaia?' Aris

asked the tactician. He anxiously caressed the silver ring of protection on his finger, which he'd taken from Aegisthus.

'No, Yahweh,' the tactician was pleased to inform, 'but —'

'No!!!!' Aris yelled as he watched the huge chunk of asteroid blasted away from its moving target and placed its focus in the heart of Chailidocean.

'I fear there is little point in going to the aid of our human brothers.' Aris was resigned to the disaster. 'There is trouble beyond our scope headed their way.'

Orestes had fled Chailidocean, with his peace offering from the Dark Lodge, in the fastest, most luxurious airship in his fleet and was currently headed east beyond the kingdom and mountains that Lugal had once ruled.

He'd indulged himself for hours with Pandora's beautiful form and now Orestes was snoozing peacefully on the bed.

Pandora was so deliriously happy that she could not sleep and as she lay awake admiring her young lover, she was filled with a sudden curiosity regarding the vase that Shamash had given her as a dowry.

The Nefilim lord had told her that the vase was invaluable, but rising from the bed to observe it, Pandora didn't think the workmanship was that extraordinary; she'd seen many finer vases during the brief glimpse she'd been awarded of the Chailidocean palace.

'Perhaps my Lord Shamash was hinting that he'd placed some riches inside?' Pandora whispered to herself as she hurried over to check. She couldn't believe that she hadn't thought to remove the lid and view inside her dowry earlier, but then her new master had been keeping her gainfully employed since they'd set foot upon his transport.

Lifting the lid Pandora reached inside the vase and was excited to find a large item wrapped in black silk. She unwrapped her treasure carefully whereupon a sold silver dagger fell into her hands. Pandora gasped, for its jewels were bedazzling. She found the weapon most enchanting and was gripped by a compelling lust to use it.

'Again my love?' Orestes felt Pandora return to the bed and rolled over to oblige her with more love play. 'I feel rested now and I —'

It was only through a reflex action that Orestes' right arm deflected the pending strike of the dagger and he only sustained a bad cut to the lower arm. Orestes rolled out of bed away from his attacker, horrified to realise that it was his shot at future happiness that was trying to do him in. 'Why, Pandora?' he appealed to her, his heart truly broken. 'I betrayed my father's memory so that we might have a life together.'

'Do I need a reason?' Pandora licked his blood from her blade and pounced at him to try again.

She did not manage to draw blood this time and as Orestes struggled to take the weapon from Pandora their airship was hit by a great shockwave. The power failed and the ship fell into darkness.

'Pandora!' Orestes yelled as she was cast away from him in the blast. He felt himself begin to float when their vessel began plummeting out of control towards Gaia's surface and then the sound of Pandora sobbing, a fair distance from him, reached his ears. 'Pandora, why do you weep now?'

'I don't know why I tried to hurt you,' she spluttered, 'you made me so happy.'

The power restored itself and Orestes hit the ground with a thud that near shattered his bones. As he moved to raise himself, he noted the blood on his hands and a trail of red droplets on the floor of his cabin.

He followed the trail to find Pandora with the dagger stuck through her chest. Orestes fell to his knees and wept for the woman he'd traded his soul for. Remorse consumed him with violent intensity. He'd lost his kingdom, betrayed his people, forsaken his sister and best friend. He'd failed to avenge his father's death, and he'd bargained with the murderous sorcerer to save both their skins.

As one of the Shar's advisors entered, Orestes rose to state his resolve. 'Turn the ship around. I'm going back to face Aegisthus.'

'But my Shar, there is no point,' his servant urged, his brow as wrinkled as could be when he spied the maiden on the floor. 'Our data indicates that the shockwave stemmed from there. We shall be lucky to outrun the wall of water headed our way as it is.'

Orestes was dumbstruck. 'What kind of a weapon puts out such a shockwave?'

'Only the gods have such power.' The advisor humbled himself.

Orestes glanced back at his dead lover. 'And they have punished us.'

* * *

Shamash stood at the large windows in the private quarters of his spaceship, laughing heartily as he watched the chaos erupting below. 'This is marvellous, just spectacular.'

The landmasses on one side of the planet were cracking into pieces like a jigsaw puzzle; some were being engulfed by water, others by fire and lava. All the ash spewing into the air was starting to darken the atmosphere and hinder the view of the surface.

'It's certainly going to take some time for the dust to settle.' The lord turned to his guest.

Atlas was not so amused. 'You promised me Atlantis for the seal, that was the bargain.' The Titan slapped one hand into the other to demand payment.

'Relax,' the Nefilim assured. 'The impact of that small asteroid will cause a bit of an axis tilt. By the time everything settles on the surface, your kingdom will be a prime piece of real estate.'

'But my family, my subjects, they shall all have perished.' The realisation of his stupidity and betrayal had a shocking effect and Atlas fell to his knees filled with remorse and sorrow.

'So you outlasted them all, Atlas. You are the last of the Titans!' Shamash tried a little cheerfulness. 'Don't brood. Not all humankind will have perished and when you return to Gaia, they will worship you as a god!'

'I don't want to be a god!' he snarled, clambering to his feet.

'That is not what you said when we had our first little chat.' Shamash's tone advised the Titan to tread cautiously. '"I would give anything to rule the City of the Golden Gates", I believe were your exact words.'

'But I am not to rule Chailidocean, am I?'

'Poor, poor Atlas.' Mahaud startled the Titan with her array of harsh voices and her horrifying appearance. 'Left to uphold the world.' As she loomed before him, Atlas backed away. 'I bet you wish you'd aided Prometheus now.' She gave a chuckle at his pain, for she felt nothing any more. 'Upon the urging of the Dark Lodge I have released the beast from its captivity and thus you will have the reign of terror you have so long desired. And I shall be there to encourage the worst of you *unto your death*.'

'No, I am finished with the Dark Lodge.' Atlas backed away from the demon. He had seen and done enough damage for one lifetime. 'Do you think I want them finding out about my part in this?' Atlas added in his own defence. 'Take me back to Gaia's surface to suffer along with my people, and I shall gladly disappear into obscurity.'

'No one can hide from the forces I have unleashed, Atlas,' Mahaud grinned, satisfied that he would get his comeuppance. 'But you shall live to try.'

'Shamash kept his word to me … for a while at least,' Electra added. 'He did not send me back into the sub-planes as long I did not do anything contrary to his interests. I was bound to answer his summons above all others. When he did see fit to banish me out of his service on Gaia, Shamash had my legend placed in secret chambers under some of his temples of worship for men of evil intent to seek and discover over the ages; for them to copy and spread afar.'

'To be found and utilised by men like my uncle, Cadfer,' Maelgwn concluded.

'Men like Viper.' Electra brought the topic of the conversation round to more current matters.

Maelgwn nodded, although he was not yet ready to return to the present. 'How did you find out about Yahweh Aris?'

'Atlas,' she replied. 'I chased him up on Gaia, once I was at liberty to do so without Shamash finding out. He spilled the beans on the Dark Lodge and the trainer of their Grand Masters through the ages.'

'And do you know what became of Prometheus?' Maelgwn felt he was pushing his luck in asking.

'The Noah myth tells us that Prometheus's son survived to sail the Ark. But for unknown reasons Prometheus didn't accompany his son on the voyage.'

'After he'd seen his son safely away, perhaps he headed back to Chailidocean to save you,' Maelgwn posed.

Electra shrugged at the supposition. 'In any case, he founded Athens in Greece, which was where Orestes turned up. Whether or not they ended their days as friends I do not know,' she concluded, sounding bored with the subject.

'You met the Prince of Darkness, you said earlier.' Maelgwn raised a topic he felt may be equally interesting to them both.

She fixed her eyes upon Maelgwn and nodded. 'You need to speak with Mahaud about that.'

'Thank you, Electra, for enlightening me to a great many things I had forgotten,' Maelgwn said in parting and gave a nod for the crone to return to the fore. The red glowing eyes, demonic voices and dark presence of Mahaud returned to haunt Tory's body once more. 'Continue,' he instructed.

'Following our encounter on the moon, the Night Hunter sent me into deepest Density, so deep that I broke through the barrier of nothingness into an illuminated region beyond. I came before a great throne and upon it sat the chief of demons himself.'

'How did you know it was Lucifer?' Maelgwn queried.

'Because the part of me that was Electra remembers speaking with the most beautiful of Logos's angels and Satan far surpassed them all.'

It was strange to hear Mahaud speak of beauty and Maelgwn considered that perhaps she had a different ideal of what was beautiful these days. 'And did Lucifier speak to you, Mahaud?'

'He did,' she informed dryly. 'He told me that as I had endured all darkness had to teach, I must find a way back to the path of light or be consumed completely by darkness. For darkness absorbs energy into one point of eternity. Much like your black holes have collapsed into a point, a singularity, I would damn myself and create a cessation, a suffocation, where space-time and I would relinquish existence. This is the true meaning of being damned. "You're no good to us here," were Satan's exact words.'

* * *

'And I know why!' Viper moved to a different soft-light screen.

'Shall I give the command to fire, Lord Viper?' His second-in-command reminded Viper that their spacecraft's photon missiles were locked on the targeted area.

Viper shook his head as he reviewed the footage of the conversation that had passed between the Dragon and Mahaud. It was the segment where Electra exposed her scars that Viper was looking for. He honed in and sharpened a picture of the seal carved on her belly and then chuckled to himself delightedly. 'Mahaud never mentioned she had a seal of obedience.' This meant that Viper no longer needed utensils to summon or hold the crone, and this latest development did away with the need to bargain with her. He turned to his second-in-command to advise. 'Wait for my word before firing.'

As his 2IC nodded, Viper departed to his room of summons, back on the Aten.

'Thus the Bringer of Light touched me and back I came into Viper's service,' Mahaud concluded. 'Just as Viper and myself had arranged back in Gwynedd of old. But my perception of my purpose here, in the physical realm, had changed since Viper and I first spoke and I knew that this time around I was not to serve the darkness, but to seek my liberation from it. Thus, I chased you up once again, Prometheus, knowing that you would be my liberation, just as you had been my doom. So you see, the dramatics are not necessary,' she looked to the cloud churning above them, 'as I do not intend to resist your intent.'

Maelgwn looked to the sky, confused. 'But I thought you were responsible for the turbulence?'

Mahaud went to shake her head, when a vision of the all-powerful seal Shamash had used to bind her to his service, via her evil elemental entourage, filled her perception. 'It's —' she tried to warn Maelgwn, but her being was snatched from the body that held her. The charm around Tory's waist snapped, and her body fell to the ground unconscious.

This is it, my love. Tory's spirit was close at hand to give Maelgwn strength.

In a great flash of light and heat, the earthly bodies of Maelgwn Gwynedd and Tory Alexander were scattered to the earth and four winds from whence they had come.

'NO!' hollered Rhun as he witnessed the blast, and the large hexagon in Taliesin's Otherworldly abode then went blank.

All the Dragon's boys were equally upset and began entertaining notions of taking the chariot back in time in order to get their parents' bodies away from the site in time.

'Mother and father both knew this was going to happen.' Lirathea barged into the middle of her brothers to get them focused. 'Remember father's last instruction to you,' she told Rhun. 'That the present is of no concern to us. You must go back and save Mahaud and what has unfolded here today will be completely altered.'

'I want to come with you,' Avery requested more than demanded for a change.

'Over a long distance, I wouldn't risk overloading the chariot with any more than two passengers,' Noah advised Rhun, before he made the decision.

Rhun draped his arm over his brother's shoulder, in touch with his reasons for wanting to come. 'You promised Lahmu you'd watch over Fallon and I cannot take her with us.'

Avery winced, knowing Rhun was right and he shouldn't argue, but he did anyway. 'We will be back within a few minutes and as I am apprentice to Gwyn ap Nudd, I may be of some aid when it comes to dealing with the elemental pets of the Dark Lodge.'

Rhun looked to Sparrowhawk and Zabeel, who both seemed prepared to allow Avery to go, albeit reluctantly.

'All right then, it's settled.' Rhun slapped his hand down on Avery's shoulder, inwardly relieved by the decision.

PART 3

MASTERS

CHARACTER LIST

PART 3

Leader of the Fallen Ones	Azaz'el,
Other Fallen Angels	Sammael
Armaros	
Viper's 2IC	Tareena
Doc Alexander's sons	Luther and Morgan
Doc Alexander's wife	Vanora
MIB Agent	Zero
The Christ	Lord Maitreya
Chohan of the Sixth Ray	Sananda
Buddha	

Prologue

Finally the writer was making a living from doing what she loved most — using her imagination. Her first trilogy had far surpassed sales expectations and she had a stand-alone novel nearly ready for publication. Work had already commenced on the next novel, a stand-alone also, which the writer was adapting from an unfinished film script.

It was a little tricky working her career in around a new baby, but her daughter was such a contented infant that somehow the writer kept managing to churn out a book a year.

The writer had become friendly with a clairvoyant, from whom she would request a reading every six months or so.

The clairvoyant reminded her of one of the wise, all-seeing druids from her tales. He had the ability to reach into the back of the writer's mind and pull out the ideas and lessons, past and future, that were valuable for her to note or pour energy into, and the oracle was rarely wrong with his predictions.

At this reading her clairvoyant's advice was proving particularly unwelcome, as it was threatening to throw her life into chaos.

'There are another three Tory Alexander books coming,' the oracle told her outright, as if the writer had no choice in the matter.

'Don't say that,' begged the writer. 'After three epic novels surely —'

'There's another three books,' he repeated. 'Just sit down and write the synopses and you'll see that I'm right,' he challenged.

'But I'm contracted to write another novel, and I've already begun.' The writer changed tack to protest again.

The oracle shook his head. 'It doesn't matter. By the time you write the synopses, your publishers will be asking you for another Tory trilogy.'

The writer didn't want to consider such a huge commitment. Having written a trilogy already she knew the hard yards that were involved, and this time she had a baby to consider. Still, this man's soothsaying was always precise, and he hadn't been so adamant about a prediction since he'd foreseen the writer falling pregnant — only three weeks before the fact. The writer had been equally adamant that now was not the right time to be having a family, with her career just taking off, and she had told her clairvoyant that his guides must have their lines crossed. Of course, the oracle had been right, and now the writer took more notice when he was resolute. 'How can you be so sure about the second trilogy?'

The oracle took a deep breath and went silent before answering her query, as he often did to listen to the advice of the spirits who came forth with messages for his clients. 'Tory Alexander is real,' he said at last, and winced. 'I don't exactly know what they mean by that.' He fell quiet to listen to the spirits once more. 'You are ...' he began and then hesitated, his frown deepening as he strained to make sense of the message. 'Tory is a part of your soul-mind living in another inter-dimensional reality.'

At this stage, the writer tried not to mock. 'Now you're sounding like my readers ... most of them feel that this particular story is real somehow.'

'That's how!' The oracle pressed his view and that of the spirit advising him. 'Tory is your muse whenever you write about her.'

The writer couldn't deny that Tory's attitude did overshadow her when writing her tales and the writer did like being influenced by Tory's strength, courage, conviction and knowledge.

When the writer had been working on the stand-alone novel, she'd been pregnant and had not really felt her normal self, nor had she felt Tory's warrior influence. Their beautiful cat, Arthur McCloud, had unexpectedly died just before she'd commenced her latest novel, and the writer couldn't help but feel that Arthur had been the muse behind her recently published work in which he'd featured as a character.

'Tory and co still have much they can teach you.' The oracle encouraged the writer not to reject the idea because of the enormity of it. 'It's very important that you do this.'

'Important to who?' The writer wanted to know. 'Me?'

'It's important to the evolution of consciousness in this dimension,' he stated in all seriousness and the writer gave a laugh.

'I'm not a spiritual guru,' she argued in typical Tory fashion.

'No, you're not,' the oracle granted, 'you're just an open channel. Every individual is, to differing degrees, and if you don't write this second trilogy, your muse will move on to the next open channel to achieve her aims.'

The writer didn't like that idea, not when the first trilogy had been so popular with readers and she had learned so much from the adventure.

'Listen.' The oracle sought to alleviate her apprehension. 'Everything about these books, from the content to the colours and designs on the jackets, has been carefully conceived of by the cosmos to stir things in the deeper consciousness of your readers ... feelings, inspiration, ideas, *memories*. That is why your readers feel the stories are real, as you are not the only one with memories of other dimensions. Some of your readers have no doubt been involved in the different events of the inter-dimensional reality Tory has been channelling through to you, and when they read your tales they remember their involvement.'

'Well!' The writer was dumbstruck. 'That's some theory you've got there.' Her eyebrows raised as she considered it further and then melted into a smile. 'Could make one hell of a story.'

18

INCOMPLETE

The intense light and heat of the blast dissipated, leaving Tory and Maelgwn facing one another in the ethereal foyer of the outer court of Shamballa.

'That wasn't so bad now, was it?' The Dragon smiled as he observed their sparkling etheric forms and how liberating it felt to have shed his physical world body for good.

'We are still separate entities?' Tory was surprised and a little disappointed.

'Your soul-mind still has tasks it wishes to perform before it unites and departs this world to do other work.'

Tory didn't have to look to know that it was the Count who had spoken, nor to know that DK was present with him, for the individual energies each master exuded were very distinctive. 'I'd almost forgotten about our musing duties.' Tory was reluctant to return to her charge, as she'd been led to believe that the shedding of physical world form represented an initiation passed, opening the second door that led to the middle court of Shamballa. When Tory did turn her attention to the masters, DK was grinning, for he knew what his charge was thinking.

'Look up,' he advised, pointing in that direction.

The ceiling above appeared as a wall of fire, not unlike that which Tory and Maelgwn had both passed through in order to enter the outer court of Shamballa. The fiery surface was gradually bearing down on them and Tory and Maelgwn waited to be consumed with delighted anticipation.

Your striving, self-mastery, endurance, patience and sacrifice for the cause of Good, Beauty and Truth have brought you here. The voice of the Master Kuthumi filled the minds of the initiates. *Greet the fiery angel that guards the central city of Shamballa and enter the Door of Will.*

The gentle cleansing fire washed over Tory and Maelgwn and was accompanied by an electrical phenomenon that surged over and through their etheric bodies.

The lightning destroys age-long accumulations of darkness, the last bond of the self to matter. Its gift is enlightenment, the birth of the soul, the ability to see and contact the greater soul in every man. All your chakras now resonate to their proper colour and vibration, forming a vessel for the blessings of the Sanat Kumara.

More liberating than the shedding of the physical body was the purification of the soul. As the fire passed down over their forms and dissipated into the celestial floor, Tory and Maelgwn had shed their ethereal forms and now occupied glowing astral forms which had a slight ultraviolet hue. The couple became aware of other beings around them. The foyer of the outer court was still present and its architecture had not changed at all, only now it was filled with other etheric spirits all calmly moving about on their own business.

'Welcome to the central jewelled city of the Isle of White,' Kuthumi greeted the couple, as he now stood alongside the Count and DK.

'Pleased we could make it,' Maelgwn mumbled, straining to concentrate on the masters, as alien beings passing by threatened to divert his attention with their unique features.

'I've been here before.' Tory recognised some of the extra-terrestrial beings. 'This is where Raziel brought Electra's consciousness to witness the meeting of the Black League.' All three masters gave a nod to confirm her hunch. When Tory spotted a being with dragon-like features she was confused. 'He's an Orion.'

'Yes, that's right,' DK granted.

'But are they not the force behind the Dark Lodge?' Tory wondered what such a being was doing here, where no dark intent could infiltrate.

'You were once a force behind the Dark Lodge,' DK reminded her. 'The Orions are gradually learning how to tread the path of light, as are we all. The Orions were also the force behind the Aryan race and you wouldn't say all Aryans were evil, would you?'

Considering that Aryan blood had once run in her veins, she had to agree with the master, although the information was rather perplexing.

'Just because a body might appear Aryan, that doesn't necessarily mean that the soul-mind is the same as the consciousness that spawned the race. Not all the white Atlanteans were of Pleiadean consciousness, now were they?' he remarked. 'That is why you can never judge a man based on his racial background, for there will always be exceptions to the rule. Human consciousness is a melting pot for all the physical world intelligence that is on the road back to the Creator.'

'And what of Yahweh Aris?' Tory wondered, in light of the fact that the Electra incident had occurred nearly twelve thousand years before. 'Has that soul-mind made it to Shamballa?'

'Not yet,' DK answered, although all the masters were very excited by the question. 'His service in the Dark Lodge of the Materialistic has been extensive and very beneficial to the plan.'

'Far more than even he realises,' the Count added. 'He has served to keep all extra-terrestrial operations on this planet a secret, by distorting the facts of UFO sightings, using charlatans and extremists. Anyone who has found hard evidence of extra-terrestrial existence, his Dark Lodge has gone to great lengths to intimidate and silence.'

'Yahweh Aris heads the Men in Black,' Tory

concluded, looking to Maelgwn to catch his reaction, although he was not really paying attention.

A group of male spirits, four in number, approached Maelgwn and greeted him warmly.

'Dragon,' exclaimed the beautiful spirit in the lead, who rather resembled their son, Rhun. 'How splendid that you are through your trial and are now fully dedicated to the subjective. We have relayed our objective to our charges, who are readying themselves for their return to Atlantis.'

When Tory noted that each spirit resembled one of her sons she guessed the group to be the Oversouls Maelgwn had been working with, just as she had been working with Astarleia.

'I should go.' Maelgwn turned back to Tory to bid her farewell with a smile.

'I'll be reading about you all,' Tory directed the comment to the group of guides representing the men closest to her during her life, 'and I know you'll make me proud, as always.'

'We had a fine teacher,' granted Rhun's Oversoul, whereupon he and the spirits in his company bowed to Tory and Maelgwn before they led her husband away. Five paces across the foyer, they all vanished.

When Tory turned back to the masters, DK stood alone; the Masters Kuthumi and the Count had both departed.

'You are wondering what effect your sons' quest to save Mahaud from coming into being will have on your ascending soul-mind, now that you realise that your time in the darkness was essential to your spiritual perfection?'

'Yes.' Tory was amused by how accurately DK described her thoughts when she hadn't even formulated her query.

'I told you before: it doesn't matter in what inter-dimensional reality you play out your karma to the Logos, no venture is ever lost in the great scheme of things.' He smiled broadly and, motioning ahead, he invited her to walk with him for a spell. 'You see, although your sons might save Electra when they return to Atlantis, which will surely affect Gaia's present reality, your time in darkness has already been played out and so that understanding shall never be lost to you. Still, if your sons can free Electra, that will be one less elemental spirit bound for oblivion.'

'But what of Maelgwn?' Tory theorised. 'Would he not have to have served time in darkness in order to understand it?'

'The Dragon has served longer and endured darkness and torment longer than any.' DK sounded most sypathetic.

Tory gasped, feeling that DK was dropping hints. 'You're not implying that Maelgwn is Yahweh Aris, are you?'

'No,' DK confirmed gently, put on the spot. But he was spared the problem of getting around the topic when they reached the exterior doors and Tory was granted her first glimpse of the paradise beyond.

Tory had seen some Otherworldly gardens in her time, but none could compare to the rare beauty of the trees, flowers, and colours of this place. There were buildings, composed of a glowing astral substance, which had miraculous architecture. These dwellings rose up like walls on either side of a huge expanse of wilderness, with waterfalls, hot and cold springs and walkways that appeared to go on forever. Looking up, Tory was surprised to find beautiful crystal stalagmites hanging from the cavern roof high above. 'We're underground?'

DK was nodding and about to comment when Tory noticed a couple of people walk by her who seemed to have a physical body. Their eyes were open and yet the iris had no colour whatsoever. A bright centre of light hung over their third eye area, and as the pair nodded in greeting and recognition of Tory on their way past her, she suspected that they were perceiving her through their third eye area, rather than with their physical eyes. 'Physical humans can find Shamballa?'

'Sometimes,' DK commented. 'You nearly made it here with your physical body still attached. But the residents you are curious about are the more adept world teachers of the Inner Earth tribes.'

'Like Neraida and her once underground Middle Eastern clan?' Tory wondered whether the tribes were related.

'Neraida's people were not really classified as an Inner Earth tribe, as they frequented the underground *and* the surface of Gaia. They found and utilised two old subterranean passageways in the Middle East, abandoned by the Inner Earth people after it was decided that the great underground complex of Giza would be sealed up and reopened when humanity was ready for the secrets contained therein.'

'So there is a time capsule under the plateau.' Tory smiled as she considered how excited Noah would be to know this. As she noted how many Inner Earth people seemed to be wandering around the place, her brain spat forth a possible explanation as to where they came from. 'These are the descendants of the refugees of Atlantis.'

DK was delighted by her guess. 'But you know that the deluge recorded in your history was only the last phase of the sinking of Atlantis. The continent known to you as Atlantis was originally connected to Lumeria, which began sinking some eight hundred and fifty thousand years before the catastrophe Electra was involved in. As humankind developed, people were continuously drawn towards the dark path of the materialistic —'

'Which was necessary in order for humanity to understand itself and the physical realm it found itself in. Once understanding advanced, then humankind could develop ideas and take its part in the creation of the physical human environment and evolution,' Tory reasoned.

'Indeed,' DK emphasised. 'As the bodies of humankind developed, the flame of thought was introduced into their minds.'

'By the Logos?'

'By his request,' the Tibetan master explained. 'The great Cosmic Lives, or Solar Angels if you prefer, who were overseeing other more advanced civilisations in other regions of the physical universe came to our Logos's aid. It was the second wave of these divine beings coming to view human development that exposed man to thought.'

'The Nefilim Logos, Anu?' Tory took a stab at guessing.

'Correct,' DK granted. 'Anu's interest guided his race here and they further developed the apeman already existing on Gaia, and in fusing Nefilim genes with primitive man, the capacity for thought was planted. But it was the third wave of Solar Angels who finally entered the etheric sphere of the human being. Many humans existing at this time could not hold the charge of power generated by these beings and their brains were burned away. But for those who did hold the charge, a great awakening began.'

'Enki's fourteen perfect humans.' Tory felt a great awakening begin to stir in her being now. 'And the Solar Angels who sparked this great awareness were from Sirius, the Pleiades and the Orion systems. Their commitment to human consciousness guided the extra-terrestrials to our solar system, where they could watch over their investment and guide it,' Tory reasoned. 'And the other human tribes who were developed on Gaia and then redistributed throughout the galaxy by the Nefilim, have benefited from these cosmic spiritual outpourings too.'

'Every planetary spirit in the universe is a Logos in the making, and each spirit has a centre like Shamballa that feeds cosmic energy through it and to the occupants of the planet they nurture, on every level of awareness ... everything is interconnected.' DK could not stress this strongly enough. 'Still, Gaia is the mother planet of human consciousness and thus will always remain the focus of the struggle for the perfection of the species.

As mankind developed, the more spiritually adept humans of each era were directed to the Inner Earth cities which had been constructed by the extra-terrestrial races involving themselves in human evolution.'

'But how is it that the Nefilim were never aware of the presence of the alien invaders?' Tory wondered.

'You forget that the Nefilim were not always a permanent fixture on this planet. There were tens of thousands of years between some of their visits. Every time a deluge occurred on Gaia, the Nefilim would pack up and head elsewhere and that's when other extra-terrestrials made themselves at home in the Inner Earth.'

They had walked quite a way from the building of initiation and the underground civilisation just seemed to go on forever. 'It's huge!' Tory commented. 'How many Inner Earth cities are there?'

'Almost as many as there are biodome cities above on the surface,' he informed.

'And all these cities are connected?'

'Almost.' His smile lost a little of its sparkle. 'The cities that once existed in the South American region were invaded and seized by the Dark Lodge soon after Atlantis's demise. This area was conducive to the purpose of the Lodge as this is where the dregs of Shamballa energy end up ... and after it has filtered through humanity, it has a more negative charge than a positive one. With any luck the next Shamballa Impact will have an advancing effect on humanity's consciousness, instead of the delaying or salvaging effect it has had in the past.'

Tory recalled Electra's tale of when she had watched the senate meeting of the Brotherhood of Light where the Pleiadean member had used this term. 'But if Shamballa is feeding energy to the etheric matrix all the time, then what is a Shamballa Impact?'

'Not all the etheric data that we receive from other systems is deemed suitable for human soul-mind consumption at the time we receive it. These inspirations are held over until such time as they are truly needed. And then they are only released when there are more souls incarnate on Gaia, both inner and outer, who are on the path of selflessness rather than the path of the materalistic. This ensures that even though both the Brotherhood of Light and the Dark Lodge will benefit from the information —'

'As polarity demands,' Tory cited.

'The path of light will prevail,' he concluded, and then raised his eyebrows to inform: 'Shamballa energy has been released directly to humanity only three times without first being filtered by the Masters of Wisdom and their adepts, who have forever stood as mediums between humanity and Shamballa.'

'Let me guess.' Tory loved this kind of challenge. 'The final sinking of Atlantis has to be one instance.'

'Actually, it marked the second Impact,' DK confirmed, 'The complete destruction of the human soul-mind was imminent, thanks to the retarding ways of the Dark Lodge. Hence Shamballa interfered and the civilised world was destroyed, leaving only the meek to continue the evolution of human consciousness on the surface of the planet.'

'So it was not the devil Mahaud released into the world.' Tory saw beyond her age-old misconceptions and beliefs. 'It was Shamballa energy, but due to the amount of evil in the world, the impact was bound to be converted to its destructive aspect.'

'Now you're beginning to see the bigger picture,' DK granted, pleased for her. 'The first great outpouring of Shamballa energy was actually —'

'When the Solar Angels entered etheric human consciousness,' Tory politely interjected, having figured the answer.

'The birth of the human soul,' he confirmed. 'The third Impact happened in 1944AD, to bring about the end of World War Two.'

'And a great many other inspirations that took longer to formulate and realise,' the master added, to outline that the Impact had short-term and long-term effects. 'The industrial movement had a huge kick-start at this time. Hitler was defeated and the United Nations was formed.'

'So this Impact was more successful than the one before it,' Tory considered. 'In so far as much good was achieved from all the destruction and a solid worldwide code of ethics was established.'

'It was a very close shave. Had the Dark Lodge chosen the Germans over the Americans to supply the information to, the world would be a very different place.'

Tory's eyes parted wide with surprise. 'The Dark Lodge are working with Gaia's world governments?'

'Since the seventh century,' he told her, as if it were

common knowledge. 'Although at that time they would have been known as the illuminati. There exists two different Leagues of the Illuminati, though: one dedicated to the cause of light, the other to the cause of the materialistic.' DK noted Astarleia approaching and waved to her to make Tory aware of the Oversoul's presence also. 'I was just bringing her to you,' he advised, as the silvery-haired spirit attired in shades of mauve and violet joined them.

'I didn't think you were bringing her back,' Astarleia said in jest but there was an underlying concern in her tone. 'Our charge's previous muse returned —'

'The film writer?' Tory queried.

'Yes. He wanted to try his hand at a manuscript, and when you did not show up on schedule, I allowed him to start re-writing one of his old film scripts into a book,' Astarleia said.

'Are you saying I'm out of a job?' Tory was flabbergasted at the thought of having to adjust to working with a new subject when she'd already instilled so much information into this one. 'Astarleia, please, I know I let you all down by getting sidetracked, but it was essential to our story that —'

'Relax,' the beautiful Oversoul reassured the muse. 'I found this wonderful oracle, and I took the liberty of having him inform our girl that she had three more Tory Alexander books she'd better start researching.'

Tory was filled with relief and excitement by the announcement. 'And she listens to this clairvoyant?'

Astarleia's smile broadened, knowing what an amazing aid this would be to Tory when trying to convey the details of her tales. 'He's a close friend of the family and is very confident about his craft. The oracle has given our charge very accurate information in the past, so she takes his words very seriously.'

'And she is seeing this oracle often?' Tory could barely contain her anticipation.

'I'll leave you ladies to your scheming.' DK bowed to them both. 'You know where to find me.'

Tory had questions for her guide, but they would keep and perhaps they were meant to. She bid the master farewell and turned back to her associate, who appeared to be most delighted about their reunion.

'To tell you the truth,' Astarleia admitted, 'I am dying to hear the rest of your story, as are the rest of the guides with our charge. And as our publishers are wanting to contract this next trilogy because of reader demand, I'd say there are many souls waiting to hear how it all ends.' The look on Tory's face prompted the Oversoul to question her. 'You do know the ending now ... don't you?'

'Who knows where it will all end? It's an adventure,' Tory said blithely. 'I have the completed books that the Master Kuthumi gave me, so, although I do not know the ending at this point, we can rest assured that we do have one.'

In his room of summons Viper held Mahaud captive. With her seal of obedience projected onto the central circular screen of his ornate ring of protection, Viper had the crone in his service and had ordered her to sleep.

She appeared different to him now, for Viper saw her for what she truly was, an elemental spirit lost from human soul-mind evolution. In other words, Mahaud was a mere shadow of the soul-mind to which she had been connected. Once parted from the elemental demons bound to her, and as her presence was no longer attached to the soul-mind that was the divine light source, there was nothing to prevent Mahaud's damned soul from being sucked into oblivion. The elemental entities that protruded from the crone's form were now clearly visible to Viper. Mahaud had always kept these entities hidden in the past, which gave the beholder the illusion that the crone harnessed vast amounts of dark power. In truth, she drew all her Otherworldly power from her elemental beasts, which was another reason to keep them secret — if no one knew of their existence then she could not be disposed of before she figured a way out of her dead-end predicament.

'You can wake up now, crone,' Viper instructed his captive from his reclining position on some large floor cushions — outside the circle of summons in which Mahaud's spirit was contained.

Viper! she thought, as she was too weak to form a physical body and the vocal cords with which to speak; the Dragon's light-filled presence had drained her stores of evil energy.

'You never mentioned that you had a seal of obedience.' Viper shook a finger at her, although the smile on his face was broad. 'I'm afraid Prince Charming will not be releasing you from your curse, Electra. I am quite sure of this, as the Dragon is all blown up.' The Falcon lord chuckled, rather impressed with himself. 'I know now why you were so eager to get hold of the physical body of your Chosen incarnation ... because if you are liberated from those creatures dragging you around whilst still attached to your soul-mind, you have a chance of being reunited with your divine light source. But ... sorry, no, that can't happen either, as the body of Tory Alexander was destroyed along with her mate.'

The only reason Mahaud did not appear devastated by the news, was because in her current state she felt nothing. Her only chance for redemption had been taken away; she had nothing left to lose, no hope left.

'But not to worry. I've had a better idea.' Viper closed the old book he'd been reading and sat up. 'Let us suppose that the Dark Lodge still exists on Gaia and that Yahweh Aris is still leading them. I bet he'd be delighted to have his elemental pets returned to him after all this time. And I feel sure he'd know how to separate you from your source of dark power and would be happy to send you on to join the damned.'

After a few moments in Viper's dark presence, Mahaud felt strong enough to project her thoughts aloud. *If you think Yahweh Aris knows more about the dark path than I do, you are mistaken.*

'Do you really expect me to believe that romantic drivel you sold the Dragon, about the unsurpassing beauty of the Prince of Darkness?' Viper scoffed, feeling angry and ripped off. 'I want that ring Aegisthus stole from you.'

I don't know for sure that Yahweh Aris has the ring, Mahaud warned. *That was just my theory.*

'He's an obvious ally on Gaia that you should have told me about,' Viper snarled and then immediately calmed. 'Oh, but that's right, you've switched sides since our first meeting, in order to get a date with our adversary! You're as bad as my damn sister!'

Why do you want the ring? Mahaud queried. *It will not grant you any power over the Fallen Ones.*

'Ah ... but according to the book of Solomon there are chants and seals, just like yours, that bind the Fallen Angels to service,' the Dark Lord grinned. 'Yes, Viper has discovered Gaia's vast store of esoteric literature.' He raised his eyebrows a couple of times to vex the witch. 'I need the ring for protection.'

Gaia's theologians have it all wrong. Catholicism misinterpreted the ancient doctrine and —

'Yeah, yeah ... and you're the only one who knows the truth, I suppose,' Viper stated with much sarcasm. 'The trouble is that you are a compulsive liar, Mahaud.'

And you think Yahweh Aris will be better able to advise you? Mahaud sneered at the idea.

'I shan't know of what aid he can be until we meet,' Viper retorted, disregarding her scepticism.

I don't know where he can be found, Mahaud was pleased to advise.

Viper smiled. 'But I have a fair idea.'

The first two books of her second trilogy had fallen into her computer like a dream.

The research for the second book had started to get a bit heavy going for a while there, but the writer had managed to wrap her head around the theories with a little aid from her clairvoyant, who had started divulging plot information at her readings. Of course, the oracle had no idea what he was talking about, as he read her books after their release like everyone else did, yet the writer always understood what the oracle was trying to impart and sure enough his advice usually helped her bypass any writer's block.

The second book of the second trilogy was now with her editor. The writer knew all her readers would be surprised that she'd taken care of the Nefilim in this book, as they would be expecting this event to be the climax to the trilogy. The trouble was, even the writer had only the vaguest idea of what the climax to the trilogy would be. It was off to see her oracle once again.

'It's going to be a difficult one to write,' he began, which deflated the writer's hopes of knocking this trilogy on the head quickly. 'From the outset it will be impossible to see where this tale is going to take you, so don't even try to fathom your destination, just take the journey ... as you always do.'

'Any hints as to the content?' The writer fished for clues. 'I mean, Tory and Maelgwn must ascend, I know that much. The children of Dumuzi are set to cause strife, but what else?'

The oracle went silent and then nodded his understanding. 'There is one place your stories have never taken us,' he stated, 'and that is, here and now.'

'What?' The writer hoped that she didn't understand where this bit of advice was leading.

'You've had a thought or two before about bringing

the tale into the now.' He decided to confront the writer's hesitation and scepticism.

'No ...' She tried to deny that she knew what the oracle was talking about. 'It's a silly idea ... it won't work.'

'Yes, it will work,' he insisted. 'Your guides are saying it will, *very loudly*.'

The writer stared at the oracle, as if he were asking her to commit suicide. 'The critics will crucify me.'

'Who cares! This is not about critical acclaim, it never was. People have to know that the principles you put forward in these books have worked for you,' he encouraged. 'All you have to do is look at your road to success to see how these cosmic principles can work if one wills it.'

The writer cringed. 'Then we're getting awfully close to preaching, don't you think?'

'Think of it as sharing,' he suggested. 'You've demonstrated how the cosmos works in fantasy, but how does it work in reality? And, you also need to take a good look at the interplay of good and evil in your story ... find the balance.'

Now he had lost the writer. 'How do you mean?'

'In creation there is light and darkness ... there is no good and evil,' he began.

'Yes, I know, it's all in a judgement, but —'

'No angels, no devils, no definable difference between God and Satan,' he continued. The words shocked the writer, making her shut up and listen. 'Light and darkness are two halves of the same whole that is creation. Without darkness, light cannot be seen; without light there can be no shadow. We think we understand the difference between light and darkness, but it is the similarities that seem to be elusive.'

The writer, having gone to Catholic schools, was having trouble digesting what it was he was trying to suggest, but she agreed she would start delving into the books to see what doctrine she could find to support the theory.

'Tory and Maelgwn's story must end with this book.' He sounded very adamant about that.

'Tell me something I don't know,' the writer agreed wholeheartedly. 'I was prepared to end it two books ago.'

'There is a great energy centre on the planet that feeds the ley line grid ...' The oracle frowned as he waited for the location to be revealed.

'Where do you mean?' The writer couldn't wait. 'Avalon? Uluru?'

'Shh,' the oracle began. 'Shangri-La? No.' He frowned again. 'Wasn't that a movie?'

The writer shrugged. 'I'll look into it.'

'I think in legend this place is located between China, Russia and India somewhere.' The oracle handed the writer's ring back to her, as he used psychometry to do her readings. 'It was an Otherworldly place if memory serves. The valley of eternal youth, or something to that effect.'

After her reading the writer had a cup of tea with the oracle and tried to question him further about some of the statements he'd made.

'I never remember a thing afterwards, my sweet,' he shrugged apologetically.

'Well, you certainly said some pretty profound things,' the writer emphasised.

'Then you must have some pretty profound guides,' he conceded.

After doing a little esoteric research on Gaia's VR-network, Viper didn't need to be a genius to deduce where the leading exponent of the Dark Lodge was currently residing.

Information pertaining to Shamballa and its function on the planet had revealed to Viper a great coincidence; that the biodome, which he was in the process of taking over, was on the opposite side of the planet to the Gobi Desert. It stood to reason that if there was a cosmic gusher on one side of Gaia, pumping etheric energy through the ley lines, then there was also an etheric world energy centre on the opposite side of the planet that was sucking energy from the ethereal matrix.

Prior to the year 2020AD, before the advent and necessity for biodome cities, South America had been the UFO hotspot of the planet. In the mid-nineteen nineties the most extreme UFO activity occurred around the southern tip of South America. Balls of fiery lightning were commonly seen darting around in the sky and across the countryside. Aircraft and citizens alike reported strange luminous spacecraft and, indeed, entire floating cities. All manner of extra-terrestrial life forms had been reported, from the classic aliens to spacemen, and huge beasts. Small, grey, hairy, clawed creatures preyed like vampires on the livestock in the area, gutting up to two hundred animals in one sitting. Close encounters of the first, second and third kinds were relayed to the authorities in Argentina and Chile every day, as were cases of abduction and visits from the Men in Black.

No one had pointed out to Viper the possible connection between MIB and the Dark Lodge. It just seemed to follow that if the Orions went out of their way to keep extra-terrestrial activity on Gaia hidden from the human populace, then the Dark Lodge of old had clearly evolved into this organisation. The agents of MIB were reportedly men of tall stature, with sparse hair and strange scaly skin, who wore dark glasses to cover their eyes, and dressed in black. These agents, who always miraculously appeared after a close encounter to harass the witness into keeping their silence, had a temperament that was said to be cool, detached and sinister. Viper considered that the alien appearance and temperament of MIB agents could be attributed to Orion soul-minds assuming a human form and falling a little short of their goal, or perhaps they were a hybrid of the Orion-Gaia variety? Which might also explain human abduction tales of being sexually violated — perhaps MIB agents were the outcome of these matings? Either way, Viper knew he was onto something. Of course, alien sightings had greatly decreased since most of the world's population had moved indoors; still, abduction tales and livestock mutilations did continue to go on inside biodomes.

The plan for finding Yahweh Aris was simple. Viper would take one of his small recon vessels and land it in the wide open spaces beyond the Andes in lower Argentina. He suspected the Dark Lodge still tested their experimental craft in this area; only now there were no humans living in the wide open spaces to witness their trials of new technology. MIB would still be monitoring the entire area and it wouldn't take them very long to figure out that Viper's craft wasn't one of theirs and send agents to investigate. These agents would be Viper's ticket to an introduction to the head of the Dark Lodge.

Thus it was that Viper came to be standing alone in the middle of the parched barren plains of Argentina, staring at a mighty mountain range in the distance, the peaks of which disappeared into the turbulent clouds above. He chose to come alone, not to protect his kindred but to further his own personal cause, which he felt his association with the Dark Lodge would do.

Viper had assumed a human form for this meeting and Mahaud was under instruction to remain invisible, but close at hand, in case at any time during Viper's visit with MIB he required Otherworldly assistance.

When he spied the numerous black vehicles flying over the plains towards him, Viper lit a cigarette and leaned casually against his spaceship. Smoking was one of Gaia's pastimes that greatly appealed to Viper. It wasn't like it could kill him and the habit was so frowned upon by mortal men these days.

The three vehicles pulled up one beside the other in front of Viper and twelve agents climbed out to confront him.

'You took your time getting here.' Viper moved away from his ship to approach the greeting party, whereupon

493

one of the agents pulled a weapon and shot Viper several times in the chest. Blood spattered forth as Viper was thrown back against his vehicle. He laughed out loud as his wounds healed over in a matter of minutes and he approached the wall of men once again. 'I think you'll have to do better than that, gentlemen.'

A second agent drew a cylindrical weapon that shot forth a ball of etheric light, which, upon contact, caused Viper to black out.

It was his nerves twitching that prompted Viper to wake. He ached all over, had a pounding headache and felt weaker than he ever had — including when he was mortal! His eyes fluttered open to spy the several men staring down at him. Their dark glasses prompted Viper to recall his circumstances. 'What did you do?'

'Positive ectoplasmic charge,' said the man leaning over his head. 'Any human who was of the light path would have been empowered on impact. But as you fell hard and fast, we knew it was safe to bring you in.'

'In?' Viper attempted to raise himself and was aided to a seated position by several of the agents. 'Where —' he became woozy and leaning forward he threw up a glowing white slimy muck. Vapour rose from this discharge, for, as it was exposed to the air, it began to dissolve.

'Your body is rejecting the light residue of the charge,' advised the spokesman for the group. 'You'll feel better now.'

'Oh, yeah.' Viper wiped his mouth and sat upright. 'I feel bloody marvellous,' he wheezed, sarcastically, although he did feel strengthened after his up-chuck. 'I want to see Yahweh Aris.'

All the men present looked at one another, their expressions giving no indication that they understood his request.

'Come on,' Viper urged them. 'He's an Orion, just like you guys, so don't try and pretend that you don't know what —'

'Why do you seek Yahweh?' asked the spokesman, curious to know how the stranger knew about him.

'I have something that your leader might be interested in,' Viper began.

'I see,' said the spokesman.

'And I know for a fact that Yahweh Aris has something —' The Falcon lord noted the ornate silver ring that the spokesman was wearing and attempted to use his etheric sight to view beyond the spokeman's physical form. The spokesman's facade began to peel away to expose a much taller being, but Viper's psychic perception crumbled before he could make out the man's true appearance; it seemed his psychic talents were at a low ebb much as his physical strength was. He wondered if Mahaud was close at hand but dared not inquire in any way, as the men about him were almost certainly psychically gifted and he didn't want his captors knowing about his insurance policy. 'You wouldn't be trying to deceive me now, would you, Yahweh Aris?' Viper raised his eyes from the ring to look into the spokesman's face.

Is he the one? one of the agents bethought the spokesman.

If he were, he would perceive this discussion —

'I *do* perceive your discussion,' Viper boasted, to shock the gathering. 'So you may as well speak aloud. And,' he added, feeling empowered by the return of this psychic talent, 'for fuck's sake, stop with the tests! I am darkness incarnate. I am immortal. Do you people have a problem with that?'

'Hardly,' said the spokesman, a smile threatening to form on his lips, although it did not.

'That's good.' Viper stood, feeling more himself. 'Because, judging from what your friend here said, it sounds like you've been expecting me.'

'Yes,' replied the spokesman. 'In fact, we've been expecting you for so long, it is hard to believe you are real.' He admired the thick, dark shadow that interpenetrated Viper's etheric form. 'How did you achieve this dark super-conductive state?'

Viper grinned and shook his head. 'How about you tell me why you've been expecting me first?'

'I'll do better than that.' The uniform appearance of the spokesman changed, as he transformed into the dragon-like being that Mahaud had described to Maelgwn. The Yahweh was a very tall, forbidding warrior and was dressed in long, black robes of a dense artificial fibre. 'Allow me to show you,' Aris suggested, winningly.

19

MAKING AN IMPACT

The underground complex of the Dark Lodge was distinctly alien to Viper, as there was no Charichalum anywhere. The architecture was geometric and featured loads of sharp angles, spikes and jagged edges. The walls, floors and ceiling were covered with mosaics, hieroglyphs, symbols and seals — some Viper recognised from Mahaud's tuition, but most were a complete mystery to him. Orion technology was distinctly foreign to Viper as well.

'We are powered by etheric energy extracted from the matrix of this planet ... it's about the only thing the positive aspect of the Shamballa energy stream is good for,' Aris jested in a friendly fashion, which made Viper feel all the more wary of him. 'Not that there is too much positivity left by the time the divine inspiration has been drained through the consciousness on the surface of this planet. It is clear that the dark path is preferred by most of the populace living on the face of the planet, and its associated colonies in orbit, on the moon and under the sea.'

'This was the case at the time of Atlantis, no?' Viper sensed by the Orion's tone of voice that there was a problem. 'A great victory for your Lodge, was it not?'

'It was a disaster.' The Orion's mood darkened at the mention of the incident. 'We lost all our well-developed human soul-minds and were left with mere savages to educate and experiment with. But we did manage to capture this stronghold from the White Brotherhood and, as etheric field manipulation is the forte of my people, we set about damming up the etheric matrix at our end. The pure energy that once flowed out of this place and back to the cosmos, we now use to power our operations here.'

'And what of the dark energy,' Viper wondered, 'what do you do with it?'

'We've been storing it for a rainy day,' Yahweh advised, and then changed the subject back to Atlantis. 'It took us eons to recover and re-establish the dark arts after the deluge, and just when the consciousness of my people was getting a firm grip on humanity the Brotherhood of Light sent Christ into the world. Still, with Jesus came the devil concept, which has proven very useful for covering up a lot of our work here on Gaia.'

'Yes, I have read about your work.' Viper glanced at the darkly-clad men who were accompanying them on their tour, and as he could not espy any etheric dragon-like forms behind their manifestations, he figured that they were hybrids. 'Abductions, mutilations, strange experiments with genetics and technology ... I have to admit I was very impressed.'

'You don't know the half of it.' The dragon wizard stopped in front of a pillared doorway. Where the doors should have been was a dense black void, which dispersed as Yahweh Aris moved to enter between the pillars.

It was not necessary to explain the purpose of the massive complex they had entered. It was clearly an embryo nursery for an entire race of Orion-Gaia hybrids. 'Behold the future of humanity.'

Inside the millions of transparent, egg-like pods which were large enough to hold a full-sized human being, the embryos were frozen at the beginning of their development. 'These guys aren't going to be much use to you for a while ... where are the full grown ones?'

'All are presently active.' Aris began to outline his problem. 'Very few human soul-minds have proven dark enough to be attracted to an incarnation as a hybrid.'

Viper didn't understand. 'I though you said that the way of the materialistic is rampant on Gaia?'

'On the face of Gaia self-indulgence is rampant. They all want to be rich, famous, clever, powerful, sexy and decadent. But the Inner Earth people have no interest in such things. They receive and transmit Shamballa energy also, sending forth their sickeningly sweet and meaningful inspiration to their brothers on the surface. Thus, my carefully retarded flock are beginning to stray before they are evil enough to join our ranks.'

Viper knew what he'd do in the same situation. 'Then destroy these Inner Earth people.'

'I fully intend to.' Aris raised a finger and beckoned Viper to follow. 'In the past, many positive extra-terrestrial intelligences have been actively contributing and reincarnating into human soul-mind consciousness. The contribution of my people is being diluted and pacified. But, as you can see, I no longer have a need for Gaia's peoples, as the adaptation of my people into humanity is complete. Destroy all of Gaia's existing human life forms and the human consciousness of this planet will be left with no choice but to join the new world order.' Aris motioned back to his embryo army before dispersing the dark void between the pillars at the far end of the complex.

'Why do I get the feeling that the dark energy you've been saving has something to do with all this?' As he followed Yahweh into the next huge chamber, Viper grinned. He couldn't help it — the Yahweh's ambitions were terrible and most enviable.

The control deck granted views inside both chambers of the twin complex. Inside each of the huge chambers Viper could see the biggest electro-mechanical devices that he'd ever laid eyes on. Both machines were entirely different in appearance and only one of them was operational at present. The device that was not in use appeared like an oversized laser gun head.

Yahweh Aris led him to the huge windows that granted a view of the machine that was in operation.

Four large metal legs shot up from the floor to form a pyramid-shaped structure that supported a large metal ball on its pinnacle.

Around the walls of the chamber housing the structure was a metal grid that appeared to be sucking electricity from the metal pyramid. The metal ball was clouded by a dark haze, which it appeared to be extracting out of thin air.

'We call this the Polarifier, as it literally separates etheric energy into its positive and negative aspects,' Yahweh explained. 'The dark matter you see shrouding the pinnacle is actually being drawn down through the legs of the device to a storage facility beneath us. The electric, or positive charge, is being sucked into our power generators for storage and use.'

Bugger me, thought Viper, impressed by the capabilities of the Dark Lodge. If they had accomplished this then what else were they capable of? 'If you were to feed your stores of dark matter back through the etheric matrix, it would suck the light from everything on the planet. Nothing would survive.'

'Except us,' Yahweh added gleefully.

'But what use will a dead planet be to your New World Order?' Viper couldn't figure the motive behind the move. 'There must be a way to establish your new race without destroying the planet you mean to rule?'

'Rule!' Yahweh burst into laughter. 'Ruling is for pussies. It is the purpose of the Dark Lodge to destroy.'

'But why turn a perfectly good planet into a dead moon?' After a life in space and his lust for a planet to call his, Viper just couldn't fathom the idea.

'Because a dead moon will never become a sun,' Yahweh explained. 'Gaia, and every other planetary Logos, has the potential to be a Solar Logos. Thus, with every planet we devour, the cause of darkness is furthered. I know that there are other human colonies in our galaxy, and once Gaia is destroyed, I shall take my New World Order and continue to further the cause of the materialistic elsewhere.'

Viper was never so pleased to be of the dark path, and yet, he felt wary. 'Well, you seem to have everything you need to accomplish your goals here. Why have you been waiting for me, Yahweh?' The Falcon lord thought he'd see just how much bargaining power he had before he stated his own reasons for seeking MIB out.

Yahweh paused a moment to consider the question. 'We've been having a little trouble reversing the flow of the matrix.' He motioned back to the huge laser weapon that was not in operation. 'As you might imagine it's very hard to get dark matter motivated. So, for eons we've been seeking a superconductor that will empower dark matter, rather than repel it.'

Suddenly Viper noticed the Dark Lord was viewing him with relish. He took a step backwards to will himself elsewhere and felt one of the MIB agents at his back. Before Viper had even blinked he was encased in a transparent egg-like cubicle not unlike those containing the frozen embryos of Yahweh's new human breed.

'This is a little invention that I channelled to a mad scientist back in the golden age of Atlantis,' Yahweh Aris advised. 'It was used to contain a time hopping immortal who was giving us grief. It has been slightly modified and improved upon now, of course, and it will hold you in a conscious state of stasis indefinitely.'

A great pressure bore down on Viper's body in every direction. 'M...a...h...a...u...d!' he cried, but his utterance took so much effort to say that he found himself frozen in time before he could instruct the crone to aid him. A steel spike extended from his capsule and rammed itself into Viper's third eye area.

'Mahaud?' Viper heard Yahweh Aris's voice inside his head. 'Is that the name of that horrid elemental assortment that has been following you around? I thought those creatures looked awfully familiar. Don't worry, now that I know your little playmate's name, I won't have any trouble extracting my pets from her and recalling them to service.'

But you need me, Viper bethought his captor. *I can get you all of the superconductive black substance you want.*

'I feel sure your crone can help me in that department, and besides, there is far more glory in destroying a rival Dark Lord. With such potential as you have, you must understand that I cannot let you live.'

Are you some kind of idiot! Viper stalled, knowing there had to be more to the Dark Lord's motivation. *You never dispose of someone who can still be of use to you. Mahaud knows very little about those planets you seek to conquer. I know all.*

'I know,' smiled Yahweh. 'I have your entire memory on record for reference.'

Viper couldn't believe it. He'd never underestimated an enemy before. Who would have imagined that there was a dark race of beings more technically advanced than the Chosen? Still, Yahweh had said that Viper's coming had been foretold; maybe some of the lord's motivation was connected to this prophecy. *Did somebody predict I was going to destroy you, Yahweh?* Viper said this as a spiteful jest, but the look Aris awarded the Falcon lord made him think that he'd hit a sore spot. Viper would have smiled if he'd been able. *You can believe it, Yahweh … I will destroy you and your New World Order.*

Tory had finally caught up to herself in the story. As she read of the events her kindred were dealing with, the story was as surprising to her as it was to the other guides following the tale her charge was writing. She was very concerned about the last scene she'd read — Viper had got himself in a real predicament and she feared she was the only soul among the Chosen who knew what Yahweh Aris was up to. Still, Astarleia encouraged Tory not to go charging off to the rescue before they discovered how Rhun and Avery made out with their mission back to Atlantis.

'Everything in the dimension you left will be affected by your sons' quest,' the Oversoul reminded the muse.

'You're right.' Tory settled back down to work, greatly looking forward to reading all about her sons' adventures. 'Back to Atlantis *again* then,' she announced and the rest of the guides gave a little clap, just as eager to return to the story. 'To be sure the time hopping chariot was not discovered by the Dark Lodge,' Tory read, 'the Dragon's sons willed their transport to land on the Mount Duranki Plateau …'

* * *

Their arrival at the plateau had been arranged to coincide with the day Prometheus and Orestes were destined to invade the City of the Golden Gates. The two brothers were delighted to be greeted by seven lovely maidens as they alighted from their transport, all of whom they recognised as incarnations of some of the greatest females of the Chosen race. Their mother was among them.

'You have come to evacuate my sisters?' Electra stepped forward to greet them, marvelling at the men's strange attire.

'Ah, no.' Rhun scratched his head. He'd forgotten that this was also the day that the daughters of the ruler, Agamemnon, had chosen to make their escape. 'But, not to fear, I believe their rescuers will be along presently. We are actually here to see to your rescue, Electra.'

'That was not part of the plan.' She backed up, wary of the strangers and the fact that they knew her by name. 'Who sent you?'

She had to admit the pair didn't seem very frightening; one of the men was not even listening to her. He'd wandered off to admire the view of the city below, which was about to be laid to siege. And the fellow that was paying attention seemed awfully familiar to her. 'It was you I saw in my vision.'

'Again, no.' Rhun appeared apologetic as he was about to confuse her again. 'The man you saw was Prometheus, your brother's ally, who will be my father in a future incarnation and it was he who sent us to save you.'

Electra gasped and took another step backwards, not out of fear but awe. 'What?'

'And you shall be our mother,' Avery turned from the magnificent view to add, stunning the oracle speechless.

'I don't know if we really needed to share that information,' Rhun commented, perturbed.

'Mother always insisted that the truth is best,' Avery defended in his happy-go-lucky fashion. 'Basically, Electra,' he strolled back over to join the conversation, 'your life is about to go horribly wrong. And the wellbeing of our future existence depends on us preventing such a sad turn of events from unfolding.'

Rhun would have been a little subtler with the delivery, but he raised his brow, shrugged and nodded to confirm his brother's claim. 'That's it, in a nutshell.'

Clearly, Electra didn't know what to think and her sisters were certainly keeping their distance. 'As an oracle of some merit, I confess I see much light within your being,' she began. 'However, my spirit guides are very reliable and I have not perceived so much as a hint of your coming.'

Rhun opened his mouth to debate the issue diplomatically, but Avery grew impatient.

'Look ... there are only two ways this thing can go,' he informed bluntly. 'Either you allow us to help you, and you will live happily ever after. Or, you can be taken prisoner by the Dark Lodge and tortured to the point of death, and you will voluntarily choose to be joined to a group of heinous elementals and damned for eons to support the dark cause on the surface of the earth.

That is, when your soul-mind is not confined to torments of Density.'

All seven women were sickened speechless.

'How do you know all this?' Electra felt nauseous. Something inside her knew he was telling the truth.

'In our future, your damned soul confessed all to us,' Avery advised, a little more gently. 'This creature you become will be a curse on the development of your soul-mind and on everything you struggle to achieve in the name of the Logos. In the dimension from which we stem, you have served your time in darkness ... now, you must allow us to help you find the path of light or the whole of humanity in our future will suffer.'

As Electra stared into the violet eyes of the young man before her, she considered how like one of her beautiful spirits he was. 'It would seem I have nothing to lose by co-operating with you,' she resolved and forced a smile. 'What would you have me do?'

'I don't suppose we could persuade you to join your sisters in their departure?' Rhun really didn't expect her to take this option, although it was by far and away the easiest one open to them.

Electra immediately shook her head. 'I must see my brother,' she appealed, regretful to be so stubborn in light of what they'd told her. 'There is history there that I must confront. I cannot leave until I clear the air between us. If he sees fit to kill me rather than forgive, then at least I shall die before I become the monster you describe.'

Rhun smiled to reassure her. 'Fair enough. I suspect that there is someone that you really should meet anyway.'

'Prometheus?' Electra understood his implication and thought it rather presumptuous. 'You think that because I am coupled with this man in your lifetime that the same should follow here. My heart shall never belong to any one man, for it is solely devoted to the Logos,' she defended, despite Raziel, one of her most trusted spirit guides, having implied that Prometheus and herself were two halves of the same whole.

'We believe you.' Avery tried to sound convinced, although his brother and he knew the attraction was inevitable.

'Let us now take you to the High Temple, Nin,' Rhun advised, his eyes drifting upwards to view the ominous ball of fire in the sky. He had to wonder if their meddling in this affair would save the long-lost continent from destruction, but from here the outcome was impossible to predict. If the Brotherhood of Light had marked the great landmass for destruction, Rhun doubted that any force or act could prevent Atlantis's demise.

Much to Rhun's astonishment, Avery raised the vibratory rate of the atoms in his body until he became invisible and he guided Rhun through the procedure to accomplish the same. Avery had shrugged this off as a simple childhood trick, but Rhun was fast realising that he really knew next to nothing about his little brother — he'd always found it easier to ignore and underestimate Avery than grant him his due. Perhaps this stemmed from jealousy; the Logos had set Avery apart to receive the great honour of being the Night

Hunter's apprentice and the next in line to rule the Otherworld. Rhun could not deny that he envied the secret life Avery led and his command of Otherworldly energies and beings.

Disguised by thin air, Avery and Rhun watched over Electra as, on her knees, she confronted Orestes, Prometheus and a large armed force. Neither of the lads from Kila were surprised to discover that Orestes was an incarnation of their good Governor, Brian Alexander.

'Don't change the subject.' Orestes came up behind Electra, placing his foot on her shoulder to push her forward into a position suitable for execution. 'You have been found guilty of acting as an accomplice in the unholy murder of our father, the Shu Sar Agamemnon. Have you anything to say for yourself, before your head and body are parted?'

Electra held her tongue and bowed her head.

Oh my God, Avery bethought his brother.

What?

The stream of light that has fallen upon Electra, Avery advised, *don't you see it?*

No, Rhun droned, thinking Avery might be pulling his leg.

Avery observed a beautiful being descend to protect the oracle. *It's a deva,* he informed, *of the highest order.* Avery could tell by the fire-like composition of its being — devas of lower order were more vaporous in appearance. *The deva looks just like father.*

So why can't I see it?

I don't know. Avery attempted to sound bemused, but in truth he knew that he had etheric world training and know-how that his brother didn't, but to state as much would only offend Rhun.

'I'll assume your silence is an admission of guilt,' Orestes warned his sister as he raised his weapon to end her life. 'May the Logos have mercy on your soul, Electra.'

Prometheus drew his sword and blocked Orestes's deathblow.

'Stay out of this, my friend,' Orestes cautioned, most perturbed. 'This is none of your affair.'

'Look at her,' Prometheus urged his friend. 'Can you not see the light radiating from her being? This is not the face of a traitor.'

'Curses!' Orestes snarled as he was encouraged to hear Electra's side of the story, but she refused to explain herself.

'Kill me, Orestes,' she resolved. 'My life is owed.'

As Orestes raised his sword once more, Avery couldn't help but protest, feeling that Electra was trying to get killed for their benefit. 'No! You don't have to die this time around,' he shouted out loud and was stunned to find that the world around him was frozen in time and he was no longer invisible.

Look at me, Electra, the spirit that shielded the oracle had moved away from her to request. *Behold my face.*

The oracle raised her eyes as requested and gasped. 'You are Prometheus?' She frowned. 'You are me?' she ventured further, recalling what Raziel and her guardians from the future had said about the man in question.

The essential spiritual essence behind your soul-mind was carried down into evolution by my fallen counterpart,

Mikhail confirmed. *Thus, within you lies the potential for my evolution and the evolution of all our forms on every level of awareness between my home plane of demonstration and yours. Your friend here is right,* the spirit finally acknowledged Avery's presence. *In his time and place you have served the Logos selflessly and now, in order to progress, you must escape the clutches of the Dark Lodge. When your time on this earth is finally done, you shall rejoin your soul-mind who is readying to ascend to causal service. You can save yourself, your brother and your future husband, but if you choose to die now, they shall surely perish.*

Tears began to stream from Electra's eyes, for causal service was her greatest wish, and she had not saved her brother's life all that time ago to have him perish now. 'My future husband!' She was a little alarmed by this claim.

Know that Prometheus is the incarnation of your male aspect, Electra. He can teach you much about yourself, the spirit told her. *You must live on, learn and teach others how to achieve the understanding of unconditional love that you shall perfect via your association with this man.*

Electra gaped at the spirit and Avery had to smile. *We told her so, didn't we?* he bethought his brother and looked around for him. *Rhun?*

Still there came no response and when Rhun did not show himself, Avery utilised his etheric vision to discover that his brother was frozen in time like everyone else present. *Oh, terrific, something else I'll get accused of lying about.*

The Logos has carefully chosen your guardians in this affair, the spirit told Electra. *One is the Lord of the*

Otherworld, who will bring down the Dark Lodge and save you the torture of doing so.

'That would be me,' Avery confessed.

Live in light and love, Electra. The spirit remained focused on his subject.

'This is goodbye then, Mikhail?' Electra's voice wavered as the thought saddened her.

The beautiful being nodded. *For now.*

Clearly Electra wanted to protest but found the strength to accept and trust in the divine plan. 'I am the humble servant of the Logos.' She stood and walked away from her brother's glowing blade and then turned to bow to Mikhail. 'I will the divine will.'

Mikhail smiled, proud of her. *Thy will be done.*

The spirit vanished and the world came to life once more.

Avery, who'd made himself visible during the visitation, quickly vanished and Prometheus frowned, having caught a brief glimpse of Avery's form. Still, the warrior was more astounded to find Electra had miraculously moved.

'How did you do that?' Orestes demanded to know.

Electra ignored her brother's question; her eyes were fixed on his companion. 'I believe I shall be of some service to you yet.'

As soon as Electra was left alone in her cell, Avery dismissed their Otherworldly cover.

'Most well done,' Avery complimented the oracle on getting this far without having her throat cut and Electra smiled, pleased with the outcome too.

'Now all we have to do is get you and Prometheus safely away before Orestes summons you to his room of court.' Rhun recapped the plan.

'But,' Electra looked to Avery confused, 'I thought we were going to bring down the Dark Lodge first?'

'What!' Rhun protested most strongly. 'No, no, no, no, no, *no*, NO!' he insisted, as Avery had a look on his face that implied he was considering the enterprise. 'Save Electra, that was the entire directive.'

'We shall see you gone.' Avery looked to Electra to confirm that part of the plan. 'And then I shall take care of Aegisthus once you are safely away.'

'No you won't and that's an order.' Rhun attempted to pull rank.

Electra was troubled by Rhun's refusal. 'But Mikhail said you would do this and save me the trouble. So if you do not destroy the sorcerer than surely I must —'

'Mikhail? Who is Mikhail?' Rhun quickly intervened, not wanting to distress their charge.

'The deva I was telling you about.' Avery tried not to wince as he broached the topic.

'The one I didn't see or hear?' Rhun stated sceptically.

'I know this spirit well,' Electra said surely.

'You heard the crone speak of Mikhail in her tale and of how he came to protect her from Orestes's wrath.' Avery jogged his brother's memory. 'Only this time the deva advised Electra to save herself. He also advised that I had the know-how to bring the Dark Lodge down.'

'I see.' Rhun hid his feeling of insult at having been left out of the Deva's confidence.

'He speaks the truth,' Electra assured and Rhun silently nodded to confirm that he believed her.

'So,' Avery broke the uncomfortable silence that ensued, 'if you can just persuade Prometheus to abandon his quest to avenge his wife and head back to Usiqua with you, we'll take care of the rest.'

Rhun served Avery the darkest look, wondering why he even bothered including Rhun in the equation. In fact, he was beginning to wonder why he was here at all, as it was apparent that Avery could have handled the quest alone.

'But how shall I persuade Prometheus to do as we wish?' Electra didn't have very much experience with such situations.

Avery smiled, as he knew from what the crone had told his father that Prometheus and Electra were about to fall in love. However, he couldn't find a way of expressing what he knew, and Avery looked to Rhun for help.

Rhun took a deep breath to disperse his bad mood, then placed a hand on Electra's shoulder, and stated: 'Just act defenceless. Make it clear to Prometheus that you are afraid to stay in the city.'

'But what if he insists on killing Aegisthus first?' Electra implored.

'He won't, Electra.' Rhun knew his father well enough to be sure of this. 'You are, in essence, the same woman Prometheus is trying to avenge the death of. He won't risk you being harmed again, believe me.'

It was so odd for Electra to be spoken about as this Prometheus's woman when she'd barely said two words to him and had never had cause to imagine her life in that sort of context. 'I shall do my best.'

'That's the spirit.' Rhun gave her a smile in encouragement.

'And, no matter what happens, remember it's for the Logos,' Avery found the cheek to suggest.

'Avery,' Rhun scorned, although he did crack a smile.

'Just helping out dear old dad,' Avery uttered in his defence.

'Well, don't.' Rhun directed him to move away and butt out, before looking back to Electra. 'We're going to leave you to deal with Prometheus however you see fit. But we'll be right outside that door. To get to you, Orestes's guards will have to get past us ... and they will not get past us.'

'I believe you ... and I thank you, but are you sure Prometheus will seek me out?' She was wary of being left alone with this man that everyone had built up to be the great love of her life. She couldn't deny she found Prometheus attractive, but these feelings were an anomaly for her and her fear of the unknown was making her edgy.

'He is here,' Rhun announced and vanished along with Avery.

The sound of her cell door unlocking set Electra scampering for a seat on the stone block supplied for sleeping, and she attempted to look fearful, just as Rhun had suggested.

'You are under no threat of death any longer,' Prometheus assured Electra, after he eyed over her quarters.

'The spirit world disagrees with you, my Shar,' Electra lied. 'I'm afraid a truly horrid death awaits me here.' She gazed at the floor, a hopeless look upon her face.

'Then I shall take you away from here,' Prometheus offered gallantly.

Electra was inwardly excited by the suggestion, but she spoke in a flat disbelieving tone to hide her true feelings as she posed the pertinent question. 'After you destroy Aegisthus, or before?'

Rhun and Avery disposed of the guards that Orestes had posted outside his sister's cell with the stun function on their pulse lasers and locking the guards in a nearby cell, the lads from Kila assumed the appearance of the Atlantean soldiers.

As Rhun seemed to be giving him the silent treatment, Avery thought he'd try and clear the air. 'My abilities are not my fault, you realise? I have not trained to be Lord of the Otherworld all my life just so I could bug you.'

'But it helps,' Rhun commented lightheartedly, as if he didn't really mean it, and maintained the soldier's stance — his eyes fixed ahead — so that he didn't have to see his brother's reaction.

Avery was not fooled. 'You think I don't know that you have infinitely more life experience than I do? I've studied your history ... you ruled Gwynedd and then Briton as High King. You did extensive time travel, built an entire underground city from nothing and fought in the greatest battle of our history, the Gathering of Kings. Not to mention the integral part you played in the rebellion of Lahmu!' Now Avery had Rhun's attention. 'I don't have your experience, believe me, I am well aware of that. But now is my time to prove my worth and I am not going to relinquish my destiny just because you feel threatened by it!' Avery spat out, feeling better for having gotten that off his chest.

Rhun began to silently fume, when normally he had a good command of his emotions. He was about to launch into a spiel about adhering to the word of authority when he felt his father's presence close by, urging him to be calm and reasonable.

Before you cut him down in flames, know that Avery idolises you above all others and always has. He just got through telling you so, though not in so many words.

A big lump suddenly built in Rhun's throat as he realised the reason he was so angry. Could he fear losing his hero image in Avery's eyes so much that he would try to oppress his little brother rather than encourage the use of his talents? Rhun realised he was greatly in error, for encouragement was the way of light and would go much further towards sustaining any relationship than jealousy and oppression, which could only destroy. 'You do threaten me,' he confessed. 'But, I would probably feel far less irritated by the fact if you would just keep me up to date with what's going on in that cosmic brain of yours ... *before* I make a fool of myself.'

Avery's desire to assert himself vanished as his brother stopped playing games and was straight with him. 'I was afraid you'd accuse me of playing you for sport ... which, incidentally, I would never do on a mission.'

'I know.' Rhun could concede that now. 'I have been an idiot, Avery —'

'No.' Avery could not agree. 'I have given you just cause to question everything I do. I do play people for sport at times and that has been my own undoing —'

'Christ, Avery, slow down.' Rhun urged his brother to quieten. 'Such revelations coming out of your mouth are making my head spin!'

The persona Avery was wearing smiled broadly. 'Ditto, brother, I thought you'd never realise I was an adult.'

'Well, I kept waiting for you to realise it.' Rhun just had to have one final dig.

But as the brothers stood smirking at each other, both wondering if Avery's comeback was going to destroy the breakthrough they'd just had, a large force of soldiers was heard to enter the long curved corridor in which they stood.

Rhun pulled his weapons. 'Time to start proving your worth.'

As the force rounded the bend in the corridor, there appeared to be roughly twenty men to contend with.

'I'll bet you dinner at Patrick's that I down more of them than you do.' Avery willed his weapons to manifest in his hands and began firing.

'Ha-hah!' Rhun joined the assault, charging forth with lasers blasting. 'You're on.'

All the noise brought Prometheus charging out of Electra's cell with his sword activated and ready for battle. But by the time he arrived on the scene only two guards remained standing and they were highly amused about something.

'It was even, I'm telling you.' Rhun turned to see Prometheus eyeing them with concern. He knew that look on the warrior's face. Maelgwn always got the same look when he was about to attack. 'No, wait!' Rhun resumed his own appearance and Avery followed his cue.

'You!' Prometheus gazed at Avery. 'I saw you in the High Temple.'

'These are my Otherworldly guardians, Prometheus,' Electra informed as she joined them in the corridor. 'They are going to help us avenge your wife.'

'What!' Rhun and Avery both protested at her implication in unison.

'No, no.' Rhun made haste towards the couple. 'We shall take care of the Dark Lodge after you two have departed the city.'

'Deukalion?' Prometheus nearly had heart failure as he saw his son in the considerably shorter Otherworldly lord before him.

It took Rhun a second to remember who Deukalion was. And as Prometheus's son was to become the Noah who built the legendary Ark, Rhun was stunned and proud — he really had to do more past-life regression. 'Your son is no doubt a past-life incarnation of me.' Rhun attempted to ease Prometheus' panic. 'Just as Electra is a twin soul of your wife.'

Prometheus struggled to accept the idea, although it was pleasing to him. 'Is that possible?' He looked at Electra, for the oracle's view.

'My spirits support their claim, therefore I must believe that what they say is true.' Electra turned back

519

to Avery and Rhun to inform them: 'I have vowed to Prometheus to aid his cause.' Electra took hold of the warrior's arm.

Rhun was about to object when Prometheus did.

'No, this changes everything. We must get you out of the city at once.'

Electra backed away from Prometheus when she realised he wasn't planning to leave with her. 'Not without you.'

The boys from Kila, having heard this argument all through their childhood years, already knew how it would end. Prometheus would not abandon his quest and Electra would not abandon Prometheus.

'This isn't the way this was supposed to go,' Avery mumbled as he pulled Rhun aside for a quiet word. 'Electra's concern for her own wellbeing last time around sprang from selfishness and fear ... perhaps that was her undoing? Let us suppose that her desire to aid Prometheus this time around, is just reinforcing her courage and selflessness, which has got to be a good thing, hasn't it?'

Rhun had a think about this and moved back to consult with Prometheus. 'The Nefilim Lord Shamash is waiting in Orestes's room of court. He has enchanted Electra's brother into trading her to the Dark Lodge, in exchange for a beautiful maiden that the Nefilim designed specifically to attract Orestes. As soon as your brother sleeps with this woman, she will attempt to murder him.'

Electra gasped, having foreseen the coming of her brother's enchantress.

'We can prevent that by disposing of the vase,' Avery thought out loud and Rhun nodded.

'The vase?' Prometheus frowned, finding the conversation, and this whole scenario, a little hard to swallow.

'But Shamash has an even bigger surprise in store for you,' Rhun enlightened Prometheus, and the Titan forgot the other matter. 'To dissuade you from aiding Electra, Shamash is going to threaten to destroy your capital city, your son and his secret project along with it.'

Prometheus was doubly shocked that the Otherworldly guardians knew about his son's work for the Lord Enki, but the knowledge of Shamash's threat was far more alarming to him.

'Now, obviously, if Shamash wants Electra he's not going to carry out that threat until he has her. Still, I doubt our chances of eluding the Nefilim and the Dark lodge long enough for your son to complete his project for Enki,' Rhun summed up and as everyone was looking a mite concerned, he thought he'd better say something encouraging. He looked at Avery. 'So, perhaps we could take the chariot back in time, find Lugal and get Enki's plans to Deukalion sooner.'

Avery nodded, as Prometheus knew what Lugal looked like, yet they risked having an even greater effect on the future if they messed about too much. 'Or ... we could attempt to put Chailidocean in stasis for a couple of weeks.'

Rhun was stunned by the suggestion, but for a change he did not scoff at his brother's idea. 'You can do that?'

Avery shrugged. 'Electra's spirit did it —'

'Who was a deva of high order,' Rhun reminded him.

'And I know the Night Hunter had the ability,' Avery added, rather bravely. 'If all his abilities have passed to me then surely I must be able to achieve the feat too.'

Rhun considered this would be a simple solution. 'Well, let's hop it over to the Mount Duranki Plateau and give it a burl.' Rhun gripped Prometheus's arm and Avery took hold of Electra.

'Electra?' Prometheus appealed for reassurance as he was suddenly engulfed by bright etheric light.

On the plateau, Avery positioned himself in the centre of the huge, carved amethyst crystal stones that marked the perimeter of the circle of this sacred site. He glanced at his brother who stood beyond the stone circle with Electra and Prometheus and Rhun gave Avery the thumbs up in encouragement.

The Otherworldly apprentice turned to face the north and took a moment to focus on his objective. He then mentally issued his summons into the etheric world, just as the Night Hunter had taught him.

North wind and the elements of earth
lend me the secrets of past and future.

Avery perceived a mass of glowing green vapour, filled with tiny light beings, rising out of the natural landscape beyond the sacred site to the north and the ethereal mist floated towards them on a northerly breeze.

Rhun saw nothing of what his brother saw, but he did note the breeze arise from the direction his brother faced and this made him smile — it was an encouraging sign that their plan might work. He waited with bated breath to see what would happen now that Avery had turned to the west.

West wind aid me with your mist,
inspiration of water and light.

A blue mist arose like a great tidal wave out of the waterways of the city of Chailidocean. It crashed down at the base of Mount Duranki and then proceeded to slither its way up the mountainside like a great serpent.

As a wind began blowing from the west, Rhun's smile grew more confident.

East wind send the spirits of air,
to speed my thought, my will.

A golden streak of wind whipped past Avery, exhilarating him with its velocity.

Rhun's smile was wiped from his face as this third wind moved over the plateau, threatening to spin the other two winds into a twister.

'Perhaps we should take shelter in the doorway,' Prometheus suggested, motioning to the entrance of the secret passage that led through the mountain to the plateau.

'A good idea.' Rhun battled the winds to lead the couple in that direction.

'Your brother is very powerful.' Electra admired the young man from the safety of the doorway, as Avery turned to face south. 'I have never seen the elements commanded to the cause of light before, only ever to the cause of darkness.'

'In the future that will change,' Rhun assured her, realising that he was planting the seed for a whole new course of study for Electra.

South wind of primordial fire,
blow forth from the dawn of life
and fulfil your Lord's request.

Avery saw this elemental wind take the form of a ball of glowing orange fire, and it combined with the other winds to form a tornado around Avery, who stood in the eye of the storm.

'Will he be all right?' Prometheus yelled over the gale to Rhun, who nodded with certainty.

'He's in his element, as it were.' His joke was personally amusing, and as Electra understood the jest she smiled too. Prometheus was only bemused, but he trusted that his company were more informed about such matters than he was.

Inside the whirlwind the elemental creatures maintained their assigned direction, and four large faces formed in each body of substance to address Avery.

The face of fire spoke first; his voice was raspy and harsh. 'This pubescent human thinks he's Gwyn ap

Nudd.' The huge face of flame burst into laughter as did all the elementals.

'The Otherworld is timeless,' challenged Avery, 'therefore I know you must be aware that I assume rulership of the Otherworld after the Night Hunter withdraws from the ethereal realm.'

The elementals only laughed harder at this. The reason the elementals did not recognise Avery was because, as he'd said, the ethereal realm was timeless; they had no sense of time past or future as they lived an eternal now. Unless, of course, an elemental being broke away from its group soul and entered the service of the Lords of the Materialistic, whereby the being could manifest in the physical realm and gain some concept of time.

'Who is the Night Hunter?' Fire queried his fellow elementals, who all pouted and shook their heads, none the wiser.

'I hate to say it, sonny,' the watery spirit garbled, sounding as if it were speaking underwater, 'but I think our master has led you a merry dance if that is what you believe. A human guardian of the Otherworld,' it suggested in jest and started another fit of laughter from all bar the Earth elemental.

'We should inform our lord of this impostor,' the glowing green face suggested in a booming voice.

'I am on to it,' the golden face of air spirits immediately calmed down to advise in a speedy manner.

'Is this part of my initiation?' Avery wondered out loud.

'The Night Hunter is here,' announced the Earth elemental as the Lord of the Otherworld passed through it to stand in the calm inner circle of the whirlwind to confront Avery.

Avery was so relieved to see his mentor that he wanted to hug him, but refrained. 'Night Hunter, I am so pleased to see you.'

'You are out of time, lad. No one here calls me by that name.' Gwyn folded his arms and frowned, most disenchanted. 'Who are you, and what do you want?'

'He claims he's your successor, lord,' Earth boomed for his information.

'But that won't happen for eons, yet,' Avery added, as the Night Hunter seemed to be most affronted by the statement. 'You were right, I am out of time. The future —'

'Eons, you say?' Gwyn was most infuriated. 'My forefather's are going to leave me stuck in this realm for eons!'

Avery was intrigued by the Night Hunter's response. 'Well, it takes that long for the rest of your kindred to finally give up Earth-bound existence, so I guess your Logos figured your soul-mind had nowhere better to go until then.'

Gwyn was clearly impressed by the extent of Avery's knowledge. 'You are very clever, for a human being,' he granted.

'Maybe that's why I was chosen to be your apprentice.' Avery ventured to be a little cocky, a trait he knew Gwyn ap Nudd was well disposed towards.

Avery couldn't tell for the life of him if the Night Hunter was testing him, or if he really didn't remember him. One possibility was that the Night Hunter had yet to fully develop all his etheric world abilities, including future sight. It sounded to Avery like the Night Hunter's Logos, Anu, was withholding certain details of the divine plan until such time as the Lord of the Otherworld was deemed ready to be made privy to it. For the first time in the whole of his tuition, Avery began to wonder: 'What did you do, Night Hunter, to become the King of the Otherworld? Did you ever belong to the physical world?'

The query seemed to spark something in the lord and he became perturbed. 'I did not come here to be interrogated. It is you who are trespassing in my realm and thus I shall ask the questions.' The Night Hunter, who was a good foot taller than Avery, walked forward to tower over him. 'Now, what is it you want, boy? I'm very busy.'

Fortunately, Avery was not easily intimidated and so floated up into the air until he equalled the Night Hunter in height. 'I was hoping to put this city to sleep for a couple of weeks, and then bring down the shield that is protecting the Dark Lodge.'

Gwyn had never been impressed by a human before — certainly not a male of the species, anyway. 'But that would aid humanity, which is not my department.' He sidestepped the request.

'Well, whose department is it?' Avery argued, although he knew what the answer would be.

'The White Brotherhood,' Gwyn replied, predictably. 'And they don't want Atlantis saved.'

'Ah! But they do want Electra and Prometheus spared,' Avery shot back.

'Then I shall get them safely away,' Gwyn offered.

'Prometheus won't leave without destroying Aegisthus first.'

'Then he shall lose his second chance at love and his son's mission will fail,' Gywn shrugged. 'I don't interfere with the evolution of man. They are making their own bed and they will lie in it.'

'*Quid pro quo*,' Avery suggested as the Night Hunter turned to depart. 'If you help me, I shall tell you anything about your future that you want to know. Everything that your Logos has kept from you.'

The Night Hunter stopped in his tracks and slowly turned back to the lad. 'You assume too much. Don't try and call my bluff, boy, or you'll find yourself rotting where the sun don't shine.'

'Then forget doing this for humanity,' Avery suggested. 'Do it for those god-ignorant elementals that are being drawn into the service of the Dark Lodge. Are they not your responsibility?'

'Yes, sire. Vast numbers of our underdeveloped beings are being attracted to the promise of the quick physical manifestation that the dark path offers,' Air confirmed.

'It is of their own will that man and elemental alike flock to the service of the materialistic.' Gwyn washed his hands of the issue. 'It is humanity that is retarding elemental growth, not I,' he reminded the elementals around him, as they seemed to be disappointed by his words.

'And who retarded humanity's behaviour?' Avery argued. 'The Nefilim, of whom you are one.'

'You should get your facts straight, boy,' Gwyn

fumed, and the large elemental faces that towered around them started to look a little worried. 'Firstly, I was never physically one of the Nefilim, but a Silent Watcher. I perform a different task in the great scheme from my kindred inhabiting the physical universe. And secondly, the Nefilim only ever affected human behaviour on a physical level. Other extra-terrestrial intelligences are to blame for humanity's consciousness. So, my cocky young friend, you're on your own.'

'And what of elemental consciousness?' Avery called after the Night Hunter. 'As man must learn unconditional love of all things, so must the denizens of your kingdom learn it.' Suddenly Avery realised what Gwyn ap Nudd's task in the great scheme was. 'Is that not your mission for your Logos? To come to an understanding of the love principle that was spawned on Gaia. Ah, that's why you choose to keep your office here,' Avery guessed.

'I'd do just fine if humans didn't keep confusing the issue,' Gwyn snapped. 'Go back to where you belong and do not anger me further.'

'I know you succeed in your quest,' Avery blurted out.

It took a moment, but the Night Hunter calmed down as he considered the claim. 'But to understand love I would have to —'

'Fall in love, yes,' Avery confirmed. 'Although legend has it that you do have a few misadventures before you settle down.'

'Tell me more.' Gwyn was definitely interested.

'Put Chailidocean in stasis and I'll have two weeks to fill you in,' Avery said, fully expecting to get the offer thrown back in his face.

'Granted.' Gwyn dismissed the elementals with a flick of his hand, whereupon they rushed off over the city and everything froze in its place. The Night Hunter manifested a luxurious lounge to sit upon and made himself comfortable. 'Now talk.'

Avery was a little stunned by his quick reversal of fortune and looking around he saw that Rhun, Prometheus and Electra were frozen in time with everything else. 'I need those people —'

'Should have said so before,' the Night Hunter dismissed the objection. 'Talk.'

The clouds in the sky above Avery's head were still moving, as was the sun, but their shadows were the only thing that moved in Chailidocean.

In the future I shall be capable of such a feat. Avery was suddenly overcome by his own potential.

The Night Hunter caught the lad's thought. 'What's your story, anyway? How did you get chosen to succeed me?'

Avery shrugged nonchalantly, although in the midst of a revelation. 'You knew I was coming before I was born. You never told me why I was chosen, but maybe it was because of this very instance.'

'Well, you've not impressed me a great deal so far.' Gwyn lied for he knew damn well the lad had nearly enchanted his elementals from beneath him. Had he not given them the order to aid Avery, they may well have joined his cause against Gwyn's will. The elementals were well disposed towards this human. 'I can withdraw my favour as easily as I bestowed it ...' He urged the human to get over his sense of wonderment and get on with his tutorial.

'Sorry.' Avery snapped to it. 'Where do you want me to start?'

Gwyn served the lad a presumptuous look. 'Tell me of my love.'

20

BE-AT-ONE

The days and nights rolled past as Avery talked himself hoarse about the future events that Gwyn ap Nudd would be involved in.

On the morning of the final day of the agreed time period, the Night Hunter seemed fairly satisfied with Avery's effort and so assured him that Prometheus's son had completed his mission for the Master Enki. Deukalion was now well prepared for the great deluge that would be forthcoming after this day.

'So Atlantis will be destroyed no matter how my brother and I interfere with her history?'

'What the Great Lodge has deemed necessary for humankind's advancement, cannot and should not be changed.' Gwyn advised. 'Personally, I don't care either way, as I am involved in elemental and devanic evolution, which humans facilitate no matter the lodge they are dedicated to, dark or light.'

'You mean to say that you don't care whether Gaia becomes a Logos filled with enlightened souls or a dead moon incapable of sustaining life?' This was not the same Gwyn ap Nudd that Avery knew and respected. 'You'll just sit on the fence and watch the great plan go to hell?'

'You wanted to know how I became Lord of the Otherworld.' Gwyn raised the subject to clarify something. 'It is because I have no real desire to be involved in this human evolutionary scheme, either materialistically or spiritually. That is why I am stationed here in the ethereal realm of non-movement. Whatever wraps this up and gets me home fastest, I'm all for it.' The lord rose from his lounge to have a stretch.

Avery was irked by the lord's attitude. 'Then why did you bother coming to Gaia at all?'

'I came because my kindred came. I am here to aid them with their passage back to Anu ... human consciousness is none of my affair.'

'After all I've told you about the future, how can you say that? It is humans of advanced consciousness who guide your stray brethren home.' Avery was very disappointed, and frustrated.

'It was a charming little tale,' Gwyn admitted. 'Perhaps things will unfold as you say and perhaps they won't.'

The rumbling of the ground beneath his feet caused Avery to refrain from arguing. 'What is that?'

'This site marks a ley crossing and as my spell is wearing off, I think you'll find that the rumbling is a build-up of the Shamballa energy that has formed beneath the plateau during the last two weeks,' Gwyn informed him casually. 'Probably something you should have considered before making your wish.'

Avery was thunderstruck; he was going to ask the Night Hunter why he hadn't informed him of this when Avery had made his request to put the city to sleep, but the answer was obvious. Gwyn ap Nudd didn't like human beings.

'Only once before has Shamballa released a large pulse of inspiration to the planet, bypassing the hierarchy that stand as mediators between humanity and the Logos — an "Impact" as it is known in the Lodges. Yet, while we spoke —'

'Oh no,' Avery begged not to know what was coming.

Gwyn nodded. 'Once my spell wears off completely this dammed energy is going to come bursting forth. If something doesn't channel it out into this world in an orderly fashion, an etheric volcano will erupt out of this mountain and the Logos only knows what kind of repercussions that will have on the physical landscape of Atlantis.' Gwyn teased the lad. 'I've never dammed up Shamballa energy before, but I'm betting that the force will be enough to sink this shaky landmass, as per the wish of the White Lodge.'

'What kind of channel do I need?' Avery glanced at Electra, knowing that she'd channelled the energy in a parallel existence, but she had been Mahaud at that time and she'd had Otherworldly protection in the form of the elemental beings with whom she'd been joined.

'I know what you're thinking, my cocky young friend,' Gwyn's grin grew wider, 'but that option is not open to you this time around. However, if your boast of being my apprentice is true, why don't you act as a channel?' He planted the challenge.

'I could do that?'

'To be a Lord of the Otherworld you would have to have very highly developed subtle bodies which would act as a magnet for Shamballa energy.'

'Have you ever done anything like this?' Avery queried, hoping to find out what he could expect from the experience.

'Hell no.' Gwyn suppressed a laugh. 'This kind of enterprise is reserved for the Master Rays and the highly adept. The reason being that the channel — you — will tune the Shamballa energy to your own vibration, which means your heart had better be in the right place when you attempt the feat, to save landing your future in a worse predicament.' The Night Hunter succumbed to his amusement and gave a mighty laugh, making out that he did not fancy Avery's chances.

'But surely my spiritual state of being will serve the future better than Mahaud's did,' he reasoned out loud, hoping that the Night Hunter would back him up on this.

'Your perspective has been warped by your physical world association,' Gwyn snapped. 'Mahaud was serving both Lodges when she channelled the energy, completely non-biased as to who profited from the

Impact. She willed the divine will. You shall never be a Lord of the Otherworld until you too cease to judge the great plan of the Allied Logoi.'

'I don't understand —' Avery appealed as the Night Hunter began to fade.

'Are you so full of yourself as to believe that you know better than the Logos?'

'But by favouring the path of light and love, am I not serving the Logos?'

Gwyn ap Nudd vanished and Avery knew he wasn't coming back. The rumbling had intensified, but as Rhun, Prometheus and Electra had yet to become conscious, the spell had obviously not completely worn off. Avery timidly floated into the centre of the site. 'I will the divine will.' Avery tried to prime his brain and spirit by taking deep breaths. He focused on switching off his emotions, which didn't seem to be working. 'Father!' Avery cried out in panic, as the rumbling grew louder. *Help me*. He focused his prayer inward. *Tell me what I must do to serve the great plan?*

Send love to those you consider your enemies and wish them well.

Avery calmed down immediately, knowing his father was with him.

And to your dark side, most of all, wish all good things to come to pass, for only then shall he see the light.

Avery had never seen Viper's true appearance and he found it difficult willing love to someone he couldn't imagine. But as a feeling of great expectation filled his soul, and heightened quickly to a sense of complete liberation, a clear picture of his adversary took form in his mind. On seeing Viper for the first time, it was extremely difficult for Avery not to resent the villain. Then he saw that his adversary was in a podlike tube in stasis and Avery, feeling Viper's fear and panic, wished him strength and hope. *He is me,* Avery reminded himself, *only all battered and torn. I do feel compassion and gratitude for what he has been through for the benefit of my evolution ... for what he still endures for my sake. I shall never judge him until again we two are one.*

The powerful force reached the surface of his manifestation and shot directly upwards towards the sky. Then a steady flow of energy split into hundreds of streams of light that shot out across and through the landscape in every direction.

Rhun and company awoke in time to witness the event.

Avery was suspended in midair, seemingly unconscious and shaking like a leaf.

Closing his eyes, Rhun focused on his third eye area to employ his etheric sight.

His brother balanced on a great force of etheric light. The fountain of energy entered his back where his heart chakra was located, and then shot out into the world from his chest in all directions until the light burst suddenly ended and Avery dropped to the ground with a thud.

'Christ almighty,' Rhun muttered, already sprinting for the centre of the site, where he collapsed beside his violently quivering younger brother. 'Avery?' Rhun rolled him over and was surprised to find the lad coherent. 'Holy mother. What have you done to yourself?'

'No time,' Avery stammered. 'I released Abbadon.'

Rhun looked into the sky, knowing that the last time this happened a mysterious force had beset the laser weapon of an Orion craft, which detonated a force that would sink Atlantis. 'Save Orestes, and then get them,' Avery nodded towards Electra and Prometheus, 'out of here.'

'But —' Rhun couldn't just leave Avery in this frightful state.

'Come back for us all,' Electra suggested. *'Do as he tells you.'* The oracle's presence became very authoritative suddenly and it startled Rhun, as she was so like his mother.

'And hurry,' Electra added.

In Orestes's room of court, Rhun found Shamash looking very impatient. Orestes was looking a little worried about losing the virgin on offer from the Dark Lodge.

'I am sorry,' Rhun announced as he manifested in their midst. 'But Electra and Prometheus have been unavoidably detained and have sent me to negotiate on their behalf.'

Who the hell are you? Shamash was worried, as the intruder was obviously psychically adept and human.

Whomever you fear me to be, Rhun responded, using the same thought projection process that the Nefilim lord was using in an attempt to intimidate Rhun. He crossed the room and took hold of the vase that Pandora clutched in her hands, whereupon it vanished into thin air.

'My dowry,' Pandora objected.

'You'll be much happier without it,' Rhun assured the past-life incarnation of Kila's Governess, before looking back to find Shamash absent. 'Oh no.' Rhun couldn't figure if the lord's absence was fortuitous or not. *I prefer him where I can see him.* Rhun willed himself after the lord to no avail — either Shamash was using some primitive form of NERGUZ to protect him from detection, or he had returned to the protection of the Dark Lodge's fortress.

'Take my hands,' he ordered both Orestes and his female companion. 'Do you wish to live?' he prompted them as they hesitated. The couple complied and took hold.

Rejoining his brother on the plateau, Rhun found Avery had recovered the use of his body and was staring out over the city with Electra and Prometheus.

'What, in the name of the gods, did you just do to me?' Orestes demanded to know as he recovered from the shock of being teleported.

'He is trying to save your life,' Electra informed him bluntly, none too amused that her brother had been willing to trade her, body and soul, to the Dark Lodge. 'And if you would be silent now, that would be helpful.'

'The shield protecting the Dark Lodge is crumbling,' Avery informed his brother. As the shield gave way, Rhun's eyes fixed on the now visible ominous-looking tower which dominated the fortress-like structure.

'Did you do this?' Rhun queried. This development also echoed the original story of this city's demise.

'No. Nor was I the one who put this city in stasis.' Avery would have once found this hard to admit.

'Gwyn ap Nudd,' he answered to his brother's unspoken question. 'But I doubt he would do this, as he cares not for physical world events unless they threaten his kingdom. The elemental forces in this area overheard me speaking with the Night Hunter and could be aiding me of their own accord ... but this would be against their lord's wishes, so —' Avery gasped as he had an awful thought. 'What if ...?' Verging on having a panic attack, Avery looked at Electra. 'Conjure in your mind an image of Aegisthus.' He gripped hold of the oracle's hand to perceive the sorcerer.

'Avery!' Rhun ran to tackle his brother and prevent him going anywhere. He slammed into Avery whereupon they were both set off balance.

They landed on a marble mosaic of occult design.

'We don't have time for this,' Rhun hissed as they scampered to their feet to look around the opulent tower room.

'Oh no.' Avery floated over to view the occupant of a throne-like chair that was facing away from them, in the centre of the large mosaic. 'It is as I feared.' He backed away upon viewing the seal carved in blood on the sorcerer's stomach and the heart ripped from his chest.

'Oh! For pity's sake.' Rhun cringed at the carnage, and then gulped on his shock as he recognised the soul-mind behind the sorcerer. 'Dear Goddess, it's ...'

'En Noah,' Avery confirmed, having realised Aegisthus's true identity the second that he'd perceived Electra's impression of the wizard. 'There is one thing I really don't get,' Avery frowned.

'Only one thing?' Rhun joked to break his own mounting tension.

'Electra mutilated herself to command the elements into her form in order to bring down the shield wall,' Avery persisted with his thought. 'But how did Shamash convince Aegisthus to cooperate?'

The husky sound of a demon seething and the creepy sensation that Rhun had always associated with Mahaud alerted him to more trouble. 'This is very bad.'

The two brothers turned to find the newly formed elemental force that the spirit of the Dark Lord was now inhabiting.

'A bad move coming here, boys,' he hissed in a choir of sinister voices. 'Now that I know what you two meddling brats look like, I shall not forget. How did Shamash talk me into it? I have become more powerful than the *gods*, more powerful than *you*.'

'Is that what Shamash promised?' Rhun sneered, while the screams of the Lords of the Dark Lodge being massacred in the complex below echoed up through the tower. 'I think you would do better to save your pupils.'

'I'll have others —' The creature moved in for the kill.

'Not if I can help it.' Avery stretched his arms and aimed all ten of his fingers at the sorcerer, quietly willing the force of the Pan Ray to channel through his person.

The Pan Ray was an earth elemental force and, being of the earth, it granted access to the densest parts of the ethereal world, where such lowly elementals as the one threatening them were best kept.

The reaction to Avery's summons was instantaneous. A green mist filled with light beings came to encircle the abomination, although the force was not flowing forth from his fingertips. He looked aside to find Gwyn spinning his ethereal magic. 'Night Hunter! This is a good sign for us,' Avery whispered to his brother. By 'us' he meant all mankind.

The dark spirit wailed furiously as it was sucked into a funnel of whirling green vapour. 'I know you, boy!' the spirit yelled out. The vapour promptly consumed itself and vanished.

A mighty explosion cracked the sky above.

'The asteroid!' Rhun and Avery guessed at once, realising a huge hunk of rock and metal was aimed right at them and would be upon them any moment now.

'Sorry.' Gwyn approached and clamped a hand down on each of their shoulders. 'But you're out of time, lads.'

Rhun tried to wriggle out of the Night Hunter's grasp. 'But Electra, Prometheus —'

'Your friends are already in Greece,' Gwyn informed them and then a bright blue-white light obscured the ancient world.

'Nothing has changed,' Tory said, bemused by what she read. 'All that has happened is that Noah's soul-mind has replaced my own and now *he* is in torment instead.'

'You're assuming a great deal,' Astarleia warned.

'No, I'm not assuming anything.' Tory held out the book she was reading from. 'It says so right here, first line of this section ... Nothing has changed.'

Astarleia smiled as she read on a little. 'But the object of the mission was to free Mahaud. This, for you, is a very important alteration indeed.'

Tory was feeling a little vague suddenly and wasn't really taking in what Astarleia was trying to convey. Tory was more worried about Viper.

In all probability, Aegisthus had just replaced Mahaud in history and Viper had raised this demon instead. Only now, the sorcerer probably thought Viper was Avery, and may have willingly sold Viper out to MIB where the dark Falcon lord was being held prisoner.

'I must warn Maelgwn,' she mumbled, and a very clear image of her soul-mate came to mind.

'Goodbye, Tory.' Astarleia waved as she saw her fading. 'I'll finish up here, not to fear.' The Oversoul held up the book they'd been channelling through to their charge. 'Thanks for everything, be-at-one.'

Be-at-one! Tory's heart chakra near leapt into her throat. Could it be that their time in the sub-planes had come to an end?

All Tory's concerns for the state of the physical world in which she'd been embroiled dissipated rapidly when she realised she stood next to Maelgwn's soul-mind. On a physical level they were located in the midst of a mostly oriental crowd, although many of Gaia's races were represented among the minority. On an etheric level, Tory perceived many other life forms in attendance — Orions, Pleaideans, Siriens, and some beings Tory couldn't pin a race name to. There were also spiritual beings present, representing the Inner Earth people, who were easily distinguished from surface-dwelling humans by their highly developed third eye chakra, through which they viewed everything while their other eyes remained permanently closed.

The entire gathering stood in a large oval-shaped valley, facing east towards a long, narrow gorge at the end of the valley. Awesome mountains towered to each side of them.

Is this the Wesak Valley? Tory had read about this place in the Master Kuthumi's library. To Hindus and Buddhists this valley, and the snow-capped Mount Kailas alongside, was regarded as the metaphysical centre of the world. It was here that the Sanat Kumara joined with Buddha and Christ in a triad of force, directing the energies of Shamballa to pour through the assembled masters and, eventually, through them onto humanity. This ceremony was a once a year occurrence, celebrated in the East when the full moon is in Gemini.

In front of the gorge in the east of the valley, a great rock rose out of the ground like a huge altar.

Tory and Maelgwn were silently and inexorably drawn towards this altar around which the Masters were gathered, Master El Morya, the Count and DK among them.

The guides who had steered them through their brief subjective service were smiling at the couple as they neared. Three figures were in front of the altar facing the gathering — two standing and one floating. Of the two Masters standing, Tory recognised the first as the Master Kuthumi, guardian of the Second Ray of Love-Wisdom. The other master, Tory suspected to be Sananda, the Lord Jesus himself, who was the Chohan of the Sixth Ray of Abstract Idealism or Devotion.

He smiled and nodded to Tory as if he knew her personally — and perhaps he did? The master who was floating on air, whose radiance set him apart from the others, Tory recognised from the statue in the foyer of the outer court of Shamballa. This was the Christ consciousness, made manifest in an etheric body as the Lord Maitreya.

Maelgwn and Tory floated to a stop behind the rows of master adepts facing the altar, instinctively knowing that it was not yet time to proceed further.

The three lords before the altar-stone stretched their arms towards the heavens and at the far end of the long gorge behind the altar, a celestial figure appeared in the sky and began to float towards the raised landmark.

Tory knew from her studies that this mighty being was the Master Buddha, come to seal the breach between this gathering and the Sanat Kumara. As Christ was the Lord of Love, the Buddha was the Lord of Wisdom, and neither was more important than the other in the great scheme.

A great beam of light fell from the heavens upon the celestial body in the sky and the light flowed through the Buddha and onto the Christ, his adepts and the Masters beyond.

When the extra-terrestrial force came over Tory, her being felt washed backward and then drawn forward towards the source on a tide of pure love, wisdom and peace.

It was the ultimate liberation, and Tory's being bowed low at the feet of the Christ consciousness, overwhelmed by her audience with such pure and divine company. She did not even realise that Maelgwn was still alongside her, as she bowed low to the ground, totally unaware of her surroundings.

The door of Monadic Sense, of Essential Duality, is open to you, the illustrious lord declared to Tory and Maelgwn, as if they alone were present. *You have become universal in your attitude, and to all forms of life in the cosmos. Thus you have reached an understanding of the isolated unity that is the Sanat Kumara. Before you leave this earthly realm for the great lodge where kindred spirits await to bestow on you Shamballa's final and most precious gift of Brotherhood, be-at-one; recall now the name of your true essence and proclaim it to all here so that humanity may know you and commend your contribution to the plan.* He placed his hands upon the heads of the initiates.

The high vibratory rate of the lord's energy set Tory's world into a spin and she felt as if she were succumbing to unconsciousness. Her life began flashing before her eyes, although she seemed to be reliving it in real time. She recalled that the last time she had died this same experience had occurred whilst her subtle bodies were disengaging, but this time she began recalling Maelgwn's life as well, from his perspective. She recalled memories of their childhood in Gwynedd, long before she'd ever arrived in the Dark Ages, and recollections from their time as a warrior, during which time they'd been separated and she had remained on Earth. And then her memories turned to their other lives in the future and the past, all the way back to Adama and Eve.

Back further, much further, in time, their consciousness passed and they were a being of rainbow fire, which Tory had met in the mental realms of existence and again on Kila at a place she called devaglen in honour of the celestial being. This being had many more memories of incarnations spent on other planets in Gaia's star system and beyond. Evolution after evolution they had braved the savage development of the soul-mind via a body, incarnating into each evolution again and again until they achieved spiritual perfection and found paradise with the great Cosmic Logos, in whose eyes they were a prince among princes. For they, at the request of the most high, had given up paradise numerous times and taken the painful journey down into Density to teach the evolving consciousness.

> *You are that angel;*
> *proud enough to believe yourself God,*
> *beautiful enough to have adorned yourself in full*
>   *divine light*
> *strong enough to reign in darkness amidst agony,*
> *and brave enough to buy your independence*
> *from the Cosmic Logos,*
> *at the price of an eternity of suffering and torture.*

Their true identity became clear to the spirit then, as it became aware of standing in the holy valley before the Christ and the righteous assembly. The soul-mind was no longer a man or a woman, but one whole which had discarded all its lower bodies and appeared now as an angel that burned with rainbow fire.

I am that angel of anarchy,
who led a hierarchy of pure spirits,
down into the dense realms
to amend our defilement of the plan.

For introducing the negative ego to humanity,
our names have been slandered,
and used as scapegoats,
for all the wrongs of humankind.

We have been depicted as devils
when no such beings exist,
beyond the minds of such entities
who have the need to place blame.

I am the Dragon of old
I am the Morning Star
I am the Bringer of Light
and the Prince of Darkness.
My name is Azaz'el, Lucifer, Leviathan,
Venus, Beelzebub, Satan, Abaddon.

My energy has dominated Gaia,
Since I took human evolution
Into my own hands
And created a disaster.

To amend, I volunteered
to spit my soul and tempt
the Adama and his Eve
into exercising their free will.

I was once the greatest believer
in the power of darkness
of the evolutionary processes
of conflict, trial and chaos.

I thought I knew better
than the Cosmos.
I see now this is impossible
for we are the same.

Gaia will soon be rid
of the shadow I cast upon her.

With my return
to the side of the Logos,
may the breach between
worlds be sealed.

'So let it be!' the gathering chanted in joyous strain, as the mighty deva ascended past the Buddha, who gave his blessing, and onward to the inner sanctum of Shamballa — the first station of the spirit's long journey home to the Cosmic Logos.

The writer is having a great day!

It took until May but her plot has finally come together and her characters have just provided the perfect scene for the jacket of the book. *Praise the Goddess*, she thinks, as she'd been concerned about which event to depict on the jacket design and the ascension scene certainly fitted the criteria. It would also fit the title of the book, *The Cosmic Logos*.

The writer wonders if perhaps she is feeling some of Tory's elation and that is the reason that she feels so inspired this afternoon ... so at-one with the universe. More likely, the elation is due to knowing her plot is sound ... it could also have something to do with the satellite dish that was just installed on the writer's house. After three years of no TV she can finally watch the X-Files!

In any case, this adventure may have been over as far as Tory and Maelgwn were concerned, but for the writer the story has a way to go yet. Thus, she ceases to waffle on about her great day and gets on with the telling of the tale.

21

LOVE THY ENEMY

In the year 2088AD, in the room of hexagons in Doc's Otherworldly abode, Rhun and Avery's mission back to Atlantis took but a blink of an eye for those awaiting their return.

No sooner did the two dragon brothers leave on the time hopping chariot, than they returned to base without it.

'Where is the chariot?' Noah, who was normally so composed, freaked!

Avery and Rhun looked at each other having not been given the opportunity to consider that little detail before the Night Hunter had whisked them away from Atlantis.

'I am sorry, En Noah.' Rhun assumed responsibility for the loss, because his sidekick in this affair was overwhelmed by the embrace of his betrothed. 'The chariot has been blown up, I expect.'

'Blown up,' Noah wheezed, horrified.

'Or Gwyn ap Nudd might have it?' Avery thought of a more positive possibility as he hugged Fallon tightly to reassure her that he was fine.

'I think you two had better sit down and tell us exactly what happened back there,' Noah requested, and was surprised when both lads seemed hesitant about his suggestion.

'I'm going to my communications room to see what impact they've had on the present,' Doc advised, and Noah nodded to second Doc's course of action. Hayden Ingram followed his colleague to the door, desperate for news of his son.

'Perhaps you should go with Doc, En Noah,' suggested Lirathea gently, as she emerged from a trance state.

Noah was now very confused and was even tempted to feel a little hurt. 'What have I done?' He looked to Rhun and Avery for an explanation.

'I will speak with you after I have consulted with my brothers,' Lirathea advised, and her intervention clearly set her brothers at ease.

Since all Noah's students were now members of Lahmu's council, he was obliged to follow Lirathea's instruction, no questions asked. 'As you wish.' He smothered his feelings to follow Doc and Hayden, and the doors to the room of hexagons closed behind them.

'What, in the name of the Logos, was that all about?' Sparrowhawk spoke up as soon as En Noah had left, furious that they would treat their mentor so.

'Our brothers' mission has had two major impacts on the present.' Lirathea walked calmly forward to confront Sparrowhawk's anger and confusion. 'And as the law of polarity demands, one of those effects was positive. The other impact was not so beneficial for we Chosen.'

As Rhun took a seat on the ground to hear Lirathea out, all those present did likewise. Sparrowhawk, who knew he was a spiritual novice compared with his half-sister, backed up to where Gazelle was leaning against a wall.

Gazelle's only desire at this point was to stay out of the way until she managed to fathom what the hell was going on. Her feeling of awe at being in this company just seemed to triple with every hour that she passed with them.

'Electra, Prometheus, Orestes and Pandora did make it to Greece, where Electra became the first Oracle of Delphi. Only, in this case, Electra became more than just an oracle, and the priestesses of her secret order developed a doctrine for the advancement of the devanic kingdom in order to combat the harm that the Dark Lodge was doing. This secret society has survived to this day and will soon bring their knowledge forth to bestow on all of humankind.'

'Will this underground order counteract the harm that the Bloodlust cult will cultivate in the future?' Rhun voiced a theory.

'That depends.' Lirathea's eyes turned to Avery. 'I cannot tell you why,' she combated his curiosity before it arose, 'but in freeing Mahaud, our parents were done a great service. However, now En Noah's soul is in the same peril.'

'What!' Sparrowhawk was riled again, looking to his brothers for an explanation.

'Shh,' Lirathea advised Sparrowhawk, who acquiesced to hear her out. 'Our parents are at-one now, and have been welcomed by others of their soul group into the greater Lodge of Shamballa.'

'What!' All four sons of the Dragon stood.

'No!' Zabeel protested. 'They were supposed to come back. What went wrong?'

'This was the impact we made that was unfortunate,' Avery assumed, so upset he couldn't think straight.

'No, nothing went wrong. This was the objective all along and our parents knew that and willed it,' Lirathea corrected him. 'Their union has brought Gaia the opportunity to close the etheric gap that exists between the physical world and the astral, which will greatly advance the consciousness of the masses to whom this planet gives host.'

'They must have been a soul-mind of great importance.' Avery mumbled his thinking out loud, to console his brothers.

'The whole planet is going to ascend to a higher plane of consciousness?' Rhun seemed a little bemused by this notion.

Lirathea smiled away her older brother's uncertainty. 'You're not going to suddenly have high-flying businessmen wandering into the astral realm, or hardened criminals chasing wood nymphs through paradise!' She could see these horrifying images running through the minds of all present. 'The vibratory rate of Gaia's body will rise to attune to an astral vibration and the peoples of Gaia will in turn receive a boost in awareness. This awakening will draw disenchanted souls to the path of light, where they will discover the subtle realm that will soon be connected to their own physical world reality. This simply means that things like astral projection and psychic talent will become commonplace. There is no void between these planes on Kila, which is why the occupants of our planet are all so attuned to the righteous path and that is why our planet was chosen by the Cosmic Logoi for the Chosen Ones. This breach between realms was closed on all the planets under Lahmu's guidance at the time of his appointment. When this shift occurs in the consciousness of those living on Gaia's surface, then the Inner Earth tribes will return to the surface to teach their brothers and sisters and lead them onto the next great phase of human evolution.'

'But that all sounds beautiful, doesn't it?' Bast didn't understand the issue of negativity.

'I am the way between worlds ...' Avery was granted a sudden burst of awareness and he trembled. 'The closing of the netherworld between the planes will mark my passing of the Otherworldly initiation. Gwyn ap Nudd told me once of the sacred trinity, the three major centres which carry out the will of the Logos and who safeguard the Gaia scheme. He named these three centres as Shamballa, Hierarchy and Humanity. He said that one day Gaia would shift from three planetary centres to two. Only Shamballa and Humanity would remain, and human souls would stand where solar angels now stood in the great plan. Upon relieving the great fiery Kumaras of their burden, they would return to the service of the great Cosmic Logos, whom they love and serve in all things.' Then, another revelation. 'Our parents were one of these Kumaras, who were original Fallen Ones,' Avery had to conclude.

When Lirathea nodded, Rhun looked at Avery, feeling for his little brother and the huge responsibility that was being placed upon his shoulders. 'Jeez, all I had to do was prevent a few wars and stop a witch.' Rhun attempted to make light of the announcement.

'Father is no longer our muse in this affair,' Avery gathered, and the fact scared him.

'It was father's task to heal the rifts between his children, so that we could function as a unit capable of supporting Avery through this,' Lirathea informed them. She could see by the way Rhun and Avery regarded each other that their sibling rivalry had transformed into a much deeper bond. The advent of Gazelle had also cleared the air between Avery, Sparrowhawk and herself, and as Zabeel cherished his family, he was hopelessly devoted to them all.

'What is it I must do?' Avery was almost too afraid to ask.

'The answer to that question lies within you,' Lirathea told him surely, and seeing how this reply dismayed Avery, she added, 'I can only steer you in the right direction.'

'Please,' Avery begged for any clues, 'should I seek out Viper and confront him, or what?'

'No!' Fallon clung to Avery, not liking that idea at all.

'Actually, that is exactly what you should do,' Lirathea was sorry to advise him. 'You must seek Viper because you love him and care about his wellbeing.'

'What is the point of that?' Fallon asked. 'Viper won't come around. You think Avery can convert him to the righteous path when I couldn't? Neither could Gazelle.'

'And how hard did you try to convert him?' Avery pretended to take offence at Fallon's point and make light of her worry.

'Avery, this is serious.' Fallon appealed to his good sense.

'Yes, it is,' he confirmed, 'and you're supposed to be supporting me, remember?'

Fallon went to protest, but then recognised fear and jealousy as her own motivators, and changed her tune. 'I'm with you no matter what you must do.'

Avery kissed her head in appreciation, managing to appear far more at ease with the situation than he felt. 'Back in Atlantis I was granted a vision of Viper,' Avery mumbled, as the image of Viper in stasis flashed before his eyes. 'I feel he is in trouble at this time.'

His statement made Lirathea smile and brought Gazelle creeping out of the background.

'What kind of trouble?' As Viper's sister she was concerned for him. 'Has that witch betrayed him?'

'That witch is now a warlock, and a very cunning one at that,' Lirathea informed those who were a little hazy on the issue.

'Not En Noah?' Sparrowhawk nearly choked on the suggestion, having finally got the gist of what had happened.

Lirathea nodded. 'This represents the negative impact of the Atlantis mission —'

'You idiots!' Sparrowhawk couldn't contain his protest any longer. 'The most learned man in the known universe and you two have damned his soul?'

'En Noah was Aegisthus,' Rhun retorted loudly so as to be heard over Sparrowhawk's seething anger. 'Avery was pushed to the limits of his endurance several times over back there —'

Avery grabbed Rhun's shirt to bring his defence to an end. 'Please, you're scaring the women.' He motioned with his eyes to Fallon beside him, her concern mounting once more.

'Pushed to the limits of your endurance?' Fallon squeaked.

'Ah, what I meant to say was,' Rhun backpedalled furiously, 'um, that Avery performed magnificent feats of Otherworldly magic, which quite frankly defied my humble imagination. But at no time was the situation beyond his control and at no time was he in any danger.'

Sparrowhawk was left gaping. If Rhun would say this about Avery then something truly phenomenal had taken place during their mission.

'Tell me of the trouble my brother is in, please.' Gazelle stepped into the pause in the argument to appeal to Avery.

'In the image I perceived,' Avery obliged Gazelle as gently as possible, 'Viper was frozen in stasis.'

'And immortals don't need stasis, so Viper has no reason to put himself under.' Sparrowhawk figured why Avery suspected foul play.

'Exactly,' Avery confirmed with a click of his fingers, and Sparrowhawk was rather impressed with himself.

'So is this new warlock in league with my brother, or against him?' Gazelle raised another of her unanswered questions. 'Because, quite frankly, I can't think of anyone else powerful enough to contain my brother like that ... present company excluded, of course.' She gave a shy smile.

'I'm guessing Mahaud's replacement is working against Viper.' Avery looked to Rhun for his opinion.

'Of course!' Rhun frowned. 'Aegisthus probably thinks Viper is you.' He shook his head, unable to wipe the smile from his face as he considered how vexed the creature had been with them by the time they'd parted company. 'Viper's in trouble all right.'

'Then help him,' Gazelle demanded in her usual tough-nut fashion, but realised how rude that seemed, and fell on one knee before Rhun to implore him: 'Is it not our duty to defend everyone. It's not Viper's fault that he is the way he is —'

'Gazelle.' Rhun crouched down to stop her. 'Of course we will help your brother. In fact, I'd go so far as to say that Viper is now our primary objective.'

Everyone nodded, in accord.

'How do we find him?' Gazelle wondered, hoping that one of the Dragon's sons would know of a means.

Everyone looked at Avery. 'If he's in stasis, that's as good as wearing a NERGUZ and I won't be able to teleport myself to him. I could seek the Count. He might know of a way of locating him?'

'I hate to sound egotistical,' Lirathea suppressed a grin, 'but I know where you may begin your search.'

All the dragon boys were taken aback by their little sister's claim, but smiled proudly as they waited to be enlightened.

'It must be a very evil force containing Viper —' she began.

'The Orions,' Rhun stated bluntly. 'They are still on Gaia?'

'It would seem so,' Lirathea said. 'The reason that Gaia's consciousness has not been progressing as well as could be expected is because her etheric body has been dammed.'

Avery didn't believe it. 'No, the Night Hunter would never let that happen.'

'We all make mistakes,' Lirathea told him. 'Shamballa releases energy to the ley grid ... follow the etheric matrix to where all ley lines cross on the opposite side of the planet and see if I am wrong.'

'So, can En Noah be trusted?' Sparrowhawk wondered why their mentor had been sent from the room. 'I think he has a right to know what has happened, and we may need his help to fix this.'

'The warlock will know no more about En Noah's movements than Mahaud did about our parents,' Lirathea clarified. 'However, if this creature is now in league with the Orions, Yahweh Aris *does* have the know-how to separate him from the demons, but only if Yahweh knows the secret name that Shamash dubbed the creature upon its creation.'

'So what you're saying,' Rhun rubbed his brow to ease his distress, 'is that Yahweh Aris could have the power to damn Noah's soul forever.'

'Who knows,' Lirathea shrugged and attempted to look on the bright side, 'Aris might suddenly find compassion, and upon separating the elemental force from the wizard he might send Noah's soul back to the light and save us the trouble of a rescue.'

Everyone looked very doubtful of this ever happening.

'There is also the possibility that the Yahweh doesn't know the creature's secret name.' She added another positive note.

'But Viper must know it,' Avery reasoned. 'And if Viper spills the beans ... which, if betrayed, he surely will,' he concluded. Avery turned his fearful gaze to Rhun, feeling responsible.

'Strategy time.' Zabeel clapped his hands to dispel the fear in the room and then looked at Avery, having read his mind. 'It is not your fault that En Noah's soul-mind was once the darkest sorcerer known to man ... so don't blame yourself for this.'

'Good call,' Rhun agreed, calming himself also. 'This is what I propose.'

If Viper was being held in stasis somewhere on Gaia, then he was not on the Aten and Rhun saw this as the perfect opportunity to reclaim the space station and search it for Rainer Ingram. Rhun appointed Doc, Bast, Sparrowhawk, Gazelle and Fallon to see to the recapture of the time hopping space station, but of course there were objections.

'But my father ordered me to stay with Avery,' Fallon said.

'I want to go to my brother's aid,' Gazelle told Rhun.

'Do you girls think that Commander is just a nickname I go by?' He didn't have to raise his voice and smiled as he asked. Neither woman wanted to take the issue further. 'Avery, Zabeel and myself will take care of Viper and the wizard. Gazelle, I need you on the Aten to try and persuade your people to surrender peacefully.'

Gazelle nodded to agree with his reasoning, and yet she obviously had doubts that she dared not voice. This dilemma was written clearly on her face.

'Out with it,' Rhun demanded.

'How can I be sure that you will fight as hard to save Viper's life as I would?' She swallowed hard, feeling that she had some nerve after all these folks had done for her.

Rhun could not think of an assurance that would satisfy her and looked to Avery for an answer.

'The fate of the future rests on me reconciling myself with your brother,' Avery informed the girl who still looked like his sister did in school. 'He is my initiation and I will not fail it. Do you believe that?'

The Dragon's sons had done everything they had said they would since Gazelle had fallen into their company. 'Of course,' she stated with certainty, to emphasise her faith in them.

Avery gave a slight bow. 'You have just assured our

success,' he told her with a large smile; Gazelle was unsure whether to take him seriously or not. 'If you do not doubt yourself through this trial, I swear by the Logos that your faith shall be rewarded. Can you do that?'

Gazelle was rather put out by the request. 'I think so.'

'Not the answer we were looking for,' Rhun announced, as all present got into the game, shaking their heads with disappointed smiles on their faces, which reduced Gazelle to nervous giggles.

'I absolutely believe that this entire mission will be an unprecedented success,' Rhun said, to rally the troops. 'Do you believe that?' He asked everyone present in turn and each of the Chosen responded enthusiastically in the positive. 'Do you believe it?' He came to Gazelle, who'd sobered somewhat.

She pulled her sleek new weapon, loaded with gold Orme darts and hit the load button. 'We're going to save some souls, Commander.'

'So be it!' they all cheered in accord.

Horace was getting hungry and he knew that was bad. Immortals didn't need food, so by his own reasoning he concluded that the she-devil, Bast, was starting to wear down his resistance to the righteous path.

No one had ever gotten inside his head like she had; no one had ever wanted to. Why did this mighty ruler care how he felt about his past and his identity? He'd cursed her, insulted her and attempted to repulse her in every way he knew how and not the slightest rise did he

563

get from her. It seemed there was not an angry atom in her whole body.

The door to his containment cell opened and Bast came striding in, decidedly determined. 'All right, my lovely.' She came to stand over the prisoner to stare into his eyes. 'Time to be the righteous cat that you took yourself for, before Viper messed with your priorities. Now, in your own *personal* opinion, Horace,' she tried a different approach to her interrogation, 'do you think Rainer Ingram is still alive, yes or no?' From the way the question was phrased, she knew he couldn't answer with his standard 'I don't know'.

'Yes,' he conceded after a moment.

'Why?' Bast backed off a little.

'I like it better when you're close.' He avoided the question nicely; there were ways and means around the restraint of the NERGUZ.

Bast straddled his lap and drew his face close. 'Why?' she repeated.

'Such a prisoner could come in useful in the future.' Horace tried to fight the admiration that was welling in his chest for this magnificent woman who knew no fear.

'The Aten is a big ship, so where, in your *personal* opinion, would Viper have stashed Rainer?' She ventured a slight smile to show that she appreciated his co-operation.

Horace shut his eyes and leaned away from Bast. 'I was never on Viper's security staff.'

'Wimp.' Bast climbed off. 'You nearly showed a glimmer of promise then, Horace.' She backed up slowly, so sure that she'd been getting through to him. 'I must have been imagining it.' Bast turned to exit and Horace released a pained cry, whereafter he, and the chair he was bound to, fell backward to the floor and then onto one side.

Bast's faith in him lightened Horace's heart, but pained his groin terribly. Horace didn't want to let immortality go, as he was much older than his present guise. He liked the attention that Bast awarded him as a younger man and he knew she'd never look at him twice were she to see him for the middle-aged cat he was. And yet, he wanted to help Bast and make her proud of him.

'Are you all right?' By the sound of his moans Bast knew that this was a stupid question and rushed over to see if she couldn't make him more comfortable.

'Viper has a room of summons on the Aten and off that one is another.' Horace gritted his teeth and spoke his mind. 'This was where they took me to be converted.'

Bast dismissed Horace's bindings with a thought and leaned down close to look in his face, desperately trying to think of something that might distract him from his pain. 'Would you like me to kiss it better?' she offered, sporting a cheeky grin.

Even in agony this mental picture was amusing to Horace. 'Yes,' he replied, hoarsely, and Bast planted her lips on his.

'Bast, I really don't believe you sometimes!' From the open doorway, Fallon objected to her sister seducing the prisoner. 'Can we go?'

As Bast moved to rise, Horace gripped her vest. 'Don't hurt my people … some of them deserve a break.'

'*Our* people are safe with me,' Bast assured him, as she backed up and left. 'I'm going to make all their dreams come true,' she boasted, blowing him a kiss on her way out the door. 'Everything is going to be fine, you'll see.'

'For some, perhaps,' Horace uttered, having mixed feelings about this conversion. He may have been left less than a man for his efforts, but he felt better, more human, than he had in some time.

He'd never believed in a Cosmic Logos, or, rather, he'd never believed any divine force was watching over him or his people. His father had beaten Horace all his young life, so if a higher power was watching over him, it did a lousy job in his opinion, and being blackmailed into joining Viper's cause had really confirmed Horace's disbelief — until he'd witnessed the divine at work in Bast.

He began to consider that, were it not for his misfortune, he would never have met her. Suddenly, it didn't matter that his private parts were disappearing, or that he was again physically ageing into his mid-fifties. All that mattered was embracing the wonderful warmth in his chest; his faith in the divine was beginning.

A couple of Doc's eldest sons, Luther and Morgan, joined the Chosen team who were out to reclaim the Aten. In everyday life these two were prominent players in secret security forces on Gaia. Luther was American secret service and Morgan was British secret service; no one on Gaia's surface knew the men were related. The brothers were very excited to be joining Lahmu's task force for this mission, as the event seemed rather like a promotion from international security agents to intergalactic warriors.

The members of Doc's team all assumed their true appearance before manifesting in the security station of the Star Chamber complex on the Aten. Viper had doubled the personnel since Noah and Candace had rescued Cordella, because four men were now manning the surveillance room. Still, as their team now numbered seven, the four men were outnumbered. Viper's men sweetened somewhat once hit with a light Orme dart. As Lahmu and no one else had the right to deem any of Gazelle's kindred one of the Chosen, the darts contained only enough golden Orme to counteract the effects of the dark Orme that Viper had administered to his people. To avoid any retaliation, Viper's people were rendered unconscious with a laser bullet and laid safely out of the way.

'Now,' Sparrowhawk waved Gazelle forward to use her palm print to access information from the security database, 'where are the rest of your kindred hiding out?'

'They're probably in the closest bar,' she commented, sarcastically, requesting a view of the quarters that had once been the private abode of the Lord Marduk. Sure enough, a large gathering of her kinsmen and women were partying hard therein. 'What did I tell you?' She sounded disappointed to be proven right.

'They may have allowed themselves to be led astray,' Sparrowhawk granted, 'but if they know no better you can hardly blame them.'

'I managed.' Gazelle felt the Chosen lord was too easy on them.

'Which only proves how extraordinary you are,' he complimented, and Gazelle's attitude softened. 'And now the Logos is granting you the opportunity to show your kindred that there is an alternative to the life they have been leading.'

'We'll need to take the leader to control the masses,' Doc suggested. 'Who would Viper have left in charge in his absence?'

Gazelle commanded the database to pan around the room, and she zoomed in on a Leonine-Nefilim woman who was dancing on the bar. 'That's her ... Tareena. She was Viper's choice to play host to the witch, until the witch could have Lirathea's body. Tareena's time at one with the witch was probably voluntary, as she always was a nasty piece of work.'

'Perfect.' Bast eyed the competition on the screen and noted that their target was now leading several men out of the room. 'She's exiting the crowd. Let's get down to the corridor and surprise them.' Bast was eager to get on with it.

'Morgan, Luther,' Doc instructed his sons. 'Stay here. Keep this station secure and your eyes on us.'

'You got it.' Luther took a seat in front of the numerous soft-light screens which Gazelle had instructed to keep track of her movements.

Lahmu's people manifested in the corridor behind the party that had just exited Marduk's quarters.

With Tareena were four men, one of whom carried a

young Leonine girl under his arm; she couldn't have been older than seven.

'Time for you to learn a few of the facts of life, my pretty,' he informed the struggling child as he slapped her on the butt.

'No, father,' the child pleaded as she struggled, and was unexpectedly released as her father cried out in pain, along with everyone else in their party.

'Shit!' The large Leonine pulled the dart from his butt, and then grabbed hold of his child's arm as she attempted to flee. 'Come here, you little —' He became aware of a pulse laser in his face and the woman behind it.

'Let her go, or I shall make you,' Gazelle threatened, so committed to her cause that her voice went hoarse.

The Leonine laughed heartily at this. 'We are all gods now, Gazelle.'

'Then why don't you disappear?' she suggested, struggling to suppress her confident grin.

'We can't.' Tareena tried to break free from the hold Bast had on her. 'What have you done to us, you fucking traitor!'

Gazelle was still focused on her target, and willed her pulse laser to switch from stun to kill. 'Let the girl go, or die.'

'Gazelle.' Sparrowhawk worried for her mental state, as she could have just achieved her goal by blasting the Leonine unconscious. 'I know this man's intent has angered you, but he cannot learn better if you kill him today,' he reasoned.

No matter how she tried, Gazelle could not hold her anger in the presence of such love and understanding.

'You're right,' she conceded, willing the pulse laser back to stun mode.

The large Leonine male smiled triumphantly, having never let go of his girl's hand.

Gazelle fired at point-blank range and he fell like a stone to join the other males Tareena had led from the bar, who were also sprawled on the floor.

'What have you done with Viper, bitch!' Tareena kicked out in Gazelle's direction.

'The Chosen have sent a team to rescue him from the clutches of that witch,' Gazelle informed her, as the young girl rushed to the only familiar face among the strangers and Gazelle hugged the child at her side.

'What witch?' Tareena scoffed. 'Liar! You're a fuc—' Bast conjured up a gag, which she clamped over the mouth of her captive and the strap self-attached around Tareena's head.

'Mahaud is a he now. Remember?' Sparrowhawk explained to Gazelle, who nodded vaguely in recognition as she crouched to talk to the young girl and reassure her. 'Now what?' Sparrowhawk looked at Doc, who'd been placed in charge.

Doc mulled this over, and looking at Bast, who was sporting a huge smile, he suspected they were having the same idea.

When Tareena returned to the bar with three of the males she'd left with, only a couple of her kindred were curious about the absent one.

'Where's Miki?' A large Leonine-Nefilim male stepped into Tareena's path.

'I'm not his mother,' she said smartly, spreading her fingers over his face and shoving him out of her path. 'I have more important matters to attend to.' She raised her voice over the din, and the noise halved.

When one of the males in Tareena's company whistled loudly, the room silenced to a few garbled comments.

'I have heard from Viper,' she announced and there was a mixed response to the news. Some present sounded pleased, some doubtful, but most were perturbed. 'By the sounds of it, our leader was right to remind me that many of you here require prompting to his cause and it is at Viper's request that I ask all of the unfaithful to line up for a shot of the bad stuff.'

There were many moans and groans of protest.

'And may I remind you all that if you do not comply,' Tareena added in a sinister strain, 'we, Viper's darker adepts, will be forced to offer you and your family as a living sacrifice to the elemental force our lord has been entertaining.'

As the three men with Tareena began rounding up the unfaithful, who moved to one side of the room as per Tareena's further instruction, the diehard supporters stayed where they were. They laughed at the plight of their weak kindred, those who kept being drawn towards the path of light!

It was the handful of diehards who were fired upon first.

As this was unexpected, the larger mass of people remaining looked at Tareena fearfully, wondering if she was seizing leadership from Viper.

'What about the rest of them?' questioned one of Tareena's supporters.

'No.' Gazelle lost her male disguise and exposed herself to the masses. 'I will not allow my people to be tricked into anything any more. They deserve to be told what is happening and given the chance to decide their own fate.'

A perfect silence fell as her companions revealed themselves and holstered their weapons.

'Listen to me.' Gazelle climbed up onto the bar. 'The potential to be one of the Chosen lies buried within the heart of every one of you. I have spoken to Lahmu, who has agreed to instruct those who are willing in the ways of the Chosen. The righteous will join the ranks of the Chosen just as I have.'

There was a gasp from the audience and garbled mutterings as they quietly debated whether to believe her.

Bast was stunned that Gazelle's tactic was working so beautifully and looking at Sparrowhawk — who was very proud of Gazelle — Bast served him a wink for all the good he'd done the rebel and he gave a shy smile in return.

'We'll never give up Viper's cause,' yelled one of the diehard minority, pulling the dart from his person and heading towards Gazelle to stab her with it.

Sparrowhawk intercepted the Falcon-Nefilim male, who attempted to fly around him. 'Be at peace, my brother,' Sparrowhawk suggested, relieving him of the dart. He squeezed a pressure point in the troublemaker's shoulder, and quiet was restored as the culprit passed out. The other diehard supporters refrained from protest when Sparrowhawk looked their way. 'It's not polite to interrupt when a lady is speaking.' He let their comrade drop to the floor and then landed himself.

'So, I suppose killing her would be out of the question then?' jested the gamest of the men.

Sparrowhawk nodded to assure him he presumed right. 'But killing you is not.'

22

MERGER OF WORLDS

Avery went ahead of his brothers to South America. He followed the ley-grid through the Otherworld, from the Shamballa centre in the Gobi Desert around the world to the opposing polar point where all the ley lines came back together.

The more sparsely populated areas did a better job of empowering the flow of energy to the grid, as the humans who inhabited such places had more space to stabilise their own energy without the interference of other people's emotions and so found it easier to maintain a positive view. In the densely populated areas the lustre was sucked from the grid. As people were so drained of energy themselves, and unable to draw on the abundance of vibrant energies to be found in nature to stabilise themselves, they were forced to suck the energy from the ley-grid and each other. Thus the inspiration of the natural power grid of the planet was depleted as it neared the opposing point on the other side of the world, and the negativity collected en route represented the Dark Lodge's contribution to the grid. Sadly it appeared that there was more shadow than light in the energy stream that managed to flow to this side of the etheric matrix. Avery was aware of the Inner Earth tribes on this planet, and that they contributed much light and love to the etheric grid and to their brothers and sisters living on the surface. Avery knew this was Gaia's saving grace.

At last, the Otherworldly lord arrived at a great cavern, located on the edge of a mountainous region. Around the mouth of the cave, the energy of the grid, good and bad, just dissolved into the ground and disappeared.

Avery lowered his vibratory rate to attune with the physical realm and then telepathically summoned his brothers to join him as he moved into the chasm and lit a flare.

Rhun arrived to find his little brother illuminated in green light and staring up at a large Mayan-style column that was protruding from the earthen wall. Despite the awesome size of the column, the first thing Rhun noticed was the forbidding presence of the place Avery had led them to. 'Dammed is right,' he commented.

Suddenly, Avery swung around to warn Rhun, 'Don't step back!' The panic in Avery's voice startled Rhun, who began teetering off balance, as he looked aside to see the great gaping crevice that ran straight through the centre of the dark cavern.

Zabeel grabbed hold of Rhun's weapon's belt and set him back on his feet. 'Forward is this way,' he chuckled, moving off towards Avery.

'I can't believe Gwyn ap Nudd allowed this to happen.' Avery sounded completely devastated.

'Hey, earthquakes flatten temples all the time,' Zabeel appealed, 'that's nature's way.'

'What is going on here is not nature's way, I can assure you.' Avery's tone was aggrieved indeed. He even sounded a little fearful. 'Don't you feel it?'

'Feel what?' Zabeel appealed.

'Exactly!' Avery confirmed. 'This place is dead! It is literally damming Gaia's energy.'

'Explain,' Rhun urged, motioning towards himself with both hands to indicate urgency.

'Instead of the planetary energy flowing back into the cosmos as it should, it is being dammed here for some dark purpose.'

'How do you know it is a dark purpose?' Zabeel wondered if Avery was just making an assumption, or had good reason to think this.

'A loving centre of energy once existed here,' Avery told him. 'If this was still the case, Gaia's energy would be being cleansed and returned to the cosmos, from whence it originally came, with love and knowledge that the Cosmic Logos could benefit from. But we feel a dreadful nothing.'

'So, in a sense, our planetary Logos has been cut off from the chain of command,' Rhun mused. 'There's information coming in but no line out.'

'Yes.' Avery nodded and conjured up a smile, pleased

to be understood. 'But that could also have been part of the great plan,' he realised as he spoke. 'The White Brotherhood knew that the planet was going to go to the dogs for an eon after Atlantis, and maybe by allowing the Dark Lodge to seize control of this place, they were protecting the higher realms from infection.'

'If you haven't got something positive to say, then don't say anything at all.' Zabeel quoted some parental advice that seemed fitting in this instance and both his brothers nodded, relating to his sentiment.

'The big question is,' Avery hesitated to pose it, 'is it time to pull the plug?'

All three brothers took a deep breath and looked at each other, wondering who was game enough to take responsibility for the answer.

'We are here to rescue Viper and the Wizard, so let's just follow the chasm and see where it leads us?' Rhun suggested finally and it was agreed.

The cavern led underground, deep underground, and Avery flew on ahead most of the way to check the path was clear for his brothers.

Zabeel couldn't help but think it was too clear. 'Is it just me, or does this look like a road to you?'

'Watch out ... vehicle!' Avery cried out in warning as he spotted it.

Rhun and Zabeel both dived aside, but the hovering vehicle stopped short of hitting them, and two men in black suits climbed out with guns blazing.

Unfortunately for Zabeel, he'd been forced to dive off the crevice side of the road and was now hanging from the ledge by his fingertips.

Rhun had pulled his weapons, but in the heat of the moment blasted his attacker with an Orme dart instead of a pulse laser bullet.

The dark agent pulled the dart from his chest and looked at Rhun, somewhat bewildered.

The second man in black approached the ledge from which Zabeel now hung and, taking aim, fired at Zabeel's hand.

'Youch!' Zabeel found himself hanging by one arm as his shattered bones repaired.

The black agent took aim at Zabeel's good hand, and with a smile fell to the ground unconscious. Avery came to land beside the fallen man and reached down to hoist his brother out of his fix.

'Cheers, Pan man. How is Rhun?' Zabeel asked, as he got a foothold.

They moved around the vehicle to find Rhun having a little chat with the other agent, who was crying like a baby.

'I didn't wanna do it,' the man in black sobbed. 'I didn't wanna be left behind. Just cause I'm a bit thick ... I still have stuff to contribute.' He gripped hold of Rhun's shirt, desperate for a solution. 'I don't wanna die!'

'And you won't ... what's your name?' Rhun sidetracked a second.

'Zero,' he replied and Rhun tried not to laugh as he found the name rather unfortunate.

'Well, Zero, if you help us do our job, then no one will die.' Rhun hoped he wasn't making promises he couldn't keep.

'What did you mean "you didn't want to be left behind"?' Zabeel couldn't contain his curiosity.

'All my people have been evacuated into space,' Zero told them. 'They just left me and One,' he motioned to the unconscious agent, 'to ensure the reversal comes off without a hitch.'

'The reversal!' all three brothers gasped at once.

Rhun shoved Zero into the driver's seat of the hovering vehicle and his brothers dived into the back. 'Let's go, pronto,' he instructed their new friend, 'to the base.'

Zero complied with gusto, throwing everyone back in their seat as the hovercraft spun quickly round, skidded along the side of the crevice, and took off down the road.

Avery peeled himself off the back seat to lean forward and question Zero. 'You haven't seen a guy that looks like me hanging around your facility here, have you?'

'There's only one guy left in the place,' the agent informed. 'He's got somethin' to do with this reversal, but I dunno what he looks like.'

'Take us straight to him,' Avery instructed, and was again thrown back in his seat as their vehicle picked up speed.

Zero sped through the empty base until the tighter inner doorways would no longer grant their vehicle admittance. The agent then led them straight to the complex that housed the Polarifier, and the huge gun head with which the Orions planned to reverse the energy flow of the etheric matrix. The Polarifier was not active today. The huge laser gun head that Viper had seen was aimed down into a massive funnel. The funnel was lodged in a pit of seething black energy which was being whipped into a frenzy around the exterior of the funnel.

'Holy smoke,' mumbled Rhun as he saw the extent of the technology here. 'I was hoping these Orions were having visions of grandeur.'

'So where's Viper?' Avery prompted their dark friend to explain.

'He's inside the funnel, I think.' Zero pointed to the towering structure into which the weapon head was aimed.

The whirlwind of shadows around the funnel began to reach out towards the conductive metal rod that shot up from the top of the gun head. The black lightning-like tentacles startled the brothers.

'I've never seen a black electric charge before,' Zabeel gulped. 'What the hell is that stuff?'

'It's pure destruction, pure negativity, pure darkness,' Avery explained. 'A black hole in every particle.'

'Then how the hell did the Orions contain this energy?' Rhun had to wonder.

'Use your etheric sight,' Avery advised, for he could see a light matrix reinforcing the metal walls that housed the seething pit of vaporous blackness. 'The Orions must have figured out how to manipulate etheric world energies. We've never come across this kind of technology before.'

'Oh, goodie.' Zabeel forced a smile. 'A new challenge. Just what we need.'

'This stuff usually just lies about doing nothin', beyond making ya feel bad.' Zero referred to the thick dark mist and scratched his head. 'Somethin's got it all worked up today.'

Avery gripped his head. 'They're using Viper as a superconductor to mobilise the dark mass! Can the funnel be blocked off?' Avery asked Zero, as they didn't seem to have too much time.

'Probably ... but I'm not very technical. I don't know how the controls work.' He backed away, fearful of Avery as he took to the air.

'Never mind.' Avery closed his eyes and willed himself to the huge weapon head.

'Avery, no!' Rhun was not fast enough to stop him and closed his eyes to go after his brother.

'No, Rhun.' Zabeel gripped his older brother's arm to keep him present. 'We both know this is Avery's gig.'

Rhun looked to the core of the dark whirlwind to see Avery narrowly escape a dark bolt of lightning that fell short of the metal rod it was reaching for. 'Where does the funnel lead?' He looked back to Zero for a response.

'Everywhere,' Zero shrugged. 'To the ley-grid of the inner and the outer world.'

'Oh no.' Rhun ran for the controls. 'We've got to close that funnel.' He pressed several buttons, but nothing was responding. 'They've locked the system off. Shit!'

Avery flew down the funnel to find Viper spreadeagled across the passage in a horizontal position. His hands and feet were bound to the wall and a dark abyss descended behind him. Metal cuffs were about his

MASTERS

ankles and wrists, fastening him in place via beams of light; this form of restraint was new technology to Avery. 'Viper?' Avery hovered over his twin, whose head hung backwards as if he were unconscious.

The Falcon-Nefilim outlaw looked up and laughed out loud when he saw Avery. 'Come to gloat? Well, go ahead, have a go! There ain't nothing you could do to me that hasn't been done.'

Avery smiled, as Viper was wrong. 'I'm here to rescue you.'

'So I can go face Lahmu's wrath, no thanks.' Viper hung his head back once more to await his demise.

'All Lahmu will ask is that you forgive yourself, Viper,' Avery explained and received a grunt of disbelief in response. 'You're me, you know,' he commented, wondering how he could sway his darker self. 'What happens to you, happens to me.'

'Bullshit!' Viper snarled. 'You have everything, I have nothing!'

'Because that is what we chose for us this time round. You have learned lessons we needed to learn!' Avery emphasised.

'I didn't choose this —'

'Yes, you did. And why?' Avery gripped hold of Viper's jacket to get his full attention. 'So you could know that the hell you've known to date is not what you want for us for all eternity!'

'All that creating your own reality stuff is crap!'

'But you've been creating your own reality all along,' Avery pointed out. 'You've just been doing it for the wrong cause.'

'Well, you had the monopoly on sweetness and love,' Viper jeered.

'I know.' Avery could see his point of view and how unfair it must seem. 'And that is why I can be so determined about saving you. If you are damned, I am damned! And when all that shit that is brewing out there hits you, we're both going straight to hell.'

'Then piss off!' Viper recommended.

'It won't make any difference, you'll still damn us! I have to get you out of here —' Avery looked up, distracted by the sound of an electric current. The dark matter now had a firm hold on the magnetic support legs for the gun head and was inching its way towards the rod. Avery flew to the wall and by covering the porthole from which the beamed chain extended to the prisoner's wrist, Viper's left arm was freed.

'Whoa!' Viper's arm fell backward. 'Forget it, fairy, it will re-bond as soon as the hole is uncovered.'

Avery removed his hand to discover Viper was right. 'Damn it!' He flew back to look into Viper's face. 'Will yourself out of here. *I'll* will you out!' Avery gripped Viper's arm and willed them to Lynn Cerrig Bach.

'There's too much electromagnetic disturbance in here.' Viper explained the problem and forced a smile. The rod at the top of the gun head blackened with its electric charge and he knew that death was imminent. 'I've played my role and as expected, I failed.'

'No! You took all the hard knocks for us,' Avery told him. 'I'm the one who failed.'

'Go!' Viper didn't need to hear this now. Tears were welling in his eyes. He'd never had someone stand by him, ever, but there was no way he was going to die crying like a baby.

'I'm not leaving you.' Avery turned to shield Viper from the dark force of energy that was about to explode forth from the weapon above.

'There's no way to stop it, you crazy son of a bitch!' Viper yelled, shocked that Avery wasn't flinching.

Avery suddenly realised why the Count had insisted on training him before he charged off to face Viper, for the Master Ray's tuition had revolved around the conversion of dark matter to light matter. 'Never say die, my friend, we still have a few tricks up our sleeve.'

'What are we going to do?' Viper was sceptical. '*Will* it to disperse?'

'Better than that, we are going to will it to return to light.'

Viper laughed, seriously amused by the notion. 'You're really not right in the head, are you?'

'All you have to do is be light of heart for one moment,' Avery looked imploringly over his shoulder at Viper, 'and we can pull the plug on the entire Orion project.'

'Well, that sounds peachy, but I'm not exactly feeling jovial right now.'

Avery turned to face Viper. 'There must have been one moment in your life when you felt happiness and love? Just one thought of pure love, that's all I ask.'

'Fallon's breast on my lips felt pretty good.' Viper tempted fate, as was his way.

Avery ignored his impulse to be jealous and angry;

he could not afford such a mistake. 'She's pretty fine, our girl.' He grinned, recalling Fallon's memory of the brief encounter, and when Viper returned the grin, Avery knew he had him on side. 'Don't allow Aris to defeat us. We can do this.'

Viper nodded, determined. 'Here goes nothing!' he warned his superhuman shield, and Avery spun around to confront the dark energy beam as it shot forth into the funnel.

'Avery!' Rhun slammed the glass observation window with both his fists, as the laser activated and all the dark energy in the chamber was sucked up into the weapon head and beamed forth into the funnel. He willed himself to Avery immediately but there was no response. 'Where the hell is Gwyn ap Nudd?' he seethed.

'I'm right here.'

Rhun and Zabeel looked at Zero, who transformed into the Night Hunter. His presence instantly infuriated Rhun.

'You could have prevented this!' He charged on a collision course with the Otherworldly lord, who vanished. Rhun nearly collided with a control panel, but flipped over it to land on his feet. 'Coward! Traitor! Cheat! You've been playing both sides all along.'

'Even so, there is only one cause. I played both sides,' he granted, 'because that was my service to the great plan. And now, they are ready for the challenge.' He motioned back to the funnel where all was now quiet and still. 'Although it will be a whole new ball game once I leave.'

'You expect Avery and Viper to survive that? They'd have to transform eons of negativity into light matter.' Rhun cocked his head, considering this a big ask, but as it was his only chance of seeing his little brother again, he was praying the Night Hunter was right.

'I expect a transformation, to be sure.' Gwyn approached the windows, when a deep rumble was felt and then heard.

Either the dark matter was sucking up everything in its path, or Avery had managed to repel the force — Rhun and Zabeel weren't leaving until they knew.

A great burst of etheric light, that would have been invisible to the naked eye, shot from the funnel. The force blew the weapon head to bits as it forged onwards through the ceiling and the earth above to find daylight. The glass observation window shattered inward upon those in the control room and the dust and rubble falling in the huge metallic pit beyond showered down everywhere.

'Crude, but effective.' Gwyn raised his eyebrows and gave a smile of pride. 'If they'd just centred their energy in the etheric world, it would have been perfect.'

'But ...' Rhun straightened up and looked about as he brushed off the glass splinters and dirt. 'Where are Avery and Viper?'

Avery floated up to stand on the top of the funnel, feeling a little out of it in the aftermath of his ordeal. This event had been his initiation and Avery felt empowered — as if he was somehow more than he was before. 'Not bad going for a supposed Dark Lord,' Avery commented down the funnel to Viper, who he figured was still flying his way up. Avery knew Viper had survived the ordeal as they'd kept communicating through the blackness of the event.

'Where the hell are you?' Viper queried, looking about, unable to see his brother in arms from where he stood on the top of the funnel.

'Hang on.' Avery felt himself over and Viper did too. 'We're … one?'

Suddenly, all of Viper's horrendous memories went flooding through Avery's mind. Alternately, Viper was bombarded by the happiness of Avery's life. 'Oh, my …' Avery felt giddy as he slowly put his hands up to his shoulder blades, and began to sway when he realised he had wings.

Rhun observed the winged figure wavering on the top of the funnel, which he assumed was Viper, even though he currently looked more like Avery. Rhun figured the ordeal had sent the Falcon-Nefilim's brain into a whirl and so had confused his identities. 'Where is Avery?' He looked to the Night Hunter for an answer, but the lord only shrugged, directing Rhun's attention back to the winged man, who swayed and suddenly fell back into the abyss of the funnel. 'Do something!' Rhun appealed to the Night Hunter.

'I'm not at your beck and call, dragon boy.' Gwyn became agitated when expected to do everything. 'I cleared the base and led you straight to Viper. Now you're on your own.' He proceeded to fade from Zero's person, wearing a broad smile on his face. 'I suggest you get off your lazy butt and try something new, I'm going home. Ciao, boys.' Zero was returned to his normal form and fell unconscious to the floor.

Rhun looked at Zabeel, bemused. He'd never learned how to fly. He'd tried a few times in private, envious of Avery's ability, but Rhun had never succeeded. 'We should have brought Sparrowhawk.'

'Well, we didn't.' Zabeel gripped Rhun's upper arms tightly. 'The Night Hunter would not have suggested you do it, if you weren't capable. So try, damn it! Try now!'

Rhun willed himself to Avery and found himself plummeting through the darkness. Above, the speck of light grew smaller. Reaching out, he gripped someone's arm and pulling the free-falling body close, he began willing himself towards the speck of light above. To his great surprise, it began to grow larger.

Rhun ...?

Rhun telepathically perceived his brother's groggy query. 'Yeah, I've got you.'

Avery's body vibrated as he gave a slight chuckle. *But who has got you?*

'You're not the only wonder boy in existence, you know,' Rhun scoffed and he felt Avery chuckle again. 'You're pretty damn elite though,' he granted, for he felt Avery's weight intensify as the exhausted Otherworldly lord passed out once more.

23

A CHANGE OF HEART

Back on the Aten, Gazelle's people were keen to take Lahmu up on his offer. After what they'd all been through, even if Gazelle was lying, whatever Lahmu did with them all would be far more humane than their lives to date.

'We were fools not to integrate ourselves into the new federation when asylum was first offered by Lahmu twenty years ago,' one of the older members of the crowd said, and it seemed odd that he had physically aged. Everyone else, besides Viper's diehards, was still under the youth enhancing influence of the dark Orme.

Perhaps he was one of Viper's diehards? Bast, who had dropped her Tareena disguise, looked to the men they'd hit with a light Orme dart and they were all still cowering before Sparrowhawk.

'Instead of chastising Cordella and Gazelle, we should have been praising them for showing us a way out of the hell we created for ourselves.' The elder continued to state his view. 'By clinging to our divine ancestry and the perverted ways of our common ancestor, segregating ourselves from humanity, we have forgotten what it is to be human ... and that wondrous capacity to love and trust that we inherited from that half of our family tree.' The old Leonine walked over to stand by Gazelle, who was still on the bar, to show his support of her cause. The hooded figure standing alongside the Leonine-Nefilim elder followed him when he moved.

It took a moment, but Bast finally figured out where she'd seen the man before. *Horace?* Her eyes moistened upon seeing him so aged. No wonder he hadn't wanted to give up his dark immortality and she knew damn well that she was the reason he'd made the sacrifice. How did he get here? Her curiosity turned to the hooded figure alongside Horace.

'All those in favour of surrendering this stolen craft to its rightful owners, and giving Lahmu's Chosen our full co-operation, raise your hands.' Horace prompted an almost unanimous show of support and all those in favour cheered as they lined up to be fired upon by the Chosen and relieved of the effects of the dark Orme.

Gazelle jumped from the bar to hug Horace. 'You're a pretty cool cat after all. Thanks for the support.'

He nodded to let her know she was welcome, although it was a sad smile he wore.

Gazelle fired upon her kindred to aid with the

conversion and before long all her people had been returned to their mortal state of being.

I think you're all forgetting one very important factor. The growling voices of the wizard brought the festivities to a grinding holt.

Lahmu's people were rather unnerved, as they had never heard the wizard speak before. All Viper's people cowered, knowing the voice all too well.

I don't wish to cause any alarm, the unseen entity advised.

'Yeah, right,' Bast scoffed on the quiet.

But I thought you might like to know that an alien force has commandeered this ship.

'You haven't got any power over us.' Sparrowhawk raised the amulet En Noah had given him to ward off evil. Bast flashed hers too, to help comfort the uneasy crowd.

I wasn't talking about me, the wizard was heard to chuckle.

Then Fallon appeared in the doorway under the restraint of a tall man dressed in a black suit. One hand was around Fallon's throat; in his other hand was a gun of sorts, with a transparent barrel filled with a slimy black ooze.

'Damn it, Fallon.' Bast was panicked and angered. 'Will yourself out of there!' She didn't expect to have to point out the obvious, but maybe Fallon had gone into shock and wasn't thinking straight.

Fallon served Bast a look of apology.

'If she disappears,' the dark agent advised in a monotone voice, 'we kill the girl.'

Several men in black suits filed into the room, one of them towing the traumatised seven year old. Tareena strolled in behind the force, looking very pleased about their arrival.

'If you do not drop all weapons and withdraw,' the man who had hold of Fallon droned, 'I pump your girlfriend full of this stuff and you can all watch her disintegrate ... body, mind and spirit.'

Lahmu's team saw no choice but to do as he asked. None of them wanted to risk willing the weapon from the man's hand, lest they cause him to fire. And no one wanted to ask what was in the gun, as it sure as hell didn't look very pleasant.

As they threw down their arms, the apparition of the wizard and his pets manifested near the ceiling and hovered over the thwarted crowd laughing hysterically.

So, who was the darkest of the dark,
to the end, one step ahead of the rest?

The warlock raised his arms in the air and every weapon in the room hit the roof, including the one at Fallon's neck.

It was that cunning sorcerer,
who defied the Yahweh, Aris.

The Chosen snapped out of their shock and an all-in brawl erupted — the MIB agents, Tareena and Viper's diehards versus everyone else in the room.

From under his hood, Noah watched the

pandemonium with a broad smile on his face. 'A stroke of genius,' he commented, feeling satisfied that his plan was coming together well.

'What are you playing at?' Sparrowhawk flew up to confront the evil abomination, once the bad guys had been overpowered and restrained. 'Where is Yahweh Aris?'

The wizard shrugged in response to the first question. *I believe the Yahweh fancies himself as the next Antichrist. And as he finally managed to con the entity, Power, into disclosing the seal that will summon the leader of the Fallen Ones, I suspect that you'll find the Yahweh in Viper's room of summons, dancing with the devil, as it were.*

'Oh, my stars.' Sparrowhawk was shocked by the information and suspicious of a lie. 'Why are you aiding us?'

Because of what's in it for me, the creature hissed, so wanting to rebel and screw everyone, but knowing he would damn himself in the process. The wizard didn't intend going back to the sub-planes. *I've been cutting a few deals of my own, birdman. And if you don't believe me, then why don't you ask your mentor to verify our arrangement?*

'En Noah?' Sparrowhawk queried with disbelief.

'It is the truth, we have struck a deal that is beneficial to both parties.' En Noah removed the hood from his head to expose himself and get their force moving. 'So let's not waste time chewing the fat.' He looked to Gazelle to lead them. 'Where is this room of summons?'

* * *

'How did you do it?' Sparrowhawk asked on behalf of all Noah's students, as they made their way to Viper's room of summons. 'How did you contact your damned self without knowing his name?'

'Some old mutual friends put us in touch,' Noah replied, a little secretive. 'And now I do know his name, which might explain how I got the wizard to agree to aid us.'

'You're going to free him from the elementals,' Fallon came forward to guess, 'and send him back to join your soul-mind.'

'Only if he's good,' Noah replied loudly enough for the wizard, who was trailing along behind their party, to hear.

You won't damn yourself, the creature growled, hating to be obliged to anyone.

'I would make that sacrifice to save my kindred,' Noah stated in all honesty and the wizard snarled, annoyed, knowing that the Sage spoke the truth.

Easy to say when you've never resided in the sub-planes.

'I have experienced Density.' Noah shocked one and all with the claim. 'What is meant to be, will be.'

Esoteric claptrap, the creature grumbled to itself, having no choice but to play along. *You had just better hope that you can keep that bloody Yahweh away from me, or we're both up the creek.*

'This is it,' Gazelle announced as they arrived at huge double doors.

'Let's take a look and see what he's up to,' Doc came up front to suggest to Gazelle. 'We'll pop back to security and use the cameras —'

Gazelle shook her head. 'Viper had all surveillance removed from these quarters.'

'It's all right.' Noah placed a hand on Doc's shoulder to reassure him. 'I don't believe we have anything to fear here. Why don't you go back and check on what has become of your sons?' Noah knew this was Doc's underlying concern. 'We'll take it from here.'

As the rest of the gang supported Noah's call, Doc gave a nod and smile of gratitude and vanished at once.

'Shall I go in first, En Noah?' Sparrowhawk felt obliged, as he was the only male warrior left among them.

'I believe our first problem will be getting the door to open,' Noah commented. They may have appeared like solid timber doors, but being activated via the telepathic plate on the wall, the door would not be kicked in.

Gazelle tried her luck with the control plate but there was no response. 'Only Viper had entry.'

'Then how did Yahweh Aris get in?' Sparrowhawk asked, and everyone looked to the wizard.

Am I expected to do everything? With a wave of the apparition's hand, the door vanished and Lahmu's party was granted a view of the goings on within.

A force of dark Otherworldly power blasted the team off their feet and into the wall opposite. A dark elemental being filled the doorway, snarling and growling to discourage any thought of entry.

'Oh goddess, what is it?' Fallon rose, her back hard pressed to the wall. Bast, Sparrowhawk and Gazelle slid up to stand on either side of her.

Noah looked to the wizard to urge it to respond with an answer.

A density shield. Dark Lords cast them to prevent forces of a good nature from listening in on, or interfering in, their business dealings.

'Can you overpower it?' Sparrowhawk insisted upon a response. 'Or can we?'

Nope, no one but the caster can dismiss it. The apparition of the wizard laughed, as did all his extra appendages. *Nothing to fear, eh?* He mocked Noah's claim.

Noah rose, unfazed by the development or the mockery.

'Do you get the impression he knows something we don't?' Fallon uttered aside to her sister, who would have responded had she not noticed the dark elemental extending its ugly head and upper body towards them.

'Scatter!' Bast suggested, breaking left as Sparrowhawk and Gazelle went right. Fallon, in the middle, was not fast enough off the mark — the entity reached out and grabbed hold of her around the waist.

'No!' She pulled against the force drawing her into itself, when someone gripped her from behind.

'Vanish, or face the consequences,' a familiar voice boomed, and the elemental withdrew immediately.

Fallon's heart leapt into her throat as she turned to view her love. 'Avery?' she queried, stunned that he was sporting Viper's wings.

'Viper?' Gazelle crept closer, wondering what had become of her brother if Fallon was right.

'Night Hunter,' Noah bowed his head in greeting. 'Congratulations on your appointment.'

'What?' Fallon gasped, her welling joy spurring her to the brink of tears.

Avery kissed his lady's forehead and smiled at all his kin. 'Later.' He headed for the open doorway to the room of summons, but stopped to reassure Gazelle on the way. 'Fear not, your brother is alive and well,' and served her a cheeky wink.

'Rhun?' Fallon looked at him for some clue as to what was going on.

'He did good,' he admitted, as he fell in behind Zabeel and Avery, motioning the others to follow them inside.

Gazelle and Fallon stared at each other, not knowing what to think.

'You heard the Pan man. Forget it for now,' Bast strongly suggested. 'Let's get with the program ... girls.' She urged them hither as Bast followed the dragon boys into Yahweh's lair.

In the centre of the room of summons, a beam of dark red celestial light ran between the ceiling and the circular screen on the floor. This screen currently displayed a very intricate seal design, which everyone assumed was the secret symbol that would summon the leader of the Fallen Ones.

As Avery entered the chamber the density shield vanished completely and the Dark Lord found himself exposed to the intruders. Still, he had cast a circle around the tool of summons and himself and felt safe and superior therein. 'You're too late, Beelzebub is here to wreak havoc upon you all!'

There was an explosion of light within the illuminated tube of deep red, which turned orange then yellow, green, blue, indigo, violet and, at the last, shimmered silver — this presence was spectacular but not harmful to the eyes of the Chosen Ones.

Yahweh Aris, however, shielded himself from the lustre, cowering behind the silver ring on his finger. 'Impostor!' he cried out. 'Where is the Prince of Darkness?'

A devanic being took form within the shimmering silver beam of light, and burst into rainbow flame as the features of its body became defined.

'Father?' all the dragon boys uttered at once, amazed and confused by his presence.

'Indeed.' Noah confirmed their doubts and explained another little mystery. 'The mutual friend who put me in touch with my dark self.'

'Ah ...' Bast, Fallon, Sparrowhawk and Gazelle raised their eyebrows, enlightened.

'Prometheus,' Aris uttered in a malign voice. 'What trickery is this?'

No trickery, Yahweh ... the Prince of Darkness no longer exists in the lower realms of Gaia's evolutionary scheme, and never really did in the form you were expecting. The segregation of dark and light on Gaia is dissipating. Her consciousness has learned all that utter darkness and density can teach and must now start upon the long road back to the clear light of the Cosmic Logos.

'Light cannot exist without darkness,' Yahweh insisted.

Darkness isn't going anywhere. It will just start integrating itself with light, rather than segregating itself from it. Take the Night Hunter. The celestial being motioned to Avery, who was the only one of his party game enough to approach the conversation and enter the circle Yahweh had cast. *He is now the perfect balance of light and darkness. He understands both and judges neither.*

'Only darkness in its purest form will cease to exist on Gaia, just as it no longer exists on any of the allied planets under Lahmu's rule.' Avery gave the telepathic command to open the shield windows, which granted a breathtaking view of Gaia beyond.

'Oh my Goddess!' En Noah mumbled, reflecting the awe of all around him, who gasped as they saw how the entire planet now glowed just like the Chosen did when they were spiritually awakened.

'The breach between Gaia's physical and emotional bodies has been healed, Yahweh.' Avery turned to confront the sorcerer of old. 'Your etheric dam has been destroyed and Gaia is once again contributing to the great universal scheme. Your service to the plan is thus at an end here, my beloved.'

'We'll see about that.' The Orion raised his arms to vanish and was enraged to find he was refused passage.

'My elementals will no longer support you,' Avery advised, as the deva took on its feminine persona.

Everyone present saw Tory Alexander, except Yahweh Aris, who recognised Electra. *Gaia's elementals are being attracted in droves to the Four-fold Chapter, which perfected its art under my guidance at Delphi and then moved into underground societies the world over, from that time to this.*

'No ...' Aris pleaded, angered that he'd never gotten wind of this hidden enemy.

Humanity has waited a long time for this day, Aris. Your people will also prosper, for Orion knowledge will be invaluable when used to further the cause of light, the Deva lovingly conveyed.

'I don't want to prosper,' Yahweh spat out in disgust, 'or serve the cause of light!'

'There's only one thing for him.' Avery looked to the fiery being resembling his mother, who nodded agreement.

'You can't harm me.' Yahweh held the ring out towards the fiery being to use as a shield.

'And where is the ring that protects you from me?' Avery questioned, feeling the Viper side of his character coming out. He silently prayed he could control him. Still, he felt more empowered, confident and in control than he ever had before.

Yahweh moved backwards to collide with Avery's brothers, who had him surrounded.

'It really has been a long time between Devachanic rest periods for you, hasn't it, Aris?' Avery neared and the Orion cowered.

'NO!' he cried in horror, shrinking to the floor, hoping to escape the Night Hunter's reach. 'Not my memory ... it's taken eons to gather the knowledge my soul-mind contains.'

'Now there's nothing to worry about.' Avery tried not to tease him, but couldn't help himself. 'You'll get to keep all the good parts.'

'There'll be nothing left!' Aris cried in horror as the dragon brothers hoisted him up to face Avery.

'Do hold still.' Avery placed a hand over Yahweh's third eye area. 'This won't hurt a bit.'

600

Yahweh struggled only a moment before his physical form disintegrated into one small ball of light, which floated in the palm of Avery's hand.

'Peace be with you, brother,' Avery said, cupping his hands together. When the Night Hunter opened his hands once more the being was gone and a cheer sounded out from his kindred.

Avery's first thought was to address and thank the Deva for its aid, but the entity had vanished during the commotion.

Rhun glanced from Avery to the glowing planet, then to the seal on the floor and back to En Noah. 'Could you please explain to me what on earth is going on?'

Noah smiled to encourage Rhun's frown to leave. 'It's all good,' he told him surely. 'The mission is all but over.'

'All but what?' Rhun queried and Bast gasped as she recalled the oversight.

'Rainer Ingram.'

Rainer was discovered in the adjoining room, just as Horace had suggested, and although the young man was clearly not well, he'd live, and he was very glad to have been found.

Doc had taken Luther and Morgan back to Lynn Cerrig Bach to recover from being shot with negative ectoplasmic charge, which had rendered them unconscious. They would awake before long and after an up-chuck of black slime, would feel as right as rain.

Avery had one hell of a time trying to explain to Fallon and Gazelle what had happened to him.

Thankfully, his brothers helped with the tale, and filled in most of Avery's blank spots. Lirathea expanded on the spiritual reasons for what had happened to Avery and Viper.

'This soul-mind's feat was unprecedented,' the oracle advised everyone, very proud of her twin. 'It literally split itself into three soul-minds: two of opposing polarities — both male, and one neutral incarnation — a female.

Fallon gasped as she learned where she figured in the equation. 'That's why my destiny has remained veiled … in order that all three of us could be tested.' She took hold of Avery's arm and twisted her hand down to take hold of his.

'It was the fastest way to gather the experience you require to assume the guardianship of the Otherworld.' Lirathea rarely became emotional, but she felt the tears welling with her next sentence. 'You two were always meant to be together.'

'Aw,' sighed everyone, repressing tears as Avery kissed his bride-to-be.

'And where's that sister of mine?' Avery questioned, letting go of Fallon to put his arm around Gazelle's shoulders.

Sparrowhawk was a little jealous of Avery's sudden excuse to get close to Gazelle and she was obviously still uneasy about her brother's supposed transformation.

Avery led Gazelle aside to speak in private. 'I'm sorry for …' he leaned close to whisper in Gazelle's ear. As he spoke quietly to her, Gazelle began to choke on her tears, hugging Avery close to accept his apology.

Sparrowhawk had seen Gazelle cry but never like

this, nor had she ever let him get so close to her. She and Avery had sunk to the floor, and she was uttering her grievances back into his ear. Her emotion turned hostile suddenly and she hit Avery a few times, before abruptly hugging him tight once more to cry away her grief and happiness on his shoulder.

Lirathea was quietly clearing the room, to give their brother and sister some space, but Fallon seemed to be as wary about leaving Avery with Gazelle as Sparrowhawk was.

'They have things to sort through,' Lirathea advised Sparrowhawk and served him a large smile as she diverted his attention to herself. 'You'll have your chance to make her feel part of the family soon enough.'

Sparrowhawk would normally have been embarrassed by the comment, but he was worried about other things. 'You and Gazelle aren't going to suddenly become one, are you?' He allowed Lirathea to lead him from the room.

'In some distant plane of awareness,' she supposed. 'But until then, we have very different lives to lead.'

'That's good.' Sparrowhawk couldn't cope with having Gazelle and Lirathea in the same room, let alone the same body!

'Oh, I don't know,' Fallon grinned as she considered that she was kind of pleased by the 'two for the price of one' deal she'd been dealt. 'Now I get the things I like about both the men in my life, all rolled into one husband. Perfect!'

The door to the room of summons closed behind them and Sparrowhawk was shaking his head — he admired Fallon's sense of adventure. 'I'd be happy with just the one.' He glanced back at the closed door, trying not to sound put out.

Lirathea chuckled at his jealousy and placed a hand upon his cheek in comfort. 'You really have no idea, do you?' She kissed his other cheek and left him open mouthed.

Sparrowhawk found himself alone in the corridor, his emotions surging in all directions, fuelled by the adrenaline from the mission that was still coursing through his veins. He was *so jealous* ... jealous of Avery, and *angry* ... angry that Avery was always coming between himself and those he held most dear. He was *tired* ... tired of competing with the Lord of the Otherworld for attention.

The door to the room of summons opened and Avery emerged alone. He smiled when he spotted Sparrowhawk waiting outside.

It struck Sparrowhawk as odd that Avery's smile was warm and sincere, and not smug and forced, as per usual.

'Gazelle wants to speak with you.' He motioned back to the room where she awaited. 'I'm going to the Star Chamber to summon Eli back to take us home.' A cheeky grin crossed the Night Hunter's face as he backed down the corridor. 'We have a few other problems to sort out with the Orion's —'

'Can I assist in some way?' Sparrowhawk was concerned.

'No, no, we can handle it,' Avery assured. 'It will probably take an hour or so to organise ourselves for departure ...' He tried to say this without too much innuendo, and then vanished.

Sparrowhawk was stunned. 'Was that Avery being *nice* to *me*?' It was too much for the system to handle. 'Maybe Viper actually did him some good?' He wandered into the Star Chamber to find Gazelle gazing out through the huge window at the beautiful glowing planet below.

She turned and smiled as she heard him enter. 'Is the universe not an amazing place?' The question was more of a statement. 'My people are free, my brother is sane and *in love*, what's more! And I am one of the Chosen.' Sparrowhawk stopped a little way away from her, and did not seem to know how to react. After that little scene with the Night Hunter she wasn't surprised. 'So what happens now?' Gazelle asked, to encourage him to speak.

'There seems to have been a break in the action,' he advised, watching intently as Gazelle closed the distance between them.

'So we are at leisure?' She came to a stop rather closer to Sparrowhawk than she was usually comfortable with and gazed up at him to await comment.

'It would seem so,' he replied, then became a little awkward as he attempted to say more. 'Gazelle, there's something I've been wanting —'

Gazelle placed her hands either side of his face. 'Sorry to interrupt, but do you think you could kiss me first and talk later?' she demanded, and her impatience, so akin to his own feelings, prompted Sparrowhawk to oblige her immediately.

'Praise the universe,' Gazelle mumbled with relief, going back for seconds and thirds. In the midst of her delirium, Gazelle took hold of both Sparrowhawk's hands and, placing them on her body, she encouraged them to explore.

'There is no rush, if you are not ready.' Sparrowhawk was amazed he could say this about something he wanted so badly. Gazelle's demeanour suddenly saddened and he felt her fear of rejection. 'I have waited so long for you to come into my life,' he thought to explain, 'that I would wait forever for your favours. It is only your company I need to sustain me.'

It was the most beautiful thing anyone had ever said to her and Gazelle nearly choked on the sudden emotion of love in her chest. Love that was empowering and not a weakness; love that inflamed her being, instead of leaving it cold. 'Well,' she swallowed back her tears, feeling there was no need to weep any longer, 'that's where you and I differ, my friend. For I have been dreaming of this moment too long. It's simply screaming to become a reality, I'm afraid.'

Her smile was like a revelation to him, pure joy. 'I am in complete sympathy, believe me.' Sparrowhawk drew her closer, daring to be a bit more liberal with his hands. 'But surely this place is not the location you had in mind?'

Gazelle shrugged, indifferent. 'Might clear some of the bad energy in here?' she suggested, moving in for another kiss. 'And who needs a grand bedchamber when you have wings?'

Oh please, master, don't make me get back in there, Eli the elestial pleaded from the rim of the pit that once housed and connected him to the Aten's time teleportation function.

'Don't be silly, Eli.' Avery motioned him to the pit.

Noah and Rhun had returned Rainer to his father, and his rightful place in history, and as all team members were now on the Aten, they were eager to get moving.

'I have every intention of sending you back to your family as soon as we get this space station back to its rightful place in time.' Avery didn't want to force the crystal elemental into doing it.

But how do I know you're not just saying that? The crystal was not convinced.

'Eli, it's me, *Avery*! I am the one who freed you in the first place. Remember?'

But Viper is in there with you, and he was the one who trapped me.

'Eli.' Fallon came forward to calm the big rock, which was easily five times her height. 'You trust me, don't you? I've never lied to you or done you harm, have I?'

True, he granted.

'I promise you that the Night Hunter will keep his word.' She placed a hand on the big guy. 'So why don't we get this little chore over with and then we can all go home.'

All right ... I'll trust you, Eli stated for the record, and then jumped into the pit, his landing sending shock waves through the Star Chamber.

Avery gave the mental command to the Star Chamber to engage the crystal, and Eli was heard to gasp on contact.

'It's all right,' Fallon told him, softly, 'it will all be over soon.'

Avery floated up to a seat on the throne-like formation atop Eli's head. 'You know the drill, Eli ... take us home.'

As you say, Sire.

'Was that what I think it was?' Gazelle panted in the wake of her outpouring of emotion and energy, clinging tightly to her lover as they fluttered back to earth.

'That was sex,' Sparrowhawk stated frankly, knowing that wasn't what she meant.

'No!' Gazelle swiped his chest with the back of her hand, 'I was referring to the great flash of blue-white light just now, and that great swooshing sensation.'

'Don't you get that every time you make love?' he teased.

'No, never,' she stated in all seriousness. 'It must just be you.'

'Me ... and the Aten time drive teleporting us forth twenty years,' he admitted, amused by Gazelle's escalating delight.

'Whoo-hoo!' She cheered their achievement. 'I bet nobody else can say they've made love for two decades!'

Sparrowhawk's silly smirk was starting to make his face ache.

'Maybe it's karma,' Gazelle posed, 'to make up for the rest of my miserable life.'

'The rest of your life is going to be anything but miserable,' Sparrowhawk told her surely, twisting her implication to a more positive note. 'I intend to see to that personally.'

'See that you do,' she threatened playfully with a kiss.

'Marry me?' The words popped out before he'd realised what he was doing, and the stunned, blank look on Gazelle's face made him wish he could take the proposal back. 'I am sorry. It's too soon —'

Gazelle, realising she was giving him the wrong impression, burst into a huge smile. 'No, it's not too soon.' Her heart was pounding so loudly in her throat she could barely hear herself think. 'I just never thought I'd hear any man say that, let alone you!' She tightened the hold her arms had around his neck. 'I also never imagined that my answer would be ... yes.'

In the year 2108AD Gaia time, most of the team from Kila dropped in to see Doc at Lynn Cerrig Bach for an update on the state of the planet. Sparrowhawk and Gazelle stayed with the Aten, whilst Noah disappeared to attend to his half of the bargain with the merlin.

'How did we do?' Rhun queried Doc, as he manifested before him in Doc's conference room.

The diplomat's smile was enough of an answer. He motioned his guests to the double doors at the far end of the room, which opened on cue. 'You remember my lovely wife, Vanora?'

A woman entered beind a light-form made up of little beings and this vaporous body rushed into the room to dance around Rhun and his party, delighting all present. Elemental beings were nothing new to Avery, but these little entities were very unusual in that they all had a four-fold nature. In a cosmic sense this meant that they had evolved beyond the lower planes of Gaia's existence. And yet they were still here?

'I see, Night Hunter, that you wonder why an elemental would choose to stay and serve on Gaia once its service here is done?' Vanora found the delight and amazement of her company most pleasing.

Rhun could hardly believe that the radiant, calm, priestess-like woman before them had once been Vanora, a student of Mahaud. A long dress flowed down and around her tall, slender figure and she moved with such grace that she appeared to float. Long, dark curls cascaded over her shoulders, and her eyes, once black as night and just as cold, were now a vibrant shade of violet.

'Come and see why, for yourselves,' Vanora invited. The light body of little beings surrounded Lahmu's people to teleport them to the current physical reality on Gaia's surface.

The light body of mist cleared to reveal a huge virgin forest, untouched by man. The sky above had an ultraviolet glow about it, as did everything under the sun.

Rhun thought the surroundings lovely, but then, the scenery on Gaia was always breathtaking when seen from the Otherworld. 'So what's the physical realm look like?'

'This *is* the physical realm.' Avery looked about him, suitably impressed with the transformation. 'All this progress in just twenty years?'

'It was largely your doing.' Vanora's eyes took in the entire team, although her grateful gaze came to rest on

Avery. 'I have been working with the secret organisation known as the Four-fold Chapter since you cleared the blockage in the etheric matrix. The elemental spirits of this planet have not been abandoning her once they have matured as we once assumed ... they have been entering the service of the Inner Earth tribes. All the long-lost species of flora and fauna have been cultivated and preserved deep within Gaia. Highly adept nature spirits aid the Inner Earth tribes with this growth, waiting for a time when the surface conditions and the human consciousness of the surface dwellers would be sufficient to assist with the repair of the outer world here.'

'The Inner Earth tribes have returned to the surface of the planet?' Lirathea held both her hands to her heart, overjoyed. This was beyond her expectations.

Vanora nodded. 'They come and go freely now. It's some of the older inhabitants of the biodomes who we've had trouble getting out into the great outdoors.'

As the older generation of the planet had never known anything other than a life in a biodome, it was easy to figure why the adjustment might be difficult.

'As you've probably already realised, the Bloodlust cult never came to be.' Vanora began to walk them through the beautiful forest. 'What was once known as the demon dome is now a spiritual centre for young people, known as the Sanctuary ... needless to say you all left quite an impression on Rainer Ingram and his father. The occupants of the Sanctuary dome are light workers dedicated to the cleansing of Gaia's energy field and the restoration of the planet's physical body. For another cult was spawned in the stead of Bloodlust —'

'The Four-fold Chapter.' Zabeel, being highly telepathic, jumped in with the punchline.

Vanora winked at him in confirmation. 'You see, when you cleared the matrix, many long serving souls were released from Gaia's plan to return to cosmic service. But Gaia's cleansing also cleared the way for a whole new wave of advanced souls to be born into this scheme. These children have highly evolved third eye vision and psychic ability.'

'The Inner Earth people are reincarnating into the surface population!' Lirathea was so excited, she had to refrain from squealing.

'Indeed,' Vanora conceded. That was it in a nutshell. 'So, instead of being addicted to cyberspace, these exceptional children have been conscripted by the Four-fold Chapter and taught the art of working with nature spirits and divine light to heal the planet and themselves. These children are then encouraged into the outside world where their healing talents are put to good use. In developing these skills and serving Gaia, the young souls are developing their light bodies and have begun their ascension process. Hence, their bodies, reinforced by divine light, are immune to the toxins that are slowly being dismissed from Gaia's atmosphere.'

'Just like we Chosen,' Rhun commented, pleased that the rest of Gaia's population were beginning to find their way back to the Logos.

'When these young light workers are introduced to members of the Inner Earth tribes for the practical side of their instruction in healing the surface of Gaia, they sub-consciously recognise these people as kindred, being born of the same soul group. Thus, this is how this new wave of adept surface dwellers are sealing the breach between the Inner Earth tribes and the biodome addicted people of the previous generation. The older people in biodomes are wary of the strange new glow of the outside world and suspicious of the Inner Earth people who have returned to the surface of the planet to train their children. Still, given time, these suspicions will fade and every soul on earth will benefit from the beautiful new world being built here. These children will lead the way to a mass ascension of the inhabitants of this planet, but all these souls have no intention of ascending. They will draw the Christ consciousness down into themselves and create heaven on earth as was always intended. The mentality of today's youth is that it is far cooler to work with Otherworldly beings to create a better reality than to waste time building a cyberspace that will never truly exist.'

'This is a good thing,' Rhun conceded, as he looked ahead through the trees and noted in the distance two craggy hillocks that were familiar. 'Oh, my Goddess,' he gasped, 'it's Degannwy. We're in Gwynedd!' he announced with great excitement to his younger kindred, rushing off ahead of them to take in the landscape that had once been so familiar.

Throughout the valley, between the forest and the rise that had once housed Gwynedd's capital, were many young people working in co-operation with all manner of nature spirits. Each young student was being overseen by a hooded figure. These tutors were easily identified as members of the Inner Earth tribes — their robes entirely covered their bodies to protect their skin, unused to being exposed to natural sunlight. Their eyes were permanently closed, as they perceived everything via the glowing violet vortex of light over their third eye area, which could easily be seen by the naked eye.

The team from Kila watched in amazement as the damage sustained through the ages was undone. Huge trees sprouted from dead rotted roots, and vegetation spread over the parched earth under the guidance of human and deva working in co-operation with the mineral, plant and animal kingdoms.

'So this is what Gwynedd looked like before we got here?' Rhun had come to a stop to take in the scenery.

'Looks just like home,' Bast commented, looking up. 'Except for the sky being indigo.'

Avery smiled broadly as he basked in the rays of the sun. 'The Master R has made himself at home.' *Speaking of whom?* 'Excuse me, will you?'

'Where are you going?' Fallon wondered why he would want to miss the briefing Vanora was giving.

'I need to check in at the office. If I miss anything, you can fill me in later.' He kissed her cheek in parting, and as she was amused, Fallon allowed him to get away without further protest. 'Back soon,' he promised, and vanished into a large tree trunk. Having watched her brother depart, Lirathea also begged her leave.

Avery raised his vibratory rate before departing Degannwy, to pass through the tree and enter the Otherworld, and he was not surprised to find he could scarcely tell the difference between one plane of existence and the other. 'As above then so below,' he uttered with a smile and, thinking of Templeton, he found himself at the vale that was once the base of Gwyn ap Nudd in Briton.

'What's news, Templeton?' Avery took great joy in assuming Gwyn ap Nudd's usual seat on a rock by the river.

The upper torso of the elemental creature that was Templeton emerged from the tree by the river. *Congratulations, master.* He bowed to Avery. *Your mission was a grand victory. Gwyn ap Nudd could not have done a better job of it.*

'Aw,' Avery waved off the accolades. ''Twas nothing.'

'I wouldn't say that.'

Avery looked to his right to find the Count sitting alongside him, smiling broadly and flashing those perfect teeth.

Beside the Master Ray sat Avery's brother Sparrowhawk, who gave his brother a friendly wave. He had his Homo sapien guise on today and was looking rather more angelic than usual.

'What are you doing here?' Avery queried his brother more than the Count, but it was the master who replied.

'I thought you'd like to meet the new Master of the Seventh Ray and the violet flame.' The Count motioned to Sparrowhawk.

'That's not possible.' Avery didn't mean to sound insulting but Sparrowhawk was a spiritual novice.

Sparrowhawk began to chuckle and then transformed into their sister Lirathea. 'Just stirring,' she

615

chuckled again. 'The look on your face!' She couldn't explain the horror of his expression, she could only laugh. 'I am the new Master of the Violet Ray,' she informed him.

'But you're a woman,' he objected. 'All the Masters are male.'

'No,' Lirathea corrected, 'that's just a persona, suitable for the present mindset on Gaia, that the master's find appropriate to project. For every male Master Ray there is also a lady Ray Master. And I am not really a female, that is just how I incarnated this time around.'

Avery couldn't wipe the silly smirk off his face. 'So the new Chohan of the violet flame was guiding me all along,' he realised and Lirathea nodded.

'The Master R was training me for this appointment long before my soul-mind was born on Kila, but the memory of my destiny only matured once I did.'

'Well, good for you.' The new Otherworldly lord roused a round of applause from all the nature elementals in close proximity, as he applauded his sister's achievement.

'And how can you say what you did was nothing?' Lirathea awarded Avery his due. 'All the Rays can now express themselves in synthesis, and thus the highest aspect of divine light penetrates down into the physical realm. And not just on Gaia either,' she informed, matter-of-factly, 'but on every evolving planet in the physical universe. This finally clears the way for the opening up of many new chakras in the human body, as there are many more energy centres in the subtle bodies of human beings than the mere seven that have been activated to date. These energy centres will promote communication with all those extra-terrestrial soul-minds from which human consciousness was spawned — and which still involve themselves in the evolution of that consciousness — on this and other planes of awareness. Orme will no longer be required to speed the enlightenment and immortal state of human beings. These capabilities are open to every living thing, and always were. Only now, the believers outnumber the non-believers for the first time since the golden age of Atlantis, and that, my dear brother, is *something*.'

Avery nodded to show he understood. 'Not bad going for the sons of Satan.' He served the Count a sideways glance in question.

'Lucifer was not so much a part of the plan on Gaia, as an alternative to the plan. He served long, for he had much to atone for. Always the rebel, he constantly sought to speed things up.'

'But my parents were so perfect. Everyone adored them.' Avery was confused. He loved his parents, so was he a devil worshipper then?

The Count burst into laughter, delighted by Avery's reasoning. 'Of course your parents were perfect. That was Lucifer's whole purpose for incarnating into the human race ... to overcome the negative ego that he introduced to human consciousness. The achievement of this goal sets a precedent. It demonstrates that anyone, no matter how great their sin, can find their way back to the Logos. You see, Avery, it was Lucifer who guided the Nefilim towards this planet, and by so doing he did speed up the perfection of the human vehicle. However, this also served to expose the underdeveloped human psyche to Nefilim injustice, cruelty, debauchery and so on.'

'That would seem to explain why my parents led the rebellion against the Nefilim,' Avery conceded. 'And why they volunteered themselves as Enki's first perfect human beings. I understand that it took some time for the Nefilim to perfect the human vehicle and many unfortunate creatures were created in the attempt. When Adama and his brothers and sisters were created, any soul-mind with any sense would have stayed well away from the human consciousness experiment.'

'Indeed,' the Count agreed. 'Satan led a band of fiery beings known as the Grigori to incarnate into human consciousness, and aided the advanced human form through its painful transition into a thinking species, able to comprehend the harsh injustice of the Nefilim. At this time the Grigori were renamed the Watchers as they split their consciousness into numerous incarnations throughout Gaia's key eras of development and went about stirring human beings to rebellion against all injustice, Nefilim included. But this may not have been necessary had the physical evolution of Gaia been left to run its own course. Still, we of the earth scheme are all in this together. There is no judgement or blame, only a divine sense of purpose which all of us shall be more open to from now on. With all this talk of karma, it does make you wonder why you led the rebellion against Yahweh Aris, doesn't it?'

Avery was shocked into standing up, as he'd just

been wondering how to deal with the Orions that remained in Gaia's star system. 'I am Yahweh Aris?'

'No, no,' the Count advised to disperse the worried look on Avery's face. 'Your soul-mind ascended long ago, a graduate of the great lodge on Sirius. But having been of Sirian descent, you have been forced to deal with Orion energy before. As all living things have a higher self, so too does Gaia. Sirius is that Oversoul and when Orion energy began to take hold of Gaia, our extra-terrestrial ancestors sent one of their finest ... not to defeat the Orions, but to conscript them, and bring them to an understanding of the negative ego that is driving them.'

'You're talking about Sacha?' Avery figured that the Deva entity that had taken him over at birth in order to aid his parents to combat the Nefilim, was the ascended master within himself to whom the Count was referring.

'You and Sacha are one, with many other soul-minds working on different levels of awareness, in many different universes ... the great scheme is more vast than you or I can imagine.' Lirathea emphasised.

'I guess that answers my question about what to do with the Orions then.' Avery tried not to sigh as he said this.

'Well,' the Count cocked an eye, 'we've tried containing them in their star system in the past ... unsuccessfully.'

'No.' Avery knew this was not the solution. 'If there is one thing that the children of Dumuzi and the plight of Gaia have taught us it is that there is only one solution to combat the overabundance of negativity in

619

this galaxy, and that is inclusion. No more brushing difficult cases into the corner and hoping that it won't accumulate into a god-awful mess. Perhaps if the Orions already settled in this star system could come to an understanding of the love principle, then they might feel compelled to enlighten their brothers and sisters still in turmoil in the Orion system?' Avery pulled a superior face to express how impressed with his own suggestion he was, and Lirathea wore a broad smile of agreement.

The Count laughed out loud and gave a clap. 'Now you sound like Sacha.'

The King's Men stone circle in Oxfordshire appeared to be in immaculate condition, as if the stones had only just been erected. Trees and vegetation were everywhere, the cloud had cleared and the landscape basked in the light of the Logos.

Noah was forced to wonder if he'd wandered into the Otherworld.

What are you smiling about? the beastly sorcerer grumbled, as the Sage stood staring at the monument. *How do you know I haven't coaxed you here to finish you off?*

Noah's smile only broadened. He couldn't possibly have wandered into the Otherworld and still have this creature in tow. 'If you kill me, then you'll be stuck with those elementals for good ... you can't trust anybody else to do the honours and not betray you. If you kill me, then you shall be forced to find a whole new scheme in which to exist. For, as new chakras, Rays and higher planes open up to human consciousness, the Talas of this scheme are being shut down and you shall have nothing to feed off. You will run out of energy and cease to be. I heard the Orion system is very favourable for those of your nature,' Noah teased and the creature responded with a garble of vile noises to reject the idea.

Millions more just like Aris. It was repulsed by the notion.

'Our other alternative, of course, is that I could dismiss you into Density before it is shut down,' Noah suggested, knowing this wouldn't appeal either. 'Then we can wait for another suitable evolution in which to indulge your nastiness.'

A whole planetary scheme filled with the likes of me … that's even worse. It finally conceded that Noah's way was the only option.

'I agree. A long stay in the purgatory of the lower astral realm will serve us far better.' Noah entered the circle and came to a stop in the middle. 'Once you've come to terms with all your negativity, you shall have a blissful, cleansing hibernation in Devachan to look forward to before you rejoin us.'

You're trying to make me vomit, aren't you? the creature seethed. *Can we just get on with it?*

Noah turned around in a circle. Four torches appeared and ignited, each in one of the cardinal points, so that the circle was reinforced with his own positive energy. The Sage then pointed to the ground to either side of him, whereupon two circles of vegetation cleared and out of the earth inside them rose a design — two seals of summons, practically identical.

What are you planning, Sage? From being over-eager the beast was suddenly wary and was careful to remain floating outside the circle.

'This,' Noah motioned to the seal on the ground to his right, 'is the seal taken from a digitally enhanced image of Electra's stomach.'

Electra's stomach? the creature queried, having not heard that name in many eons.

''Twas another dimension and is not important.' Noah waved off the query. 'What is important is that *this* seal,' he motioned to the symbol on his left, 'is the seal that Shamash used to summon you, and although the seals look identical, there are a few subtle differences.'

As Noah said this, the sections that were identical to the seal Electra had used to summon the elementals into her fell away and only the alterations Shamash had made remained.

'This is the key to your freedom, Aegisthus — your seal,' Noah told the creature, which, for the first time ever, was speechless. It had not heard that name in a long time.

How did you get Shamash's seal? the creature demanded to know.

'Well,' Noah grinned, having predicted the creature would want to know, 'Shamash had a rather long stay in the Otherworldly prison of Gwyn ap Nudd, which is located on Gaia's moon ... just a thought away from here,' Noah clarified, pointing a finger towards the sky. 'In that prison, Shamash used the seal to summon you forth to his service. And, although he chiselled the secret seal from the stone ground in which he'd carved it, there are a few stony critters hanging about the detention centre who hold no love for you and have an excellent memory.'

The mineral kingdom's answer to rats, those gargoyles. The wretched being cursed them to avoid having to praise the Sage's ingenuity. The sorcerer had never even considered that Shamash might have pulled a fast one and tampered with the original seal of summons — without this vital piece of information, the Sage may not have been able to part him from the elementals. By changing the seal, the Nefilim lord would have had the last laugh and damned the sorcerer forever. *All right then, get on with it!*

'You would have to come into the circle first,' Noah pointed out, and the reluctant subject dragged his beastly appendages, snarling and growling, into the positive energy Noah had rallied to aid his cause.

Separate elemental
from your human host
Dismantle the abomination
known as 'Mematros'.

This was the secret name that Shamash had given to the sorcerer when the beast was created — much the same as he'd renamed Electra Mahaud. This piece of vital blackmail information had once again been supplied by the gargoyle Tobit and his mineral mates on Gaia's moon. Noah wished he could take credit for the brilliant idea of visiting the Otherworldly prison, but he had in fact been summoned there by the recently ascended Prince of Darkness.

Noah closed his eyes to focus his will.

Denizens to your seal
Release the sorcerer's ghost.
to confront his misgivings
before the throne of the Logos.

The shrill of agony the beast released prompted Noah to open his eyes.

The etheric creatures tore themselves away from the sorcerer's spirit as they were sucked towards their seal of summons and Aegisthus's being was left quivering in the wake of his great loss of power.

Lost denizens,

Noah turned to focus his attention on the mixed bag of low-consciousness etheric world entities, who had been conscripted into the service of the Dark Lodge for far too long.

by the flame of fire,
power of the air,
cleansing of the water,
stability of the earth,
I command you to disperse
and forbid any reunion.

'I pray you find your way back to your group soul and the light of the Logos before you cease —'

You're setting them free! The sorcerer made it sound like a protest, although he was, in fact, surprised.

The entities fled in all directions before Noah had the chance to respond or change his mind. 'It becomes very easy to walk the path when there is only one path to walk. Lucifer and his associates, myself included, only confused the issue and now it will be simplified once more.'

Are you going to set me free? Aegisthus asked, hopefully.

'I am free,' Noah responded. 'Therefore, yes, you shall be freed, on many levels of awareness. But this must be your choosing, Aegisthus.'

The sorcerer whined, put out by the condition.

'Move to your seal of your own will, for I will not force you to comply.' Noah stepped back to await Aegisthus's decision.

The sorcerer gave a laugh, realising he had the option to take flight into the physical realm and see if he couldn't establish himself once more — maybe the Sage was lying about the Talas? Given leave to use his abilities, Aegisthus willed himself invisible to vex his Chosen incarnation, who only stood patiently awaiting the spirit's return — as if it were inevitable. By the very fact of having a Chosen incarnation the sorcerer knew that he would bend to the cosmic will and that the Sage knew it too — attempting to prolong the fact would only make the Dark Lord appear naive.

The spirit appeared over the seal. *You win. So let's not pretend I have a choice.*

'There is always a choice.'

But I don't have to like it!

Noah shook his head slowly. 'Still, a wise soul would love it ... be at peace, care for and love unconditionally all things living in the light of the Logos.'

The sorcerer was screwing his nose up at the suggestion.

'It's your choice, of course, but your journey back to us will be a whole lot easier if you do not cling to your past.'

I'm still here, aren't I? Aegisthus looked at Noah, giving him leave to send him on his way.

Noah served the sorcerer a smile of encouragement, for Aegisthus did not need his permission. 'Just make the wish and we shall be healed.'

24

FULFILLED

W hen word of the victory on Gaia reached Lahmu via his now returned team, Brian had Doc Alexander and Vanora brought forth to Kila, where they were invited to sit as Gaia's representatives on Lahmu's council. Doc would represent the human face of Gaia and Vanora the nature realms, with whom the Four-fold Chapter were intimately involved.

The humans on Gaia were going to need a little preparation before being informed about their interstellar neighbours. Brian could see many long conferences ahead to plan Gaia's coming out into intergalactic society. But it would happen, very soon.

Gaia's guardians graciously accepted the appointment, doubly thrilled, as this represented their official pardon and gave them leave to join intergalactic society themselves. To this day, all of Doc and Vanora's attentions had been focused on repaying their karmic debt to Gaia and this had kept their physical bodies planet-bound there. But their penance was done now and the couple greatly appreciated the excuse that their new position would give them to familiarise themselves with all the planets in Lahmu's alliance.

Aris's mothership had been commandeered and flown into the Aten for teleportation to the future by Rhun, Zabeel and Bast immediately following Aris's demise. The MIB prisoners, numbering a few hundred in all, were detained in a prison complex on the outer island ring of Kila, along with the children of Dumuzi. This prison had only ever had a handful of poachers stay there in the city's seventy year history. The complex was specifically designed to cater for immortals, being equipped with a PKA teleportation shield lock. Some of the Orions had been psychically adept before being hit by the Orme dart which rendered them mortal, so the choice of accommodation was just a precaution. Their dark powers could not serve them, in any case, on a planet where there had been no illwill to speak of.

Lahmu saw each of the prisoners in turn after Rebecca had prepared her report on them. Brian may not have been able to lead the latest quest of the Chosen, but in the few days his Vice-Governor and team had been absent, Brian had been working on developing his etheric sight; now he could tell the true intent of any subject just by looking at them.

The Orions were going to need a lot of TLC before

gold Orme would take to their systems and restore their immortal status via the path of light. Only a handful of Viper's diehards were refused Chosen status, but their cases would be reviewed after a year under the tutelage of Noah and the cleansing processes of the healing Orders. All of the new Chosen Ones would be cleansed and prepped for governmental training and service for a minimum of a year. This would give the new residents of Kila time to decide on which planet they wished to settle, and what vocation suited them most. The only exception was Gazelle, who had been given Lahmu's blessing to wed Sparrowhawk in the near future and settle on his home planet of Tarazean.

Brian was much relieved when the long line of prisoners came to an end. Still, he'd seen the dreams of many come true and that was very satisfying. Even his daughter, Fallon the ever-sullen, was suddenly outshining her sister. Engaged to the ruler of the Otherworld, Fallon had discovered her calling, won her love and found true happiness. Brian was overjoyed for the couple, and sad to be losing another daughter from his household so soon.

And while he was on the subject of sadness, the news of Tory and Maelgwn's physical destruction and ascension had completely rocked Brian. Could he believe that his sister and her husband's soul-mind added up to be Satan, and that all fourteen of the souls who started out together in Eden, himself included, were Fallen Ones, incarnating into human consciousness to make amends for the Nefilim? And, if Tory and Maelgwn were Lucifer, then who was he?

'Sammael. The ruler of the fifth heaven and the planet Mars.'

Brian went into deep shock upon viewing Maelgwn sitting on his office lounge, appearing the same as he ever did.

'Hence, Lahmu,' Maelgwn added, as Brian appeared at a loss for words.

'Are you an ...?'

'Apparition?' Maelgwn asked, and Brian nodded. 'Yes, I am toying with your perception. You perceive that my physical body is present, as I thought you'd find that more comfortable.'

'More comfortable than what? No, don't answer that.' Brian decided he didn't want to know. 'So, you're not really here?'

'Not in body, no,' Maelgwn clarified, 'but in spirit.'

Brian was only mildly comforted by this. 'Are you really ... *Satan?*' He whispered the name as if it were still taboo.

'It seems so,' Maelgwn nodded. 'I really thought that I was driven by divine purpose to achieve all I did, and it turns out that we are all just repaying our debt to Gaia for speeding up the perfection of the human vehicle.'

'Well, I'm sure we thought we were doing mankind a favour,' Brian defended.

'Frankly, Sammael, we didn't give two hoots about mankind. It was earthly pleasure we were interested in.' He grinned mischievously and Brian did too — this explained a lot about his own promiscuous nature in the past.

'But where did our interest in the human vehicle

stem from when the perfect human had yet to be fashioned?' This was the one point Brian failed to understand after hearing the report from his Vice-Governor and En Noah.

'In this dimension,' Maelgwn clarified. 'And there are many, many different inter-dimensional realities to this scheme,' he went on. 'In one reality the Nefilim never came here and neither did we.'

'And what is life in that reality like?' Brian was curious.

'Pretty much the same as it is today, only Gaia was never abused and so never needed healing — mankind worked in co-operation and understanding with nature's spirits all along. Of course, the other human tribes were never created, Kila was discovered and mined by the Nefilim and the Chosen Ones never existed, for indeed, every soul on Gaia was aware of being a divine entity ... as will be the case on Gaia soon.'

'So, with all we did, we've only restored Gaia to how she would have been if we'd never interfered!'

'That's about the size of it,' Maelgwn granted. 'Still, it was an honest mistake we made. The Nefilim had always treated each other fairly well. We weren't to know that subjecting them to Gaia's emotional principles would have such an adverse effect on their morals and character. By the time they'd fashioned the perfect human body, no soul in heaven wanted to risk exposure to the heartless wrath of the Nefilim. Our desire for the materialistic experience, rebellious nature and accountability for the grievous mistake of guiding the Nefilim here made us the perfect volunteers for the job of getting rid of them ... long and arduous as that task promised to be. And yet here we are, our mission completed.'

Brian felt kind of elated by the news, but puzzled. 'So why haven't all of the fourteen of us ascended?'

'Oh, but you have,' Maelgwn informed him. 'I will represent the last of us to return to the Logos.'

'But?' Brian frowned and Maelgwn preempted the query.

'There is no time beyond the earth plane,' he explained.

Brian's frown faded, as he partially understood the premise. 'Where is Tory?'

'I am here.' Maelgwn spoke with Tory's voice as his appearance changed into that of Brian's sister.

'Goddess!' Brian reared back, rattled by their unity. 'Doesn't that feel strange?'

'Not at all,' she assured. 'Just think of it as knowing the one you love very well.' She waited for Brian to get over his shock and approach her.

'So, this is it then, you're leaving.' He ventured to take hold of her hands and was relieved when they felt warm and solid.

'We're just off to join you and the others, at long last,' she explained with a smile. 'I feel quite sure that you'll be glad to see us.'

'So, you're not planning on coming back here, at all?' Brian asked, unable to imagine life without them.

'Well, if father and Taliesin have returned to earth service after they've ascended, then you never know?'

632

'What?' Brian found his smile. 'Have they?'

Tory was pleased for him and kissed Brian's cheek. 'Ask your new son-in-law-to-be to introduce you,' she suggested and vanished before the good mood could evaporate.

'Father!' Bast came charging into Brian's office, unannounced. 'I've just come from seeing Nin Rebecca, who tells me that you declined the prisoner, Horace, the right to Chosen status.' She came to a stop, with hands on hips. 'May I ask, why?'

It was clear to Brian that Bast was playing the daughter and not the diplomat. When in a meeting of the council, Bast would not dare to conduct herself thus, so clearly this inquiry was personal in nature. *Interesting*, thought Brian, recalling the prisoner in question was of the Leonine Nefilim persuasion. 'Actually, we only advised him that a delay might be best, and he chose to take our advice.'

'That doesn't answer my question,' Bast persisted. 'Why, father?'

There was a silent pause as Brian took a seat on his lounge. He was having one hell of a day. 'Sweetheart,' He waved her to a seat but she refused. 'Horace still has a great darkness in his heart, and we suspect that he resents Viper —'

'No,' Bast disagreed, calmer now. 'It's not resentment. It's just plain old sadness.' She dwelt on this a second, seeming satisfied. 'Was that all that was amiss with him?' Bast checked.

'Apart from the low self-esteem he's experiencing due to his injuries at the hands of Viper.' Brian shifted in his seat, disturbed just thinking about it. 'His heart is the only other problem.'

'Then without the heart problem he would really have a good case for a compassionate claim on his Chosen birthright.'

'If you think you can fix the problem, sweetheart, then I'll review his case,' Brian granted, figuring she couldn't get in too much trouble with the man at present.

Bast smiled broadly and then crouched down in front of her father to kiss his cheek. 'Thanks, daddy. You're the best.'

'Hey, hold on,' he objected as she quickly made for the door, for he'd realised she'd just managed to weasel confidential information out of him. 'This coversation never took place.'

'What conversation?' she grinned broadly and blew him a kiss of appreciation as she left.

Once alone, Brian wondered if his sister was still hanging about. 'Perhaps our double wedding is going to turn into a triple!' he commented. When there came no retort, his good mood left him, and he sank back into the lounge. 'Miss you guys already.' He gave a heavy sigh to expel his sadness. 'And you're right, I will be very glad to see you when next we meet.'

His wife, Candace, entered his office carrying afternoon tea on a tray, looking more beautiful than ever, and Brian's spirits immediately lifted. He realised how preoccupied he still was with material pleasures and if this meant that his conscious perspective was focused in Kila's physical realms for a while longer, then so be it in his opinion — Brian could only be happy about that.

* * *

Bast tracked Horace down at the Institute of Immortal History, where he had begun a course in cosmology as part of the term of his sentence for Lahmu.

The one-time outlaw was seated in the beautiful, stepped courtyard of the Institute and was studying alone, a thought recorder in one hand as he jotted notes on a pad.

'You can just record your notes on another orb,' Bast offered her advice. 'On windy days thought recorders don't blow away.'

Horace appeared to be disconcerted by her visit, although he raised his ageing bones to greet her, as was polite. 'To what do I owe this honour?'

Bast sat down to give Horace his leave to sit. 'I never got a chance to thank you for speaking up for us back on the Aten. You really saved our butts.'

'You represented the first real shot my people ever had to escape the nightmare we created for ourselves.' Horace planted himself down again. 'We should have seen that twenty years ago when everybody else did.' He looked out over the sparsely populated courtyard to avoid eye contact with Bast, and she got the distinct impression that she made him uncomfortable.

'Any plans as to what you're going to do after you finish your service on Kila?' She kept the conversation light.

Horace suppressed a laugh. 'Like you're interested.'

'Why would I be here, if I wasn't?' Bast retorted, gently.

'A very good question.' Horace grabbed his study tools and stood. 'Why are you here, *highness*? If this is some sort of power trip for you, then, please forgive my bluntness, the last thing I need right now is a tease.' He turned and walked off.

Bast was gobsmacked a second and was tempted to retaliate. But then she had to ask herself why his comment had riled her so — could it be that he could see right through her? Was she just teasing him? As she watched him walk away, determined not to chase him, the words of En Noah's prophecy sounded in her mind. *True happiness lies with a man that you will have to pursue.* Bast gasped, reminding herself of all Horace had been through in his life and of all he was still sorting through. 'I see.' She stood and spoke up. 'You'll talk about the welfare of your people, but when the opportunity to take action tries to present itself, you'll turn your back on it.'

Horace stopped in his tracks and did an about-face. 'You're here to offer me a job?' All the colour drained from his face as Bast nodded and he realised his grievous error. 'I am so sorry —'

'Forget it.' Bast waved off his discomfort. 'I was coming here to seduce you also, but, as you're obviously not going to buy into that, I thought I'd just stick to the job offer, for now.'

Horace had to assume she was joking to make him feel better and he cracked an uncomfortable smile.

'But if you can't stand the thought of working with a tease then ...' Bast gave a sigh of regret, 'I'll have to find somebody else with your mature outlook and first-hand knowledge of the history of your kindred.'

Horace thought this a nice way of referring to his old age. 'What is the job?'

'Well, I figured that there are representatives of your kindred on every planet they might wish to take up residence on. Gazelle is on Tarazean, Cordella is on Lura ... but there is no one to represent your people on my home planet, Nugia,' Bast outlined in a professional manner. 'I feel sure father would permit you to serve your term in Nugia's service, especially as it would be to the future benefit of your people. I can tutor you in the ways of the Chosen, and you can advise me on how best to integrate your people into Leonine society.'

Horace had never felt honoured before — Bast could have picked any one of seventy other members of his kindred for the position. An emotional lump welled in Horace's throat which made it difficult to speak. 'It is my greatest wish —' He choked on his emotion and so left it at that.

'Mine, too.' Bast slapped her hands together, pleased to have achieved her objective — Horace wouldn't have that dark cloud over his heart for very much longer.

The tunnel of rainbow fire, formed by the synthesis of the divine rays within the soul-mind, dispersed into a white light mass.

Azaz'el?

The name stirred many memories of study and service, but only fragments. No recollection was completely stable. They just presented themselves and then vanished into the recesses of the soul-mind's foggy consciousness.

I think our fearless leader is nearly with us.

Well, praise the Logos for that. We can finally get on.

The soul-mind became aware of floating in a chamber, his form contained within a shaft of light. Beyond the lightbeam floated three other beings: two of rainbow fire, and the other an ascended master still employing a subtle human form. This being moved closer and with a wave of his index finger the barricade of light between them vanished.

Welcome home, Azaz'el, said the master, and the other two beings echoed the sentiment. *How was your trip?*

Djwhal Khul? The soul-mind recognised the master. *My trip?* Azaz'el dwelt on this idea for a moment and was bombarded with a string of earth memories. *It was successful, I hope?* Azaz'el realised that the master was in a far better position to answer that question.

Hell yes, it was a success, Sammael confirmed enthusiastically, when the other fiery being with him, who Azaz'el had known as Noah, Selwyn and the Sage of Eridu, corrected Sammael: *We don't use the 'H' word any more … let's not tempt fate.*

A thousand apologies, Armaros, Sammael granted. *I'm just a bit excited at the prospect of working on a new enterprise.*

Azaz'el was preoccupied with the architecture of the chamber in which they stood. It was more colourful, light-filled and impossible than anything on earth — and hauntingly familiar, with its tall, spiralling columns. These appeared not unlike glimmering, ivy-bound trees whose branches unfolded at the top to support the ceiling. At the foot of the column, roots spread across the ground and disappeared into the floor. The beam of light that had surrounded Azaz'el upon arrival here was simply the point of entry to the celestial city, and this beautiful chamber was the entrance foyer.

Seeing this place brought the situation into focus for Azaz'el. *So the damage done to human consciousness has been righted?* Azaz'el sought verification before getting too excited.

The master nodded. *The Sanat Kumara awaits you in the Great Council chamber to welcome you home, and his great city is open to you once more.*

This was very uplifting news.

You have gone where most angels fear to tread, and although it may have been done as a punishment, your deeds have taught us much and did advance the human consciousness experiment with the advent of the other human tribes.

Bonus points! Sammael clenched a fist and raised it in a gesture of might.

We have been recalled to cosmic service, Armaros further enlightened, appearing very pleased about the event.

Sirius, here we come. Sammael did a little dance.

So, the split soul principle worked? Azaz'el figured. *Our female halves kept our male halves on the straight and narrow.*

Azaz'el recalled that this had been the only condition of earth life that had bothered the Grigori — splitting their soul-minds into male and female aspects before entering the human consciousness stream.

And continues to work, Armaros stated surely.

The fact was most amusing to his associates as well. *The Great Lodge knew exactly what they were doing*, Sammael granted. *You think they would have risked sending us down without a sound contingency plan for getting us back?*

I found the whole double perspective experience to be most beneficial. Armaros offered his view.

Yes, Azaz'el smiled fondly at the memories, *it was rather wonderful. I could even venture to say I might miss it.*

Oh, I just love it when the plan comes together. DK slapped his hands together, delighted by their banter.

Azaz'el cocked an eye, curious about the master's enthusiasm. *Why? What has the Logos in mind for us next?*

That will be your choice, of course, DK assured.

Uh-huh. Azaz'el suppressed his amusement. *I've heard that one before.*

Understanding the jest, DK only smiled. *Join us in the Great Council chamber at your leisure. You will be updated with the current state of the plan and all your questions will be answered.*

Azaz'el nodded, knowing that it was not the master's place to answer such questions.

We have missed you, Azaz'el, and your minions, DK said, before leaving. *It is a joy to see you returned to us a wiser and happier soul.*

It is a joy to be thus. Azaz'el and the master bowed to each other and Djwhal Khul departed.

My friends. Azaz'el turned to Armaros and Sammael. *Where are the rest of us?*

They are awaiting our debriefing in the ante-chamber of the Great Council of the Sanat Kumara, Armaros informed.

You could say they are chomping at the bit to find out what our future prospects are, so, we shouldn't keep them waiting, Sammael advised. *They'll be real glad to see you, just as I am.*

Ditto, Armaros smiled.

Azaz'el nodded to confirm he felt the same. *We did well and have learned much. But I think that from now on, it would serve us better to have a little more patience and just stick to the plan.*

His associates wholeheartedly agreed.

Epilogue

'The End.' What a ridiculous term. It sounds so final and yet according to esoteric doctrine it is redundant. For nothing ever really ends or dies, it just changes form.

The first question my readers will ask is — is that the last we shall ever see of Tory and Maelgwn? And the honest response is ... you never can tell. Still, the writer feels that there are other muses with amazing tales to tell and wisdom to teach, who have already been put on hold for too long.

Will the writer be sad to see these characters go?

Absolutely — but without change there can be no growth. When I think about all that these characters have taught me in the seven or so years we have spent together, my mind boggles! They have literally changed the way I live my life and view the world. They have led me to eras, places and people who have had a profound effect on my life and my career, including my latest chance encounter.

One morning early this July I awoke, made a cup of tea and went to check my email, as per usual. Only with this morning's email came a message from the ascended Master Djwhal Khul (DK) which had been committed to email through a spiritual teacher in Australia (the Reverend). The Reverend had aided me with some esoteric research I'd been needing to complete this last book of the triad. I consider the Reverend to be a trustworthy source, being that he is to be a guest speaker at the forthcoming (Western) Wesak celebration, held every year in California, and is to be the vessel for the Master Rakoczi at the holy assembly.

Djwhal now here, at your service beloved.

To really walk the talk so to speak, we must all find the time to nurture the innerness that is the GOD Within amidst the activities of the form life. Only the negative ego will try to tell you otherwise. The conscious communion with the stillness of the wordless realities of the inner planes can only serve to make the whole book creation process more refined, efficient and joyous. So we offer to assist you to deepen your inner connection, to allow you to flow more with our guidance and our love, for we see that your medium for expressing a greater reality within the written word will serve to gently generate interest in growth, the Masters, and the Path of Ascension. Yet the ego places feelings of unpreparedness, or busyness, or unworthiness as a barrier to further expansion. To relieve yourself of such unnecessary obstacles and have made known that which is currently veiled, you must remove the veils, we will assist, but you must perform within thyself, the necessary alignment and attunement to approach us. So meditation is the key, and we know that you are able to do so or we would not have suggested this, for to have done so would be to dis-empower which is not our style of doing things. So remove potential distractions, prepare a sacred space wherein you feel 'safe', ask for my protection and guidance, be 'heart open' and follow the procedure that the Reverend shared. Be without expectation, simply know that the inspiration will come. It is TIME!

Blessings of abundance to you in this most exciting time in your world's history and heart.

I AM Djwhal Khul.

I have read enough of DK's books to know this master when I read him, and yet my mind would not accept that this could be happening to me. *You're being had*, I decided, or at least it was easier to believe that.

A reader, who was a close personal friend of the Reverend, had been the one to put me in touch with him. Hence, I wrote a letter to the reader who'd been the catalyst in this affair, voicing my reserve about this correspondence. The reader replied to say that she'd received several emails from Masters via the Reverend and understood that I might be doubtful. She suggested that I might like to do a weekend workshop with the Reverend and decide for myself if he was legitimate? I have never been a good pupil, as I've always been a self-teach kind of girl. The reader cum go-between then reminded me that even Tory Alexander had a Merlin to guide her.

Trying to decide whether or not to take up the offer, threw me into complete turmoil and I could not sleep that night — for hours I pondered these events unfolding in my life. When my clairvoyant had said that 'I could not possibly predict where this story would lead,' I had assumed he'd been referring to my characters, not me! The meditation the Reverend had given me to do to inspire the information for the scene I'd been having trouble with, worked like a charm. Still, having been a visionary all my life, I wondered how to define the difference between my own imagination and divine inspiration? Was it the same thing? It came from the same source. I'd always said that it felt like I was merely taking dictation when I wrote.

When I first started writing *The Ancient Future* I asked myself the question, 'If an ascended Master opened a door for you, would you step through it?' I'd always fancied that my answer would be 'yes'. Now here I was being offered the chance to become the heroine I'd so long admired. Would Tory have walked away from this challenge? I thought not. A million reasons why I couldn't take up the offer raced through my mind and yet every time I considered declining, my heart felt like it was breaking. When I considered doing as my reader had suggested, my heart settled and felt at ease. By 2.30 in the morning I decided 'What the hell!' The tossing and turning was driving me nuts! What kind of writer would I be if I did not investigate this for myself? My readers had often asked me if my tales were all true — well, there was only one way to find out.

The following morning this email from the Reverend awaited me.

Greetings my friend!

So your world is somehow new again, I sense your wonder and the wondrousness of the answering of your call for awakening. Yet the activity of the ego and its analysing mind nags with its fears of loss of control. There is no judgement, there is only love and a longer or a shorter journey home. Are you ready for the express ride? Ask and you shall receive. When the pupil is ready, the Master appears. This is your time, if you but choose.

much Love, your friend and spiritual brother

Well, I was gobsmacked, especially when I noted the time that the email had been sent: 02:29:01. The Reverend knew the exact moment I'd decided to take him up on his offer. And in typical Cosmic Logos style, I'd been given proof of the master's abilities after I had decided to leap into the void and not before. Even my husband had been interstate the previous night, thus no living soul knew about my late night of procrastination or my resolve. When I'd been tossing and turning over what to do, my cynical mind had wondered if the Reverend knew the turmoil he'd thrown my being into. Judging from this turn of events, it would seem so. Not to mention that practically every statement in the email was a line straight out of my books, and I knew for a fact that the Reverend had never read any of my work. This was enough to convince me that the universe was definitely supporting my decision to go do this weekend workshop.

Thus, two weeks later, I headed off to an unfamiliar city, *alone*, to meet up with people I'd only known via email and do a course with a fellow I'd never met. What's more, I felt incredibly good about this, which in itself was a miracle. The wondrousness of the cosmos that I'd so missed, locked in my office writing away for six years, was making itself felt once more.

I once heard a quote, 'Write and you don't live, live and you don't write.' I considered this an accurate summation of my time as an author, up until this point. For a change, it was me who was off on a little adventure and, although my deadline was fast approaching, I decided that my characters could put their lives on hold for a change.

I hinted at what was unfolding in my life to the wonderful readers who have been frequenting the Message Board on my website. Little do they know that the reader-go-between that started me on this roller-coaster ride has been chatting with them too (I bet they can guess who). It is amazing to hear their stories about strange occurrences in their lives, sudden bursts in awareness, and how many of them have dreamt about these tales. It seems that the more honest I am about the bizarre events of my life, the more open others are to talk about their experiences and impressions. I love that my readers now have an outlet to discover that they are not weird, or nut cases, if they have seen a ghost, someone's aura or felt at one with the infinite — strange and wonderful stuff happens to everyone, not just those of us who get to write about it ... praise the universe for that!

I have come to realise that my purpose for meeting the Reverend had little to do with a piece of research information I was lacking. I am normally able to imagine anything, but I just couldn't get a grip on this particular scene — well, in retrospect it seems that the inspiration eluded me just so I would get in touch with this man. After I had made contact, the inspiration flowed freely and I agreed that I would give credit to the Reverend for his aid. That was right before he actually began to have a stronger bearing on the sub-plot of the tale. That's when I had another *huge* realisation. When the ascended Masters of the Far East and the Master Rays entered into my story, I'd been treating them like mythological characters that I could pluck out of fiction and manipulate to suit my plot, rather than conscious living entities and incarnations working on this planet today. And although Goddess knows I did some heavy research to write this book, most of my trusted references were over a hundred years old! When you are talking about a living, evolving planetary hierarchy, there are bound to be a few changes in the structure in a century. What I needed was someone who was up to date with the state of the planetary hierarchy at present. Well, what a coincidence, hey? The perfect consultant had just been introduced to me — the universe always provides. I was able to breathe easier knowing any errors I may have made about the Masters or their teachings would not go to print and even my agent agreed that asking the Reverend to proofread this manuscript was the right thing to do.

So, you have to figure that I was fairly impressed by the Ascension weekend workshop. The Reverend wasn't joking when he said I would be getting the express ride — I felt like I'd literally been scoured by cleansing energy at the end of it. The discourses in cosmology made me realise just how much my esoteric library needs updating. It was very disconcerting for me to be confronted with updates on the work of the masters on this planet, mainly because it was as if my ability to create my own reality was suddenly rather more extensive than even I'd imagined — for here was my plot unfolding in reality. I came away from that weekend without any doubt that I had spent it in the company of a truly adept man with some highly beneficial teachings.

How much of the sub-plot about the writer is true? The information about my guides I pieced together from various experiences and psychic readings I've had over the years. The story of my success has been recounted with as much truth as I can tell it. This was my attempt to demonstrate how the principles I learned about via the fantasy could work in reality — or at least they've worked for me.

I am now making a living doing what I love most and, without too much public exposure or media support, these books have just sold themselves. From where I sit now, I have to wonder how a girl who left school in fourth form with a D in English, who can't spell and is dyslexic, became a best-selling author — that does seem like a fantasy.

I have heard from, and know, many others who have taken their reality into their own hands by learning to trust in the universe to support their pure intentions and aspirations. This does require a re-training of the brain, however — it is simply amazing how much negative programming we entertain in our everyday thinking.

It has taken many years of consciously addressing those nasty little voices in my head telling me 'I'm not good enough', or 'not smart enough' to fulfil my desires. I cut the phrases 'I can't' and 'it's too hard', and the like, from my vocabulary and replaced them with phrases like 'no fear', 'the universe always provides', 'it's a test of character', and 'what is meant to be will be, and what is not, won't ... so why worry?'

It seems very apt that at the conclusion of writing a series of books exploring the occult history of our Earth, I should receive a spiritual wake-up call myself. I know that since that weekend workshop I have been calmer, more open to the needs of others, including the planet and creatures with which we share it. 'Write and you don't live, live and you don't write,' was a very true statement for me. My clairvoyant told me once that it was not enough for me to write about Tory Alexander, I had to be her! 'We lead by example, relaying the theory is not enough.' I believe my introduction to the Reverend was the universe's way of insuring that I don't forget my own development and the concerns of the real world — the fight for the survival of our beloved Gaia. This battle of negative and positive forces is unfortunately far from over in our inter-dimensional reality. When John Lennon wrote 'all you need is love' never a truer statement was made. All Gaia needs is love; if we could only do every task in our day for the love of it, all would be well with the world.

The line between fiction and fantasy has always been a little blurred to my way of thinking, but as time and my investigations into the cosmos roll on, my stories seem to contain less and less fiction. How much of it is real to others, is up to each reader to decide and investigate, if so inclined. Still, I am here to tell you that if you are lusting after a life of cosmic adventure in the manner of Tory Alexander, it is all out there for the taking. In my own investigation of religion, mythology and esoteric texts, all roads lead to Shamballa and to the teachings of those Wise Men of the Far East, whose writings have so strongly influenced my own. The world is a truly amazing being and never has it been easier to seek out information about Gaia and her greater mysteries.

As for the writer, she will continue her spiritual journey and delight in weaving her discoveries through the plot lines of her tales. For this has been a wondrous adventure, and I look forward to those that lie ahead with great expectation.

BIBLIOGRAPHY

Bailey, Alice A. *The Seven Rays of Life*, Lucis Publishing Company, London, 1995.

— *The Seventh Ray — Revealer of the New Age*, Lucis Publishing Company, London, 1995.

— *Initiation, Human and Solar*, Lucis Publishing Company, London, 1922.

Blavatsky, H.P. *The Secret Doctrine*, Theosophical University Press, 1988.

Bletzer, June G. *Encyclopedic Psychic Dictionary*, Donning Co, Virginia, 1986.

Briggs, C. V. *Encyclopedia of Angels*, Penguin Group, New York, 1997.

de Laurence, L.W. *Lesser Key of Solomon* Kessinger Publishing, USA, 1916.

Hope, Murry. *Practical Greek Magic*, Aquarian Press, England, 1985.

Lindsay, Phillip. *Masters of the Seven Rays*, Apollo Publishing Aust, 2000.

— *The Shamballa Impacts*, Apollo Publishing Aust, 2000

Saraydarian, Torkom. *The Legend Of Shamballa*, Saraydarian Institute, US, 1976.

Stone, Dr Joshua. *The Easy to Read Encyclopedia of the Spiritual Path: The New Dispensation of Ascended Master Teachings for Aquarius*, Light Technology Publishing, Sedona, Arizona.

REFERENCES

The author gratefully acknowledges the authors of the following quotations, references and inspirations.

Part One, Page (9) — 'Knowledge dwells in …' Sir Frances Bacon.

Part One, Page (122) — *The Great Invocation* by Alice A. Bailey and the Tibetan Master Djwhal Khul (DK).

Part Three, Page (547) — The seven line verse 'You are that angel' Inspired by the words of the Kabbalist — Eliphas Le'vi. Sourced from *The Secret Doctrine* by H.P. Blavatsky, Part 2, Page 505, Para 4.